Praise for Steven Harper's novels of The Silent Empire

Dreamer

"This exceptional first novel in a new series is a satisfying and complete work in itself. A diverse array of memorable characters and worlds makes this a book [to] relate to and enjoy." —*School Library Journal*

"This series opener should appeal to lovers of far-future space opera and sf adventure." —*Library Journal*

"In terms of narrative and world building, this is definitely a well-told tale, and Harper's skill at characterization is significantly above average. Moreover, his extrapolation of aboriginal Austrialian myth freshens the shopworn theme of telepathy. Even the future slums he imagines are memorably vivid." —*Booklist*

"A fresh, original story . . . a clever concept . . . an exciting tale." —BookBrowser

"Harper is a promising writer." —On Spec

continued . . .

The Silent Empire

DREAMER
NIGHTMARE
TRICKSTER
OFFSPRING

OFFSPRING

A NOVEL OF THE SILENT EMPIRE

STEVEN HARPER

A ROC BOOK

ROC
Published by New American Library, a division of
Penguin Group (USA) Inc., 375 Hudson Street,
New York, New York 10014, USA
Penguin Group (Canada), 10 Alcorn Avenue, Toronto,
Ontario M4V 3B2, Canada (a division of Pearson Penguin Canada Inc.)
Penguin Books Ltd., 80 Strand, London WC2R 0RL, England
Penguin Ireland, 25 St. Stephen's Green, Dublin 2,
Ireland (a division of Penguin Books Ltd.)
Penguin Group (Australia), 250 Camberwell Road, Camberwell, Victoria 3124,
Australia (a division of Pearson Australia Group Pty. Ltd.)
Penguin Books India Pvt. Ltd., 11 Community Centre, Panchsheel Park,
New Delhi - 110 017, India
Penguin Group (NZ), Cnr Airborne and Rosedale Roads, Albany,
Auckland 1310, New Zealand (a division of Pearson New Zealand Ltd.)
Penguin Books (South Africa) (Pty.) Ltd., 24 Sturdee Avenue,
Rosebank, Johannesburg 2196, South Africa

Penguin Books Ltd., Registered Offices:
80 Strand, London WC2R 0RL, England

First published by Roc, an imprint of New American Library,
a division of Penguin Group (USA) Inc.

First Printing, November 2004
10 9 8 7 6 5 4 3 2 1

Copyright © Steven Harper, 2004
All rights reserved

Cover art by Tristan Schane

RoC REGISTERED TRADEMARK—MARCA REGISTRADA

Printed in the United States of America

To Aran, my own child

ACKNOWLEDGMENTS

Gratitude forevermore to the Untitled Writers Group (Karen Everson, Anne Harris, Jonathan Jarrard, Lisa Leutheuser, Erica Schippers, Catherine Shaffer, Shannon White, and Sarah Zettel) for sympathetic ears and unsympathetic critiques.

Gratitude also goes to Deirdre Saoirse Moen, and Christina Stitt for critiques of the early chapters. Jim Morrow's advice was also greatly appreciated.

Jana Sibson, Esq., gave valuable advice about custody cases involving children, both born and unborn.

CHAPTER ONE

"Playing games helps children understand to live by rules and understand the difference between fair play and exploitation."

—Irfan Qasad

The game representative flashed a killer smile, and Father Kendi Weaver shifted uneasily in his office chair. Killer smiles always made Kendi uneasy.

"We're offering generous terms," the game rep continued earnestly. "A five hundred thousand freemark advance against three percent royalties on the first two million copies, four point five percent on every copy after that. You don't have to offer anything but your endorsement. We do all the work—writing, developing, marketing. You just sit back and rake it in. Easy money. But we have to know now so we can get production moving, strike while the iron is hot."

Kendi tapped his fingers on his desk and looked at the holographic models on the table in front of him. One was a representation of himself, a tall, dark-skinned man with tightly curled hair, a flat nose, and a whipcord build. Australian Aborigine to the core, though Kendi preferred the term "Real People." Next to Kendi's hologram stood a model of Ben. He was shorter than Kendi, stocky, red-haired, and damned handsome, especially in the spring sunlight that streamed through the office window.

Kendi's office was, like most offices at the monastery, small and cramped, with wood-paneled walls and a hardwood floor. To combat the lack of room, Kendi kept his space austere. His desk was bare, and there was only one chair for guests. The windowsill, which looked out into leafy talltree branches, had a precious few holograms on it—Ben and Kendi arm in arm on a beach, a motherly woman with dark hair, a representation of Real People cave paintings. A pair of pictures hung on the walls, both pen-and-ink drawings of Outback landscapes.

A third hologram waited to one side on Kendi's desk. It portrayed a chesty blond woman, blue-eyed and beautiful. Kendi picked it up by the base.

"Who's this supposed to be, Mr. Brace?" he asked. "She looks familiar, but I can't place her."

"Ah. That would be Sister Gretchen Beyer."

Kendi almost dropped the hologram. "*Gretchen?*" he spluttered. "It looks nothing like her. What did you do, stuff balloons under her—"

"We had to modify her a little," Tel Brace said smoothly. "After all, sim-game heroes are larger than life. People have expectations."

"Anything that big would be more of a surprise than an expectation," Kendi muttered. "Why do you have a workup of her in the first place? I mean, she was important to everything that happened during the Despair, but other people were more instrumental, you know?"

"She's your romantic alternate."

Kendi blinked. "Come again?"

"Part of the sim-game involves a romantic subplot," Brace said. "This version allows the players a choice of partner—Ben or Gretchen."

"A choice of partner."

"We want to appeal to the broadest possible base," Brace explained. His golden hair shone in the sunlight, and Kendi wondered if HyperFlight Games had chosen Brace to approach Kendi because of his good looks. "There will certainly be a segment of players—male and female—who will be more interested in playing up a romance with a woman, and we have to meet that need. It's a standard development tactic."

"I see. What did Gretchen have to say about this?"

"I'm not at liberty to discuss Sister Gretchen's negotiations, Father. I'm sorry."

"What are you going to call this game again?"

" 'Dream and Despair.' Marketing predicts it'll be one of the biggest sellers in all history, rivaling even 'The Siege of Treetown.' You and your family will be set for life, Father. All you have to do is sign and watch the freemarks roll in."

Kendi toyed with the hologram in his hands. "Dream and Despair." An apt title. The galaxy had once been dependent on the Dream, a telepathic plane of existence that only telepaths known as the Silent could reach. Within the Dream, language and distance were no barrier to communication. In a galaxy where faster-than-light travel was cheap and faster-than-light communication was impossible, the Silent had become essential, allowing governments, corporations, and other entities to maintain quick communication with outlying branches, subsidiaries, and colonies.

Then came the Despair. Terrible forces had torn the Dream asunder, and the Silent found themselves exiled from its haven. Bereft of the Dream's touch, many Silent became despondent, even suicidal. Kendi, Ben, Gretchen, and several others had been caught in the maelstrom of the Despair, and they had managed to keep the Dream from self-destruction, but only barely. Now only a tiny handful of Silent could enter the Dream, and the place had become a near-wasteland. Unable to communicate with their allies and subsidiaries, governments and corporations plunged into chaos. Many fell apart or went bankrupt. Some rulers grabbed power, others abandoned it. The Empress Kan maja Kalii, ruler of the Independence Confederation had, for example, disappeared without a trace.

Now a company called HyperFlight Games wanted to make a history sim-game out of it all, with Kendi as the hero.

Part of Kendi was flattered. The rest of him was suspicious. Tel Brace had a low, smooth voice and an earnest manner, both of which flared Kendi's nostrils. He also recognized the elements of a good con game—a demand for a quick decision, smooth explanations, overly friendly demeanor.

"I'll need time to think about it," Kendi said, still holding the Gretchen hologram. "Consult with some people, sniff around, you know. Leave me a copy of the offer, and I'll get back to you."

"I don't know how long I can keep the offer open," Brace said, racking up another con game point on Kendi's mental tally. "The boss is riding me, you know?"

"I'm sure," Kendi said. *Now he'll take me into his confidence,* he thought. *Make me feel sorry for him.*

"Tell the truth," Brace continued conspiratorially, "I'm really hoping you can help me out. The economy is still bad after the Despair, and I haven't been able to seal any decent contracts in months. I'm worried about my kids. Things got even rougher after their mother left. Do you have children, Father?"

"Not yet," Kendi said, and held up his data pad. "I need time to consider your offer, Mr. Brace, so please zap me the terms. I have a lot to do today."

Brace managed a weak grin, one completely unlike the megawatt version he had used earlier. "Right. Here it is, then." He aimed his own data pad at Kendi's. A green light flashed on each, indicating a successful data transfer. Brace stood up and held out his hand. Kendi rose to shake it. Brace's grip was dry and firm.

"Keep the holograms as our gift, Father," Brace said. "I hope to do business with you soon."

After the man left, Kendi checked his messages. His public box was crammed. Four offers for speaking engagements. Sixteen requests for information about himself. Eighteen sales pitches. Twelve requests to let someone write his biography. Thirty-five people writing to say they appreciated what he had done for the Dream. Forty nasty letters asking why he hadn't simply let the Dream die. Nine marriage proposals. Two death threats. And more than a hundred solicitations for more . . . personal services.

Kendi forwarded the death threats to the Guardians, deleted the rest, and called up the HyperFlight Games agreement to skim. His brow furrowed. Was he reading it right? According to the contract, he would have no input on the final version of the game. HyperFlight would also have the right to use his name and likeness for any advertising they liked, whether it related to the game or not, and the agreement lasted one hundred years after Kendi's death. The royalties, meanwhile, came off the net profits, not the gross take. Kendi narrowed his eyes. No sim-game, movie, or music feed had ever made a profit, and the companies employed teams of accountants to prove it.

Kendi sighed and shut off the data pad. As the display winked out, his eye fell on the holograms lined up on the desk, and a thought occurred to him. A bit of rummaging in a drawer turned up a small scanner, which he ran over the base of each hologram. When he reached Ben's hologram, the scanner beeped once. Kendi glanced at the readout and shook his head with a tight smile. He looked at Ben's holo for a long moment, then tapped his earpiece. "Ben," he said. His earpiece started to connect the call, but Kendi interrupted the connection with another tap, stopping the call entirely. He waited a moment in silence, then spoke to the empty air.

"Hey, Ben, it's me. Fine. Uh huh. Well, I just met with the sim-game guy. The offer looks pretty good, I think, but I'm a little unsure. What's the savings account like? Oh. Did you talk to the bank about the home improvement loan for the nursery? Oh. That bad? What about that contract job you were bidding on? You're kidding! They gave it to *who*? All life, we needed that money. What kind of assholes would—yeah, I know. Okay. Well, maybe this sim-game offer is just what we need then. I'll see you when I get home."

With that, Kendi pocketed his data pad, exited the office building, and walked straight into a demonstration parade.

Most of the participants were human, though a substantial number were Ched-Balaar. They carried signs, both placard and holographic. FOXGLOVE AND THE FEDERALS: OUR FRIENDS! FOXGLOVE STANDS FOR JOBS! VOTE FOR FOXGLOVE AND FEED MY FAMILY! FOX 'EM, MITCH! THE CHILDREN OF IRFAN EAT WHILE MY CHILDREN STARVE! The holographic signs were decorated with images of a man with dark hair and broad, handsome features.

The humans in the group were poorly dressed. Their patched clothes hung on them as if they had lost weight. The Ched-Balaar had a scruffy, disheveled look, and there was dust in their fur. One human woman had two small girls at her side. Both were thin and ragged, and they looked at Kendi with quiet eyes. He put a hand on the gold medallion he wore around his neck, the one that marked him as a Child of Irfan. Their mother followed their gaze to Kendi in his loose brown robes. Her jaw firmed, and she raised her sign as the procession marched past. Kendi wanted to do something for her, give her money or the jade ring he wore. But her face was hard and he knew such a gesture would only make her angry. A human voice broke into song. Immediately the Ched-Balaar joined in, chattering their teeth in rhythmic counterpoint. The procession came to a halt as everyone sang.

We all are prisoners of starvation
Fighting for emancipation!
We call upon each city-nation,
One union grand.
Little ones cry for bread
With their parents cold and dead.
The Federals lead us from this dread!
It's our final stand.

A dark-skinned woman in dreadlocks and a hand-knit scarf climbed up on a balcony rail. She raised a placard that said OPEN MINDS FOR OPEN MINES. Several of the holographic signs in the procession erased themselves and called up new text. WE CAN MINE RESPONSIBLY. WE AREN'T CHILDREN—LET US WORK! A MINE IS A TERRIBLE THING TO WASTE.

"We are sitting on unimaginable wealth," the woman shouted. "Bellerophon is rich in metal—gold, silver, iron, uranium, and more! And yet our people starve. How did we let this happen?"

Cheers of agreement roared through the talltree leaves.

"Our ancestors thought they were being wise when they laid the restrictions on mining and farming and talltree harvesting," the woman shouted. "Perhaps they were. Perhaps they preserved the environment. But that was almost a thousand years ago, and times have changed. We are responsible adults, not children. We can mine the planet's resources without causing harm. Mining and farming and harvesting would mean jobs for the people!" More cheers. "Food for our children!" Cheers. "Security for everyone!" Cheers. "Mitchell Foxglove and the Federals opposed the mining restrictions long before the Despair, and he opposes them now. The Unionists and the Populists supported the restrictions, and look where it got us—frozen, starving, and afraid. Foxglove needs our vote, and we have to give it to him. Foxglove! Foxglove! Foxglove!"

The procession took up the chant of Foxglove's name and started marching again. The dreadlocked woman jumped down to join them. Protesters both human and Ched-Balaar continued along the office building walkway and tromped down a wide wooden staircase that wound around a talltree trunk. One of the little girls threw Kendi a last glance before marching out of sight.

Kendi sighed and released his medallion. The edges had dug furrows in his palm. How could he possibly get het up about a sim-game contract when people starved within ten meters of his office door? He decided to donate a portion of the sim-game proceeds to a charity that helped the hungry. Maybe the First Church of Irfan. Orphans and other needy people fell under their bailiwick.

The last of the procession cleared the walkway, and the Blessed and Most Beautiful Monastery of the Children of Irfan went back to moping through a crisp spring afternoon. The small audience that had gathered to watch the march drifted away like limp petals on a tired wind. Some were brown-robed monks—Children of Irfan—and others were laypeople who worked for the monastery, though these days there were fewer and fewer jobs. Although most of the people were human or Ched-Balaar, a fair number of other species fed into the mix as well, and the air was filled with the quiet chatter of human voices, the muted clatter of Ched-Balaar tooth-talk, and the squeaks, squawks, and quacks of other species. Gondola cars strung on overhead cables coasted by, and a monorail train snaked between the massive talltree branches. Beneath the monastery's swaying walkways lay the dizzying drop to Bellerophon's forest floor more than a hundred meters below. Overhead, the sun's great golden eye hung in a field of perfect blue, and the air smelled of green leaves.

Kendi leaned on a heavy wooden railing and looked out over the arboreal monastery. A man and a woman in brown robes passed Kendi, their voices barely audible. A teenage boy walked in silence with a being that looked like a giant caterpillar, and their steps dragged. Kendi sympathized. Before the Despair, all the monks at the monastery had been Silent, able to enter the Dream. After the Despair, only a tiny handful had retained their Silence. For the Silent, exile from the Dream was like being struck blind or deaf. Not everyone had adjusted well.

A gentle tap on Kendi's shoulder made him turn. Behind him stood Ched-Hisak, one of the equinoid Ched-Balaar. Like all of his species, Ched-Hisak was the size of a small horse. Hay-colored fur covered a stocky body and four legs that ended in heavily clawed feet. A thick, sinuous neck rose between two muscular arms that ended in four-fingered hands. His head was flat, with wide-set brown eyes and a lipless mouth filled with shovel-like teeth. His forehead sported a small hole just above and between his eyes. His forelegs were thicker and sturdier than the shorter hind legs, which gave a downward slant to the Ched-Balaar's back. One finger sported a green jade ring similar to Kendi's.

"Ched-Hisak," Kendi said with a warm smile, and held out both hands, palms up.

Father Ched-Hisak placed his hands over Kendi's and gripped his wrists in greeting. His palms felt like warm suede. Ched-Hisak opened his mouth, and his teeth clattered in a complex rhythm punctuated by occasional soft hooting sounds from the nasal opening between his eyes. Half a lifetime of living among the Ched-Balaar let Kendi understand the language perfectly, though he had no hope of reproducing it.

"I wish to make you an invitation," Ched-Hisak chattered after exchanging a few pleasantries. "It is time for Ched-Nel and Ched-Pek to leave the den, and it would please me much if you and Ben attended the ceremony."

Kendi blinked and suppressed a small gasp. "It would

be an honor!" he said. "But Ched-Hisak—are you sure you want us there? I've never known the Ched-Balaar to ask aliens to attend a Leaving for their ch—for their younger family members."

Ched-Hisak dipped his head once. "You and Ben have been good and kind friends to me and my family for a long time, and it is my wish that you attend."

"Then we'll definitely come," Kendi said. "When and where?"

"Four days from now in our home. We begin at noon. I have hope it will be a fine and festive occasion in a difficult time."

"We could use some festivity," Kendi sighed.

"It has been a difficult eight months," Ched-Hisak chattered. "Our entire civilization was based on every one of us learning to reach the Dream. Now that has been taken from us."

Kendi placed a hand on Ched-Hisak's flank. "I'm sorry. I've been so busy running around putting out fires for the monastery that I haven't had time to think about what the Despair means for your people."

"I cannot find fault with you, Kendi," Ched-Hisak said mildly. "You are the reason the Dream still exists, limited though it is. In any case, there is nothing you personally could have done. We Ched-Balaar have gone from Silent to Silenced. That is the way of it."

"Except it was humans who nearly destroyed the Dream in the first place," interrupted a third voice. "Our ancestors should never have brought humanity into the Dream. Now they have repaid our kindness with exile and despair."

A second Ched-Balaar had approached. This one was a little shorter than Ched-Hisak, with paler fur and startling violet eyes. She wore no monastery ring, and a swirling, curlicue pattern had been shaved into her pelt.

"Ched-Putan," said Ched-Hisak. "Your words only cause anger, and they solve no problems. Why are you here? The demonstration has already passed by."

Ched-Putan waved a hand. "There are so many demonstrations and marches, it is impossible to be anywhere without seeing one. The people—our people—have time to demonstrate because they have no jobs."

"More rhetoric," Ched-Hisak said. "What do you want here, in this place at this time?"

"I have come to meet with the Council of Irfan. I will talk with the Ched-Balaar who walk with the Children."

Kendi's eyes widened. Ched-Putan had used the actual word for *children*. The Ched-Balaar used that term only rarely. In fact, the Ched-Balaar term for the monastery's people technically translated as "the Family of Irfan" though everyone mentally translated it as "the Children of Irfan." The Ched-Balaar, meanwhile, pretended that the human word *child* meant "young family member." Kendi himself had heard a Ched-Balaar use the term *children* only once or twice in his entire life.

Ched-Hisak raised his head high, and his fur stood up in outrage. "Ched-Putan, your rhetoric takes you too far. You use offensive language and anger all those who hear you."

"That is my wish," Ched-Putan responded. "Our people have been too mild for too long. The Dream is empty, kinsman, and you do not see that this is our chance to reclaim it."

"Reclaim it?"

"We can preserve the Dream for the Ched-Balaar," Ched-Putan said. "It is nearly empty now, and we must prevent the other species, especially the humans, from finding it again. Mitchell Foxglove is a human, but he agrees with us, and when he wins the upcoming election—"

Kendi waved a hand in front of Ched-Putan's face. "Hello! Human standing right here. Silent human."

"And look what Silence did to your people," Ched-Putan said, rounding on him. "It made you a commodity. Your own species kidnaps you, treats you like animals for breed and for sale. When the slavers destroyed your *child*hood, Father Kendi, did you find yourself grateful for the 'gift' of Silence?"

Kendi's jaw tightened. He was about to snarl at Ched-Putan when a warm hand on his shoulder restrained him.

"There is no point in arguing with this person," Ched-Hisak said. "You will not change her mind, and she will not change yours. Your words will matter for nothing."

Kendi fought his temper and finally beat it back. His old teacher Ara would have been proud. Still, he couldn't resist saying, "You're right. As much try to persuade a maggot not to eat rotten meat."

He turned his back and marched away before Ched-Putan could reply. A scrape of claws on the wooden walkway told him Ched-Hisak had followed. They walked in silence for a long moment. Then Ched-Hisak said, "I feel I should apologize on behalf of my species."

Kendi shook his head. "Not all Ched-Balaar are like her."

"Perhaps not all," Ched-Hisak said. "But certainly a growing number. Almost every member of my species was Silenced by the Despair, and they want to blame someone. Just as the humans who have lost friends and family and jobs to the Despair want to blame someone. The Freedom Confederation Party—and Mitchell Foxglove—is capitalizing on that."

"Keep the species separate," Kendi said. "I've heard the rhetoric. It makes me sick. What do they think, that after all this time, Bellerophon will splinter into enclaves based on planet of origin?"

"Stranger and more frightening things have become law. Slavery, for example."

Kendi pursed his lips. "You have a point," he said. "I should know that people don't change. Not even after a thousand years."

"They don't change," Ched-Hisak agreed. "They are evil, cruel, misguided, and absurd. They are also brave, noble, kind, and giving. We have to find the latter qualities while we fight the former, and it would be foolish to expect anything else."

Kendi reached up and placed his hands on either side of Ched-Hisak's face in a sign of affection. "I know. Thanks. And thank you for the invitation."

They parted company, and Kendi's feet took him toward home. Before he got much farther, his ocular display flashed. A high-priority message was waiting for him. Kendi tapped his earpiece.

"Display message on ocular implant," he said. His eyes tracked back and forth as text scrolled across his retina, and a smile broke out on his face. "Well, what do you know?"

*   *   *

Ben Rymar sat on the floor and stared at the holograms on his coffee table. The first showed a pretty woman, with pointed features and a long, brown braid. She wore a formfitting jumpsuit with a small captain's insignia at the shoulder. The other hologram portrayed a short, stocky man. His straw-blond hair and enormous blue eyes gave him a boyish look. A handsome guy. Ben puffed out his cheeks and held up a hand mirror so he could compare his reflection with the hologram's. His hair was sunset red, but Ben and the man shared the same long jaw, the same stocky build, the same square features. Their eyes were the same shade of blue.

There was something of the woman in Ben's face as well. Ben made mental comparisons. Same eye shape, same mouth, same nose.

Ben set the mirror down and drew his knees up to his chest. The base of the woman's hologram was inscribed with the words Irfan Qasad. The base of the man's hologram said Daniel Vik. They had died almost a thousand years ago, and they were his parents.

He sat on the hardwood floor for a long time, trying to wrap his mind around this impossible concept. Irfan Qasad. Captain of the colony ship that brought humans to the planet Bellerophon. First human to speak to the alien Ched-Balaar. First human to accept the Ched-Balaar's gift of Silence and enter the Dream. Founder of the Blessed and Most Beautiful Monastery of the Children of Irfan.

Daniel Vik. Yeoman to Captain Qasad and eventually her husband. Second human to enter the Dream. Father of Irfan's children. Genocidal maniac who had tried to murder every Silent on Bellerophon.

Ben got up and went to the kitchen, poured himself a tall, tart glass of juice, and took it out onto the balcony that ringed the house. The early spring sun had finally chased away the heavy winter clouds. Voices, both human and Ched-Balaar, chattered, clattered, and hooted in the distance. Beyond the balcony stretched the talltree forest, with its hundred-meter trees above and giant lizards below. Neighboring houses peeked out from the branches one tree over. The original colonists of Bellerophon had taken to the trees to escape the local lizards—inevitably dubbed "dinosaurs"—and their Tree-town descendants had never gone back to the ground. Some of the structures, built of iron-hard talltree wood, were reputed to date back to the time of Irfan Qasad herself.

Irfan Qasad. Ben set the juice glass on the balcony rail. The news felt unreal, as if it had come to someone else, as if—

"You are brooding," said a voice behind him. Ben spun, upset the glass, and caught it just before it fell over the rail. Juice spattered the leaves below.

"Harenn," he yelped. "You scared the life out of me."

"Perhaps I should scare some life *into* you," said Harenn Mashib. She was leaning against the door jamb, her dark eyes half-closed, her arms folded. At her feet lay a star-shaped piece of computer equipment. "I knocked, but no one answered."

"I didn't hear."

"You hear very little lately," she observed. "Kendi has noticed, you know. He asks about you, wants to know if I have any idea what bothers you, and then I have to lie and tell him I know nothing. I dislike lying to him, Ben, especially about something so important. You have to tell him."

"I will," Ben protested. "I just . . . it hasn't been the right time."

"This begs the question of when the right time will come."

Ben sighed and boosted himself up to sit on the balcony rail. Harenn remained in the doorway. She was a shortish, pretty woman whose choice of clothing ran to voluminous, and she covered her hair with a blue scarf.

"I don't know," he said finally. "How do you say something like this? 'Hey, love, I just thought you ought to know that Harenn found out who my biological mother is. Can you believe it's Irfan Qasad?' Sure."

Harenn picked up the bit of equipment and brought it over to the balcony. "That information will not change Kendi's feelings for you. And it does not change who you are."

A crisp spring breeze ruffled Ben's hair. He took the cryo-unit from Harenn's hands and stared down at it.

The information didn't change who he was. The problem was, he didn't *know* who he was. Or maybe it was that he *did* know.

System lights blinked in a familiar pattern across the readout. Ben knew the cryo-unit itself wasn't a thousand years old, unlike the embryos frozen inside. Those embryos were mere clumps of tiny cells, yet they managed to raise countless questions. Why had Daniel Vik and Irfan Qasad created them? Who had stolen them away? Why had the thief later abandoned them?

Ben knew part of the story, of course. Ara Rymar, on a mission for the Children of Irfan, had found a derelict ship orbiting a gas giant. A brief examination had proven the ship empty except for the cryo-unit. Back on Bellerophon, Ara decided she wanted a child of her own and had one of the embryos implanted in her womb. Nine months later, Ben came into the world, red hair, blue eyes, and all.

Although a simple scan had revealed that all the embryos were Silent, Ara had never bothered to run a full genetic comparison on Ben or his frozen siblings. No point. The derelict ship had been nowhere near Bellerophon, and it seemed unlikely such a scan would reveal any relatives at the monastery.

After Ara's death, however, Ben had gained custody of the cryo-unit and its contents, and once he and Kendi had decided they wanted children together, it seemed the most natural thing in the world to turn to the cryo-unit and the tiny riches within.

Ben had always wanted to raise his brothers and sisters as his own children, wanted it with an ache so intense it sometimes awoke him late at night when the only sounds were Kendi's deep breathing and the secret cry of unborn infants.

Kendi, however, had been less poetic and more practical. Unknown to Ben, he had asked Harenn to run a full genetic comparison to make absolute sure everything was all right with the embryos. The results had wrenched Ben into a strange and different universe.

"I am tiring of lying at your request, Ben," Harenn said. "I lied to Kendi when I told him that the database yielded no parental matches. I lied to him when he asked me if I knew what was bothering you. Lucia has joined in these lies, and she finds it a strain because she still holds the famous Father Kendi Weaver in awe, and she fears what will happen when he learns she has concealed the truth from him."

Lucia dePaolo. Ben ran his fingers over the familiar shape of the cryo-unit. Lucia and Harenn had volunteered to be host mothers for the embryos, and Lucia had been present when Harenn had broken the news to Ben.

"You are causing your beloved great pain with this secret," Harenn said, "because he believes you are unhappy about something. You must tell him so his pain will end."

"It's not that easy, Harenn," Ben protested. "If this information gets out, do you know what will happen to me? To them?"

"Tell me what you think will happen."

"Devastation," Ben said bitterly. "God, Harenn— Irfan Qasad is the most famous human being in all history. She changed society across the universe. Without her, humans would never have entered the Dream. People have built religious cults around her. Hell, Harenn, Lucia and her family worship Irfan as a goddess."

"They worship her as a mortal incarnation of divinity," Harenn corrected gently.

"You know what I mean," Ben said. "If this came out, half the universe would show up on the doorstep to have a good gawk, a quarter would probably want to kidnap me and the children for study or worship or whatever, and the last quarter would probably try to . . ." He waved a hand.

"Assassinate you," Harenn finished. "Because Daniel Vik was your father. Or because some people like to target the famous."

"It won't affect just me. It'll affect the kids. And I don't want to be famous. It scares me, Harenn. Enough people already know who I am and what I did during the Despair. Everyone calls me a hero. They stare in public, and they ask questions, and I hate it. I don't want this for me, and I don't want it for our kids."

"I still fail to see the problem," Harenn said. "Telling

Kendi is not like telling the world. He would not give the secret away if you didn't wish it. Kendi will be the father of these children, Ben. Perhaps not biologically, but certainly in all ways that matter, just as Ara was your mother in all ways that matter. He deserves to know."

"I know," Ben sighed. "Every time I try to say the words, they won't come. And, no, I don't want you or Lucia to tell him."

"You have a deadline," Harenn said. She took the cryo-unit from him. "By the end of the week, my body will be ready to receive your first child. I will not go through the procedure if Kendi remains ignorant of the baby's nature."

A door slammed inside the house and a voice called, "Ben?"

"Out here, Kendi," Ben called back. Then, to Harenn, "Not now."

"As you say," Harenn replied. "But you have my opinion and my deadline."

Before Ben could say more, Kendi strode out onto the balcony with an excited bounce in his step. Kendi favored the brown tunic and trousers often worn by the Children of Irfan, and the jade ring on his hand indicated he had reached the rank of Father. Like Ben, he was in his late twenties, but the excitement on his face made him look younger. Ben found himself sharing the excitement, even though he didn't know what it was about. Kendi could still do that to him, communicate a mood by his very presence. Ben liked that. He kissed Kendi hello, then backed up a step. Kendi's eye fell on the cryo-unit in Harenn's hands, and his face went tight.

"Is something wrong?" he asked.

"We were discussing parenthood," Harenn said, "and I was using a visual aid. No need for alarm."

"Ah."

"All right, out with it," Ben commanded, changing the subject.

"Out with what?" Kendi said innocently.

"There's something you're dying to tell me," Ben persisted, "so go ahead."

"Sound advice," Harenn murmured. Ben shot her an

alarmed look, but Kendi was too excited to notice. "And what is this news, then?"

"You should check your messages, Ben," Kendi said. "Grandma is running for governor."

Ben stiffened. Then his knees went weak, and he grabbed the balcony for support. Salman Reza was actually Ben's grandmother, not Kendi's, but she had pressed Kendi into using the designation as well.

"Are you all right?" Kendi asked, taking Ben's elbow. "It can't be that much of a shock. All life—she's been talking about it for weeks."

"I was just hoping she wouldn't go through with it," Ben said.

"Gonna be a fun ride," Kendi observed. "We'll be famous. Again."

"Yeah," Ben muttered. "Famous."

"I must be going," Harenn said diplomatically. "Bedjka will be home from his playmate's house any moment, and I must start supper." She gave Ben the cryo-unit and a hard look, then withdrew. Ben stared over the cryo-unit and balcony rail into Treetown. Cloth rustled as Kendi moved to stand beside him. After a long moment, he rested his dark hand on Ben's light one.

"I should've realized," he said quietly. "I'm sorry. I didn't mean to upset you."

"I'm not upset."

"Liar." Kendi's voice was gentle. "She hasn't made the official announcement yet, you know. You might be able to talk her out of it."

"I'd have better luck telling a carnosaur to go vegetarian," Ben snorted. "If she wins, we'll be part of Bellerophon's first family. Or don't grandchildren count as firsts?"

"Dunno." He squeezed Ben's hand. "Is this all that's upsetting you?"

"What do you mean?" Ben asked, though he knew perfectly well.

Kendi sighed. "I know this is usually not the best way to approach you, love, but I don't know what else to do. Most of the time I know you'll tell me eventually. The quieter you get, the faster you say something. But this time . . ." Kendi shrugged. "It's been two weeks since we got back from SA Station, and you've barely said a word except when I ask you a direct question. I'm getting scared. What's wrong, Ben? Are you having second thoughts about becoming parents?"

The answer died in Ben's throat, and he shut down. He sometimes envied Kendi's easy use of words, the way he could blurt out whatever was on his mind. Ben knew what he wanted to say, knew he had to say it eventually. But his mouth wouldn't form the words. It had been like this ever since he could remember. He stared down at the cryo-unit in his hands without speaking.

"Fine," Kendi said at last, a note of anger in his voice. "Where do you want to order dinner from tonight? Can you at least tell me that?"

Ben's stomach twisted. He hated it when Kendi got upset, hated it even more when it happened over something Ben himself had done. Was doing. "Maureen's," he muttered. "A number twelve for me."

"Sure." Kendi turned to go, his face hard as talltree wood. Ben's mouth was completely dry, and his hands were cold on the cryo-unit.

Say it, stupid, he ordered himself. *Just open your mouth and say it.*

The words still wouldn't come. Kendi reached the balcony doors, his back rigid. Ben already knew what was coming. They would eat a tense dinner from take-out cartons, after which Kendi would prowl restlessly through the Dream while Ben hid in his computer workshop or lifted weights. Ben would go to bed early, Kendi would stay up late. Ben would stare sleeplessly at the ceiling until Kendi finally came in to bed, whereupon Ben would feign sleep, even though Kendi knew Ben was faking to avoid talk. This would go on until Ben finally told Kendi what was bothering him. These little spells were rare, but the pattern was always the same, and suddenly Ben hated it. Kendi had to know, and Ben had to tell him. It was as simple as that. Still, he had to cough to get his voice to work.

"Kendi," he said. "Wait."

Kendi turned, his face expectant, yet uncertain.

"There is something going on. It's not bad. At least,

I don't *think* it's bad. But . . ." Ben took a deep breath.
"I just don't know how to tell you. It's . . . it's that . . ."

"Just say it, Ben. Hey, there's nothing you can say
that'll make me love you any less. Blurt it out."

"Yeah. Okay." Ben clutched the star-shaped cryo-unit
hard. The polymer was smooth, the corners sharp. Sometimes it seemed like he could hear eleven tiny voices
calling to him, begging him to let them out. He wanted
to. His mother had told him about his origins and about
his frozen siblings as soon as he was old enough to understand, and Ben was glad of it. It had been obvious
from the start that he was different. Mom's entire family
had ultimately sprung from the Middle East back on
Earth, and Ben's red hair stood out like a torch in the
rain forest. Finding out why was a relief. Ben used to
pretend his brothers and sisters were just sleeping, and
one day they would wake up, ready to join his family.
Now he had the chance to make fantasy into reality.
First, however, he had to tell Kendi the truth.

"It's kind of a family thing," he began. "See, I learned—"

"Attention! Attention!" said the house computer. "Incoming call for Ben Rymar and Kendi Weaver. Caller
requesting high priority. Attention! Attention! Incoming
call for—"

"High priority?" Kendi interrupted. "Irene, who is
calling?"

"Senator Salman Reza."

"Isn't she out of town?" Kendi said.

"We better take this," Ben said, uncertain whether he
was relieved or not. He strode into the living room and
tapped one hardwood wall. "Irene, connect."

The wall glowed briefly, and Salman Reza's face appeared on the screen. She was eighty years old but
looked closer to sixty. Her face was round and only
lightly lined, and thick silver hair made a firm helmet on
her head. Her eyes were dark, and she was smiling. For
a moment Ben saw his mother, Ara, on the screen, and
a small lump came to his throat. Ara Rymar had died
almost eight months ago, but grief still struck Ben from
unusual directions. He did like Grandma Salman a great
deal, though growing up he had usually seen her only at
major holidays and family gatherings.

"Welcome home, Grandma," Ben said. "What's going on? We got your other message."

"So you know I'm going to declare my candidacy," Salman said. "I'm sure you've figured out that it's going to have a big impact on this family, yes?"

"It had crossed our minds," Kendi said wryly. "Going to put yourself through the ringer, eh?"

"I live for pain, hon," Salman said, equally wry. "But I think the Unionist Party is the best choice to lead Bellerophon right now."

"And as head Unionist, that would put you in the governor's chair," Ben said.

"By sheer coincidence," Salman agreed, still smiling. "Which means we really need to have a family meeting, my ducks, and the sooner, the better. Dinner at my house tonight? Six o'clock. No need to dress."

Ben checked his fingernail for the time. "We'll barely make it."

"I'll send a flit. See you soon." Her image vanished.

"No room for argument," Kendi grinned. "No wonder she's party chief."

"We better hurry and dress," Ben said, already moving toward the bedroom.

"What? But she said—"

"You know Grandma," Ben interrupted. "When she says 'no need to dress,' it only means you don't have to wear formal robes and I don't have to wear a tuxedo."

Cora Haaseth, age ten, peered around the spiral slide. Nick was nowhere in sight, and the talltree branch they had designated as home base was in clear view. Cora narrowed her eyes. Nick played hide-and-seek to win. When he was It, he sometimes hid so he could guard his base from a safe vantage point, leap out, and tag anyone foolish enough to make a dash for home. Right now Cora couldn't see him anywhere, and that made her suspicious.

A scattering of other kids played on the playground, filling the air with shrieks and yells. A series of platforms connected by rope ladders, stairs, ramps, and slides wound its way around the talltree. Swings and merry-go-rounds occupied some of the platforms, along with hopscotch courts, flimsy-ball loops, and catch-em bars. It was a pretty fun place, though Cora had the opinion that she was outgrowing it. Cora caught sight of Sammy Fishman, who was peeking out of a series of interconnected plastic tunnels. He looked ready to run for it. Cora nodded to herself. She could watch Sammy go first, let him spring any trap Nick might have set.

"Excuse me, young miss," said a voice behind her. "Can you help us?"

Cora turned in surprise. A human man and woman stood behind her. The man was holding a small holographic image generator on his palm. Above the generator hovered the image of a puppy with big paws and floppy ears.

"What's wrong?" Cora asked.

"We lost our puppy," the woman explained. "And we need help finding him."

"You have a puppy?" Cora said, fascinated. Bellerophon was a city of platforms and walkways, and dogs were difficult to care for in such an environment. Cats, which could be litter-trained, were easier to deal with. Cora's family had two of them, in fact, but she had always wanted a puppy.

"He ran away," the man said. He was tall and blond, and his blue eyes crinkled up when he smiled. "He's probably hungry and scared. Have you seen him?"

Cora shook her head. Mom had warned her about talking to strangers, but these people were obviously nice. And they had lost a puppy.

"Maybe you can help find him," the woman said. She had black hair. "If we give you a copy of the holo, you could show it to your friends."

"Sure," Cora said. "I'll ask around."

"Thanks," the man said. "We've got copies of the holo over here. Come on—we'll give you one."

As Cora followed the couple away, she took a glance over her shoulder. Sammy Fishman had left the safety of his hiding place and was running for all he was worth toward home base. At the last moment, Nick jumped out from around a corner and tagged him. Cora smiled to herself, glad she'd been too smart to fall into that trap.

CHAPTER TWO

"Family secrets are sometimes even kept from family."
—Daniel Vik

The automated flitcar rushed through the cool spring air. Kendi looked out the window. The sun had become a lonely orange ball dropping to kiss the horizon, and the talltree forest below was already in shadow. A few lights shone here and there amid the canopy, looking isolated and forlorn. Before the Despair, Treetown had been a bright, vibrant place after dark, with plenty of house- and streetlights to banish the shadows. Most people in the post-Despair depression, however, burned as few lights as possible in an attempt to scrape up a few more pennies for food. The flitcar was the only vehicle in the sky, another indicator of the new poverty that crushed Bellerophon and her people. Kendi felt a stab of guilt. He was riding high above want and need in a hired flitcar.

Ben sat beside him, face stoic. Kendi sneaked a glance at him. Although Kendi was burning with curiosity about Ben's news, whatever it was, he knew better than to press for details right now. Visiting Ben's family was stress enough for him. It could wait until they got home.

To pass the time, he called up a newsfeed text on his data pad. Ched-Pirasku, the Populist party leader, had just declared his candidacy and was now part of the race for governor. The Guardians were looking for a ten-year-old girl who had disappeared from a playground near the monastery. Foul play was suspected. An advice columnist advised a husband to be creative in order to spark his wife's waning libido. And the Treetown Carnosaurs had beaten the Othertown Pirates 5-2 at soccer.

"We're almost there," Ben said, and Kendi shut off the pad.

The little flitcar approached an enormous house with a circular landing pad on the roof. It circled once, landed, and opened the door. Kendi smoothed his blue silk tunic and slid out into the chilly air. Ben, dressed in midnight black from head to toe, followed. Down among the trees it was as if the sun had already set, though Senator Salman Reza kept lights on her roof, and they shed a warm golden illumination.

The moment Kendi and Ben cleared the flitcar, its door snapped shut, and the car fled back to the sky in a silent rush of wind that ruffled Ben's sunset hair. Kendi gently combed the thick strands back into place with his fingers.

"You," he said, "look damned amazing in black, Mr. Rymar."

A hint of red colored Ben's face. "And you look fantastic fine in electric blue, Father Weaver."

"Then let us grace this party with our august presence." Kendi threw an arm across Ben's solid shoulders, and they moved toward a large painted circle marked LIFT. Darkening azure sky stretched above them, and the tops of the talltrees made a green carpet that stretched all the way to the horizon. Ben's body was warm next to Kendi's, and he gave an inward sigh as they approached the lift. Ben was Kendi's rock, hard and solid, always there. And like a rock, Ben could be stubborn and silent. Kendi had been surprised when Ben started to talk about what was bothering him, and the computer call had seriously pissed him off. If it weren't for the high-priority request, Kendi would have simply ignored the call. What could be so horrible? It must have been something that had happened since they got back from Silent Acquisitions, Ltd. Maybe it was the raid. No, Ben had said it was a family thing. Maybe it had to do with Kendi's brother and sister.

Several months ago, Kendi had learned that his brother Keith and sister Martina, captured and sold into slavery when they were children, were being held by a corporation called Silent Acquisitions, Ltd. Kendi, Ben,

Harenn, and Lucia had put together a risky plan to get them out, a plan that sometimes still made Kendi sweat in retrospect. In the end, however, after two months of effort, they had come away with not only Kendi's brother and sister but an entire shipload of escaped Silent Acquisitions slaves to boot.

After fifteen years of separation, Kendi abruptly had a brother and sister again. Keith and Martina were currently sharing a small house that had belonged to Ben before his mother had died, and Kendi spent a fair amount of time visiting them.

A thought struck Kendi. Maybe Ben was jealous. Kendi turned the idea over in his mind. It made sense from several sides. Ben wasn't used to sharing Kendi with anyone. And Kendi had been spending almost every spare moment with Keith and Martina lately, helping them acclimate to the Monastery of Irfan, showing them what it meant to be free again, and just getting to know them once more.

A family thing. Jealousy? Ben doubtless felt uncomfortable admitting he was jealous, since he knew Kendi had missed his family horribly and it wasn't fair to expect him not to see them often. Ben, shy to begin with, hadn't made a big effort to insert himself into the relationship, and Kendi, idiot that he was, hadn't noticed.

The more Kendi thought about it, the more sense it made. Poor Ben! No wonder he'd been upset. Well, Kendi would have to reassure him once they got home. Then there would be the make-up session in bed—a fine prospect in and of itself—and everything would be all right again. The revelation put a slight spring in Kendi's step and a wide smile on his face.

"What?" Ben asked, noticing the change in Kendi's mood.

Kendi kissed him on the cheek. "I'll tell you later, love. For now, we only have to—"

Another silent blast of air hit them from behind. Both men turned. A second flitcar was landing on the roof. The door opened, and a male-female couple emerged. They were both in their late fifties, running toward plump, and wearing brown robes. Both of them wore amber rings. Ben groaned. Kendi grimaced.

"Well, we knew it would happen," he said. "A family meeting brings out the family."

"I'm just glad we aren't technically related," Ben muttered as the pair approached.

"You don't have a single asshole gene in you," Kendi agreed.

"Not even after all those times we—"

Kendi tightened his arm around Ben's shoulder. "Company manners, love. Hello, Brother Hazid. Sister Sil."

Hazid and Sil Lemish—Ben's aunt and uncle—paused uncertainly. Kendi gave a prim smile. This was a purely social situation, but Kendi had addressed them by their monastic titles, throwing everything into a more formal mode. Sil uncertainly brought her fingers up to touch her forehead in automatic salute, then stopped herself when she realized what Kendi was doing. Hazid merely glowered.

"Very funny, Kendi," he growled. "So it's going to be like this tonight, is it?"

"Is it ever any other way?" Kendi replied, not bothering to keep the contempt out of his voice. He felt Ben tense beside him.

"I don't know why you have to snipe all the time," Sil put in. Her voice was high and whiny and made Kendi's teeth ache. Her hair was styled into an old-fashioned helmet like Salman's.

"When you figure out why I do it, I'll stop," Kendi said. He drew Ben closer to him, turned his back, and stepped onto the lift. Ben's mouth was tight. "Down," Kendi ordered before Sil and Hazid could join them. The lift sank into the roof, leaving the other couple behind.

Once Ben's and Kendi's heads dropped below roof level, a door slid shut above them, and the lift descended gently to the floor of an entry foyer. The interior of Salman Reza's house was all white plaster walls and deeply carpeted floors. Expensive paintings hung in tasteful places, and the furniture looked more elegant than comfortable. Kendi dropped his arm from Ben's shoulder, and they stepped off the lift together. It rose back up toward the ceiling to fetch Sil and Hazid.

Ahead, the foyer opened into a formal sitting room, and Kendi's attention was immediately drawn straight to a hovering easy chair and the woman seated therein. Senator Salman Reza. She had silver hair, pale gray eyes, and an absolutely straight posture. The senator was a large woman, and her presence permeated the room. When she sprang to her feet to greet Ben and Kendi, her movements crackled with fierce energy.

"Come in, ducks," she said. Her voice filled the space around her. "Your aunt and uncle should be here any moment now."

"They're on the roof," Kendi said, and kissed her on one soft cheek. She reminded Kendi of Ara Rymar, her daughter and Kendi's longtime teacher. Ara had also been Kendi's surrogate mother from the time she had freed him from slavery at the age of fifteen. Her death had dealt him a heavy blow, one that still made him reel at times.

Elsewhere in the room, fresh flowers made splashes of scented color among the furniture, and in the corner a floor-to-ceiling cage swarmed with dozens of tiny Bellerophon tree dinosaurs, each one yellow as sunshine. They chirped with musical softness. On a sofa that floated a few centimeters off the floor perched younger versions of Sil and Hazid—Zayim and Tress, Ben's cousins.

Ben gave his grandmother a kiss of his own while Kendi turned to the cousins.

"Brother Zayim," he said formally. "Sister Tress."

Neither of them rose to the bait. Zayim got up to shake hands. Tress kept her seat. Her eyes were tired, almost vacant, and she looked unfocused and dim, especially with her grandmother in the room. Still dealing with the aftermath of the Despair, Kendi thought.

The lift came down again, and Sil and Hazid entered the room, looking defiant. More greetings were exchanged. Ben said very little, pulling inward tight as a turtle. His handsome face remained expressionless, though Kendi's practiced eye saw the misery. It made Kendi's blood boil to see Ben like this, and fresh anger burned in his chest. Ara Rymar had been active among the faction of the Children of Irfan that traveled about the galaxy, seeking enslaved Silent and doing whatever it took to free them. Ara had used bribery, theft, blackmail, extortion, and an endless supply of con games to pry Silent chattel away from their owners and bring them back to Bellerophon.

This meant, of course, that Ara had been away for long periods when Ben was a child. During those times, Ben had usually stayed with his aunt, uncle, and cousins. Ara had hoped that Tress and Zayim would turn into a brother and sister for her only child, but it had never worked out that way. Not only did Ben look completely different, he was also the only family member who wasn't Silent. Tress and Zayim had made his life miserable, and Hazid and Sil had turned blind eyes to it. Had contributed to it. Kendi kept hoping that one of them would finally give him an excuse to use an uppercut. Or a groin shot.

Everyone settled back into couches and chairs, which adjusted their elevation for optimum comfort. A tray of hors d'oeuvres sat on the etched glass coffee table next to a selection of chilled flasks and bottles and a steaming tea set. Kendi knew the rule—no one but Salman touched that tea set.

"Help yourselves," Salman said. "Dinner will be ready soon. I don't know about all of you, but I'm tired and starving."

"Long trip?" Hazid said.

"Fourteen days of speaking, pleading, cajoling, and even roaring like a dinosaur," she said. "And I'm not a hatchling anymore."

"So what's this meeting about, Grandma?" Kendi asked, pouring himself a glass of juice. "As if we didn't know."

"When will you be making the formal announcement?" Tress asked. Her voice was low, barely audible.

"Soon," Salman said. "Within a few days. There are things to discuss first, my loves."

"Such as?" Ben asked, and Kendi could hear his apprehension.

"The impact my candidacy will have on this family." Salman picked up a teacup and saucer in her large hands. "Bellerophon's population numbers about ninety-eight million people. Just over half are human. The Ched-Balaar make up approximately forty percent, and the rest consist of other sentient species. I want to be their governor. This means that millions of people are going to be watching me and mine very carefully. Unfortunately, this also means that you'll come under a certain amount of scrutiny as well. Sil, you're my only . . . my only child now, and the press will try to take a hard look at you."

"Let them," Sil said airily. "I have nothing to hide."

"What about all those recreational drugs you took last year?" Kendi asked.

"How dare you!" Hazid snapped, half-rising.

"I never did any such thing!" Sil said.

" 'Candidate's Daughter Denies Taking Drugs,' " Kendi intoned like a newscaster. " 'Details at ten.' "

Ben said, "Ouch." Sil stared at Kendi, her mouth open.

"He's right, Mother," Tress said quietly. "We have to be ready for that."

"I can, of course, let the press know that my family isn't involved in my politics and that any reporter who bothers you will never have access to my administration," Salman said, "but that sort of protection only goes so far, and it's an empty threat to the scummier newsfeeds that know they'd never be allowed inside the governor's mansion anyway. Everything you say, everything you do, is a potential story. If you accidentally belch in a restaurant, there'll be a vid of it on the feeds within minutes. If you step outside with your fly unfastened, they'll beam a close-up into every living room on the planet."

"What about personal safety?" Kendi asked.

"Safety?" Zayim echoed. "You mean we're in danger?"

"We have ninety-eight million people in the world," Salman said, "and some of them talk to trees. Or wear foil hats. Or think they're the reincarnation of Irfan Qasad."

Ben snatched up a napkin and coughed wildly, drenching the cloth with a mouthful of soda. Kendi thumped him on the back.

"You all right?" he asked, concerned.

"Fine. Sorry, Grandma."

Salman nodded. "Since the Despair, the number of mental patients has skyrocketed," she continued. "Some of them fixate on public figures and may—I stress, *may*—want to harm you. And, of course, I have political enemies who might try to influence me by threatening you."

"I don't want bodyguards," Zayim said. "Do you think I need bodyguards?"

"We'll talk specifics in a moment," Salman said. "Right now I'm just laying out the topics of discussion. We also need to go over privacy issues, what's likely to come out in the press, and how to behave in public. Especially you, Kendi."

"Me?" Kendi said, startled.

Zayid smirked while Hazid nudged Sil in the ribs. They exchanged knowing looks.

"You aren't known for your tact, hon," Salman said, and Kendi shifted a little under her penetrating gaze. He was surprised to find himself flushing. "What you did during the Despair has granted you a certain amount of leeway—"

"You mean the fact that I saved the universe means people give me a little slack now and then?" Kendi said, despite his warm cheeks. "Imagine that."

"Now that's exactly what she means," Sil said. "You can't shoot your mouth off whenever you like, Kendi, or lord your status over the rest of us like a spoiled child. If you want to be a part of this family, you can't go around saying—"

"*If* I want to *be* a member?" Kendi interrupted. "Let's get one thing straight, Sil. I was dragged kicking and screaming into this den of dysfunction. Ben is the only one of you lot who's worth a—"

"That's *enough*!" Salman's voice boomed like a cannon. "You listen to me—all of you. I know damned well that this family has two enemy camps. I also know that if I'm going to win this election, we have to present a united front. I don't give a flying shit-fit if it's a fake front or not. What you do and say behind closed doors is your own damn business, but in public, you *behave*. Or do you want Michael Foxglove in the governor's mansion?"

Her fury silenced the room. Kendi clenched a fist. Tress had drawn her feet up and tucked them underneath herself on the sofa. Sil and Hazid sat rigidly next to each other, and Ben's face was carved from stone. The stillness lay thick as dust.

"Grandma's right," Kendi said at last. "We can't let Foxglove anywhere near the governorship."

"I never liked the fighting," Tress said softly. "Not since the Despair, anyway. Ben . . ." She took a deep breath. "Ben, I want to apologize. I treated you like dirt when we were kids, and I wasn't any better when we grew up. I was dreadful, and I'm sorry."

Ben stared, clearly unable to speak. Kendi squeezed his hand. It was sweaty.

"Tress!" Zayid said. "What the hell? We weren't any meaner than kids in any other family."

"Yes we were," Tress said. "We treated Ben like an outsider and a bastard child just because he wasn't Silent. Well these days he's Silent and we aren't, and now I know what it's like. So I'm apologizing."

"To make yourself feel better?" Kendi burst out. "Assuage some guilt? All life—is he supposed to forget everything you did and said to him just because you say you're *sorry*?"

"Kendi," Ben said. "You're hurting my hand."

Kendi instantly relaxed his grip, though he couldn't keep from grinding his teeth. Tress expected a single sentence to undo more than twenty years? What kind of trick was she trying to pull?

"I accept, Tress," Ben said gravely.

"Thank you," Tress replied.

Kendi started to speak again, but Ben squeezed his hand hard, and Ben's hands were *strong*. Kendi suppressed a wince and shut his mouth.

"Let's continue, then," Salman interjected from her chair. Every head swiveled toward her. "I'm afraid very little of this is going to be pleasant, my ducks, and I want you to remember that I love each of you very much. The public, however, may have a different view."

"What do you mean?" Zayid said.

"Let's start with the news media. They're going to dig into our pasts to look for delightful and interesting facts to air on the feeds. We need to anticipate what will come up and how to handle it.

"First, Zayid, they'll make hay over your four marriages, your four divorces, and the child you had from that one-night stand."

Zayid paled. "How did you know about that?"

"And Tress," Salman continued, ignoring the question, "they'll learn how your studies at the monastery were delayed while you underwent rehabilitation. Sil and Hazid, you separated for six months and got back together again, but only after Sil spent time in a psychiatric hospital. None of this should cost me the election, but it *will* come out, and you need to be ready for it."

"What about Ben and Kendi?" Sil said, her face hard. "They aren't perfect, you know."

"The circumstances of Ben's birth will come under scrutiny, yes," Salman said. "As will his and Kendi's role in the Despair, though that's already gone through the feeds a thousand times. If there's anything else you can think of that might come out, you'd better tell me, either here and now or soon and in private."

The room remained silent. Kendi thought about his checkered past at the monastery, his angry teenager days. He'd stomped on several dozen rules and almost been expelled twice. Or was it three times? Maybe he should mention that to Salman.

"Remember," Salman continued, "that the media are extremely resourceful and persistent. If there's anything to find, they'll find it, and they'll make it public. It's easier to deal with such things if we know about them in advance, my loves."

On the couch beside Kendi, Ben tensed. A flush crawled over his face, and subtle movements of his jaw told Kendi he was chewing the inside of his cheek. Did Ben have a dark secret? A skeleton in the closet? No. Kendi knew Ben's past like he knew his own, and it contained nothing Grandma hadn't already mentioned. Kendi considered asking him. Then he caught sight of Sil and Hazid, whose faces bore an odd mix of stubbornness and anticipation. They were dying to hear some tidbit about Kendi and Ben, something they could snicker and snarl about. Kendi's own stubborn streak came to the fore, and he clamped his lips firmly shut. There was no way he would give Hazid and the others the satisfaction of ferreting out some nugget of scandal, especially one attached to Ben.

"I'll talk to each of you later, then," Salman said. Her words sounded ominous. "Also remember that reporters will almost certainly dog your steps every moment of every day once I declare my candidacy. The four of you"—she made a gesture that took in Kendi, Ben, Tress, and Zayim—"can expect less attention because you're 'only' my grandchildren, though Kendi is already a celebrity."

"Senator," said a gray-clad maid at the doorway, "dinner is ready."

They rose and went into the dining hall, where they took places at a long, polished table beneath a crystal chandelier. Salman sat at the head. The first course was clear onion soup covered with a mild, melted cheese. It was delicately seasoned and delightfully salty. Kendi savored each mouthful and wished that Ben liked to cook. Or that Kendi himself *could* cook. Ben, however, remained supremely uninterested in culinary matters. As for Kendi, every time he even glanced at the kitchen, food smoked, shriveled, vaporized, or exploded. Eventually the two of them had given up and run up tabs at all the local take-out places. Ben called it their duty to the local economy.

Salman continued her speech as they ate. "In answer to Sil's earlier question," she said, "Sil and Hazid will indeed need bodyguards. It would be foolish for you to go out in public undefended. The Guardians will work with you, of course, and keep the disruption to a minimum."

Hazid groaned and Sil covered her mouth with a napkin, but neither one of them questioned Salman's assertion.

"What about the rest of us?" Kendi asked.

"As a rule, grandchildren of high-ranking government figures don't need bodyguards. However, if any kind of threat arises, we'll provide security to you."

"How much will all this cost?" Hazid asked.

"The bodyguards are government employees," Salman

said. "No cost to you. And that brings us to the next thing—blathering personal opinions."

The maid took away the soup bowls and replaced them with small fish fillets drizzled with a creamy mushroom sauce. Kendi picked up his fish knife and suppressed a smile. He had grown up in the poorer section of Sydney, Australia, back on Earth, running half-wild with his older brother and younger sister on the grimy streets. His parents had fought to get him to use a plastic spoon to shovel beans down his throat. Now he was eating a fish fillet at a table decorated with enough cutlery to arm a small nation. Life was a strange thing indeed.

"The media will ask you about this issue or that problem," Salman said. "And they'll be relentless. Just acknowledging their presence will start a frenzy, and they won't leave you alone."

"Well, that's all to the good," Sil said. "I have a few things to say about—"

"*No*," Salman interjected firmly. "That's exactly what I'm warning you about. Never, *ever* talk to a reporter or newsfeeder. Even a comment that seems innocuous at the time can have earth-shattering repercussions for my campaign. Kendi already showed you how easily they can twist words. The only thing you should ever say in the presence of a reporter is—"

" 'Get the hell out of my way'?" Kendi asked.

"I was thinking a firm 'No comment,' " Salman replied. "You need to understand that even the slightest slip can damage my party and my chances."

"How many Senate seats do the Unionists hold right now?" Ben asked.

"We have thirty-two," Salman said. "A little over a third. Foxglove's Federals hold only twenty-five, but we're both outnumbered by Ched-Pirasku and the Populists, since they have the remaining forty-one."

Kendi did some math. "Ninety-eight seats total. When did the Senate lose one?"

"Just after the Despair," Salman said. "Enough people died that we had to remove a chair. The Federals were the losers, thank heaven, and you should have seen the fight they put up. Redistricting everyone was war, especially because we were trying to run this place on our own for the first time. We still don't know what the hell we're doing half the time."

Kendi nodded. Just a few months ago, Bellerophon had been a part of the Independence Confederation, a powerful government that encompassed dozens of worlds. The Bellerophon Senate had run local affairs but ultimately answered to Empress Kan maja Kalii, a benign and popular ruler. After the Despair severed all interplanetary communication, however, the Confederation fell apart, and Bellerophon was left to its own devices. Political parties rose out of the chaos, and the Senate decided to elect a planetary governor imbued with the powers once held by the empress. To avoid giving any one party too much power, the Senate also decided that the governor would be elected by popular vote and not appointed by Senate majority.

"The real struggle is going to be defeating the Populists," Salman said. "They hold the most seats, and Ched-Pirasku's popularity is pretty high right now."

"But together the Unionists and the Federals outnumber them," Tress pointed out. "That has to be some kind of advantage for you."

"Not as much as you'd think," Salman said. "We're polar opposites. My Unionists are out to keep Bellerophon a united planet, and we've *got* to build up the military and find some allies. It'll mean more jobs, for one thing. For another, Bellerophon has more functioning Silent per capita than any other planet in the galaxy, and you can be sure someone out there will realize that we're ripe for picking without the empress to defend us. An invasion is inevitable. But Foxglove and his pet Federals are pushing that separatist nonsense. They want to pull away from the rest of the galaxy and retreat into racial enclaves. Foolishness! This isn't the time to entrench—it's time to expand, to reach out toward other—"

"We're on your side, Grandma," Zayid interrupted. "You don't need to give us the speech."

Salman's mouth snapped shut. Then she gave a small smile. "Sorry. Rhetoric is a hard habit to break."

"How are the campaign finances doing?" Hazid asked, changing the subject.

"Could be better," Salman said. "There isn't much to go around these days."

Kendi looked down at the remains of his fish and saw the face of a hungry little girl.

THE CHILDREN OF IRFAN EAT WHILE MY CHILDREN STARVE!

People were going hungry around the galaxy, even on this very planet, and Kendi was eating gourmet food from china plates with silver flatware. Grandma Salman wasn't hurting. Neither were he and Ben. But they were exceptions. The Despair had Silenced almost all the Children of Irfan, the very people who provided Silent communication for hundreds of governments and corporations in all corners of the galaxy, and the revenue generated by this essential service kept the Children and their employees highly solvent, even wealthy. Now only a tiny handful of Children could enter the Dream, and they produced only tiny handfuls of money.

"I'm running fund-raisers," Salman continued, "but it's hard to get people to cough up. That's another problem. The Populists are bigger, so Ched-Pirasku is outgunning me financially. The Federals are smaller, thank heavens, so Mitchell Foxglove is an even worse position than I am. I'll be exploiting that, my ducks, you may be sure."

The fish was replaced with a char-grilled steak tender enough to cut with a fork. Three splinters of bone placed discreetly on the plate told Kendi the meat came from a mickey spike, an herbivorous dinosaur the size of a truck. Mickey spike meat was always served with three bone slivers on the side. No one knew exactly why, though folklorists argued endlessly about it.

"We're all waiting for the High Court's ruling on Othertown's mining rights," Salman said. "That'll have a tremendous impact on my campaign."

"I don't understand the connection," Sil said, setting her bone slivers aside and cutting a piece of meat. "I know you've been trying to get the rights halted, but—"

"We can't allow Bellerophon to become another Earth," Salman said. "It was extremely wise of the original colonists to put severe restrictions on mining and tree farming and anything else that might hurt—"

"You're giving another speech, Grandma," Ben said. "What's it got to do with your campaign?"

"Money," Salman said, and popped a bit of steak into her mouth.

"It always comes down to that," Kendi said. He remembered the dreadlocked woman and the little girl, and a thought struck him. "Before you explain, Grandma, tell me if I'm right."

"Oh, here we go," muttered Zayim. Tress waved her wineglass to shush him.

"If the Othertown district is granted better mining privileges," Kendi said, "it will mean a boom in the mining industry. That'll open up new jobs. The people who are out of work in Treetown will move to Othertown to find employment. And *that* will mean another redistricting. Correct so far?"

Salman nodded, chewing. "Very good."

"An exodus will cost Treetown plenty in the way of political power and hand it to Othertown," Kendi said. "So it's definitely in Mitchell Foxglove's interest for that law to pass."

"And he's pushing hard for that to happen," Salman said. "Before the Despair, the High Court thought more like I do. But the Despair balanced the bench, and the mining decision could go either way now. I can't say I blame them for changing their minds, but it's a short-term solution that'll create long-term problems."

"What are you planning to do?" Ben asked.

"Lobby," Salman replied. "But indirectly. Lobbying the High Court is a no-no, but there's the food lobby and the drinks lobby and even the dessert lobby."

"What's that all about?" Sil said.

"High Court justices work long, torturous hours, poor things," Salman said. "And it's my duty as a citizen to ensure my justices have plenty of delicious food and drink at their fingertips for those late-night sessions. I have informants at every restaurant and food market within walking distance of Justiciary Hall, so I know their favorite dishes."

"Isn't that . . . bribery?" Tress said.

"It would be," Salman said with a bland smile, "if food counted as money. And it doesn't. Keep that in mind the next time you want me to do something for you, my ducks."

That garnered small chuckles, and the conversation turned away from politics. Kendi began to relax, if only a little bit. Naturally, Salman dropped a bombshell in the middle of dessert.

"I have one last request," she said, digging her fork into a meltingly soft chocolate cake. "Ben and Kendi, it would be a great help if the two of you would publicly endorse my campaign."

Ben froze, a forkful of cake partway to his mouth.

Kendi nodded. "I was wondering when you'd get around to asking that."

"No ego problems *there*," Zayim muttered.

For once, Kendi ignored him. "What did you have in mind, Grandma?"

"You'd tell everyone you can what a wonderful governor I'd make. There'd be fund-raisers, advertisements, speeches—the usual."

"No," Ben said.

Salman raised silver eyebrows.

"I'm sorry," Ben said, his face wooden. "But no. I'm not going to stand on a podium and make a fool of myself. Kendi's better at that than I am."

Kendi laughed. "I think that's a compliment."

"I don't suppose you're going to ask any of *us*," Hazid said. Chocolate crumbs dropped from his lips into his lap.

"I'm sorry to be so blunt, dear," Salman said, "but you aren't a celebrity. Ben is. So is Kendi."

"Only because Kendi hogs the spotlight," Zayim pointed out. " 'Look at me, everyone! I saved the whole goddamed universe! I'm a god! Bow down before me!' "

"Awwww, wook at dat, Gwamma," Kendi cooed. "Widdle Zayim's so cute when he's jealous."

"Don't you call me cute," Zayim snarled. "I'm not like you."

"Yeah—I know how to use birth control."

"Is that what you call it?"

"Time to go," Ben said, rising and hauling Kendi to his feet. "Thanks for dinner, Grandma." And he towed Kendi toward the door.

"I'll do it, Grandma," Kendi called over his shoulder. "Call me."

Ben remained silent on the trip home. Kendi didn't try to draw him into conversation, and for this Ben was grateful. It always took Ben a few hours to recover from a family visit. He was still feeling unstable from this one. As always, Grandma was loud and bossy. Sil and Hazid made Ben shake with a mixture of fear and anger. Zayim remained immature and obnoxious. And Tress! Her unexpected apology had startled Ben more than anything else that evening. He still wasn't sure he believed it. He wanted to believe it.

Kendi, on the other hand, was clearly in a bouncy mood, and he fidgeted on the seat next to Ben. He knew what Kendi was thinking. Salman had asked him to endorse her campaign, and he was excited. Ben tried to be excited for him, use Kendi's happiness to banish his own unease. It worked a little bit, but Ben still didn't feel like talking.

The automated flitcar deposited them in front of their house and vanished into the night sky. Walkways and balconies made black lattices among the talltree branches. Tree lizards chirped and squeaked from hidden places, and the night air was chilly. Ben and Kendi's two-story house, the one left to Ben by his mother, was dark. Ben palmed the lock and the lights came on inside. The usual twinge—

mom's dead and I'm in her house

—bolted through him, then faded. Maybe one day it would disappear entirely. Ben wasn't sure if that was a good thing or not.

A pair of arms hugged him from behind and a dark chin rested on his shoulder. "How do you feel?" Kendi asked.

Ben reached back and rested a hand on Kendi's rough hair. The touch settled Ben a little, and he felt muscles unclench. "Better," he said. "Now that I'm home."

"I hate what they do to you," Kendi said. "Maybe we should tell Grandma we won't do family meetings if your family is there."

Ben had to laugh. "Maybe. How about coffee?"

"That'll settle your nerves?"

"It will if you drink it with me."

They entered the spacious kitchen with its polished wood floor and cabinets. Ben pulled the coffeemaker from its niche and filled it with water. The coffee container was almost empty, the victim of an early shortage. Coffee was one of the few dishes Ben could reliably make, however, and it had the added benefit of not reminding him of his mother, an avid tea-drinker. Ben set the machine to brewing, then got out the cream and sugar. Ben wondered how long it'd be before sugar became hard to find. Kendi sat in amiable silence at the wooden table with an enigmatic look on his face. The rich smell of fresh coffee filled the kitchen. Ben narrowed blue eyes.

"What?" he said.

"What what?" Kendi asked.

"You look . . . sly," Ben replied. "What are you up to, Father Kendi?"

"Everyone suspects me of being up to something," Kendi complained.

"That's not a denial."

Kendi toyed with a sugar spoon. "I've figured out your secret, is all."

"My secret?" Ben said, confused.

"About why you've been edgy lately, why you haven't wanted to talk to me. I know all about it."

Ben's stomach clenched, and he sank into the chair opposite Kendi. "You do?"

"Hey, it's okay." Kendi reached across the table and took Ben's hand. "I'm not mad, love. I know it's been hard for you, and I can see why you'd have a hard time bringing it up with me."

"Oh. Okay," Ben said, and felt oddly put out. He had torn his hair out forcing himself to decide when to tell Kendi about his parents, and now Kendi had gone and found out on his own. He felt oddly cheated. "But how did you figure it out? Harenn didn't say anything, did she? Or Lucia?"

"Lucia?" Now Kendi looked confused. "No, it was logic. That, and the fact that I know you better than anyone else. It's a natural reaction."

"It is?"

"Sure. Hell, I should have seen it coming." Kendi squeezed Ben's hand once and released it. "But I'm not upset. You're my family, Ben, and we'll work it out. You don't need to be jealous of my family."

"Uh . . ." was the best Ben could come up with. By now it was clear he and Kendi weren't talking about the same thing. So Kendi *didn't* know. Ben's mouth went dry, and he steeled himself for what had to come next.

"Look," he said, "there *is* something I need to tell you, but it's not—"

A knock at the front door interrupted him. Kendi let out an aggravated noise. "Who the hell is coming by at this hour?"

"It's not even eight-thirty," Ben said. "It just feels later because of everything that's happened. Irene, who's at the door?"

"Wanda Petrie," said the computer.

"Wanda Petrie?" Kendi repeated. "Who the hell is Wanda Petrie?"

"No idea," Ben said.

"Irene, ask Wanda Petrie to state her business."

Pause. "Wanda Petrie says she is a publicist who is here to see Father Kendi Weaver. Wanda Petrie says she is in the employ of Senator Salman Reza."

"I'd better put another pot on to brew," Ben said, feeling both relief and trepidation. Was this a reprieve or an impediment?

"It's okay, Ben," Kendi said. "We can pretend we aren't home."

"Don't be ridiculous. Irene, unlock the door and tell our guest we're in the kitchen." He poured the coffee into a carafe and started the second pot.

"Hello?" said a woman's voice a moment later. "Father Kendi?"

"In here," Kendi called. "We're just having some coffee."

A woman entered the kitchen. Her hard shoes snapped the floorboards with quick clicks. Her blue business suit stood stiff at every crease, and her upswept brown hair was rigidly piled in a firm nest atop her head. She extended a birdlike hand to Kendi, who rose to shake it.

"Father Kendi," she said. "I'm Wanda Petrie, manager and publicist. Senator Reza hired me to handle your involvement in her campaign."

"That didn't take long," Kendi said with a wide, white grin. "We only just left her house."

"I was already on her staff, Father. The senator called to reassign me a few minutes ago, and I decided not to waste time."

"Efficient," Kendi said.

"Coffee?" Ben said, brandishing the carafe and an empty cup.

"You have coffee?" Petrie said. "I'd love some. Are you . . . ?"

"Sorry," Kendi said. "Ms. Petrie, this is Ben Rymar, my spouse."

"Of course," Petrie said, and shook hands when Ben set the cup down. Her grip was dry and forceful. "I don't have to tell you, Mr. Rymar, that Senator Reza is still hoping you'll eventually join the campaign as well. Two heroes of the Despair would be a major asset."

"Not for me," Ben replied. "Cream and sugar?"

They took up places at the table. Kendi drank his coffee with long, slow swallows. Petrie sipped quickly, like a bird dipping up water. Ben stirred his, staring at the swirling patterns that trailed after his spoon.

"We need to set a schedule, Mr. Weaver," Petrie said between sips, and set a data pad on the table. A tap called up the holographic screen, and another tap called up a calendar program. "I've already contacted a feed studio, and they can film your first commercial the day after tomorrow at eight o'clock. That should end in time for you to attend a fund-raising luncheon for the Ched-Balaar League of—"

"Wait, wait, wait," Kendi said, holding up his hands. "I'm still at the monastery, you know. I have duties in the Dream. We don't have a whole lot of working Silent these days, and I can't just—"

"Senator Reza is arranging leave for you," Petrie interrupted. "It shouldn't be a problem. After all, the Children of Irfan are backing her campaign."

"With endorsements or funds?" Kendi asked. Ben could see he was getting interested despite himself.

"Both, though their funds are limited these days."

"You said you want me to speak at a luncheon," Kendi said. "I'm not much of a speechwriter, though I suppose I could put something together if I don't have to go to work."

Petrie looked horrified. "We have speechwriters, Father Kendi. Please don't *ever* speak extemporaneously in public. Every word you use has to be weighed carefully. Casual remarks can have terrible repercussions."

"So Grandma said."

"I've arranged an extensive workshop for you tomorrow afternoon," Petrie said, and the date glowed on the calendar. "Our team will take you through what to do and not do, what to say and not say."

"How fun," Kendi said with too much enthusiasm. Subtle signs in his expression and posture set off alarm bells in Ben's head. "Gee. What else will I learn?"

"How to dress, places you should and should not visit, what to say to unexpected questions, how to modulate your voice for best effect, and similar subjects."

"Where will they insert the key?"

Petrie looked blank. "The key?"

"The one that winds me up." Kendi made jerky hand motions like a mechanical toy. "Senator-Reza-is-the-best-choice-vote-for-her-no-further-comment."

Petrie's face hardened. "Mr. Weaver, Senator Reza is running for world governor. That means the world population is going to examine her and everyone in her campaign in great detail. That includes you. You are a hero of the Despair, and the public has raised you high, but remember that the public also tears people down, especially in hard times like these. If you can't control yourself and follow the rules we set for you, you'll become a liability to the senator's campaign. In that case, we'll have to let you go and hope the senator can win without you."

Ben half expected Kendi to snort in derision and tell Wanda Petrie to get lost. Instead, he thought a moment and then nodded.

"I'll go along with what you say," he said. "But I have a few conditions of my own."

Petrie looked doubtful. "What kind of conditions?"

"Ben and I are trying to start a family," he said. "That

comes first with me. This means I can't do multiday trips, and family business will take precedence over fund-raising, speeches, and commercials. I also reserve the right to modify speeches—with the help of your speech-writers, of course. This is because I won't publicly state a position I don't agree with."

"The last part is easy," Petrie said. "The first—I don't know. Long-range flits get expensive, and we'll definitely need you to speak in Othertown and Rangeway and other places. We can probably handle it, but I'll have to check with the senator."

"And speaking of expenses," Kendi continued, "how are mine going to be met? The monastery is generous, but I don't think they'll give me paid leave for a political campaign, even one they support."

"Stipend from us." Petrie took another sip of coffee. "Indirect, of course."

"How so?" Kendi asked.

"The campaign can't pay you a direct salary," Petrie explained. "It would destroy your credibility. Instead, we'll set up a foundation, then ask some of our contributors to give money to it. The contributors pay the foundation, the foundation pays you. The campaign never touches the money."

"And I thought *I* was a con artist," Kendi said happily. "This is going to be fun."

They continued to talk about the campaign and Kendi's schedule. Ben sat at the table, toying with his coffee and growing restless. He had been prepared to tell Kendi about his biological parents all afternoon and evening, and this latest delay was grating on him. Petrie stabbed at a date on the holographic calendar, and it changed from blue to green, indicating another speech. She was a black hole, sucking up Kendi's time and energy. Ben grew more and more restless as the coffee in his cup grew cold. The words built inside him like a volcano. Abruptly he stood up.

"It's late," he said. "Could we finish this later?"

Wanda Petrie looked a bit taken aback. "If Father Kendi—"

"It's been a long day," Ben said, "and Father Kendi and I still have things to do. Thank you for coming by."

"Of course." Petrie snapped off her data pad and withdrew from her pocket a brand-new one. "Here, Kendi—a thank-you gift from Salman. All the people in the campaign are using this version, and it's half again as powerful as what's available on the civilian market. You'll like the holographics—twice as many pixies per cubic centimeter. Makes holos crisp and clear like you've never seen."

"Nice," Kendi said with pleasure. "Tell her I said thanks."

Petrie shook hands all around. "I'll be at the workshop in the afternoon, Father," she said. "If you have questions or an emergency arises, you can call me night or day."

"Thank you," Kendi said with a hard look at Ben. "I'll escort you to the door."

They left. Petrie's shoes made more clipped clicks on the hardwood floor. Ben felt suddenly nervous. He dumped his cold coffee down the drain and began cleaning up the kitchen, more out of a need to do something than any real desire for tidiness.

"That was rude," Kendi said in the doorway. He set the new data pad on the table. "And unlike you. What the heck is—"

"Daniel Vik and Irfan Qasad are my parents," Ben blurted.

Kendi burst out laughing. "That's a good one," he said. "No really—what's bothering you?"

"It's the truth," Ben said in a hoarse voice. "Harenn confirmed it."

"What?"

"She ran the gene scan three times on the *Poltergeist* and twice more after we got home from SA Station. The results were always the same."

"What?"

"We haven't been able to figure out why Irfan and Daniel made all these embryos—made me—or how the embryos got onto the ship Mom found or anything else about them. I wish we could have."

"What?"

"Harenn told only me because she figured I should be the first to know. I asked her to keep quiet because I wanted to be the one to tell you. But I couldn't find a way to say the words until now. I'm sorry."

"What?"

"Would you stop saying *What?* You sound like you're broken."

"Wha—oh." Kendi sank into a chair with a dazed expression on his face, one Ben couldn't read. "All life. Ben, you're saying that those embryos—that you—are almost a thousand years old? That you're the *son* of Irfan Qasad and Daniel Vik?"

Ben managed a nervous laugh. "Yeah."

"*The* Irfan Qasad," Kendi went on. "The first human to enter the Dream. Who founded the Children of Irfan. Who created the idea of human Silent."

Ben sat down with a nod. "And Daniel Vik is my father. Yes—the man who tried to destroy all human Silent on Bellerophon. Lucia's been having fun with that one. Something about it symbolizing the good and evil found in everyone."

"*Lucia* knows?" Kendi said. "You told *Lucia* but not me?"

Ben looked down at his hands. They were twisting themselves in his lap. He had known this would happen. Kendi was angry at him. He hated it when Kendi got angry. Not because he was afraid of Kendi, but because it . . . hurt. As if he had disappointed Kendi somehow. Ben hated disappointing anyone.

"Lucia was there when Harenn gave me the results of the scan," Ben said to his hands. "Harenn said she had a right to know if she was going to be a surrogate mother."

"But *I* didn't have the right to know?" Kendi's voice was growing shrill. "All life, Ben—when were you planning to tell me? After the kids were born? At their first birthday party? Shit, I can't believe you sat on this for a goddam *month!*"

Ben stood up and walked out of the room. He strode into his study and quietly shut the door.

Kendi stared at the empty space Ben had occupied. His mouth opened and shut like a landed fish's and his mind spun in circles, trying to encompass what Ben had told him. Ben was the son of Irfan Qasad herself. It was impossible. It was preposterous. But Ben would hardly say such a thing as a joke.

"Irene, call Harenn," he said suddenly. "Mark the call high priority."

"Working." A moment later, part of the kitchen wall glowed and Harenn's face appeared on the monitor.

"Is it true about Ben?" Kendi said without preamble.

"Yes," Harenn said, not mincing words herself. "I ran the scan five times. He and the other embryos are Irfan's children. And Daniel Vik's."

Kendi flung himself backward against the slats of his chair. "Do you know what this means? It's like discovering a son of Buddha or Krishna. Not a descendant. A *son*."

"Sons are descendants," Harenn pointed out.

"You know what I mean," Kendi snapped.

"Are you unhappy about it?"

"I'm startled out of my billabong, that's what I am. I knew Ben had something on his mind, but I would never in a thousand years have thought this was it. All life, Harenn—why didn't *you* tell me?"

"I promised Ben I would not. He wanted to be the one."

"The Children are going to throw a thousand cats," Kendi muttered. "Half of them will figure it's some kind of blasphemy, and the other half will worship at Ben's feet."

"Do not forget that your children bear the same genes," Harenn said. "They are Vik and Irfan's children as well."

Kendi groaned.

"You are acting like this is bad news," Harenn said. "Is it?"

"I don't know," Kendi growled. "I can barely get the idea through my head, let alone figure out the implications."

"And how do you think Ben feels about it?"

Kendi froze. The news had flabbergasted him so badly he had barely noticed Ben's agitated exit. "I have to go," he said, and broke the connection without waiting for a response.

A moment later he stood outside the door to Ben's study. A thin line of light limned the bottom. He tried the knob. It turned easily. Kendi took a deep breath and entered.

Ben was sitting at his desk, turning an old hard drive over and over in his hands. Computer guts and arcane bits of machinery littered the room around him. Ben didn't look up when Kendi entered. Kendi just looked at him for a moment. Now that Kendi was looking for it, he could see the resemblance to Daniel Vik. It was eerie and made Kendi's skin crawl. He swallowed. Irfan Qasad and Daniel Vik had reached across a millennium to create a man named Benjamin Rymar, a man Kendi had loved for almost fifteen years.

All life, had it been that long? It had. Kendi clearly remembered the first time he had laid eyes on Ben. Ara had thrown a party in honor of several students who had entered the Dream for the first time. Kendi was among them. Ben sat on the floor in one corner, looking shy, forlorn, and striking. Flame-red hair, sky-blue eyes, large hands, and a lost-puppy expression. Even today Kendi couldn't believe he had just walked up to Ben and started talking to him, and every moment from then on, he was glad he had done it. Their relationship had survived numerous breakups, several attempts at murder, the Despair, and Ara's death.

So why are you so upset now? he thought. *He's the same person he was before. You just know more about him.*

Kendi stood behind Ben's chair and put his hands on Ben's shoulders. The muscles were tense and hard. Ben didn't respond. He had shut down again, and Kendi's heart felt as if it had dropped into a bucket of ice. Kendi leaned down to embrace him more fully.

"Ben," he said. "I'm sorry. I didn't react well. It was the last thing I was expecting to hear. I didn't mean to shout. The news must have been a shock to you, too, hey?"

Ben thawed a bit. "Kind of."

"I'm glad you told me. It must have been hard."

Ben grabbed Kendi's wrist without answering. After a moment, his head dropped back to rest against Kendi's body. Kendi wrapped his arms around Ben for a long time, savoring the relief.

"What's it like?" he said after a while. "Knowing who your bio-parents are, I mean."

Ben thought. "I don't feel any different. Sometimes it doesn't seem real. Irfan and Vik died so long ago, and they're so . . . famous. When I was little, I used to pretend Benjamin Heller—Mom's fiancé before he died—was my bio-father and that he'd come home one day and play with me."

"Wait a minute," Kendi said. "Ara once said—didn't the cryo-unit's computer record them as frozen in the same year Benjamin Heller died? Ara said it was almost like a sign or something."

"That's when the embryos were put into that particular cryo-unit, yeah. My guess is they were transferred from an older unit into that one for some reason. Maybe the old one was breaking down. Anyway, the unit's computer would record them as being 'frozen' when they—we—were put into the cryo-chambers. It doesn't mean we weren't created earlier than that."

"So who else knows?" Kendi asked.

"Just Harenn and Lucia," Ben said. "And I want to keep it that way."

"Oh?" Kendi hooked another chair with his foot and dragged it over so he could sit. "What do you mean?"

"I mean I don't want anyone else to find out about this," Ben said fiercely. "Not Grandma, not my cousins, and definitely not that publicity woman. If this got out, I'd be an instant celebrity—and a target. The idea scares the shit out of me, Kendi. God. I've had nightmares."

"What about the kids?" Kendi said. "Do we tell them? They're Irfan's children, too."

Ben started to answer, then shut his mouth and pursed his lips. "I don't know," he said at last. "I hadn't thought about it. I suppose they have a right, but . . . I don't know."

"Well, we don't have to decide now. We have a few years. Want something to eat? Or maybe we could go for a walk and talk some more."

Kendi started to get up, but Ben grabbed his hand. "I want you to swear."

"Swear what?"

"Swear that you won't ever breathe a word of this to anyone, no matter what," Ben said. "I want you to swear on Mom's memory."

"Ben, I—"

Ben squeezed Kendi's hand. "Swear!"

"I swear on the memory of Mother Adept Araceil Rymar do Salman Reza that I will never tell anyone about your parentage," Kendi said. "Good enough?"

"Yeah."

Kendi flashed a grin. "Hey, you can trust me with a secret. I'm a con artist from way back. I deal in secrets."

"That's why I had you swear on Mom," Ben said with a grin of his own. "It's the only vow I know you'd never break."

"Hey!"

But further protests were interrupted when Ben pulled Kendi down into his lap and kissed him, long and hard. His arms, warm and solid, wrapped around Kendi's shoulders, and his large hands stroked Kendi's hair. The kiss grew more intense, and Kendi felt his body responding.

"You know," Ben said, breath hot in Kendi's ear, "I think I like this. It's putting me in the mood to do something different."

"Like what?" Kendi asked. Small shivers ran up and down his spine.

"Let me show you."

Brother Carl Kirchenbaum snuck a peek into the bedroom. His wife, Larissa, lay peacefully asleep on their bed. He marveled at how different she looked now. Her breasts had grown considerably, and her stomach was already starting to round out. Carl carefully shut the door and checked his watch. He had maybe half an hour before Larissa would wake up and have to use the bathroom. Just enough time, if he hurried.

He let himself out of the tiny apartment they now shared and clattered quickly down the stairs. The building was shabby, and the hallways stank of old cooking and unchanged diapers. Carl grimaced. Before the Despair, her job and his stipend from the Children had been plenty enough to allow the two of them to rent a nice little house on the outskirts of the monastery. After the Despair, things had changed drastically. Carl himself had been Silenced—worse than being struck deaf and blind—and Larissa had lost her job when her employer went bankrupt. For a short while they'd been all right with Carl's income. Then the monastery had reduced stipends to almost nothing, meaning he and Larissa could barely afford a two-room walk-up in a bad part of Treetown.

Carl sighed worriedly as he trotted out into the night. It seemed as if he worried all the time these days. He worried about Larissa getting unexpectedly pregnant. He worried about money and medical care. And through it all, he worried that he was going to fall apart. The only thing that kept him from falling into a permanent depression after losing his Silence was the thought of what it would do to Larissa. So he kept going, even when it felt like gravity had doubled and he would fall through the floorboards like an unfeeling rock.

The night was already chilly. The height of summer had passed. That, of course, meant heating bills, something else to worry about. Carl touched his pocket, which held the precious few freemarks he had managed to scrape together by going without lunch while he hunted for a job—any job. He should probably set the money aside, just in case. But it had been so long. . . .

Brother Carl went up a set of stairs and down a walkway until he reached the store. Mrs. Porfax, the aging owner, nodded to him from her counter near the door. Carl found what he was looking for and brought it over to her, feeling slightly embarrassed. Mrs. Porfax glanced at the item, and Carl felt his face heat up.

"Do you need anything else?" Mrs. Porfax asked, opening a brown bag.

"Not today," Carl mumbled.

"Five freemarks and twenty, then."

He paid her and left quickly. Outside he opened the bag and looked in. The small carton of gourmet chocolate ice cream seemed to look accusingly up at him. *I'm too expensive*, it said. *You shouldn't spend the money*.

But Larissa loved it so much, as did he. After everything they'd gone through, they deserved a little treat together now and then. Didn't they?

"Hey, friend. Spare a freemark?"

Carl closed the bag and looked up. A shabby man and an equally shabby woman stood at the mouth of an alleyway near the store. The man was holding out his hand.

"Sorry," Carl said. "I don't have—"

The woman gave a low cry and doubled over. The man spun and caught her, though her weight was an obvious drag on him. Carl automatically stepped forward. He took the woman's arm and helped the man lower her, moaning, to the ground.

"What's wrong with her?" he asked.

"Sometimes she gets like this," the man said. "We don't know why. She hurts."

The woman looked up at Carl with pain-filled eyes. Then her hand whipped around and Carl felt a *thump* against the side of his neck. The woman's hand came away. She held a dermospray.

"What—?" Carl said. And then his world went black.

CHAPTER THREE

*"Never get into a public argument with someone who
has a microphone."*

—Irfan Qasad

Morning found Kendi in his office at the monastery. Arranging the leave of absence had indeed been easy. The Council of Irfan wanted Salman Reza to win the election, wanted her to win it very much, and the members had quickly agreed that Kendi's endorsement of her campaign would greatly increase her chances.

Kendi cleared out his mail—fifteen sales pitches, ten biography offers, twenty-eight fan letters, one death threat—and made sure the monastery's other working Silent knew they'd have to handle his communication caseload.

His eye fell on the sim-game holograms lined up across his desk. Gretchen's upper torso looked as improbable as ever. Ben's image was smiling. Kendi looked at the holo with a tangle of emotions. Ben was Kendi's rock, his grounding point, the love of his life, and the eventual father of his children. Ben was Irfan Qasad's son. Ben was also Daniel Vik's son.

So what? Ben was Ben. His *real* mother, the one who mattered, had been Ara Rymar. Kendi knew that, but it still hit him at odd moments that Ben had originally been—created? put together?—almost a thousand years ago by the universe's greatest hero and its greatest villain.

It was a powerful secret, and a part of him wanted to let a few people in on it, see the startled and amazed looks on their faces. Keith and Martina wouldn't tell anyone if he asked them not to, and it—

No. Ben didn't want anyone else to know, so no one

else would know. Kendi needed to concentrate on something else.

He picked up the Ben hologram, set it in the hallway, and shut the office door. Then he tapped an empty space on the wall. "Sister Gretchen Beyer," he said, and the wall screen glowed as the computer made the connection. Gretchen Beyer's blond head popped up. She was a plain-faced woman, tall and raw-boned, nothing at all like the busty beauty on Kendi's desk.

"Hey, Kendi," Gretchen said after initial greetings. "What's going on with you?"

Technically Gretchen was supposed to address him as "Father Kendi," but Kendi rarely pushed the issue. He and Gretchen had been through too much together for that sort of formality.

"Did a bloke named Tel Brace contact you?" he asked. "From HyperFlight Games?"

"Yeah, a few days ago. I was going to call you about it, but I got busy. I laughed my ass off over the hologram."

"Is the hologram in the room with you?" Kendi asked.

"Nope."

"Good. Listen—don't agree to anything quite yet."

"Why not? I could use the money, Kendi. My stipend doesn't go as far as it used to these days, if you know what I mean."

Kendi knew what she meant. Gretchen had been Silenced during the Despair. It flashed across Kendi's mind to offer her some money to tide her over, an idea he just as quickly discarded. Such an offer would only transform Gretchen from a proud woman into an angry one.

"Just hold off a few more days," Kendi said instead. "It'll be worth your while, I promise."

Gretchen eyed him suspiciously from the viewscreen. "All right," she said at last. "A few more days. And you owe me dinner. One just like Ara used to buy."

"Done." Kendi grinned. "I'll catch you later, then."

They signed off. Kendi retrieved the Ben hologram, sat down at his desk, and searched his computer for a single sound file. He activated it, and the soft sound of a computer alert chimed through the room.

"Father Kendi," Kendi said, pretending to answer a call that came in over his earpiece instead of on the viewscreen. He paused. "Hey, love. Yeah, I'll probably be home early. Look, I'm glad you called. I've been looking at the cost of adding a nursery, and I'm thinking we should accept that offer from HyperFlight Games. It'll more than pay for the new room, and they'll get us the money quick. Heaven knows we need the cash. Yeah. Okay, I'll see you in a while."

He tapped his earpiece again, this time for real. "Tel Brace."

Brace came on almost immediately. Kendi could have called him on the viewscreen, but he didn't feel like seeing the man's grinning face.

"What can I do for you, Father?" Brace asked in Kendi's ear, and Kendi imagined him rubbing his hands together in anticipation of a multimillion freemark contract.

"Mr. Brace, I've given your offer considerable thought, and I'd like to discuss it in more detail. Could we meet in my office at, say, two o'clock?"

"Let me check my appointments." Brace made a small clucking noise with his tongue. "I'm afraid two doesn't work for me. Three?"

"Three is fine," Kendi agreed. "I'll see you then."

Kendi disconnected and gave Brace a few more flim-flam points for controlling the time of the meeting and thereby reducing Kendi from autocrat to supplicant. The extra hour was supposed to give Kendi time to worry something had gone wrong with the deal.

A knock sounded at the door and Kendi shouted permission to enter. A man and a woman came in. The woman possessed a head-turning beauty, with fine features and wide, dark eyes. The man bore a strong resemblance to Kendi. His body was a little thicker and gray streaked his hair, but anyone seeing them together would have known they were related. Keith and Martina Weaver, Kendi's older brother and younger sister.

"Keith needs a change of scene," Martina announced, "so we're kidnapping you for an early lunch."

"I don't need a change of scene," Keith muttered. "I'm fine."

"People who sit around in dark rooms all day don't get to say they're fine," Martina said firmly. "I've lived on Bellerophon for three weeks now, and I've yet to have eaten in a Ched-Balaar restaurant. How about you show us one, Kendi?"

"Sure." Kendi pushed the Ben hologram into a drawer. "I know just the place."

Martina linked arms with Keith and all but dragged him out of Kendi's office. Kendi followed, watching Keith's slumping posture from behind. Kendi pursed his lips. He didn't like this development with Keith. Kendi, Ben, and a team of Children had yanked Keith and Martina out of enslavement to a strange cult on SA Station just three weeks ago. Keith had come out of it ebullient and happy, but his mood had lately shifted to gloom and depression. He resolutely refused to see a counselor, and in any case the monastery's psych people were overworked treating Silenced Children traumatized by the Despair. People who had retained their Silence, as Keith had, rated low priority.

Outside the office building, clouds drew a low, gray curtain across the sky, and the air was damp. Martina maintained pointedly happy chatter. Keith remained quiet. Kendi led the way. The staircase they were descending opened onto a wide platform at the bottom, where another group of people were demonstrating. Placards and holograms bobbed up and down. About half were in the curved, swooping script of the Ched-Balaar. CHED-PIRASKU—THE BEST CHOICE. MODERATION IN ALL THINGS AND THE GOVERNORSHIP. OUR ALLY CHED-PIRASKU. NO RADICALS! NO LIBERALS! JUST CHED-PIRASKU!

A Ched-Balaar with dark, almost black fur had straightened her neck, raising her head high above the crowd. Her teeth chattered like a xylophone.

"What's she saying?" Martina asked.

" 'The Federals and the Unionists want to create division and battle among our people,' " Kendi translated. " 'They do not seek a middle ground for all to stand on. We can mine the world's treasures, but we do not have to strip the earth to do it. Carefully regulated mining will create jobs without destroying the environment our ancestors worked so hard to protect. However, we will also have to regulate the factories and manufacturing industries that will use the products of the new mines. Ched-Pirasku is prepared to address those challenges with compassion and forethought for all.' " Kendi paused. "She's exaggerating Grandma's position. Grandma doesn't advocate no mining at all—she thinks we need to be careful. I agree with her. Remember what Australia was like?"

"The Real People were enslaved by miners looking for opals and ore," Martina said as if reciting a long-ago lesson. "Under mutant control, the Outback became a desert, and the Real People were forced to eat meat for the first time. Do you think that could happen here?"

"Not the enslavement," Kendi said firmly. "We don't buy and sell people on Bellerophon. But the environmental disasters—that's something else entirely."

A cheer rose from the crowd and the signs waved wildly.

"These people sure go in for their demonstrations and marches," Keith observed. "You can't run to the corner store without tripping over one."

Kendi laughed. "You've got the right of that. This is the first time Bellerophon has had free elections for several hundred years. Before that, we were a member of the Independence Confederation under the rule of Empress Kalii. The Confederation appointed local government but otherwise let us have our head. The Children of Irfan were a lucrative source of income for the Confederation, and her imperial majesty was smart enough not to upset the goose that laid all those golden eggs. Now, though, we're starting our own government practically from scratch. Everyone gets to voice an opinion, and they do."

"Especially since so many people don't have jobs to keep them busy," Keith said cynically.

They skirted the demonstration and continued on their way. A brisk stroll over several walkways and down two flights of stairs took them to the Ched-Balaar restaurant. It was, like most Treetown structures, a wooden building built on a platform amid talltree branches. A balcony set with tables ringed the second floor. None were occupied—it was still early for lunch. The name on the sign said in graceful Ched-Balaar script, *Delectibles of the Open Blossom*. Strange and delicious smells wafted by.

"What do the Ched-Balaar eat?" Keith said dubiously.

"You'll like it," Kendi promised.

"That means it's going to be disgusting."

"Stop being such a baby," Martina said. "Let's go in."

The interior was dark and damp. Moss covered the floor in a thick green carpet. More tables were scattered about, and an artificial waterfall rushed down one wall. The ceiling was high, to accommodate Ched-Balaar height. Smells of hot oil, sharp spices, and cooking meat salted the air. A Ched-Balaar with pale, silvery fur and a red head cloth turned to greet them.

"Father Kendi," chattered the Ched-Balaar. "I have the perfect table for you. Who are your friends?"

Kendi paused to translate for his family, then said, "Ched-Mulooth, meet my brother and sister, Keith and Martina Weaver. They're new to Bellerophon."

Ched-Mulooth dipped his head. His movements were slow and careful. "It is a fine thing to meet the family of the great Father Kendi Weaver. Please come this way."

He led them past a series of tables too high for humans to use comfortably. There were no chairs. A pair of female Ched-Balaar occupied one table, sitting on their haunches like dogs or cats. Two wide troughs containing purple liquid rested on the table, and one of the Ched-Balaar dipped her wide lower jaw into it to drink. A delicate slurping sound accompanied the gesture. The other Ched-Balaar glanced at Kendi as he passed, then turned back to her companion.

In the rear of the restaurant was a scattering of human-sized tables and two human-sized booths. Ched-Mulooth ushered them toward one of the latter and stood solicitously by as the Weavers seated themselves.

"The world will provide," Ched-Mulooth said, and withdrew.

"It's hard to tell," Martina said, "but I get the feeling that he's pretty old."

"Ched-Mulooth? Yeah, he's older than Irfan." The comparison made Kendi think of Ben, and he shifted uncomfortably in the booth. "He's a great host. I don't think he's cooking much these days, though."

"So what do we order?" Keith asked.

"We don't. The Ched-Balaar believe that the world will provide, and asking for specifics is rude. It's actually Ched-Mulooth's job to anticipate what we'll like and serve it. He's really good at that, which is why I brought us here."

"Apology," chattered a new voice. "Are you Father Kendi Weaver?" One of the Ched-Balaar they had passed earlier was standing near the table.

"That's me," Kendi replied. Martina and Keith looked lost, so Kendi gave a quick translation. "What can I do for you?"

She thrust a computer pad at him. "Your handprint?"

Kendi laid his hand on the pad, then scribbled his initials at the bottom with a stylus. The Ched-Balaar bobbed her head.

"My gratitude, both for your handprint and for your deeds." And she left.

"Does that happen to you a lot?" Martina asked.

"Yeah," Kendi said in a rueful voice. "She was polite, at least."

More people, both Ched-Balaar and human, were filling the restaurant around them. The mossy floor muffled both human voices and Ched-Balaar tooth-talk. Ched-Mulooth reappeared and set three troughs on the table, smaller versions of those used by the Ched-Balaar. A shiny purple liquid glimmered in each.

"You don't have to slurp," Kendi said, hoisting his trough and taking a drink. Martina and Keith followed suit. The light wine was sweet, with a distinct fruity aftertaste.

"It's wonderful," Martina said. "Isn't it wonderful, Keith?"

"It's okay," Keith muttered.

Kendi tightened his jaw. He remembered his older brother as serious but not morose. When they were children, all three of them had invented games that transformed the grimy streets of Sydney into pirate coves, opal caves, and space ships. Keith had been the best at inventing new settings, pretending to explore new things. But fifteen years of slavery had taken their toll.

And then there was the slaver named Feder. Just after their capture, the Weaver family had spent several days on a slave ship, and Feder had taken a . . . liking to Keith. Kendi had only been twelve at the time, but he still remembered the helpless rage he had felt every time Feder came to their cell and took Keith away, returning him, stone-faced and mute, several hours later.

Slavery, abuse, the Despair, Silent Acquisitions—was it any wonder Keith had problems?

"Aren't you Father Kendi Weaver?" This time the speaker was human, a young man. Kendi signed an autograph and turned back to his siblings.

"Is it going to be like this all through lunch?" Martina asked.

"Some days are worse than others," Kendi said. "Ben got our address removed from the public databases, or we'd probably deal with it at home, too. My work address is public information, though, and I get deluged with messages there."

Ched-Mulooth set three logs on the table. Fragrant steam rose in delicate, spicy-smelling tendrils from gaps in the bark, and pale ·mushrooms poked up like soggy miniature umbrellas. Bits of wet, rotten wood showered the table. Ched-Mulooth withdrew. Keith stared at the logs. Martina cocked her head.

"Explain," she said.

"Like this," Kendi said. He ripped a piece of wood away. Large red grubs glistened inside. Kendi plucked one out—it was almost hot enough to singe his fingers— and popped it into his mouth. It was juicy and meaty, like a bite of tender steak with an outer skin that broke with a slight crunch. Martina grinned.

"You used to hate grubs in the Outback," she said, tearing open her own log and selecting a blood-red specimen. "What changed?"

"The Ched-Balaar are better cooks."

"Why do they eat this stuff?" Keith said. He hadn't touched his own log.

"Look at their feet," Kendi replied. "They evolved

tearing stuff apart and digging things up. The Ched-Balaar are omnivores, like humans, but their eating habits are more . . . bearlike than monkeylike."

"Eat your grubs, Keith," Martina said, downing one of her own. "They're good."

"You're meant to eat the mushrooms, too," Kendi put in. "Ched-Balaar salad."

"Maybe I could just ask for a cheese sandwich," Keith said.

Martina made a face. "A chunk of half-rotten milk stuck between two slabs of yeast-infected seed powder? Ick!"

At that, Keith managed a smile, though to Kendi's eye it looked forced. He reluctantly ripped out a piece of wood, selected a steaming slug, and stared at for a long moment. Then he ate it.

"It's not half bad," Keith admitted grudgingly. "Could use some salt."

"Aren't you Father Kendi Weaver?"

Kendi signed another autograph and turned back to Martina and Keith. "So how are you two getting along with your teachers?"

"It's annoying," Martina said, delicately licking a shred of slug from her upper lip. "I know how to operate in the Dream, thank you very much, and don't need help with it. I can possess people and I can whisper from the Dream and my short-term recall is already perfect. But Mother Bess keeps trying to make me do memory exercises. Like I said—annoying."

"Mother Bess was Silenced, wasn't she?" Kendi asked.

Martina nodded. "It's why I haven't really rebelled against her. She looks so . . . unhappy all the time."

"I know what you mean," Kendi said. "All life, I can't imagine what it must be like to lose the Dream."

"I can barely reach it," Keith said. "And I can't stay in for very long. It's like having a hand cut off. Or having palsy. I can still do stuff, but I can't do it *well*."

"That's exactly it," Martina said. "All life, I—"

"Why do you talk like that?" Keith snapped. " 'All life' and 'Real People' and all that Outback shit?"

Martina blinked at him. After a pause, Kendi said,

"It's who we—who *I* am. The Real People got me through being a slave and losing Mom. They're how I found the Dream."

"You're angry at the Real People," Martina said. "Keith, that's all r—"

"I don't need you to tell me what's all right and what's not," Keith snarled. Then he sighed. "I'm sorry. I guess I'm not good company."

He lapsed into silence again, and a Ched-Balaar approached the table. "You are Father Kendi Weaver, true?"

Martina bravely tried to keep conversation going for the rest of lunch. Keith didn't speak, and Kendi couldn't bring himself to give more than one- or two-word answers. Throughout three years of slavery and twelve years with the Children of Irfan, he had dreamed of finding his family again, sitting with them at a meal just like this one. Kendi had fantasized about laughing together, telling stories, even having childish squabbles. He hadn't ever thought it would be like this.

"Aren't you Father Kendi Weaver?"

Kendi signed, then stood up. "Let's go. I've got stuff to do."

They exited the restaurant straight into a crowd of people. The wide platform that made up the "street" in this part of Treetown groaned with humans and Ched-Balaar. A Ched-Balaar with designs shaved into her body fur stood head and shoulders above the crowd next to a sandy-haired man.

"Not another one," Keith complained. "This is getting stupid."

"It's not a demonstration," Kendi said with groan. "It's a press conference. For *him*."

". . . these times of economic hardship," the man said in a voice that carried well above the crowd, "we need to pull back, hunker down, and find our strengths as a people. This is not a time to look outward. It is a time to look inward. Our tax money should be spent on job programs for our people, not on arms programs for our military. We Federals firmly believe that the people come first."

When he fell silent, the crowd exploded into questions

like an erupting volcano. "Mr. Foxglove, how long do you think the post-Despair depression will last?" "Mr. Foxglove, what will be your first act if you win the governorship?" "Mr. Foxglove, do you think the High Court will rule in favor of releasing mining restrictions in your district?" "Mr. Foxglove—" "Mr. Foxglove—" "Mr. Foxglove—"

"I have every confidence," Foxglove said, and the reporters fell instantly silent, "that the High Court will make a fair and just ruling to relieve the mining restrictions in the Othertown district. The reasons for the restrictions were wise nine hundred years ago, but times have changed. We can now mine the resources of this planet without harming our environment and in the bargain provide our people with much-needed jobs."

"Mr. Foxglove, what cutbacks to the military are you proposing?" shouted another reporter before the others could begin their frenzy.

"I'm not proposing a cutback," Foxglove said. "I'm proposing a freeze. The Federalist Party has said it before, and I'm saying it again: We don't need more ships. We need more jobs. We don't need more soldiers. We need more financial security. My proposal would save our government over nine hundred million freemarks without cutting jobs within the military itself."

"Mr. Foxglove—" "Mr. Foxglove—" "Mr. Foxglove, what about the Silent and the Children of Irfan?"

Kendi held his breath. Martina did the same. Keith stared at his fingernails.

"The sun is setting on Irfan Qasad's Silent Empire," Foxglove said. "I think it's time for the Silent and the Silenced to accept that their time on Bellerophon is growing to a close. We can create new enclaves for them, let them live their lives outside humanity, as they've always done. Then, perhaps, the different species can find peace."

"What kind of bullshit is that?" Kendi snarled without thinking. Several people turned. Ched-Balaar heads swivelled. Kendi found himself staring into several pairs of inquisitive eyes.

"Father Kendi Weaver!" someone shouted, and a sea of people washed around Kendi like a whirlpool. Recording devices were shoved at his face, and two floating microphones spun into orbit around his head. Ched-Balaar heads bobbed, human hands waved. "Father Kendi, do you agree with what Mr. Foxglove just said?" "Father Kendi, what's your position on the mining rights?" "Father Kendi, are you planning to run for office?" "Father Kendi, is it true that you've taken a leave of absence from the Children of Irfan?"

Martina and Keith both shrank behind Kendi. Behind them, the restaurant window filled with faces of patrons, some of them still chewing. Kendi raised both his hands, palms out, and the noise stopped.

"I'm not here to give a press conference," he said, and the microphones broadcast his words to the edges of the crowd. "I was just getting a bite of lunch with my family, if you don't mind."

"Father Kendi, why the leave of absence?" "Father Kendi, are you quitting the Children?" "Father Kendi, what do you think of Mr. Foxglove's remarks about the sun setting on the Silent Empire?"

"It's bloody nonsense," Kendi said, addressing the last question. "I don't think—"

"With all due respect, Father," Foxglove boomed from the other side of the platform, "I don't see how the Children can survive. My Ched-Balaar friends tell me they have sensed no new presences in the Dream for many months now, and one day those who can reach it now will pass away. Time moves on."

"Why don't you have any human Silent or Silenced in your campaign, Mr. Foxglove?" Kendi shot back. "Don't you think they're human enough for you?"

Foxglove gave a hearty smile. "Are you offering advice to me on how to run a campaign, young Father? I hear you're experienced at stealing slaves and wandering around the Dream, but I'm afraid that public office is another matter entirely." A small chuckle. "I suppose we can forgive the foibles of the young and the brash."

Anger boiled Kendi's chest in acid. He opened his mouth to respond when someone yanked him hard from behind, and he found himself back inside the darkened restaurant. The patrons at the window turned to stare. Kendi tried to round on Martina, but she still had a hold on his robe. Keith slammed the door and twisted the deadbolt lock. The microphones orbiting Kendi's head fell to the mossy floor and Martina stepped on them. Reporters pounded on the door, but couldn't open it.

"What the hell are you doing?" Kendi snapped.

"Saving your ass," Martina snapped back. "What are you, mad? You got into a public debate with an experienced politician with a pack of reporters looking on."

"I was about to give him a piece of—"

"Nothing," Martina interrupted. "There was nothing you could say that he couldn't counter, Kendi. That's what politicians *do*. The longer you shouted at him, the stupider you looked."

"Is *stupider* a word?" Keith asked.

"It was invented just for Kendi," Martina said, and turned to Ched-Mulooth, who was hovering nearby. "Do you have a back exit? We need to slip away."

Ched-Mulooth was only too glad to show them another way out. The trio fled down two walkways and three flights of stairs before Martina consented to release Kendi's robe. Kendi took a deep breath, trying to get his anger under control. Martina leveled him a hard look, then flounced to a bench on a secluded little balcony and sat. A patch of spring sunlight washed her in gold.

"Calm?" she asked.

"Calm," Kendi grumbled, taking a seat next to her. Another deep breath. "Okay, you were right."

"What do you say, then?"

"Thank you for saving my ass," he said.

"You're welcome."

"Adventures at lunch," Keith said. "I hate to ask what's going down for supper."

"Want to eat at my house and find out?" Kendi said. "We'll have a meal just like Mom used to make—when we ordered takeaway, anyway—and talk about old times."

Martina laughed. "I have things to do," she said. "But thanks."

"I'll have to give it a miss, too," Keith said. "Martina?"

Kendi watched the two of them leave. His brother and sister. They lived right here on Bellerophon, and he could talk to them whenever he wanted. Nothing Foxglove could say would take that away from him. Still, Kendi had to run most of the way home to vent the last of his anger.

Ben met him at the front door, his face pale as milk. His eyes were wide with panic. Kendi's stomach clenched.

"What's wrong?" he asked.

Without a word, Ben grabbed his arm and towed him toward the den. He seemed unable to speak. His hand was sweaty on Kendi's bicep. The house was dark, with few lights on, and Kendi's footsteps echoed eerily on the hardwood floor as they reached Ben's den. Kendi heard Ben's breathing, harsh and fast.

"What's going on, Ben?" Kendi said, fighting down his alarm. "You're scaring me."

Ben pointed in answer. A holographic display hovered in the darkness above his cluttered desk. It showed Daniel Vik and Irfan Qasad standing next to each other in a forest. The image was famous, and Kendi had seen it thousands of times. This version, however, had been altered. An image of Ben had been inserted between Daniel and Irfan and someone had added a caption. It read, SILENCE WILL COST YOU.

CHAPTER FOUR

"You can only blackmail someone who gives a shit."
—Daniel Vik

Lucia dePaolo rotated Kendi's new data pad, the one Petrie had given him, and examined the holographic image from all sides. Her scarred hands were rock-steady above the kitchen table. Ben's hands were clasped tightly in his lap, and his right leg bounced up and down. Kendi sat next to him, his face hard. Harenn poured herself a cup of coffee, laced it heavily with cream and sugar, and brought it to the table. It was the last of the coffee supply, but no one objected.

"It's a good job," Lucia said, pushing dark hair away from a her forehead. "But I'm sure you already know that."

"Ben turned it inside out," Kendi said. "He couldn't find any clues as to who made it. Same went when we tried to trace the message that sent it. The thing was routed through several anonymous accounts, including two scrambler services. Whoever did this knows Ben is a hacker supreme."

"Obviously they know more than that," Harenn said.

"How did they find out?" Ben blurted. "Who told?"

"I told no one but you and Lucia," Harenn said. "And each time we discussed it, our circumstances were private. No eavesdroppers. Unless someone was hanging underneath your balcony yesterday."

"A burglar with serendipity on his side?" Kendi said. "Doubt it. Lucia? I hate to be blunt, but the First Church of Irfan would kill to get information like this. Did you drop any hints? Maybe by accident at a service?"

"I haven't breathed a word of it since Harenn told me

back on the *Poltergeist*," Lucia said. Her voice was low and serene. "Not a single time, I swear by Irfan herself."

"I know I haven't mentioned it," Kendi said with a guilty little pang at how close he'd come to telling Keith and Martina. "Ben?"

"Absolutely not!"

"I did have to ask," Kendi said gently. "We'll sort this out somehow. So who else knew about the embryos?"

"Grandfather Melthine and Mother Ara," Harenn said. "But they died before we learned of the embryos' . . . origin."

"What about the people who were on Mother Ara's team when she found the embryos in the first place?" Lucia said. "They know the embryos exist."

"It's been almost thirty years since she was a part of that team," Ben said. "They've probably forgotten all about them. Besides, they wouldn't know the truth any more than Mom did."

"Maybe," Lucia said. "But they're a place to start."

"Don't forget Ben's relatives," Kendi said. "His aunt, uncle, and cousins know about the embryos, and they're the most likely lot to pull something like this."

"I hadn't thought of them," Ben said. He ran a shaky hand through his hair. "God, it does sound like something Hazid or Zayim would try, though it doesn't explain how they found out."

"You don't think Sil or Tress could be involved?" Harenn said.

Ben shook his head. "Sil doesn't have the . . . she isn't—"

"No need to be delicate, love," Kendi said. "We all know Sil's as bright as a wet matchstick. She's a champion whiner, but blackmail is beyond her. Tress, on the other hand—"

"I don't think it's Tress," Ben said. "She's changed."

"You only have her word on that," Kendi pointed out.

"Right now, we can't rule anyone out," Lucia said. "I'll put on my private investigator hat and check them all. My license is still active."

"We'll pay your usual hourly rate," Kendi said. "What is it?"

Lucia pursed her lips. "Under other circumstances, I'd

do this for free. But the PI business has been poor lately, and I can't afford to turn anything down. I've already been forced to move back in with my parents."

"Lucia! Why didn't you say something?" Kendi said, shocked. "You're going to be carrying one of our children. That makes you a member of *this* family, too. If you need a place to live or a few thousand freemarks to tide you over—"

"I won't live on largesse," Lucia replied firmly. "However, my full fee should cover my shortcomings. Five hundred freemarks per hour, plus expenses, with a ten thousand freemark advance."

"Done," Ben said.

"Then let's get started. First, I'll need the full names and addresses of your extended family, Ben. Kendi, does the monastery keep records of who went on what mission? I'll need to track down the people on Mother Ara's old team."

"No problem," Kendi said. "I can get you the information today."

"Harenn," Lucia said, "you ran the gene scans. Tell me exactly what you did and who else may have figured out what you were doing."

"No one," Harenn said. "I performed the first gene scans on the *Poltergeist* at Kendi's request, and I told no one what I was doing. The procedure is straightforward. The computer scanned the DNA of the embryos and checked it against the monastery database."

"How did you check the database?" Lucia said. "We were docked at SA Station at the time, and you couldn't have accessed Children records from there."

"I updated the *Poltergeist*'s medical computer just before we left. It contained the latest information from the monastery's databases, including genetic records."

"Why do you carry genetic records on a rescue mission?"

"Standard procedure," Harenn said. "It allows me— the Children—to check mitochondrial DNA of rescued Silent slaves and see if they have any relatives on Bellerophon."

"You ran the scans three times on the *Poltergeist*," Lucia said.

"Yes. I thought the initial results were a mistake, so I ran the test again, and then once more. When I was absolutely sure of my data, I called you and Ben into the medical bay. You know the rest."

"What about the files?" Ben asked. "The computer must have made a whole bunch of them."

"Erased and scrubbed," Harenn said. "This is standard procedure after a . . . a . . ." Harenn trailed off and her brown eyes went vacant.

"What?" Kendi asked.

"I am trying to remember if I scrubbed the backup files." Harenn's brow furrowed. "I do not remember doing it. On the other hand, I do not remember *not* doing it."

"Another place to check," Lucia said. "The team that refurbishes the ships would have access to those files. I'm not a computer expert, though. Ben, if you checked the *Poltergeist*'s system, could you tell . . . ?"

"Yes," Ben said. "Though I couldn't necessarily tell *who*. Just *when*. Or *if*."

"Let's look there first, then." Lucia rose. "Irfan willing, it'll be a short hunt."

Lucia and Ben headed for the door. Kendi and Harenn followed. Lucia halted.

"We don't need all of you," she said.

"I'm not staying behind," Kendi said. "I want to know now."

"As do I," Harenn said.

Lucia sighed. "Father Kendi, I can't work with someone staring over my shoulder. I promise we'll call the moment we learn something."

"You're not getting rid of me that easily, Lu—"

The doorbell rang and the computer broke in. "Attention! Attention! Wanda Petrie requests entry. She claims she has urgent business with Father Kendi."

"We'll just nip out the back," Lucia said, and vanished with Ben before Kendi could react.

"They settled that, didn't they?" Harenn murmured.

"Attention! Attention! Wanda—"

"Irene," Kendi interrupted, "tell Wanda Petrie she can come in. We'll meet in her the living room."

Wanda Petrie burst into the living room with a thunderstorm on her face. Her hard shoes slammed the floor with every step, and her sharp eyes looked ready to strike Kendi down. He took an involuntary step backward. Harenn withdrew to a corner chair and sat.

"Perhaps my instructions were not clear, Father Weaver," Petrie snapped without preamble. "What the hell were you thinking?"

"About what?" Kendi said.

She whipped out a data pad and jabbed at it. A head-and-shoulders hologram of Kendi popped up. "You gave an unauthorized press conference this morning. You entered into a debate with Senator Mitchell Foxglove, and he made a right fool of you. We had to assign a team of five people to spin the damage."

"It wasn't a debate," Kendi said. "We just—"

Petrie slapped the data pad on the coffee table with a *crack*. Kendi's image bobbled. "Anytime you enter into a public conversation with a candidate, it becomes a debate. The fact that dozens of reporters witnessed the entire thing made it even worse."

"I didn't say anything that—"

"Three of the feeds caught and broadcast the phrase *What kind of bullshit is that*," Petrie said. "You also called Foxglove's remarks, and I quote, *bloody nonsense*. Then you confronted Foxglove about the lack of Silent on his campaign team."

"The man is an asshole," Kendi shot back. "He as much said that Silent weren't human and that they should be shut away in their own little enclaves."

"Your opinion of Foxglove doesn't matter," Petrie growled. "What matters is that you called him names in public and made a fool of yourself in front a pack of reporters. Thank god we haven't officially announced that you're supporting Senator Reza's campaign. As it is, we'll have to delay everything to let the situation calm down."

"It can't be *that* bad," Kendi said.

Petrie closed her eyes. Her lips were pressed so tightly together Kendi half-expected to see blood. "It *is*, Father Kendi. Very bad indeed. We scheduled a press conference for Senator Reza—after inventing a reason that had nothing to do with you—and arranged for reporters who are friendly to our cause to ask questions about you so she can make light of what you said. It won't be an easy conference because you can bet Foxglove will do his best to make sure a few hostile reporters attend. You're making her sweat in front of a planet, Father Kendi, and if you can't keep your mouth shut, I'll have to recommend you be pulled from the campaign. Right now, you're more liability than asset."

"My," Harenn said from her chair.

Kendi sat in a chair of his own, feeling abashed. The last thing he wanted to do was hurt Grandma, and that's exactly what he had done. "Is there any way I can help clean up?"

"Not right now," Petrie said, still on her feet. "It's best if you stay out of the public eye for a few days. I've cancelled your first speaking engagement and rearranged your calendar. We'll have to delay the workshop, too— the man who is supposed to train you is busy cleaning up."

"For what it's worth," Kendi said, "I'm sorry."

"Sorry won't help Senator Reza." Petrie took up an easy chair and crossed her legs at the ankle. Her skirt displayed athletic legs. "But your sentiment is noted. You have to change some behaviors, Father."

"If you're going to bawl me out on a regular basis, I think you'd better call me Kendi."

"And I'm Wanda. I'm not entirely unsympathetic, understand, but my primary responsibility is to Senator Reza." She cleared her throat. "I suppose I should have known better. Politics is a new arena for you."

"I've played monastery politics for years," Kendi said. "They're just different. National elections are a new game, a con game, really, and I have to learn the rules. *Then* I can break them."

Petrie looked pained, and Kendi flashed her a grin. "Joke," he said.

"It was not," Harenn murmured.

"I need to discuss another matter," Petrie said. "With all that's happened—and going to happen—I think it would be prudent for you and Mr. Rymar to take a security detail."

Kendi froze. Did Petrie know about Ben? But she

couldn't. Not unless she was the one who was threatening blackmail. Was she playing Kendi along? He gave himself a mental shake. He was getting paranoid.

"What do you mean?" he asked instead.

"Senator Reza is receiving more and more attention, even though she hasn't officially announced her intention to run for governor. That will mean more attention for you and Mr. Rymar—and your eventual children. It would be a good idea to have someone who can . . . interfere for you."

"Guard us, you mean," Kendi said. "We haven't been bothered any more than usual lately. I'm getting the same number of weirdo messages and autograph hounds. Nothing's changed."

"Not yet," Petrie said. "You haven't officially endorsed the senator's campaign. Once that happens, people will seek you out even more. I was able to walk right up to your house, Kendi. Who knows what strange person would do the same?"

"Our address isn't listed on any database," Kendi said. "No one comes. The location of my office is public knowledge, but the monastery has pretty good security. Bodyguards would get in the way, especially since we don't need them."

"Nonetheless," Petrie said with more heat, "I've seen this sort of thing before. People think they don't need bodyguards until something happens. The best kind of bodyguards are the kind that don't seem to be needed. They take care of a situation before it becomes a crisis— before you even know something is wrong."

"I don't want someone in my house day and night," Kendi said. "My privacy is invaded enough as it is." *And bodyguards might learn about the blackmail plot*, he added silently.

"Kendi—"

"Drawbridges," Harenn put in. As one, Kendi and Petrie turned to look at her. "This house is accessible by two walkways and two staircases. Convert them into drawbridges, and no one can get in unless they can scale a talltree. Doesn't Senator Reza have such a system at her home?"

"That would help home security," Petrie said, "but not public situations."

"It'd be a good compromise," Kendi said doubtfully. "But still a pain."

"I'll call a carpenter immediately." Petrie rose. "And do consider taking on a security detail, Kendi. It would only be until the election is over."

"I'll give it all appropriate consideration," Kendi promised.

Petrie gave a delicate, birdlike snort. "That is the sort of answer you should give to people who try to engage you in public debate. I'll be in touch."

And she left.

"That was informative," Harenn said. "And fascinating. You have not received a proper dressing-down for a long time."

"I haven't missed it one bit." He picked up his data pad from the coffee table and called up the feeds. "Let's see if everything's as bad as she said."

Harenn peered over his shoulder as Kendi sifted through text. He could have called up a live news report, but it was faster to read. A Child of Irfan named Carl Kirchenbaum had gone to the store for ice cream and not returned. Two Ched-Balaar researchers had discovered a new way to block pain without medication. And Kendi had gotten into a verbal sparring match with Mitchell Foxglove. The latter story appeared on several different feeds, Kendi came off looking foolish in all of them.

"Not the first time I've looked like an idiot in public," Kendi said philosophically. "Ben's going to love this, though."

"How are things between you and Ben?" Harenn asked. "I have had no chance to talk with you in private except during frantic phone calls. I've had two of them in two days, come to that."

"I think we're fine," Kendi said. "I groveled and he forgave me for being an ass. I don't mind telling you it scared—scares—the hell out of me. It's the biggest secret in the universe. I almost told Keith and Martina. I'm glad I didn't. If this comes out, it would kill Ben."

"Ben is stronger than you think," Harenn said.

"And more breakable than *you* think," Kendi countered. "Do you honestly believe the only reason I suck up the spotlight is ego and self-interest?"

"It had occurred to me."

Kendi grimaced. "It's all a front, Harenn. Ben hates being in the public eye. You didn't see the panic attacks before the newsfeed interviews. You didn't nurse him through the stress headaches, the nausea, and the insomnia. I think he was as relieved as I was when the Children gave us permission to disappear for two months to rescue your son and my siblings."

"So you accepted the heavy burden of fame to distract public attention from Ben?" Harenn said. "How noble. I'm sure you hate every moment."

"Fame does have its perks," Kendi said, refusing to rise to the bait. "Fame also has its problems. I jump up and down and shout 'Look at me!' Then I give interviews, I handle offers to do books and games about my life, I read fan mail and death threats, I sign autographs and put up with interruptions in public places. Ben, meanwhile, gets to drop out of sight. The arrangement works."

"I see."

"My, we're coming across all skeptical today."

"It is a function of hunger," Harenn said. "I have not yet eaten lunch. That, in case you missed it, was a hint."

"There's no food in the house," Kendi said. "We can order from Maureen's, though."

Harenn went into the kitchen while Kendi called up a menu on his data pad. From the kitchen came the sound of cupboards opening and closing, followed by the noises of someone rummaging inside the refrigerator. Harenn gave an uncharacteristic squeak of dismay, and the refrigerator slammed shut.

"Sorry!" Kendi called. "Should've warned you about the vegetable drawer."

"The two of you live like bachelors," Harenn called back. "How do you expect to raise eleven children in a house with no food?"

"By means of a wonderful thing called takeaway," Kendi said. "Maureen's chick-lizard sandwich is good, but the mashed potatoes are fake—shortage of real ones—so you might want to get the beet salad instead. I already ate, but I could do with a snack. Maybe some fried *ben-yai* leaves."

Harenn emerged from the kitchen, wiping her hands on a dish towel. "You are completely unprepared for parenthood, do you know that? You cannot run a house on restaurant food. Not only is it less nutritious, it is also foolishly expensive."

Kendi shrugged. "I don't know what else to do. Ben can't stand cooking, and I'm so rotten at it, I can't even make morning coffee."

"I will speak with Lucia," Harenn said. "In the meantime, I believe I will order a sandwich and beet salad from Maureen's."

They ate lunch and busied themselves with small matters surrounding the implantation. Kendi, Ben, and Harenn had already worked out the legal aspects of Harenn's surrogacy. Harenn had originally refused a stipend, but her job had disappeared into the Despair, so she had reluctantly agreed to take one. Bellerophon law allowed for more than just two parents of record, so all three of them would be the child's legal parents, but Ben and Kendi would be awarded sole custody. Harenn would be granted "arranged access" to the child, meaning she could visit whenever she wanted as long as she called first—in theory. In practice she would be in and out of Ben and Kendi's house all the time. Harenn—and Bedj-ka with her—already came and went without knocking, though Kendi couldn't say how or why that had begun. It had just seemed natural for Harenn's household to combine with Ben and Kendi's. The arrangement had begun soon after Ara's death, so maybe that had something to do with it—an ease of grief.

A small icon flashed at the bottom of Kendi's vision, and he shot to his feet. "All life, I forgot!"

"What is it?" Harenn asked.

"I'm supposed to meet with that sim-game bloke in my office at three o'clock. The blackmail hologram dumped it right out of my head."

"It isn't quite two-thirty. You have plenty of time."

"I have something else to do first."

Kendi left the house, rushed to the office building, and skidded to a halt in front of it. A knot of reporters was waiting on the wide balcony that ran the length of the building. Two Guardians, their silver medallions gleaming in the dappled sunlight, flanked the main doorway. The reporters stampeded forward and thrust questions at him—"Father Kendi, did you mean to condemn Senator Foxglove's campaign with your remarks?" "Father Kendi, would you support Senator Reza for governor?" "Father Kendi, is it true you feel Senator Foxglove's positions are nonsense?" Kendi pushed through them, chanting "No comment," until he could slip inside the office building. He stood in the foyer for a moment, resisting the urge to pant. It was post-Despair all over again. He had been hounded like this for weeks after word about his involvement had gotten out. Kendi would just have to get used to going through it again. At least this time he knew it would only last until the election.

The Initiate staffing the reception desk pressed his fingertips to his forehead in salute. "I called the Guardians when those reporters showed up, Father. We booted them outside. I hope that's all right."

"Yes, and thank you," Kendi said. "Pray for a cloudburst."

As he passed down the hallway to his office, a woman with graying mouse-brown hair stuck her head out of her own door and caught sight of him. "I thought that might be you, Kendi," said Mother Bren. She had been Kendi's history teacher when he was an Initiate. "I saw you on the feeds a little while ago. Quite the shouting match. Rumors are flying."

"I'll bet. And if you're fishing for information, Bren, you're in for a long time on the lake. I'm under strict orders not to open my mouth in public anymore."

Bren laughed. "That'll be the day."

In his office, Kendi checked the time. Fifteen minutes before his meeting with Tel Brace. He hummed to himself and made rustling noises around the desk for a few moments. Then, with a glance at Ben's hologram, he suddenly said to empty air, "Father Kendi Weaver. Uh

huh . . . You're from which company? . . . Oh . . .
Oh! . . . Well, I feel I should tell you I'm already in
negotiation with HyperFlight Games, and I'm supposed
to meet with them in a few minutes to—no . . . No, I
haven't signed it yet. . . . Uh huh. . . . Look, I wouldn't
want to do anything to jeopardize the deal with Hyper-
Flight but—" He paused. "*How* much? . . . Well, you've
got my attention. I suppose I could put off signing with
HyperFlight until we talk. Should I tell him that you
called me? . . . Why not? . . . I see. Okay. . . ." He gave
a small laugh. "Well, I won't say anything if you don't.
How about we meet tomorrow morning at nine? . . .
Great! See you then."

Kendi drummed his fingertips on the desktop. This
was going to be fun.

Thirteen minutes later, a chime sounded. *"Father
Kendi, a human named Tel Brace is here to see you,"* said
the Initiate's voice. *"He says he has an appointment."*

"Send him up," Kendi called.

Tel Brace entered the office, looking breathless and
windblown. Kendi rose and greeted him with a firm
handshake.

"Right on time," Kendi said without a trace of irony.
He was pretty sure Brace had originally intended to be
late, pushing Kendi further into the role of supplicant.
Clearly Brace had changed his mind in the last few
minutes.

Now why would he do that? Kendi thought smugly. "I
hope the reporters outside didn't give you trouble," he
said aloud.

"Not at all," Brace said. "So you had the chance to
examine the offer more closely?"

"I did, but . . ." Kendi put a sheepish look on his
face. "I'm sorry, Mr. Brace, but I'm waffling again. Some
other . . . factors just came up. I'm not ready to sign
just yet."

"Not another offer, I hope," Brace said with a jovial
grin.

"No!" Kendi said a little to quickly. "Nothing like
that. It's just that I'm nervous about putting more of my
life on public display."

Brace sucked at his teeth. "Perhaps we can alter the offer a bit," he said. "Raise the advance to seven-fifty and up the royalties half a percentage point."

"Really?" Kendi popped open his data pad's display and made the changes on the agreement. "That's generous, Mr. Brace."

"But only if you sign today," Brace said. "I'll have to talk fast to the boss, but I think it'll fly."

Kendi deflated. "Oh. I can't sign today, Mr. Brace. I'm really sorry. Is the original offer still good?"

"Yes, but . . ."

"But what?"

"I don't know for how long. I mentioned before, Father, that I'm under pressure to close this one, and I hope you can help me out."

Kendi bantered with Brace for almost an hour, pretending he was on the edge of signing before backing away. Then his earpiece chimed softly. When Kendi answered, Ben's voice broke in.

"*Meet me at home,*" he said in a desperate voice. "*Hurry!*"

Kendi's stomach flipped over. "What's wrong?"

"*Just meet me at home as fast as you can get there.*" The call ended.

Kendi's bantering demeanor vanished. He all but shoved the startled Tel Brace out of his office and ran all the way home. Walkways trembled and balconies thudded beneath his feet. Humans and Ched-Balaar alike snatched themselves out of his way, and twice he almost knocked someone over. When he burst into the house, he found Ben, Harenn, and Lucia in the living room with a data display hovering over the coffee table. Their faces were tight and pale.

"Wha—what—" he gasped, trying to get his breath.

"Another blackmail letter arrived," Lucia said. "Ben got the notification while we were investigating the *Poltergeist.*" She gestured at the display with a scarred hand. Kendi read, mouth dry.

WANT YOUR SECRET TO STAY SECRET? it said. THEN GIVE ME SOME MONEY. JUST POP TEN THOUSAND HARD AND HAPPY FREEMARKS INTO A PLAIN CLOTH SATCHEL

(FASHION NIGHTMARE, I KNOW, BUT WHAT ARE YOU GOING TO DO?) AND TAKE THAT LITTLE DARLIN' TO THE WALKWAY IN FRONT OF THE HOUSE AT ULIKOV 10832-15. AT EXACTLY TWO P.M. TOMORROW, THROW IT OVER THE RAIL. IT'S A NASTY NEIGHBORHOOD, SWEETIE PIES, SO WEAR YOUR GANGSTER REPELLENT. NOW I KNOW YOU'RE THINKING OF GIVING THE COPS A TEENSY LITTLE RINGY-DINGY, AND THAT WOULD BE A REALLY BAD IDEA. MY FINGERS ARE JUST ITCHING TO DO THE TWO-STEP OVER MY KEYBOARD AND TELL THE WHOLE WORLD THAT OUR BOY BENJI HAS THE MOST DYSFUNCTIONAL FAMILY SINCE . . . WELL, SINCE DANNY AND IRFAN MADE THE BED BOUNCE. LOOKING FORWARD TO SEEING YOU—AND TO COUNTING THE SMALL FORTUNE YOU'RE DYING TO GIVE ME.

—A FRIEND

"What the *hell?*" Ben said.

"Unorthodox," Lucia said, "but the meaning is clear. It's certainly no surprise."

Kendi tasted anger and bile. "So what do we do?"

"We pay it," Ben said. "In hard, happy freemarks."

"And what," Harenn said, "would prevent this person—or people—from demanding money again and again?"

"Nothing in the world," Lucia said. "Which is why we have to act. The address is Treetown, not monastery, so perhaps we should quietly alert the Treetown police and let them—"

"No!" Ben shouted. Everyone stared at him. He was on his feet, his face painted with a sheen of sweat. "If we bring the police in, they'll want to know what the blackmail is about. We can't afford to tell them—the more people who know, the more likely someone will tell."

"All right, all right," Kendi soothed. "But Ben—you know we can't let them get away with this. Harenn's right. It'll only get worse."

"The weak point in any anonymous blackmail plan is picking up the money," Lucia said. "The blackmailer has to be in a certain place at a certain time, meaning some-one can set a trap."

Ben sank to the couch. Kendi sat down as well, and

Ben leaned into him. Kendi put an arm around Ben's shoulders and was surprised to find him shaking. Kendi wanted to wrap his body around Ben, shield him from the fear and pain. Hatred for whoever was causing this stormed over Kendi, and he ground his teeth.

"What do we do to catch this bastard?" he said.

"Can you get your hands on that much hard currency?" Lucia asked.

"I think so."

"Then we'll use the tried-and-true. I will put tracer units on the bag and in the currency. You and I will set watch. When Ben makes the drop-off, we will grab the person who tries the pickup."

"You mean when *I* make the drop-off," Kendi said, hugging Ben harder. "Ben doesn't need to be involved."

Ben sat up. "Yes, I do. I want to be there."

"Are you sure?" Kendi asked. "You don't have—"

"I'm sure," Ben said.

"What about me?" Harenn said. "I can be present as well."

"You're going to be pregnant by tomorrow afternoon," Kendi said. "The doctor's going to tell you to sit home with your feet up for a few days, you know that."

"All right then," Lucia said before Harenn could respond, "let's find the drop-off point." Lucia called up a map of the area. Treetown surrounded the monastery like a lake surrounding an island. Technically the monastery was its own political unit, a city within a city with its own police force, governmental representatives, and municipal works. In practice, however, Treetown and the monastery tended to blend together. Both had the same postal service and utility companies, for example, and the monastery worked closely with Treetown schools and libraries to provide education.

The drop-off address was Ulikov 10832-15, and Kendi automatically split the number into its component parts. The first three digits indicated how high up the building in question was. The lowest anyone was allowed to build was a hundred meters above the forest floor. Every meter was a level, so 108 meant the house was on level eight, one hundred and eight meters up its talltree. The

32 meant section thirty-two on a grid arbitrarily drawn over Treetown and the monastery nestled within. Each sector had a name as well—Ulikov in this case—but the post office insisted on numbers. Ben and Kendi lived in Irvine—section six—which put them out of walking distance from the pickup point. The last two digits were simply the house number. So 10832-15 was house number fifteen on level eight in section thirty-two. Lucia highlighted the spot with a stylus. It glowed an angry red that matched Kendi's mood.

"I don't know that part of town very well," he said.

"I do," Lucia said. "It's a poorer section, with a lot of run-down apartment houses. It's gotten worse since the Despair. I'll scout it out and figure out the best layout for a trap. Then I'll get back to work on the *Poltergeist* people."

"Did you find anything out?" Kendi asked.

"I ran a check," Ben said. "There definitely used to be a backup file. It was erased only a week ago."

Harenn paled. "Oh, god," she whispered. "Ben, I am so sorry. This is my fault."

"Didn't we dance to that tune already?" Kendi said. "You tried to take the blame for the way Martina and Keith disappeared. It wasn't your fault then, and it isn't your fault now. It's the fault of the asshole who's blackmailing us."

"We did get a list of eight people who had access to the *Poltergeist*'s computer," Lucia said. "As I said, I will follow up on it. I'll also interview the spaceport staff. It may also be that someone who *wasn't* supposed to have access broke into the ship, and the staff may have seen something suspicious. Leave it to me, Father Kendi. If there is anything to find, I will find it."

Sitting there in his living room with her firm hands and serious face, Lucia came across as supremely confident and competent, and Kendi felt a bit better.

"Thank you, Lucia," he said. "But if you're going to be carrying one of our children, I think you'd better call me Kendi."

Lucia blushed slightly and looked less confident. "I . . . I will try. But it'll feel strange."

"Speaking of surrogacy," Harenn put in, "perhaps we should put off my appointment tomorrow in light of everything that's happened of late."

"No!" Ben and Kendi said together, and Kendi managed a laugh. "I won't interrupt our lives for this guy's bullshit," he said. "Besides, everything will be sorted out one way or another long before the baby is born. We shouldn't wait."

"Famous last words," Harenn said, but didn't disagree.

"We should call Vidya and Prasad," Ben said.

"What? Why?" Kendi said.

"Well, what I really mean is that we should call Sejal," Ben said. "Sejal didn't lose his mutant Silence in the Despair. He can still possess people, Silent and not, willing and not. He'd be the perfect person to catch a blackmailer. And he won't ask us questions if we tell him not to."

"I should have thought of that myself," Lucia said.

"Stressful times." Kendi got up and tapped the wall. "The Vajhur family."

"*That was quite a press conference,*" Vidya said on the viewscreen a moment later. She had long, silver-streaked hair and mahogany skin that showed stress and worry lines around the eyes and mouth. "*You looked even more foolish than—*"

"Thanks," Kendi interrupted. "Is Sejal around? We need to talk to him."

Vidya Vajhur's face went blank. "*Sejal is not here. He hasn't been for quite some time.*"

"Oh? Where is he?"

"*Away. I do not know where, exactly. It is a secret he has chosen not to share with me. I only know someone has hired him for a 'secret mission' for which he is being well-paid.*"

"Is this why he couldn't help us rescue Keith and Martina?" Ben spoke up. "I talked to him in the Dream and asked for his help, but he got all evasive and finally ran off."

"*I imagine that is the case,*" Vidya said. Her words were short and clipped, clearly angry. Kendi could understand why. Vidya had been forcibly separated from her husband Prasad and their baby daughter when she was pregnant with Sejal. As a result, she had raised Sejal alone in the roughest slums on the planet Rust in the Empire of Human Unity. Seventeen years later, the entire family had been reunited on Bellerophon. Vidya had just gotten her daughter back; Kendi couldn't imagine it would sit well with her to lose her son.

"Do you expect him back anytime soon?" Kendi asked.

"*I have no idea,*" Vidya said.

They exchanged a few unrelated pleasantries, and Kendi disconnected.

"So much for the easy solution," he sighed. "Now we play commando."

The door slammed in Gary Kyle's face. He stared at it for a moment, fuming, then picked up the baby carrier and turned toward the stairs. Mark didn't stir from his nap, for which Gary was grateful. A screaming baby would make an already bad situation unbearable. Why did Pandora have to be so difficult? You'd think she'd be *glad* to have him take Mark on the weekends so she could have some Alone Time. That was what she always called it—Alone Time, complete with capital letters. Trouble was, two months ago Gary had discovered her spending Alone Time in company. A whole lot of company. It had ended their marriage.

Gary had kept the house, but he still couldn't believe the court had granted Pandora primary custody of Mark. Wasn't Gary the one with intact Silence? Didn't he have the better income? Didn't he spend his evenings and weekends at home?

As Gary carried Mark out of the apartment building and onto the walkway, he worked to clear his thoughts of anger. Mark was just a baby, but Gary was sure he could feel the tension between his parents, and Gary was determined that his child should be as unaffected by it as he could manage.

Unfortunately there was no doubt in Gary's mind that Pandora would bad-mouth him to Mark once the boy was old enough to talk. A breeze stirred his brown robe, and Gary sighed. Maybe he could find some kind of evidence proving Pandora was an unfit mother. She took Mark into *bars*, for god's sake. How could the court possibly—

"Excuse me, Brother. I seem to be lost. Can you direct me to the monorail station?"

The speaker was a blond man. A dark-haired woman stood near him, looking around and trying to get her bearings. It would be easy to lose them—so many of the streetlights were out these days.

"I'm heading for the station right now," Gary said, glad of the distraction. "It's not far. Just follow me."

"Thanks," the man said.

"What a *darling* baby," the woman said. "Yours?"

"My son," Gary said, unable to keep from smiling. "He's nine months old tomorrow."

"What a sweetie," the woman cooed, bending over the carrier. Mark slumbered on. "And so handsome. But where's his mommy?"

"Divorced," Gary said shortly. "Look, if you want to catch the next train, we should probably—"

Something cold pressed against the back of his neck, and Gary felt a thump. He spun in time to see the man lower a dermospray. Gary stared at him, uncomprehending. Then a wave of dizziness hit him. He barely had time to set Mark's carrier down before he dropped like a stone.

In the morning, Kendi, Ben, and Harenn coasted in a gondola toward the medical center. Kendi usually loved the gondolas. The pulleys on the overhead wire were silent, allowing them to slide from station to station without a sound. It was like floating among the talltrees and houses in a balloon. The walkways and balconies hummed with human voices and Ched-Balaar chatter. Fresh-smelling spring breezes swirled gently around them, bringing the relaxing scent of flowers and bark and leaves. Today, however, Kendi felt unsettled. He and Ben had spent a restless night, neither able to comfort the other very well. Ben had wanted to be held, but Kendi found himself unable to lie still for long.

Today they were supposed to be excited. But Ben looked pale, Kendi felt tense, and Harenn worked her jaw. They spoke little. Ben held the star-shaped cryo-unit in his lap.

Dr. McCall was a round woman topped by a fluff of pale hair. Kendi and Ben stepped into the hallway outside the examination room while she gave Harenn a final checkup and got her onto the table and draped in a green sheet. Then Ben and Kendi rejoined her, standing near Harenn's head. Her face was placid, her hair hidden by a surgical cap. The room was a bit chilly and smelled of antiseptic.

"Ready to become pre-parents?" McCall asked merrily.

"Ready," Kendi said, and took Ben's hand. Ben reached down for Harenn's hand, and she gave him a small smile.

McCall touched a control on the cryo-unit, and the top slid aside. With a hiss of cold steam, a metal ring rose a few centimeters above the unit. Eleven cloudy ampules poked upward. Kendi peered at them, though he knew he wouldn't be able to see anything.

"The readouts say there are six boys and five girls," McCall said. "Do you have a preference for sex or for which embryo you want implanted?"

"Let the universe decide," Ben said. It was the same thing Ara had said on the day of Ben's implantation. Kendi squeezed his hand, and Harenn nodded.

"As you like," McCall said. She plucked an ampule at random and closed the cryo-unit. The ampule went into an instrument that looked like a cross between a pistol and a syringe. "We just have to wait a few moments for the bioimplantation unit to thaw the—ah! We're ready. Please relax, Ms. Mashib. You'll feel a slight pressure, but it shouldn't hurt."

Harenn took Kendi's other hand and squeezed it. He grinned down at her, feeling like he should say something important but unable to think what. Harenn was being implanted with his child, his son or daughter. In nine months, he'd be a father. So would Ben. Harenn would be its mother, and Kendi liked that idea.

It would also be a child of Irfan Qasad and Daniel Vik. Kendi wasn't sure how to feel about that. He was knowingly bringing into the world a child who, if the truth came out, would become instantly famous. Kendi had heard plenty of stories about famous children cracking under the pressures of celebrity and turning to drugs or theft or arson or worse crimes, and he swore a silent oath that this would never happen to his sons and daughters. Perhaps they deserved to know the truth when they were grown, but the world never would. Kendi looked at Ben's blue eyes and knew that he was thinking the same thing.

"Done," McCall reported, and stripped off her gloves. "You should avoid heavy lifting for the next forty-eight hours, but other than that, you're fine."

"Thank you, Doctor," Harenn said.

"Do you know for certain it took?" Kendi asked.

"Oh, yes. Miscarriage used to be a problem in these cases, but not anymore. Barring accident, injury, or disease, Ms. Mashib will bear a fine, healthy child. Do you want to know the sex now?"

"No," Ben said.

"Yes," Kendi said at the same time.

"I thought we already talked about this," Ben said.

"Talked about, yes," Kendi said. "Decided, no."

Harenn sat up as McCall took her feet from the stirrups. "I seem to recall," she said, "that you had indeed agreed to keep the baby's sex a surprise."

"Hey!"

"You're outnumbered," Ben said.

"However, I feel I should point out," Harenn continued, "that you could check the cryo-unit to see how many embryos of each sex are left."

"Don't even," Ben warned.

"You're a vile temptress, woman," Kendi growled. "But a promise is a promise. Even if I don't specifically remember making it."

McCall helped Harenn down from the table, and Ben and Kendi took refuge in the corridor again so she could dress. Kendi swept Ben into a hug.

"Hey, Dad," he whispered.

"Hey, Dad," Ben whispered back.

They parted, and Ben said, "What are the kids going to call us? It'll be confusing if we're both Dad."

"*You* can be Dad," Kendi said. "I'll be their Da."

"Works for me."

"That way," Kendi finished, "all their first words will probably be about me."

When Harenn emerged from the examination room, Kendi was cowering in a corner. Ben was pummeling him mercilessly.

"A fine pair of role models, the both of you," Harenn said.

"That's why we have you." Kendi grinned, straightening. Ben gave him a final thwack. "Shall we go?"

The gondola ride home was a little more cheerful, despite a stop at the bank for the blackmail money. Kendi couldn't take his eyes off Harenn. She looked the same—dark skin, pretty face, brown eyes, blue head scarf—but she also seemed different. When Harenn had first been assigned to Ara's team years ago, Kendi hadn't liked her much. Her verbal barbs and readiness for violence had put Kendi off. It wasn't until much later he had learned the source of her cynicism—her ex-husband had kidnapped their baby son Bedj-ka and sold him into slavery. The knowledge had changed the way he'd seen her. Harenn had stopped being a bitch and became more like a crusty maiden aunt. Later, when Kendi took over command of Ara's team and headed out to rescue her son, Harenn became something like an older cousin who worked in the family business. Now she was . . . what?

"Did I grow a third eye?" she finally asked. "Perhaps an extra nose?"

"You're going to be our child's mother," Kendi said. "I guess I'm rearranging how I see you."

Harenn put a hand on her stomach. "You will see plenty more of me soon."

The hiss and thump of resin guns greeted them when they got home. A team of human carpenters were swarming over Ben and Kendi's house. The two staircases leading to the building—one up, one down—lay in pieces, and a carpenter was running a measuring scanner over the walkways. Another worker pulled a sonic cutter from his pocket and with a quiet *zip* cut a board neatly in two. Pieces of electronic equipment littered the area, along with pulleys, cables, and other objects Kendi couldn't identify.

"I'd forgotten all about this," Ben said. "Why does everything have to happen at once around here?"

"We'd get bored otherwise," Kendi said, shifting the satchel slung over his shoulder.

"*You'd* get bored," Ben corrected.

They talked briefly with the supervisor, a brown-haired woman with sawdust in her eyebrows, before going inside. Smells of rich tomato sauce, sauteed chicklizard, and fresh-baked bread assailed them.

"Attention! Attention!" said the computer. "Lucia dePaolo used her access code for entry."

"In the kitchen," Lucia called.

"I'd guessed that," Kendi called back, inhaling appreciatively.

The kitchen had transformed into a domestic scene. Thick, spicy smells bubbled from a large pot on the stove. Meat sizzled in a pan next to a kettle of boiling pasta. Golden-brown rolls heaped a serving bowl. Lucia was grating pungent Parmesan cheese into a pale mound.

"I thought I'd test your kitchen," Lucia said, "to see if it still worked. And I needed to release some stress."

"I'm too nervous to eat," Ben said, dropping into a chair.

"What do you know, Lucia?" Kendi asked, tossing his money belt into a corner next to an anonymous-looking canvas satchel.

Lucia brushed the Parmesan into a bowl. "Not much. After we got the blackmail note, I went back to the list of technicians. Eight of them had access to the *Poltergeist*'s medical computer, and I ran checks on them all. No histories of criminal activity, no questionable background checks, nothing. I've interviewed five so far, and—"

"What did you tell them?" Ben interrupted. "They had to be curious about why you needed to talk."

"I only said we were trying to track down a missing file," Lucia said. "At any rate, the five I talked to claim they didn't take anything away from the ship, and they didn't see anything suspicious. They could be lying, of course. I'll talk to the other three and keep digging. Would you set the table, please? I'm nearly done here."

"What is the plan?" Harenn asked as Kendi got out plates and glasses.

"Very simple." Lucia stirred the sauce pot, tasted, and sprinkled in green herbs. "The satchel is in the corner. I take it the money is in that belt? Good. After lunch, we'll put the cash in the satchel, which also has a bug in it. The blackmailer wants you to toss the money off the walkway in front of that house in Ulikov district, so it's a good bet someone will be waiting at the bottom of the talltree to catch it and run. I'll be waiting down there, too, wearing a heat-and-light camouflage outfit. It disguises both me and my heat signature, in case they're equipped with infrared seekers. Irfan willing, I'll be able to follow and catch the blackmailer."

"So why the bugs, then?" Ben asked.

"The bugs are there in case I lose our friend. I'm there in case our friend loses the bugs."

"What about us?" Kendi asked. "What do we do after we toss the money?"

"Go home," Lucia said. "I intend to tail the culprit and find out if more than one person is involved."

"And I?" Harenn asked.

"You're pregnant," Lucia said. "You will stay here."

"No heavy lifting," Kendi said. "I'm sure that applies to sprinting after blackmailers."

"And since it seems your kitchen does work, despite many years of neglect," Lucia said, "we will eat lunch."

Although the food smelled delicious and Kendi tried to keep the talk light, no one ate much. Ben barely made a pretense of picking at his food. Kendi forced down a few forkfuls of delicious chick-lizard Parmesan and found he didn't want more. Kendi tried not to worry but couldn't help it. Any number of things could go wrong with the plan. What if the blackmailer got away and released the information? What if the blackmailer had a weapon, and Ben or Lucia got hurt? His chest felt like someone had poured sand and glass into it. Harenn and Lucia ate slowly. The clock said it was barely noon.

They passed the next hour discussing and rehearsing the plan. Lucia changed into the camouflage outfit. It looked like an ordinary green formfitting jumpsuit, though it had a hood, gloves, and a belt.

"How will that hide you?" Kendi asked.

Lucia smiled and tapped one cuff. The suit swirled into a leafy design. Another tap, and it shimmered into desert coloring. "The hood has a one-way mask on it, so I don't even have to wear makeup," she said. "I'll leave now so I can find a good vantage point."

"Are you licensed for a weapon?" Kendi asked.

Lucia patted a belt compartment. "I can carry a neuro-pistol, stun-level only. I will see you down there."

"Actually, we won't see you," Kendi said. "I hope."

"Yes." Lucia touched her collarbone, the place where she usually wore a small figurine of Irfan. "Mother Irfan will bless us, Fa—Kendi."

And she left. Kendi and Ben waited half an hour, then followed. Outside, the carpenters had finished the staircases and were dismantling the two walkways. Susan Bayberry, the brown-haired supervisor, called out an apology.

"We should be done in a few hours, sir," she said from across the gap. The polymer mesh underneath held a few dropped pieces of wood and a resin gun. Visible through the mesh were leaves, branches, and lower walkways. One of the carpenters drew a small pistol from his belt and aimed it downward. An orange beam of light touched the resin gun, and it flew upward. With a practiced motion, the carpenter shut off the beam and caught the errant gun. A sticky bead of resin clung to the end like a bit of liquid amber.

"Do you want me to show you how to use the stair bridges now?" Bayberry asked.

"Later," Kendi said distractedly. "We should be back soon. Leave instructions if you don't see us."

Without waiting for an answer, he and Ben trotted down the stairs that wound around the talltree. Ben carried the bag over one shoulder. Dirty gray clouds dragged across the sky, an omen of cold rain. Tree lizards chittered and chirped in a cheerful counterpoint to Kendi's mood.

On the front balcony of the house below, an older woman built like a hickory walking stick was scooping soil from a sack into a large pot. A flat of sky-blue blossoms waited nearby. The house itself groaned with plants and flowers. Hanging baskets spilled vines over their sides. Window boxes burst with bright colors. Ivy crawled up the walls. Kendi tried to slip past the woman without attracting her attention, but she looked up and caught sight of the two men. Kendi liked his neighbor, but he wasn't in the mood to talk. Still, he couldn't bring himself to be rude.

"Grandmother Mee," he said, pressing fingertips to forehead.

"Father Kendi," she replied. Dirt smudged her cheeks. "And Mr. Rymar. Is all that hammering up there for you?"

"We're having some work done," Kendi replied. "I hope they didn't disturb you. They should be done soon."

She waved a brown hand. "No bother. It's something different to wonder about. Now that I've been Silenced, all I have are my flowers and neighborhood gossip."

"We're in something of a hurry, Grandmother," Ben said, shifting the satchel.

"Off with you, then," she said to Kendi's relief. "But stop back and tell me what's going on in the Dream sometime, would you? I miss it."

"I will, Grandmother," Kendi promised, and let Ben lead him away.

The monorail station was a wide platform supported by the massive branches of the talltree and partly supported by thick cables drilled into the trunk itself. A pair of tracks snaked away through the leaves and branches for trains that ran in opposite directions. About a dozen people, both human and Ched-Balaar, awaited the next train. According to Kendi's ocular implant, it would arrive in the next three minutes.

"How are you holding up?" Kendi murmured to Ben.

"I'm upright," Ben said. "That's the best I can do right now."

Kendi wanted to smash something. Instead he turned and looked up the track to see if the train were coming. It wasn't, of course.

"Excuse me, aren't you Father Kendi?"

Three people at the monorail station—two human and one Ched-Balaar—asked for his autograph. A fourth tried to convince him to buy into an investment program for a fried chick-lizard franchise, and Kendi had to snarl at him before he would go away.

"Maybe we should get our own flitcar after all," Ben said as the train finally whooshed into the station like a silent dragon.

"Just filling out the forms will take months," Kendi replied sourly. "Though I'm starting to think the same thing."

They boarded and found seats in the section for humans. Ched-Balaar sat on the floor and hooked their front claws into footholds designed for that purpose. Two of them chattered quietly to each other, arms waving as one of them made a point. Kendi automatically sat next to the window, and Ben took the position next to the aisle. This cut down on the number of people on the train who might see and recognize the famous Kendi Weaver, and when had sitting like this become a habit?

Ben wound a leg through one handle of the bag and set it on the floor. The train slid forward, then put on a smooth burst of speed. The trees outside smeared into a green-brown blur.

They changed trains and finally arrived at the Ulikov station. As Lucia had said, this part of Treetown was more run-down. Tall, beehive apartment houses drooped among the talltree branches. The leaves here were thinner than elsewhere, letting in more gray sky, and some of the platforms creaked ominously as Kendi walked across them. The people were more shabbily dressed, and they didn't accost Kendi or Ben except to give them furtive stares. Kendi saw no Ched-Balaar at all. This was no surprise—this part of Treetown was known to harbor groups with anti-Ched-Balaar sentiments. The Human League, a group more paranoid than the rest, claimed that the Ched-Balaar had caused the Despair in order to force humans out of the Dream. Kendi wondered if they were the ones who had uncovered the information about Ben. The Human League was probably short on cash these days, and blackmail made a good fund-raiser.

"Spare a freemark for a fellow human?" asked a gray-faced, unshaven man. Kendi shook his head in refusal, then caught sight of the satchel hanging over Ben's shoulder. The money in that bag would feed a family of four for months, and Kendi was quibbling over a lousy freemark? He dropped a handful of coins into the man's palm and kept walking.

The pair crossed several walkways and went down a set of stairs to another balcony in front of an abandoned house. Graffiti sprawled across the door: FUCK REZA. Ben, face still pale, checked his data pad. "This is it."

"What time is it?"

"Two minutes before two."

Kendi peered over the rail. The mesh below was rent and torn like a fish net that had trapped a shark—storm damage or vandalism that the neighborhood couldn't afford to repair. Leaves and bark descended into shadow. Who was waiting down there? Ben unslung the satchel.

"Are you two in place?" came Lucia's whisper over Kendi's earpiece. He tapped it.

"We are that," he murmured.

"Do you see anyone?" Ben asked, also in a murmur.

"No, but they may be hidden as I am. Make the drop in five . . . four . . ."

"Is anyone looking?" Ben asked.

Kendi checked. A few figures moved in the distance, but the nearby balcony and walkway leading through it were currently deserted. "Nope."

Ben took a deep breath and held the satchel out over the balcony. Kendi leaned over the rail to keep on eye on it. When Lucia reached zero, Ben opened his hand.

CHAPTER FIVE

"If I lived like a dolphin, I would probably live longer."

—Daniel Vik

The satchel fell, and an orange beam of light flashed down from somewhere above Kendi's head. The satchel hovered for a split-second, then fled up the beam and disappeared.

Kendi was running before he was even aware of it. The bag had popped into an upper window of an abandoned two-story house one level up and ninety-degrees clockwise around the tree. He pounded up a staircase without looking to see if Ben were behind him and hit the house's platform. Doors and windows on the first floor were boarded up, and Kendi saw no way in. A flicker of movement on the roof caught his eye. A figure in a bulky jumpsuit was climbing out of a high window. A hood obscured the figure's face, and the satchel was strapped to its back. Kendi spotted a fire ladder running up the side of the house and dashed toward it. The figure made for the far gutter.

"Did you drop the satchel?" came Lucia's voice in Kendi's earpiece. *"I didn't see it."*

Kendi ignored her. He reached the roof just as the figure caught sight of him. It froze, then turned and ran across the shingles. Kendi followed, heart pounding, jaw tensed. A walkway for the upper level ran past the house two or three meters up and out. It had no mesh beneath it. The figure ran full tilt for the gutter and leaped. It easily snagged a support cable and pulled itself onto the swinging walkway. Kendi put on a burst of speed. He hit the edge and jumped.

Everything slowed. Kendi saw his own hands stretched

out before him. The support cable was a handsbreadth away. The figure on the walkway pulled a pistol from its belt. With aching slowness, it aimed. Kendi's hands touched the cable. The figure fired down at him. This time the beam was green, and it caught Kendi square in the chest. The air was smashed from his lungs, and the cable tore itself from his grip. Kendi flew backward and fell. Leaves and branches rushed past him and wind filled his ears. Then there was a stretching sensation, and he stopped.

Kendi hung there, dazed and motionless. Above him, weathered wood and green leaves swayed sickeningly. Kendi felt bruised and out of breath. He tried to move his arms and legs. They didn't respond. A tearing noise, and Kendi dropped a few centimeters. He gasped, and his surrounding snapped into focus. He had fallen into the tattered mesh below the rendezvous balcony. His arm had gone through one of the holes, and that was all that prevented him from sliding into a much bigger rent further down the mesh. Again he tried to move, but his muscles refused to work. Another tear, and the hole widened.

"Kendi!" Ben's face appeared in Kendi's field of vision. He was lying on his stomach to look over the edge. "Kendi! Are you okay?"

Kendi managed a blurry response, unable to create coherent words.

"I've called a rescue squad," Ben said. "God, can you—"

The hole tore some more, and Kendi jerked downward. Ben swore.

"Grab my hand!" he shouted, and thrust his arm down. It was within easy reach. Kendi tried to move but only managed a twitch. Ben slid feet-first over the edge, legs dangling, arm wrapped around a balcony strut. He reached for Kendi's free arm, but fell a few centimeters short. Ben's feet swung over empty air.

"You have to bring your arm up so I can grab you," Ben said. His voice was perfectly calm, but Kendi saw the sheen of sweat on his forehead. "You can do it, Ken. Bring your arm up."

Rip, drop. Another tear and Kendi would slide into

green oblivion. Kendi shrugged, trying to flip his arm up toward Ben, and managed a useless flopping motion.

"Almost, Ken," Ben said. "Come on. Try again."

Kendi shrugged harder. The motion brought his arm up. Ben reached. With a rotten tearing sound, the last of the mesh gave way. Kendi's stomach lurched, and he fell. Then he jerked to a stop. Ben's hand was white around Kendi's forearm. Kendi felt a rush of pain. Pins and needles stabbed his entire body, and an iron band crushed his arm where Ben had him in a death grip. Their feet swung gently over empty air. Ben groaned aloud.

Kendi hung there for a moment, then gave himself a mental shake. He could feel his arms and legs again, and that meant he could move them. He brought his free arm up. Hot pain wrenched every muscle, but it moved. He got it around Ben's neck. This brought him partially behind Ben, like a child climbing on for a piggy-back ride. The motion made Ben hiss through clenched teeth. His elbow, the one wrapped around the wooden strut, must be in agony. Kendi hung on through his own pain.

"I've got a hold," he gasped. "Now what?"

In answer, Ben let go of Kendi and lunged with his free arm. Kendi swung wildly but kept his hold around Ben's neck. Ben cried out in pain, but managed to grab the strut with his other arm. He was facing the balcony now.

"Can you climb up?" he panted.

Kendi reached for the balcony. Pain thundered through him, but his hand reached the edge. He started to climb, then lost his grip. He fell backward and only barely managed to wrap his arms around Ben's neck again. The jolt wrung another grunt from Ben. Panting from pain and exertion, Kendi reached up to try again, but couldn't even touch wood. He gritted his teeth.

"I have to lunge for it," he said. "Ready?"

Ben jerked his head in a nod.

"One . . two . . . *three*." Kendi lunged for the balcony—and missed. He was sliding down Ben's back when a hard, scarred hand grabbed his. Lucia added her other hand to the grip and pulled. Kendi made it over the edge of the balcony onto blessedly solid wood, then turned to help Ben up. The three of them lay panting on the platform, savoring the feeling of being alive and out of danger. Hardwood had never felt so good beneath his body.

Sirens wailed in the distance. Kendi sat up. "Let's get out of here," he said. "I don't feel like explaining anything."

They didn't quite flee—Kendi couldn't manage anything above a fast walk, and Ben's right arm hung uselessly at his side—but they managed to get away before the rescue squad arrived. Kendi realized belatedly that barely two minutes had passed since he's been shot.

Once they were a safe distance away, they ducked into an empty stairwell. Kendi explained what had happened while Lucia rolled up Ben's sleeve to examine his arm. The hard muscle was already darkening with bruises, and he winced under Lucia's careful prodding. Then she had Kendi lift his shirt. A rough circle was already turning purple on his chest and stomach.

"The blackmailer hit you with a gravity beam set to repulse," Lucia said.

"I figured that out," Kendi said.

"I think your arm is sprained, Ben. Harenn will have to look at it. And you, Fa—Kendi, will need analgesics. The human body isn't made to be pushed around by a gravity beam. In some ways, it's as effective as a neuro-stunner."

"Let's just get home," Ben said. "I feel like shit."

"What about the money, Lucia?" Kendi asked. "Are you tracking it?"

Lucia shook her head. "The bugs shorted out almost immediately. The gravity beam must have destroyed them."

Lucia changed her camouflage jumpsuit to an unremarkable blue, and they emerged from the stairwell to trudge toward the train station. The monorail ride home was silent and solemn. Kendi could feel his muscles stiffening. Ben sat in the hard seat, his face unreadable, though Kendi knew him well enough to recognize how upset he was. Pain mixed with guilt. Why had Kendi been so stupid? He should have let the blackmailer get away. He had come within a hair of dying, had almost taken Ben with him. Now they were out ten thousand freemarks, and the blackmailer was probably royally pissed off. That didn't bode well.

Kendi thanked his ancestors when they got home and saw the carpenters had left. Except for crumbs of sawdust scattered here and there, the staircases and walkways looked exactly the same as before. Harenn was waiting for them in the house. In the living room with her was a boy with dark eyes, hair, and skin. He was a bit short, and good-looking in a way that made maiden aunts ache to pinch his cheeks. Kendi had long ago decided the boy would one day break hearts on a dozen worlds.

"Bedj-ka," he said weakly. "What are—"

"School is out, and he can't stay home alone," Harenn said. "What happened?"

"You look awful," Bedj-ka said.

"Bedj-ka, I want you to go into Father Kendi's room," Harenn said. "You may use the sim-games there."

"Uh, not those," Kendi said quickly. "They wouldn't be—um . . ."

"There's another sim unit in my office," Ben said.

"Go, Bedj-ka," Harenn said. "Now!"

"I never get to hear anything good," Bedj-ka complained, but left.

"I'll get the medical kit," Lucia said, and disappeared into the bathroom. Kendi explained what happened, and Harenn's mouth hardened. When Lucia returned, Harenn took out the kit's little scanner and told Ben to take off his shirt. Kendi flinched at the sight. The clear line of a balcony strut was imprinted in the crook of his elbow, and Ben's fair skin showed the mark with perfect clarity. The limb was swelling. The hard, well-defined muscles of his arm and chest twitched painfully when Harenn touched them. She checked the scanner.

"Your arm is badly sprained," she said, and racked an ampule into a dermospray. She pressed it against his arm with a *thump*. "This will clear it up, though it will take several hours. You should wear a sling for the next day or so. You will need prescription painkillers, but I do not have—"

"I have a stash," Kendi said.

Harenn gave him a long look. "Do I want to know how you laid hands on them?"

"Not if you want to keep your nurse's license."

"Very well. Take what you need and no more, Ben. Lucia, help him put his shirt back on. Kendi, I need you to hold still." Harenn examined him, poking, prodding, scanning. Kendi bore the process in uncharacteristic silence. The pain had settled into a low, steady ache.

"Your assailant could have killed you," Harenn said. "If that beam had been turned up higher, it would have punched your heart out through your spine. You were very lucky."

"I know," Kendi said with look at Ben. Lucia was helping his sore arm into the sleeve, and Kendi was seized with an urge to push her away. That was *his* job.

"As it is," Harenn continued, "your muscles will be sore for a day or two. There is nothing for it except rest, a hot bath, and pain medication."

"Ben?" Bedj-ka called from the office. "Your computer is signaling. It says you have an urgent message."

There was a collective rush for the office. Harenn ordered Bedj-ka out, and he went with poor grace. Ben sat at the desk and ordered the computer to bring up the message. Kendi's mouth was dry.

YOU WERE BAD, BAD BOYS. KENDI DOES HAVE GUTS, I'LL GIVE HIM THAT. I ALMOST GOT TO SEE THEM. SORRY ABOUT THE GRAVITY BEAM, SWEETIE-PIES, BUT YOU DIDN'T LEAVE ME ANY CHOICE. AND BEN, YOU FLAME-HAIRED HUNK—BETTER START SCARING UP MORE CASH. MAYBE YOUR GRANDMA CAN PASS A LAW MAKING BLACK-MAIL A DEDUCTION. I'LL BE IN TOUCH.

—A FRIEND

"It's like being blackmailed by the tooth fairy," Kendi muttered. "Let's see if anything about this appeared on the newsfeeds."

The local lead stories included the arrest of three Ched-Balaar humans who were part of a drug ring, the opening of a new play about Renna Dell, one of the original human colonists on Bellerophon, and the disappearance of a baby whose parents were divorced. The father had vanished as well, and the Guardians were treating it as a case of parental kidnapping. There was nothing about a strange chase through the streets of the Ulikov sector in Treetown.

"Now what do we do?" Ben said.

"I think we should call the police or the Guardians," Lucia said. "These notes are very distinct, and a linguistic profile might be able to tell us something about—"

"No Guardians," Ben almost shouted. "Absolutely not."

"As you like, Ben," Lucia said, taken a bit aback.

"No Guardians," Kendi agreed, "but we might want to get someone else involved."

"Didn't you say Senator Reza offered government security guards?" Harenn said. "Why not use them?"

"They're government," Ben said. "Legal law enforcement. I don't want them near me."

"But we need someone," Kendi said.

"Why?" Ben countered. "People have tried to kill us before. Besides, the blackmailer doesn't want us dead—hard to sign checks from beyond the grave."

"What if he—or she—decides to get rid of the evidence?" Kendi said. "When people came after us before, it was on other planets. Even when the Dream stalker was trying to kill Ara and me, it was in the Dream. This is *here*, in our *home*. Where we're going to have babies."

Ben's mouth folded into a hard line, but eventually he said, "Who did you have in mind to call?"

"Lewa Tan. She retired from the Guardians a few years ago and does private security work now. Best of all, we can afford her. For a while, anyway."

"Call, then," Ben said. "And get it over with."

"Open sesame," Kendi said. A section of walkway plank, currently raised upward like a pointing finger, dropped into place. Two startled glider lizards leaped from the house gutter with matching squeaks and sailed away.

Inspector Lewa Tan (retired) gave it a critical look. "Is it just passworded?"

"Password, voice recognition, and print scanner, all set into the railing," Kendi said, tapping the wood. "The staircases do the same thing."

"A good start," Tan said. "Let's go inside."

Tan inspected the house with a careful eye and a quick hand on her data pad. Kendi and Ben followed. Harenn and Lucia had already left. Kendi hadn't realized how long it had been since he had last encountered Inspector Tan. He had seen her on and off since the Dream stalker murder case, but the visits had tapered off in recent years. Now there was a great deal of gray in her black hair, though the braid that ran down her back was as thick and heavy as before. Deep lines had cropped up around her nose and mouth, and her brown eyes were a shade or two lighter. She still moved with firm strength, and Kendi was certain she could take down most assailants before they even saw her move. Her voice had also remained the same—it grated like a rusty hinge, and she spoke like she was going to be billed for every sentence.

"Have to replace these curtains with one-way blinds," she said. "You should shut windows, especially on the ground floor. I'll arrange to have mail sent to a service for checking before it comes here. Alarm system needs upgrading. My recommendation is a guard for each of you all day and at least one in the house all night."

"I don't know," Ben said. They were standing in the living room. "It sounds like an awful lot."

"It'll keep you alive, Ben," Tan said bluntly.

"I'm used to worrying about all this on field work for the Children," Ben said. "But not here. In my own home."

"Your choice," Tan said. "You're paying for my opinion, and I'm giving it. I'm just surprised you haven't had any major trouble yet. Are there any weapons in the house?"

"In the floor safe in Ben's office," Kendi said. "We have a neuro-pistol and a needle gun. Children of Irfan issue."

Tan nodded. "Is that sling something I should know about?"

Kendi gave Ben a sidelong look. Ben remained silent, leaving it to Kendi to take the lead as he usually did when he was uncertain. It was a part of Ben that Kendi didn't always like. Kendi had to guess what Ben would want done or said. If Kendi guessed right, Ben got the benefit risk-free. If Kendi guessed wrong, Ben would have someone to blame.

"The sling isn't important," Kendi said. "It's unrelated to why we called you."

"Uh huh." Tan leveled them a stare hard as brown glass. "I worked forty years as a Guardian, Kendi. I see a lot. I see Ben's hurt. I see you're moving carefully. I see new drawbridges. I hear about a rescue crew that showed up in Ulikov and found no one to rescue. Cop instincts say all the paints belong to one picture. I can't help unless I know what's going on. I'm confidential as a lawyer, if you're worried. You hired both me *and* my silence."

Kendi bit the inside of his cheek. The Despair had Silenced Tan, and he wondered if her last remark was meant to be a subtle rebuke.

"I suppose I'd be disappointed if you weren't suspicious," Kendi said, stalling. "You could say the events are related. We . . . we aren't . . ."

"We're being blackmailed," Ben said. "We tried to catch the person when we handed off the money, but he knocked Kendi over the rail with a gravity beam and got away. I hauled Kendi back up, but it was a close thing."

Kendi blinked at Ben, then averted his gaze.

Tan folded her arms. "What are they blackmailing you about?"

"You don't need to know, Lewa." Ben held up his good hand. "You're going to quote Irfan Qasad at me: 'The greater your knowledge, the lesser your risk.' But it ultimately doesn't matter *why* we're being blackmailed."

"Tell me this much," Tan said. "Is it because you did something illegal?"

"No," Ben said. "And we've hired Lucia dePaolo to look into it. She's tracking leads right now."

"Lucia's good," Tan mused. "Why not call the Guardians?"

"No Guardians," Ben said. "And no police. That's non-negotiable."

"You're the boss." Tan flicked her braid over her shoulder. "But I can't be held responsible for anything that happens because you held back."

"Fair enough," Kendi said.

"When will you assign security detail?" Kendi asked.

"Now," Tan said, tapping her data pad. "I'll have people here within half an hour."

"I should give you contact information for my publicist," Kendi said. "She has a whole campaign schedule worked out for—"

"Attention! Attention! Wanda Petrie is asking permission to enter by the western drawbridge."

"Perfect timing," Kendi said. "Irene, lower the—"

"Stop!" Tan barked, and Kendi subsided into startled silence. "You can't do that, Kendi. Anybody could walk up and claim to be Wanda Petrie. Stay here."

Tan went to the living room window and peered around the edge of the curtain. "I see a woman with brown hair in a business outfit. She doesn't seem to be armed. Come take a look, Kendi, but be careful."

Feeling a bit silly, Kendi crept to the window and peeped outside. Wanda Petrie stood at the drawbridge with an impatient look on her face.

"That's her," Kendi said. "Can I let her in?"

"Should be all right." Tan took out her data pad. "Have to get some security cameras installed around here, too."

"Irene, lower the western drawbridge and tell Wanda Petrie to enter."

A moment later, Petrie clicked her way into the living room with her quick, birdlike movements. Kendi made introductions, and Petrie sat.

"I'm glad to see you changed your mind about the personal security," she said. "Good. I've reworked your schedule, including the workshop. Tonight Senator Reza is speaking at a Unionist rally—a *small* rally—and I'd like you to attend. As a guest, not a speaker. If anyone talks to you, smile, nod, and keep quiet. Do *not* talk to any members of the press."

"Details," Tan said over her own data pad. "Time, place, people."

"I'll zap them to you right now," Petrie said, tapping buttons. "You'll want to talk to the senator's Guardian force, too, so you can coordinate with them."

Kendi leaned back in his chair. The two women talked and argued about Kendi's schedule as if he and Ben weren't there. The air was growing stuffy, since Tan had insisted they close all the windows, and Kendi's body still ached from the gravity beam. It felt like the room, his schedule, even his body had grown close and confining. Kendi needed to get out, get away. He shifted in his chair and caught Ben's eye. Ben looked as uncomfortable and bored as Kendi felt. Kendi jerked his head toward the stairs and winked. Ben hesitated, looked at Petrie and Tan, and nodded.

Feeling like a conspirator, Ben sidled toward the stairs with Kendi. He should probably stay and listen to Tan and Petrie, but the mischievous look on Kendi's face was too . . . too . . . well, it was too cute to pass up. Ben bit his lip to hide a smile. After almost fifteen years, he still found Kendi cute.

The two of them slipped upstairs and into their room. Kendi shut the door and leaned against it with an exaggerated sigh of relief. Ben couldn't help a small laugh. Kendi's sense of humor had gotten both of them into trouble a few times, but it was one of the things Ben loved most about him.

"You're silly beyond reason, you know," Ben said.

"The road to hell may be paved with good intentions," Kendi said. "But the road to heaven is mortared with silliness."

"Mortared?"

"Silliness holds everything together," Kendi said seriously. "Without it we'd fall apart."

"I thought the Real People didn't believe in heaven."

"I'm making this up as I go. Bear with me." He slid his hands over Ben's broad shoulders, careful not to jostle his sore arm. "How's the injury?"

"Not bad. The painkillers at work."

"You look like a wounded hero in that sling. Come to think of it, that's exactly what you are."

The remark jolted Ben. For a few minutes, he had managed to forget the blackmailing, the failed plan, and the fact that some stranger out there knew he was Irfan's son. His life would be destroyed under a stampede of reporters, thrill-seekers, and religious fanatics. The idea filled him with an unreasoning terror, though he couldn't say why. In a lifetime of working with the Children of Irfan, he had faced battle cruisers, galactic empires, greedy slavers, and even a serial murderer. He had been afraid of all of them—only an idiot wouldn't feel at least a little nervous with a Unity battleship firing missiles up your slipdrive—but the idea of becoming an intergalactic celebrity filled him with a bone-shaking terror that he couldn't seem to shake. His gut twisted, and he wanted to creep into a dark corner like a cricket, letting the world pass him by except when he chose to make a noise.

"Hey, I didn't mean to upset you," Kendi said, reading Ben's face. "Look at you—scared and upset and everything else, and I blew the chance to make it stop. I'm so stupid."

"You did everything you could, Ken," Ben said, falling into a nickname he rarely used and Kendi allowed to no one else. "Don't beat yourself up. That's my job."

Kendi ran his fingers along Ben's jaw, something that always made him shiver. "I never got the chance to thank you properly for saving me," he said, and bent his head to kiss Ben. Kendi's mouth was warm on his, and it was several moments before they parted.

"You're welcome," Ben said, then leaned against Kendi. "God, I thought I'd lost you. When you fell like that . . . I thought I'd die, too. Don't do that ever again."

"I won't," Kendi promised, whispering into Ben's hair. "I'm sorry."

They stayed like that for a long time. Finally Kendi broke away. "Let's get the hell out of here," he said. "I need a change of scene."

"Where?" Ben asked. "You know that Tan won't want us going anywhere without her approval."

In response, Kendi glanced at Ben's dresser. The top was a tangle of odds and ends. Two unmatched socks and a broken comb lay among the mess. The bedroom itself was divided in half. A king-sized bed occupied the exact center—the size was a concession to Kendi, who claimed Ben was a bed hog—and each half had its own characteristic flavor. Ben's side was, like his den, a total mess. Clothing lay tumbled on the floor along with book-disks, readers, and other objects. Kendi's side was spartan. Clothes and robes hung neatly in the closet, and a short red spear hung on the wall. The high-beamed ceiling and polished wooden floors gave the room a light, airy feel despite Ben's clutter. Kendi fished a dermospray from the jumble atop the dresser and handed it to Ben.

"Ah," Ben said. "My turf or yours?"

"Mine," Kendi said. "You'd look sexy in a loincloth."

Ben blushed, then laughed and lay down on the bed, feeling a little better. He watched Kendi retrieve his own dermospray from a drawer and press it to his forearm. A hiss, a *thump*, and the drug drove home. Kendi took down the spear and fitted the sharp end with a rubber tip. He bent one knee and fitted the spear underneath it, creating a pirate peg leg for himself. The rubber end of the spear pressed against the floor. If Kendi had been outdoors, the sharp point would push into the earth to give the spear stability, but that wasn't possible indoors. Once Kendi was sure of his balance, he cupped his hands over his groin and closed his eyes in the traditional meditation pose for the Real People of Australia. No matter how many times he watched Kendi do this, it amazed Ben that he didn't fall over.

Ben pressed his own dermospray to his arm and felt the small *thump*. With a final glance at Kendi, he shut his eyes and lay back. After a moment, color swirled before his closed eyes, and he felt a warm languor spread through his limbs—the drugs at work. Ben concentrated on his breathing, emptying his mind, reaching upward and *out*.

The colors faded and cleared. Ben opened his eyes. His sling was gone, and he was standing on a white tile floor in the middle of a computer network. Organic data processing units twined up like vines, their DNA matrices glowing green and blue. Keyboards, microphones, and holographic displays made neat rows on gleaming metal surfaces. Lights flashed. Transmission lines and data portals opened in all directions, ready to transmit or receive.

It was the Dream.

Despite a thousand years of study, no one knew exactly what the Dream was, though the prevailing theory held that it was a plane of mental existence created from the collective subconscious of every sentient mind in the universe. The Silent—people like Ben and Kendi—could actually enter the Dream, usually with a boost from a drug cocktail tailored to their individual metabolisms.

In the Dream distance meant nothing. Two Silent who entered the Dream could meet and talk, no matter where in the galaxy their bodies might be. The Silent could also shape the Dream landscape, form it into whatever environment they desired. In Ben's network, every wire, every matrix, every chip was a sentient mind in the solid world, and they took on those forms because Ben wished it. Or perhaps Ben saw the Dream as a computer network because his own mind wanted him to see it that way. Philosophies differed, even among the Children of Irfan. Ben only knew it gave him a headache to think about it.

Before the Despair, the Dream had been full of whispering voices, the voices of millions upon millions of Silent. These days the Dream was quiet, like death, and a tiny handful of whispers skittered amid the hum of Ben's ventilation system. The silence was eerie, and it felt like the Dream was in mourning.

Ben shook these thoughts aside. He was supposed to meet Kendi on Kendi's turf. He concentrated for a moment and banished his network. A rush of Dream energy swirled around him, stirring his hair and clothes like a whirlpool. The network vanished, and an empty gray plain took its place. In the distance, earth merged with sky at an ill-defined horizon. The air was still and just a little stale. It was the default condition of the Dream.

Ben shut his eyes and listened to the faint whispers on the air. Practiced Silent could single out individual voices and track them down, and Ben was picking up the trick quickly, almost as if he had been born to it.

Maybe I was, he thought, unsure whether he was being resolute or wry.

One whisper, close by, felt familiar as his own voice. Ben opened his eyes and trotted toward it. His footsteps were muffled, as if he were surrounded by carpeted walls instead of empty space. Just ahead of him, the landscape changed. Rocks and hills came over the horizon, and

Ben caught a whiff of hot, dry air. The sun appeared, a hard gold coin that radiated harsh heat. Sandy soil appeared a few steps away. Ben halted and reached out to touch the place with a mental finger.

~*May I approach?*~ he asked in the ritual greeting.

~*Get in here,*~ Kendi replied.

Ben took a step forward and braced himself. When two Silent met in the Dream, they had to decide between them whose mind would shape reality. Unless one Silent were willing to let go, the Dream would warp as both minds pulled at it, sending the landscape into a Dali spiral. The stronger mind would usually win out, but experience had an impact as well. Ben let out a deep breath and released his expectations. Another rush of Dream energy, and Kendi's turf surrounded him on all sides. Sandy soil peppered with scrubby plant life stretched in all directions around him, and the sun continued to pour down liquid heat. It was the Australian Outback, or Kendi's Dream interpretation thereof. Ben had never visited the real thing.

A high scream pierced the air overhead. Ben looked up, squinting against the sun. A winged speck described a circle in the clear blue sky. Ben became aware he was wearing nothing but a loincloth. Dream etiquette—the host dressed the visitor in whatever clothing was appropriate for the climate in the host's turf, and the Real People wore little or nothing in the Outback.

The speck folded its wings and dove straight for Ben. He raised an arm. The little brown falcon pulled up just in time and landed gently on Ben's bare forearm. Feathers brushed his skin and talons pricked without piercing. A real-world falcon would have laid him open to the bone, but this was the Dream.

"I thought you were kidding about the loincloth," Ben said. "You've never put me in one before."

"Some people," the falcon leered, "shouldn't be allowed to wear clothes."

"And if I get sunburned here, it'll carry over into my solid body. You remember the term 'psychosomatic carryover,' don't you?"

"I could whip up some sunscreen."

"Kendi."

"Oh, all right," Kendi said, fluffing his feathers in a pretend pout. "Here." Khaki trousers and a matching shirt grew down Ben's body, and a pith helmet appeared on his head. Heavy boots closed around his feet. The falcon, meanwhile, fluttered to the ground. The moment its talons touched earth, its form shimmered and shifted like muddy water, and a kangaroo stood in its place. The animal had a pouch.

"Better?" the kangaroo asked.

"Much." Ben took a deep breath of spicy desert air and looked around at Kendi's Outback. The rocks and boulders cast razor-edged shadows. A group of small-leaved trees made a grove around a wide, muddy billabong that looked ideal for hiding crocodiles, though nothing stirred the water. No other animals were in evidence, and the air was devoid of birdsong. The place possessed a stark, primal beauty. "So what are we doing here, anyway?"

Kangaroo Kendi flopped down on the ground in an extravagant sprawl of fur and tail. "Relaxing. Getting the hell away from it all."

Ben sat down next to the kangaroo. "Any luck with . . ."

"No," Kendi said. "I'm still stuck in animal form. I'll keep trying, but for now it's kangas, koalas, and camels."

Ben nodded and stroked the kangaroo's soft, dusty fur. Before the Despair, Kendi had been one of the more powerful Silent in the Dream. The chief manifestation of his power had been an uncanny knack at tracking other people and the ability to create animals in the Dream. No Silent could create sentient creatures—creating and controlling such complicated reactions was too much for even the subconscious mind—but a few could handle lower life-forms. Kendi had gone one step further. His animals had been shards of his own mind, separated from his main consciousness and possessing a certain amount of autonomy. Oddly, all his animals were female, though Ben continued to think of Dream Kendi as "he." The Despair had robbed Kendi of much of his power within the Dream, leaving him able to appear there only as an Outback creature and killing his ability to create independent animals. His tracking skills had also been dulled, but there were also far fewer people to track.

The sun continued to pour down, and suddenly Ben felt itchy and confined in his explorer's outfit. "Let's go swimming," he said.

Kendi cocked an ear. "Swimming?"

"You know how, don't you?"

"Depends on my shape."

"So let's go to the beach," Ben said.

Kangaroo Kendi thought a moment. "You're on."

Ben felt the landscape around him shift and loosen as Kendi's mind relaxed its hold. Ben reached out and touched the Dream.

The Outback vanished, leaving the flat plain and a puddle of muddy billabong water. Then the puddle expanded, gushing toward the horizon with the sound of a thousand rivers until it met a distant azure sky. White sand faded into existence beneath Ben's boots. Palm trees grew toward a gentle sun, putting out leaves and coconuts like green fingers and brown knuckles. The ocean roiled and bubbled in its newness until Ben stretched a hand over it. It calmed at once, deepening to a perfect, clear blue. Ben's explorer outfit melted away, replaced by bathing trunks, sandals, and a yellow gauze shirt.

"Nice," Kendi said with admiration. "Though the palm trees look a little barmy."

"I've only seen holos," Ben apologized. "It's not something I—"

The kangaroo bolted upright, ears pricked, nostrils flared. "What the hell?"

"What?" Ben twisted around, trying to see in all directions at once. "What's wrong?"

Kendi remained motionless, a furry brown statue. "I thought I heard . . . something."

Ben listened. All he could hear was his own breathing and the gentle lap of small waves on white sand. The usual murmur of Dream whispers formed a susurrant background. "I don't hear a thing."

Kendi listened a moment longer, then gave an oddly human shrug. "Guess I'm jumpier than I thought. Ha! I didn't even mean the pun."

"Let's go in," Ben said. "The water's fine—I know."
He started to pull of his shirt, then caught himself. With
a flick of his mind, it disappeared, along with his sandals.
The soft, golden sun shone pleasantly warm on his bare
shoulders, a marked contrast to Kendi's harsh Outback.
With a happy yell, Ben dove into the cool waters and
swam several meters out before surfacing. He shook his
head and flung water in all directions, treading furiously
to keep himself afloat.

The beach was empty, the kangaroo gone. Ben shaded
his eyes and kept kicking. What the hell? Where was—

Something bumped his legs from beneath. A stab of
panic—

Shark!

—flashed through him before he could remind himself
that there would be no sharks in the Dream unless Ben
put them there. He was looking down, trying to see what
it was, when a dolphin poked its head above the surface
and blew water into Ben's face. Ben spluttered and
wiped his eyes.

"You bastard!" he said. "And since when can you
do dolphins?"

"Since now," Kendi chirped. "There are dolphins in
the oceans around Australia. My subconscious is letting
me count them as workable animal shapes, I guess. Or
maybe I'm getting stronger in the Dream. This is *fun!*"
He slipped backward into the water, then abruptly burst
upward, arcing over Ben's head and splashing down behind him. Ben laughed, and more of his tension eased.

"I don't think dolphins are supposed to giggle," he
said when Kendi surfaced.

Kendi presented his dorsal fin. "Grab hold!"

Ben obeyed. The dolphin's skin was smooth and cool.
The moment he got a good grip, Kendi took off. Ben
was flying through the water. The ocean washed over his
body, sliding under and around him like a liquid lover.

Kendi dove. Ben barely had time to snatch a breath
before they were underwater. Sound vanished, and blue
depths sank into darkness beneath them. Ben held
Kendi's fin with strong hands, the same ones that had
pulled Kendi back from deadly green depths barely an
hour ago. Ben tried to push the memory away and only

partly succeeded. He concentrated on the feel of Kendi's muscles pumping smoothly up and down as his muscular tail propelled them forward. It was exhilarating—speed without sound. Normally speed meant rushing air and some kind of roaring motor, but down here it was all silent. Even the whispers were quiet.

~ . . . ~

Kendi stopped. Ben let go of him and hung in the water, paddling gently to keep from sinking. This time he had heard it. Down here, in the absolute silence, the sound had been clear. Faint, but clear. Ben couldn't describe it, even to himself. It was the little pause before a speaker cleared his throat, a tiny intake of breath. He had never heard anything like it before. Kendi floated in the water beside him, and it was clear he had heard the same thing.

Ben's lungs called for air, but he didn't want to surface in case he missed the sound again. It occurred to him that he could create a mask and breathing collar for himself, but that would create bubbles and destroy the perfect silence.

You're not really underwater, you know, he told himself. *You don't really need to breathe. This is the Dream, and you're the son of the most powerful human the Dream has ever known.*

Ben's lungs were shouting now, and Kendi poked him with his snout, urging him to surface. Ben held up a hand. The fine red-gold hairs on his arm waved like kelp in the smooth water. Ben closed his eyes, concentrated.

The water is as good as air, he thought. *I can breathe the water. I can breathe the water* now.

He inhaled. Air burst from his lungs, and water rushed in. His chest felt abruptly heavy and he tried to cough, but the water prevented him. Panic hit. Ben's eyes popped open and he struggled. Kendi dove underneath him in a flash and pushed him toward the surface. Ben choked and fought to regain his concentration.

I can breathe, he told himself firmly. *I can breathe* now!

He gasped, and the heaviness in his chest vanished. Water filled his lungs, sweet as air. Ben pushed away from Kendi and dove downward, swimming away from the surface. Kendi rushed after him, obviously afraid Ben had panicked and was heading the wrong way, as drowning victims sometimes do. Ben held up a hand again with a grin and pointedly inhaled. The dolphin's eyes widened, and a clicking chirpy noise filled the water. Kendi's words in a dolphin's voice.

"How the hell are you doing that?" he demanded.

Ben shrugged, uncertain whether or not he could talk underwater, and decided not to push his luck. Instead he spun and swam away with a silent laugh. It was glorious! The water supported him, moved with him, let him slide in any direction he wanted. Kendi easily caught up with him, swimming around him, under him, caressing him with his sleek, muscled body. Suddenly even the simple swim trunks felt tight and confining. Ben's mind flickered, and they vanished. The sensual feel of the warm water and Kendi's smooth skin on his intensified. He wrapped his arms and legs around Kendi and let him propel both of them forward. It was like sliding through warm silk. Ben tasted salt, felt liquid course over him faster and faster as Kendi's tail thrashed the water. He was aware they were rising, rushing, flying toward the surface. His breath came faster, his lungs pumped furiously. They broke the surface, man and dolphin, and arced into the sky together, impossibly high, impossibly free. Ben hung in midair with Kendi for a tiny moment that lasted an entire day. Then they were falling back toward the ocean. They hit with a great splash that sent up a gout of white water. Bubbles tingled against Ben's bare skin. Automatically he swam upward and surfaced with a shout. Kendi appeared a moment later.

"That was the greatest!" Ben whooped, shaking his head to fling the hair from his eyes.

Kendi's dolphin grin stretched wider. "Let's do it again."

"Give me a minute to recover first. That was a hell of a ride." He lay back, tried to float, failed, and went back to treading water. Kendi nuzzled up next to him to help.

"You heard that sound," he said after a while.

"I did. What was it? You control the Dream better than I do."

"Not true. Teaching yourself to breathe a foreign atmosphere was a neat trick—difficult for most Silent and impossible for the rest. *I* can't do it. All my animal shapes breathe air."

"Do you think it's because I'm Irfan's son?"

"Could be," Kendi said. "In any case, I don't know what the sound was—or where it came from."

~May I approach?~

Ben jumped. He hadn't been expecting anyone to knock. The voice, however, was familiar.

"Martina!" Kendi called. "Come on in—I mean, if it's okay with Ben."

"Sure," Ben said.

The Dream rippled, and Martina Weaver appeared a few meters away. She wore a one-piece blue bathing suit. For a split second, she appeared to be standing on the surface of the ocean. Then she vanished with a squeak and a splash. She surfaced, sputtering and blowing salt water.

"Sorry!" Ben called. "I forgot there's no place to stand."

She splashed him in response, then lay back and stared up at the perfect blue sky. "This is a fine stress reliever. Glad I stopped by."

"What are you up to?" Kendi asked. "Anything going on?"

"I'm hard at work. Now that you're on sabbatical, the Children decided to end my training—as if I hadn't already been doing courier duty for half my life—and they put me on duty. I've been making contacts and running messages to the Prism Conglomerate all morning. Their banks are a real mess now that they can only communicate locally. Anyway, I sensed the both of you and decided to pay a visit before my drugs wear off. I wasn't expecting an ocean dip."

"Don't call your brother a dip," Ben said with mock severity. A gout of water from Kendi caught him in the face.

"How deep is it?" Martina asked, and dove without waiting for an answer. She surfaced a few seconds later. "I'm impressed. Clearest water I've seen this side of a swimming pool. Lets you see everything." She sniffed.

"Including the fact that Kendi isn't the only one doing a skin swim."

Ben reflexively jerked his arms down to cover himself, sank, surfaced, and sprayed water. He would be wearing a bathing suit. He would be wearing a bathing suit *now*. And he was. It was yellow. Ben's face went hot. Martina covered a smile with her hand as she tread water. Kendi gave a chirping dolphin laugh.

"Didn't mean to embarrass you," Martina said, then winked. "Actually, I should probably congratulate you. Or maybe I should congratulate Kendi."

"Thank you," Kendi smirked. "You're as bad as I am, sis."

"Runs in the family. Does he always blush like that?"

"It's that fair skin. Shows everything."

"Ah. Like the water did."

The ocean vanished, leaving the stark, gray plain in its place. Martina fell and landed on her backside with a squawk. Kendi thumped to the ground as well. Ben, who had been ready for the change, landed neatly on his feet. Before anyone could react further, the ocean exploded back into existence. Again, Ben was ready and tread water. Martina and Kendi surfaced at the same time, looking indignant.

"Oops," Ben said. He had wanted to say *Sorry*, but no one could lie in the Dream. "Do you think all that embarrassment made me lose my concentration?"

"Ha!" Martina scoffed. "I'm going to have a bruise on my arse when I wake up, I can feel it already."

"Better offer pax," Kendi said, "before he calls up an undersea volcano."

Martina looked down with mock horror. "Pax," she said.

"Pax," Ben said.

"I have to go, anyway," she said. "My drugs are wearing off."

"Before you leave," Kendi said, "did you hear anything . . . strange today?"

"Strange how?" Martina said. "Strange like a rumor at a party or strange like a witch doctor at a cricket match?"

"A strange noise," Kendi clarified.

"Nothing like that," Martina said. "Why? What did you hear?"

Kendi hesitated. "I'm not sure. The Dream is so different now."

"That it is. Hey, didn't you offer supper yesterday? I wasn't free then, but I am tonight. I think Keith is, too."

"Damn," Kendi said with regret. "This time *I* can't. Grandma Salman is speaking at a rally, and I'm supposed to go. It'll be scarf and run for supper. Tomorrow?"

"Oops," Martina said. "Drugs are off. Call!" She vanished. Water swirled in the spot she had occupied.

"We should probably go, too," Kendi said. "I'm sure Wanda and Lewa will need to talk to us before the rally. Do you want to come?"

"I probably should," Ben said. "She's my grandmother, after all. She'll be a great-grandmother pretty soon."

"She already is," Kendi reminded him. "Don't forget about Zayim's kid. Did you know about that?"

"That was the first I'd heard of it." He paused, tried to speak, failed, and tried again. "I wish . . . Do you think . . . ?"

Kendi slid closer to Ben, who threw an arm around him. "Yes. Your mom knows about our kids, no question."

"She'll never see them, though," Ben said. "And they'll never know who she is. Was."

"Then we'll have to tell them," Kendi said. "We'll tell them so many stories about the great Mother Adept Araceil Rymar that by the time they're teenagers, they'll roll their eyes at the mention of her name and say, 'Aw, Dad—not Grandma Ara again.' "

Ben forced himself to laugh. "It's a plan." He pushed away from Kendi. "You go on out. I want to wander around a little more."

"Okay. See you in the real world. Dad."

"Da."

Dolphin Kendi closed his eyes and vanished. Ben spun gently in the whirlpool he left behind, then let the ocean disappear. The empty gray plain stretched away in all directions, and the stale air hung motionless around him.

Ben was bone dry and clad in his usual loose trousers and tunic. It was like being indoors.

A wave of grief washed over Ben, and his throat tightened. The feeling was getting a little easier to deal with, and he wasn't sure if that was a good thing or not. Did it mean he was starting to forget her? Ben tried to recall his mother's face, and for a panicky moment his mind stayed blank. Then he remembered dark hair, round face, firm voice. Suddenly he wanted—needed—to see her again, needed it so badly it made his hands shake. He reached out with his mind and touched the Dream. A sketchy, three-dimensional outline took shape before him. Another part of his mind shouted a warning, shrieked at him to back away from this. Everyone knew it was a bad idea to call up the shapes of dead loved ones in the Dream. Ben heard it and ignored it.

The outline was too tall. Ben shortened it, made it round. He topped it with dark hair. It looked like a bad wig. A face took shape. Rounded cheeks, dark skin, a firm mouth. The chin wasn't coming out right. It was too pointed. And the ears were too big. What had the inner part looked like? Ben tried to remember, but the image wouldn't come. God—he couldn't even call up a good memory of his own mother. The shrieking part said this was why you didn't call up images, that they only made you feel worse. He wasn't much of an artist, either, and the replica looked blurry. The skin had a single tone, making it appear flat and lifeless. He worked for several minutes, adding a little blush to the cheeks and trying to put highlights into the hair. At last he stepped back. The figure looked like a bad mannikin of his mother, dull and lifeless and fake.

It isn't moving, he thought. *That's why it looks so strange.*

He raised his hand. The shrieking part of his mind begged him to stop, not to do this. But Ben ignored it. He gestured. "Speak," he said.

The new Ara opened her mouth, creating a red hole in the middle of her face. "B-e-e-e-n," she said. Her voice was thick and gluey. She twitched once, then took a lurching, monstrous step forward. "B-e-e-e-e-n. I m-i-i-i-s-s-s-s-s . . . m-i-i-i-i-s-s-s-s-s . . ." The s sound hissed like a snake. Ben backpedaled. Nausea oozed through his stomach.

"B-e-e-e-e-n-n-n-n." The creature shambled forward. One of its legs didn't have a knee joint. "B-e-e-e-n-n-n I w-a-a-a-n-n-n-t . . ."

"Go away!" Ben screamed.

The thing vanished. Air rushed in to the spot it had occupied. Ben went to his hands and knees and retched on the flat, gray ground. The sour taste of bile flooded his mouth, and grief made a cold rock in his chest. What the hell had he been thinking? He'd been so *stupid*. Mom was dead, and there was no way to bring her back. Not even in the Dream. The grief mixed with a rising anger—anger at mom for killing herself during the Despair, himself for not getting home in time to save her, anger at . . .

Padric Sufur.

Ben got to his feet. Around him, the Dream formed itself into a high canyon. Boulders were strewn over a rocky ground. The blue sky was diamond-hard and far away. Mesquite clung stubbornly to cracks and crevices. With ease born of practice, Ben put out a hand, palm down. The ground rumbled, and a statue rose from the earth itself. It portrayed an old man with a hawk's nose and a thin, whiplike body. The features were clumsily rendered but recognizable. Ben stared at it, jaw clenched. The Despair had come about because of this man. His mother was dead because of this man. Hatred burned, then blazed. He put out a hand. A ten-pound sledgehammer slapped into his palm, and he raised it high.

Ben always started at the head. A satisfying impact shock traveled up his arm when the hammer struck. He swung again and again. Rock chips flew. Without missing a swing, Ben called up a clear faceplate for himself. Chips pinged off it, and he swung the hammer again. In seconds the statue became a wreck from the shoulders up. Ben attacked arms and torso. His hands stung and ached. Sweat broke out on his face and under his arms. The air behind the faceplate grew sweaty and moist. When the statue was half gone, Ben threw the hammer aside and raised a furious fist. A bolt of lightning cracked down from the empty sky and struck the remains of the statue. It shattered into fine sand. The thunderclap crashed against Ben's bones, as it always did, and knocked him backward. He landed hard but didn't care. The pain made it real. It was his penance for surviving.

Ben lay on his back, staring upward. He didn't feel much better. The grief was getting better, but the anger was getting worse. He should tell Kendi about it, see what—

No. Kendi would only insist Ben see a counselor, and the counselors were all busy with people who had real problems. Ben wouldn't be able to get an appointment for months, and when Kendi heard about that, he would try to pull strings to get Ben in earlier, and the thought only made Ben angrier. Did Kendi think he couldn't solve his own problems? That Kendi had to step in every time Ben—

Get a grip, Ben admonished himself. *You're angry at him for something that isn't even a blip on the sensor screen.*

The weird thing was that Ben *wanted* Kendi to help him. He wanted Kendi to present him with a solution, an instant remedy, and he wanted Kendi to do it without Ben having to ask for one. Ben sighed and banished the faceplate. He clearly didn't know *what* he wanted. Except, maybe, for Padric Sufur's head in a basin of bubbling lava.

Let it go, he thought. *Being mad doesn't do you any good. Padric Sufur is a thousand light-years away on his rich-boy estate, drinking champagne to the Despair. You can't reach him and you can't do anything to him. So just let it go.*

Ben took a deep breath and exhaled to push the anger out.

It didn't work.

Finally he sat up, gathered his concentration, and let go of the Dream.

The best thing about science class, mused Matthew Secord, was that sometimes you got to run around outside and call it homework. He pointed his data pad at a passing glider lizard. It beeped once, and Matthew checked the readout. Female. Two years old. Body temperature 45 degrees Celsius. Nice.

Around him, the talltrees soared up to impossible heights. Their rough brown trunks were so big, it took Matthew almost a minute to walk all the way around one. Now that he was thirteen, Mom was finally allowing him to descend to the forest floor on his own, and Matthew reveled in the newfound freedom. He had to admit that he had been a little nervous at first. The government didn't have money these days—no one did—which meant they had cut back on the pheromone sprays that kept the more dangerous dinosaurs away from Treetown. But he hadn't seen anything remotely resembling a carnosaur, and he had come to relax.

Relax. He wished Mom would learn to relax. She had been Silenced, of course, and that made it hard for her. Matthew had just started touching the Dream himself—having extremely realistic Dreams, hearing strange whispers, feeling like he was being watched—when the Despair struck. Dad had . . . well, Matthew didn't like to think about that. Dad was gone now, and that was that. The Despair had Silenced both Mom and Matthew, and Matthew knew Mom worried about him. Losing Dad and being Silenced had almost crushed her, and she was afraid the same was happening to him. Well, Matthew was fine, just fine, and he didn't need Mom hovering over him all the time, demanding hugs and weeping into his hair. It was relief to be down here in the forest, surrounded only by the dinosaur calls and birdsong and—

"Help! Help me!"

Matthew spun. The call had come from somewhere behind and to his left. It was also quite close. "Hello?" he shouted. "Where are you? What's wrong?"

"Help me!"

Following the sound of the shout, Matthew skirted a talltree and clambered over an enormous fallen branch that was half as tall as he was. On the other side, Matthew found a dark-haired woman sitting on the ground.

"What's the matter?" he asked. "Are you all right?"

"I think I twisted my ankle," she gasped. "I can't stand up. Can you help me?"

Feeling very grown-up, Matthew knelt and looked at the woman's ankle without touching it. Then he took out his data pad and activated the basic first-aid scanner.

"It looks okay to me," he said. "No major injury. Maybe we can—"

Something cold and hard thumped against the back of his neck. Matthew twisted around and stared up at a blond man holding a dermospray. The man didn't say a word as Matthew Secord keeled over among the soft ferns.

CHAPTER SIX

"Politics is war without blood."

—Irfan Qasad

Kendi threaded his way through the crowded gymnasium. The weak breeze admitted by the open windows did nothing to ease the heat or mute the din. Humans talked, Ched-Balaar clattered, and a sprinkling of other aliens added their own unique sounds to the din. Most of the people wore the gold medallions that designated a Child of Irfan. Signs of all kinds bobbed and floated overhead. SAVE US, SALMAN! MILITARY, NOT MINES! REZA IS RIGHT! KEEP THE FORESTS, LOSE THE MINES! IRFAN LOVES SALMAN!

Kendi's goal was the empty platform-cum-stage at the front of the gym, but the closer he got, the thicker the crowd became. The air was close and stuffy. A Ched-Balaar trod on his instep with a great, splayed foot. A woman's elbow dug into his side. Every so often he shot a glance back at the main doors, where Lewa Tan stood with folded arms and stern face. She didn't seem to be watching him—her gaze was always elsewhere. After speaking with Salman's security detail, Tan had decreed the rally safe for Kendi, but that didn't mean she relaxed her guard. Her presence felt both strange and comforting.

Kendi pulled the hood of his robe further down, the better to hide his face. He didn't feel like playing celebrity tonight. Besides, it would detract from Grandma's speech. Unfortunately, it also meant he couldn't socialize without revealing his presence. Kendi never had been very good at keeping to himself, and he wished Ben had decided to come instead of begging off and staying home with one of Tan's employees, a handsome, powerfully built young man named Lars. Images flickered unbidden through Kendi's mind. The feeds were full of pornographic games and sims related to bodyguards and their charges, and Kendi couldn't keep from thinking about them. Ben and Lars. Lars and Ben. Kendi shook his head and gave a wry grin. Did all men think that way?

Probably.

The crowd was chanting Salman Reza's name, with the Ched-Balaar tooth-talk playing percussion. Wanda Petrie ascended the platform to stand behind a podium. Holographic projectors mounted on the walls sprang to life, and a giant version of Petrie's slim, impeccably dressed form exploded into being behind her. The hologram's head brushed the ceiling. A herd of reporters milled about just in front of the platform, recording devices at the ready.

"Ladies and gentlemen, may I present to you," Petrie said, "Senator Salman Reza!"

Earsplitting cheers erupted from all quarters. Salman Reza, resplendent in a deep purple robe, climbed the platform steps and took Petrie's place behind the podium. A gold medallion glittered at her throat. Kendi had almost forgotten that Salman was still a Grandmother Adept among the Children, even though she had been Silenced. It occurred to him that Salman had never talked about losing her Silence. How did she cope with the stresses of entering politics while dealing with a crushing loss? Kendi found himself admiring her strength.

"Ladies and gentlemen," she boomed into the unseen microphone, and every voice fell still. "My fellow Children. It is good to be back home at our most blessed monastery."

Still more cheering. Kendi looked over the crowd and saw a nondescript blond woman with blue eyes and blocky, unassuming features. Kendi's eyebrows went up. Gretchen had never struck him as the sort to attend a political rally. He sidled closer to her. His first instinct was to send her a text message from his data pad so he wouldn't have to talk, but he had left the pad at home.

"For the past two months I have been traveling all through Treetown, Othertown, and Rangeway, telling the folks about the facts of life. They have been interested and enthusiastic. And now they are *excited!*"

Cheers again. "Hey, Gretchen," Kendi said above the noise. "I didn't expect to see you here."

"Kendi?" She tried to peer under the hood. "When did you start playing Father Incognito?"

"About the same time you started attending political rallies."

"I have been working hard, but I am not tired," Salman boomed. The giant hologram mirrored her gestures. "The welcome I have received everywhere has sustained me. The deep conviction that I am right in fighting for the people has carried me on."

Gretchen shrugged. "I don't have much else to do. It's free entertainment, and there's food."

Sour guilt panged Kendi again. Wasn't there anything he could do for her? Gretchen wouldn't take money from him, would only get angry if he offered. But there had to be something he could do. Gretchen had saved his life a time or two, and he couldn't just let her slide into the gutter.

". . . have come back home to report to my fellow Treetowners. I bring good news . . ."

Inspiration struck. "Need a job?" Kendi asked.

"Why?" Gretchen said warily. "I won't take charity work, Kendi. Not even from you."

"No charity," he said. "You'd earn every freemark."

Several people turned hard glares in their direction, clearly ordering them to be quiet for the speech. Kendi tapped his earpiece and said Gretchen's name. When the call connected, they continued to speak subvocally. He wished again for his pad—it would have made voice communication unnecessary.

"See the woman over by the door?" he said.

"Graying hair in a braid? Yeah."

". . . cracked the Populist north. Rangeway is going Unionist. So are parts of Othertown. The people, both human and Ched-Balaar . . ."

"She runs the security firm that's guarding Ben and me—and Harenn, for that matter," Kendi said. *"Brand-new contract, and I'll bet she could use some help."*

"Guarding you would strain a platoon," Gretchen

said, eyeing Tan with interest. *"You think she'd take me on?"*

". . . what Foxglove and his Federalists stand for. They stand for separation of the species. They stand for isolationism. They stand for exploitation and pollution of our resources. Ched-Pirasku and his Populists whine and waver. They're so busy trying to keep a balance that they forget why they're in office . . ."

"You'd come with my recommendation," Kendi said. *"That's still worth something these days. It'll tide you over until that game contract comes through."*

Gretchen wavered. *"I don't know, Kendi. I don't need you to find work for me, you know."*

"I owe you, Gretchen," Kendi countered. *"After all, you delayed signing the sim-game contract for me. This lets me pay you back."*

Brief pause. *"Yeah, all right. I'll talk to her. As a favor to you."*

"Thanks."

". . . my duty and my pleasure to announce my formal bid to run for governor of our fine planet."

Kendi snapped to electric attention as cheers a hundred times louder than before thundered through the gymnasium. He hadn't known Salman was going to announce her candidacy tonight. Why hadn't she told him? Then he remembered the dustup with Foxglove, and he chewed the inside of one cheek. Petrie had probably insisted he be kept in the dark. At least now he knew why Petrie had wanted him to attend the rally. He joined in the applause and added a few earsplitting finger whistles to the noise.

Ched-Balaar heads bobbed up and down on serpentine necks. Teeth clattered, and excited hoots punched the air. Humans stamped their feet, clapped their hands, and whistled through their fingers. Reporters spoke to empty air, sending frantic stories back to the feeds. Salman stood at the podium with a modest smile, acknowledging the accolades with a nod. Several holographic signs changed to SALMAN REZA—OUR NEXT GOVERNOR.

"Well," Gretchen subvocalized, *"you don't see that every day."*

Salman held up her hands, but the audience took its

time in quieting. A Ched-Balaar with reddish fur, meanwhile, joined her at the podium.

"I would also like to introduce my choice for running mate," Salman said. "A fine person, well-qualified, skilled, and intelligent. May I present the next lieutenant governor of Bellerophon, Justice Ched-Tumaar."

Ched-Tumaar thanked the audience for its applause, then withdrew so Salman could continue her speech. Salman's voice boomed thick and powerful from the speakers, filling the gymnasium from floorboards to rafters.

"We need to look to the future, not live in the past," she said. "In the past, Bellerophon was the victim of vicious pirates trying to kidnap and enslave the Silent. Without the protection of the Independence Confederation, Bellerophon is once again vulnerable to this threat. For our protection, I intend to increase military spending once I am in the governor's mansion. Not only will this bring us security and safety, it will provide much-needed jobs in both the military and civilian sectors. Bellerophon has the power to be prosperous again—we just need to use it."

The cheering began again, and most of the crowd tried to surge toward the platform. Kendi didn't want to get caught in the morass, so he wormed toward the back with skill of long practice. Gretchen followed. Tan was only a few yards away. He met her eyes and was about to tap his earpiece to tell her about Gretchen when every light in the gymnasium went out, plunging the meeting into blackness.

A moment silence followed, followed by abrupt shouts and cries. Hard hands grabbed Kendi from behind. He started to fight back, but Tan's familiar voice barked in his ear.

"Come on!" she shouted, and dragged him away before he could argue. The rally was rapidly dissolving into pandemonium. Shadows swarmed. Humans and Ched-Balaar stumbled around, trying to get their bearings and understand what was going on. Tan hauled Kendi to the perimeter of the crowd. By now his eyes were adjusting to the dim light, and he was able to see her open a side door. She thrust him inside.

"Stay put," she ordered, and slammed it shut. The light disappeared entirely.

Kendi stood in darkness. The smell of floor wax and wood soap told him he was in a storage closet. Was the blackout an accident, he wondered, or was it sabotage? Perhaps it was part of an attempt on Salman's life—or his. Damned if he was going to cower in a closet while all the excitement was going on outside. He reached for the doorknob—and pulled back. Tan had told him to stay put, and it occurred to him that if he left the closet and came up missing, Tan would go into hyperflight mode. She'd probably alert the Guardians and the police and cause an enormous uproar, and when Kendi turned up perfectly fine, there'd be hell to pay. He sighed. Sometimes being a responsible adult sucked billabong water.

The hubbub continued outside. Something crashed to the floor and shattered. For want of something better to do, Kendi felt around the shelves and to his surprise came up with a flashlight. He tapped it, and the room flooded with light. The beam picked out bottles and boxes lining shelves above a utility sink. A moment later it occurred to him that if someone had indeed blacked out the rally in order to get at him, the light leaking around the edges of the door created a fine beacon. He switched the flashlight off, but not before his eye caught a box label. Kendi carefully turned the flashlight on for a second to make sure, then flicked it back off. An idea came to him. Tan would have a fit, but at least she would know where he was. And he really doubted the blackout was a strike at him—no one except Tan, Petrie, and perhaps Salman had known he was attending the rally.

Kendi stood outside the closet a moment later, the open box in his hands. "Candles!" he shouted. "Tallow dips! Tapers! Get your tapers here! Free for the taking! Tapers! Tapers! Can't finish the rally without a taper!"

There was a pause, and then shadowy fingers took candle after candle out of his hands. Yellow points of light flickered and shed golden circles all about the gymnasium. Tan appeared beside him with a scowl on her face.

"Can't stay out of the spotlight for ten minutes, can you?" she growled.

With an unrepentant grin, Kendi handed her the box of candles and ducked back into the closet, where he found a second box. When Tan ran out, he gave it to her.

"Tapers!" he shouted. "Come get your tapers!"

The glowing candles created a cozy, if primitive, atmosphere. Petrie stuck a pair of tapers at the corners of Salman's podium. Apparently whoever was in charge of Salman's personal security had decided that her safety wasn't in question—or she had given them orders to let her stay—because she quickly took up her post again.

"My friends," she said, shouting to be heard without the PA system, "it seems we have overcome this campaign's first obstacle." Shouts of laughter and hoots of amusement followed this remark. "My informants tell me we're able to continue today thanks to my grandson-in-law Father Kendi Weaver. Kendi, you have our thanks. Nothing can keep us down as long as we have our tapers."

The room erupted in laughter and applause. Kendi raised his candle in salute. A voice started up a chant: "Tapers! Tapers! Tapers!" Somehow a line of dancers got started, snaking through the gymnasium with their candles held aloft like trophies while everyone else chanted. Tan came to quiet attention, scanning the dimly lit crowd with experienced eyes. Kendi wondered if he should be worried, then discarded the thought. Tan acted paranoid so Kendi wouldn't have to.

At last Salman called for quiet. "Well done, my tapers," she said to more laughter. "But now we have more serious issues to address. We have a job to do and an election to win!"

And speaking of jobs, Kendi thought.

"Lewa," he said quietly as Salman continued her speech by candlelight. "I have a friend who could use a little help."

The postrally party was lavish, as befit a newly declared gubernatorial candidate. High-level Unionist senators, officials, and supporters gathered in cheerful knots of murmured conversation in the living room. Glasses of champagne and troughs of wine hovered about the room. The buffet was piled high with delicacies both human and Ched-Balaar. Kendi was able to enjoy none of it. He was currently perched on the edge of an armchair in Salman's spacious home office. The doors were firmly shut against the party, and Salman herself was furious. She didn't pace or wave her hands, but her expression reminded Kendi of a gargoyle ready to fly off its pedestal and kill something. A handful of aides scurried about, trying to look busy and avoiding her gaze. Kendi sank bank into his armchair and tried to look inconspicuous.

"I want information, and I want it now," she howled. "I want to know why the hell the power went out when it did, I want to know who was responsible, and I want to know how they're going to pay."

Yin May, Salman's chief assistant, checked his data pad. His expression was calm as a talltree. "I do have some preliminary information, Senator."

"I have better things to do than wait to hear it, Mr. May," Salman growled.

"Of course, Senator. As most buildings and homes do, the gymnasium rents its water generator from Treetown Energy, which dispatched a fusion repair crew the moment the power went out. The crew examined the generator and reported a problem in the transformer. According to their report, it overloaded and shorted out. Treetown Energy apologizes for the inconvenience."

"I'm sure," Salman said. "And who, pray tell, owns Treetown Energy?"

"The Bellerophon Energy Consortium."

"I hope you can predict my next question, Mr. May."

"Mitchell Foxglove owns a substantial portion of the BEC. He was once the chief operating officer, but he stepped down to run for office. He is still a majority stockholder."

Justice Ched-Tumaar made a chuffing noise, the Ched-Balaar equivalent of a polite cough. His immaculate reddish fur gleamed in the light of the fireplace. "Before we make public accusations, Salman," he said, "we will need some sort of proof."

"I doubt we'll find any." Salman grabbed the glass that hovered near her elbow and drained it. "If Foxglove was clever enough to sabotage the building's fusion generator and disrupt the rally, I'm sure he—or his agent—was clever enough to cover his tracks. Bastard. I should have realized something like this would happen eventually."

"You don't suspect Ched-Pirasku?" Kendi said. "The Populists have a certain amount to gain by disrupting your campaign."

"I suspect everybody," Salman replied. "But right now—"

"Excuse me, Senator." Another aide entered the office with a tiny data button. "This just came for you."

"What? Why didn't they message it to me?" Salman said. "And where's Petrie? I need to talk to her."

"A bonded carrier brought the message," the aide said. "It was no one I knew."

Salman waved at Yin May, who took the proffered button and slotted it into his data pad. Thick black eyebrows drew together as he read. Kendi's danger instincts prickled the hair on his neck, warning him of an approaching storm. Deciding he'd already been rained on enough lately, Kendi left his chair and sidled toward the door.

"Well?" Salman demanded.

"You are being cited for violating local fire codes at the rally," May said.

Kendi fled the office.

Lucia dePaolo pulled herself over the gutter and rolled onto the slanted roof. Wood shingles clattered softly beneath her. She froze, listening. Chirps and creaks of night lizards and birds chittered around her. Overhead, the talltree canopy made a black umbrella suitable for a giant. Enormous branches thick enough to hold up a mickey spike stretched into the darkness. Only a few public lights shed a golden glow, and none of the light touched the house. The air was chilly and bit damp. Nothing moved.

At last Lucia eased into a crouch and slipped across the roof, her camouflage jumpsuit automatically blending her with the shadows. The house had a pair of dormers on the second floor, and Lucia was able to reach the windows set into them without difficulty. One was lit, the other dark. The curtains of the lit window were drawn, so Lucia peeped cautiously around the sill of the dark one. The room beyond the glass was empty, as far Lucia could tell. The same was true of the house. Lucia had already watched the building for several minutes and seen no signs of life. While she was waiting, she had made several anonymous calls to the Days' home number. All had gone unanswered. It should be safe to go in.

Lucia ran a gloved hand around the edges of the first window, and the tips of her fingers glowed green, indicating the security system was inactive. It was amazing how many people left home without turning on the burglar alarm. Still, they had locked the windows.

Lucia's hand dropped to her belt and came up with a cutting tool. With exquisite care, she drew the cutter around the edge of the glass. A tap, and the entire pane fell inward to land with a quiet *whuff* on the carpet beyond. Lucia pulled the suit's mask over her face and climbed in after it.

The bedroom was the usual sleeping place—bed, dresser, closet, night stands. A collection of frilly human dolls sat on a long shelf, staring at the dim room with shiny blank eyes. Helen Day's room, then. Her brother and housemate, Finn, must have the other bedroom. The house had a sour smell to it, as if the inhabitants didn't often open the windows. Lucia made her way downstairs. Only the bathroom light was on, though it shed enough illumination to let Lucia navigate the floor freely. After some searching, she found an office area with the main computer terminal in it. She sat down and found the chair was slightly warm. The Days must have left just before Lucia arrived. Good—it meant they would probably be gone for a while yet.

Lucia conjured up the holographic screen with a tap of her gloved finger, then called up the net connection. The Irfan figurine she habitually wore around her neck seemed to glow with a serene warmth beneath the suit, and Lucia allowed herself a small smile. Like most people, Finn Day left his home computer system linked to the nets, along with his message system and general files. At his job—Finn and his sister were lucky enough to retain employment—he no doubt kept everything pass-worded and voice-coded, but here in his own home, con-venience beat out security.

Lucia cracked her knuckles and went to work. Her movements were smooth and calm, as if she were work-ing in Ben's living room instead of a house she was bur-glarizing. She came across the Days' financial records, including Helen's paychecks from the shipyard where the *Poltergeist* had been docked. Finn himself did tempo-rary clerical work for the same yard. Before that, he had been a secretary who worked at Federalist Party headquarters. Lucia had uncovered the latter fact while interviewing some of the shipyard workers. The potential connection was too great to ignore, and Ben had asked Lucia to take a closer look as a surprise for Kendi. Al-though Ben felt like a younger brother to her, Lucia still held Kendi in awe, and she found herself agreeing to Ben's proposal because it would please Kendi—despite the fact that her methods were patently illegal.

Lucia skimmed Finn's finances. No one had made any large deposits into their bank accounts recently, but that came as no surprise—Finn and Helen would be fools to leave that kind of record. With a glance over her shoul-der at the door, Lucia closed down the financial files and started a system deepsearch for the name Benjamin Rymar. She held her breath while the computer searched.

After several seconds, it chimed once and showed her two matches. Lucia's heart began to pound, though her face remained serene.

"Serene must you walk the paths," she told herself, quoting Irfan's famous proverb, *"and serene must you ever remain."*

Her heart slowed, and Lucia selected the first match. It pointed to a backup file on the house computer. The second turned out to be a record of a file transfer from disk to drive. Lucia called up the backup file and sucked in her breath. It was a genetic analysis for eleven cryo-genically frozen embryos. So either Finn or his sister was indeed the blackmailer. More likely both siblings were involved. Lucia wondered which one of them had collected the money and how they had gotten hold of a gravity beam powerful enough to knock Kendi for a loop. Perhaps Helen had stolen one from the shipyard.

Lucia scrubbed the backup gene file from the computer, then rifled the desk. She came up with several button-sized disks. The third one had the original file on it, and the file markers indicated it had originally come from the *Poltergeist*. Lucia tapped it thoughtfully on one knuckle. The main computer had the gene file in its backup sector. Where was the original? Lucia could see the Days copying the file from the disk to their computer, but why had they deleted it again? Paranoia? Except if they were that paranoid, why hadn't they also deleted the automatic backup?

Lucia ran the deepsearch again, though this time she had the computer look for files that were the same size as the backup in case the Days had renamed the file. Five matches turned up, but none contained the gene scan. Deciding it would be better to puzzle over this later, Lucia shut down the computer and pocketed the tiny disk. The latter was evidence of the blackmail, and Ben had said he would want to keep anything like it that turned up, though Lucia wondered how he and Kendi were going to explain his possession of the disk to the Guardians. Lucia headed for the stairs, then changed her mind and did a quick search of the first floor. In the bathroom closet behind a stack of towels she found the cloth sack. The money—most of it—was still inside.

Amateurs, Lucia thought with scorn. *I'd never leave this kind of evidence in my own house.*

The house's sour smell was stronger in this room—much stronger. She expected bowel smells in a bathroom, but Lucia had been in the house for quite some time and the odor was noticeably fresh. Lucia's eye fell on the shower curtain. It was drawn shut. A terrible suspicion crawled over her skin like a thousand spiders. Lucia swallowed, then reached out with a gloved hand and snapped the shower curtain aside.

Helen Day's corpse lay faceup in the bottom of the tub. She stared upward with blank, filmy eyes, and her skin was gray. Brown hair was plastered to her skull in wet clumps. A bright burn mark the size of a fist lay between her flaccid breasts. Lucia pressed a hand to her mouth.

Serene must you ever remain. Serene must you ever remain. Serene, serene, serene.

Bile pressed the back of her throat in a harsh lump. Lucia slid the curtain shut, snatched up the money sack, and dashed upstairs. She paused at the entrance to Finn's room, the one with the light on. After a split-second hesitation, she poked her head inside.

The walls in Finn's bedroom were covered with color prints of abstract art. Eye-twisting designs swooped, spiraled, and spun across paper and canvas. Sprawled on the floor lay the form of a brown-haired man. Lucia ran inside just long enough to touch his neck. Her shaking fingers found no pulse. The body was still warm.

Lucia's mind raced, and the clues she had been too stupid to see snapped into a complete picture. The deactivated alarm. The sour smell. The warm chair. The missing file. The alarm had been deactivated because the Days were home. The killer had probably knocked at the door or had perhaps even simply walked into the house uninvited. He or she had killed Helen in the shower—the burn mark reminded Lucia of a neuro-pistol discharge—and had then gone upstairs to wreak the same fate on Finn in his bedroom. Once the Days were out of the way, the killer had sat at the computer and deleted the file on Ben's siblings. Unfortunately, Lucia had broken in at that point, and the killer had been forced to flee. Lucia swallowed, remembering the body heat left in the chair, the heat of a murderer. And she hadn't even realized it.

Lucia had to get out of the house. If she were caught now, the charge would be far worse than simple breaking-and-entering. She ran into Helen's darkened bedroom, tossed the sack out onto the roof, and pressed her gloved palm to the pane of glass on the floor. It stuck to her hand. Her heart was pounding and every instinct screamed at her to run far and fast, but she climbed out the window backwards and with great care, fitting the glass back into the hole behind her. Once it was back in place, she took a stylus from her belt and ran it around the edge of the pane. The stylus secreted an epoxy that heated the glass and melded it back together. A close look would reveal something wasn't quite right, but only if someone looked. Lucia wondered if anyone would. Once the bodies were discovered and the police called in, the house would become a crime scene crawling with technicians. Thanks be to Irfan she had worn her camouflage suit and prevented herself from leaving any telltale traces of DNA.

She ran across the rooftop on shaky legs and dropped to the balcony behind it. Then she eased over the rail and dropped straight down. There was a dreadful moment when she was falling, then the stretchy polymer netting caught her. Lucia scuttled like a spider along the safety net, staying in the shadows and out of sight beneath the walkways until she judged she was far enough away from the Day house. Footsteps sounded overhead, and for a horrible moment Lucia was sure someone—the killer?—was following her. She froze, and the footsteps continued along the walkway. When she was sure the coast was clear, she hauled herself back onto the wooden path, and stripped off gloves and mask. She jogged a little further along the dark and swaying walkways.

Treetown had become a frightening place at night, dark and eerie. Most residents rented their home fusion generators from Treetown Energy, and the rent was determined by the amount of power each plant produced—more power meant more upkeep, or so Treetown Energy claimed. In times of privation people used fewer lights. Treetown itself had cut back on the number of lamps it left burning. Lucia walked the dark paths and long balconies, trying not to feel threatened. A dinosaur roared far below, and she jumped, heart pounding. She passed dark houses that stared at her with Helen Day's glassy eyes, and every time she turned a corner, she wondered if anyone would be—

"Spare a freemark, lady?"

Lucia leaped back, her hand already going for the knife she kept in her belt. The human who had accosted her stood in a shadowy stairwell. The moonlight revealed scruffy hair and a dirty coat. Her upturned palm was grubby, and she smelled of old sweat. She couldn't have been more than fifteen or sixteen.

Heart still pounding, Lucia flipped the girl a coin. She caught it with a quick snapping motion. Lucia said, "Have you tried the Church of Irfan? There's a mission not far from here. They can give you good a meal and a place to sleep."

"They're full up tonight," the girl said. "They're always full up. You got somewhere I can sleep?"

Lucia's heart wrenched. She wanted to take this young woman home with her, clean her up, feed her, give her hope. But Lucia knew that would be foolish in the extreme. She had no idea who this girl was or what she might do once Lucia got her home. It was this way all over Bellerophon, and there wasn't anything she could do about it, except continue to volunteer at the Church. She made a mental note to put in extra hours this week.

"Sorry," Lucia said, and flipped the girl another freemark coin. Then she turned and trotted away before she could respond. The girl's image stuck with her, though. What would it be like to spend your nights on the walkways, worried you could be mugged or raped or murdered for your shoes? Lucia, at least, had places to go. Despite Ben and Kendi's advance on her detective services, Lucia had decided to continue living with her family and pay them the rent she would have put toward an apartment. Mom and Dad had at first refused her offer, then had given in after minimal persuasion. In addition to her family, Lucia knew she could go to Ben and Kendi for help. Lucia had many resources. That girl had none. There had to be a way to help her and others like her. She couldn't—

Pain exploded across the back of her head. With a small cry, Lucia slumped to the walkway.

CHAPTER SEVEN

"It's narrow thinking to see the customs and manners of other people as ridiculous and extravagant when they don't resemble our own"

—Daniel Vik

"The newsfeeds are already calling us *Tapers*," Kendi said with a laugh. "It's become a nickname for the Unionist party."

"What does Grandma think of that?" Ben asked.

"Dunno. I left the party before she could explode again. It was all over the feeds on the ride home, though." Kendi picked up his data pad, the one he had left home by accident, and fiddled with it idly. "Grandma gets seriously scary when she's pissed off."

Ben shifted on the living room sofa. His posture held him inward and upright, as if he were balanced on the head of pin. Kendi wondered if he should ask what was wrong or let Ben come around to telling him.

"Grandma didn't always used to be like that," Ben said. "But then there was the Despair, and Mom's . . . death. I don't think she's taking it well—being Silenced, I mean. She never wanted anything to do with politics before the Despair, and then she sort of threw herself into it."

"Coping mechanism?" Kendi asked, setting down the pad.

"Maybe." Ben shifted again and glanced toward the door. Kendi decided to go for it.

"What's the matter?" he asked. "You're nervous about something."

"What makes you think I'm nervous?"

"Just say it, Ben," Kendi said. "It's been a long night, and I don't think I can—"

"Attention! Attention!" boomed the computer. "Emergency message for Ben Rymar. Playing now."

"What the hell?" Kendi said.

"Shush!" Ben snapped.

"Ben! Help me! I can't . . . stand up. I'm about . . . about fifty meters from the house. Southwest, I think. Can you . . . can you come?"

Ben and Kendi were out the door before the message finished. Kendi almost crashed into Lars the bodyguard, who was on patrol outside the house for the night. The drawbridges on both walkways and staircases were up, further blocking their path.

"Come with us!" Kendi ordered Lars. "Friend in trouble."

"Lucia!" Ben shouted. He slapped the scanner set into the balcony rail. "Lucia, can you hear us? Dammit, open sesame!"

The drawbridge ahead of him lowered itself. Ben sprinted across before it was completely level. Kendi and Lars followed, also shouting Lucia's name. The darkness swallowed their voices, and dark houses glared accusingly at the way they shattered the peaceful night. Kendi's nerves hummed like high-tension wires. His active imagination foresaw a dozen terrible things that could have happened to her. Ben ran beside him, his footsteps thudding on wood. Bulky Lars brought up the rear.

They found her struggling to stand in a puddle of moonlight. Ben sprinted ahead of Kendi and picked her up as if her lush body weighed nothing at all.

"Lie still," he instructed. "We'll get you home and call the rescue squad."

"What happened?" Kendi asked. "Can you talk?"

"I'll be all right," Lucia said, though her speech was slurred. "Don't call the squad. Please. I'll have to explain my outfit."

Belatedly Kendi realized she was wearing her camouflage jumpsuit. He tapped his earpiece. "I'll call Harenn, then."

"And no Guardians!" Ben said to Lars before the bodyguard could speak. "Let's get back."

He carried Lucia back to the house with Lars and Kendi trailing behind. Lucia held on as best she could, but it was clear she was in pain. Kendi looked for blood as they ran, but the moonlight made it impossible to see clearly. When they got back home, Ben laid her down on the couch. Harenn arrived moments later in a breathless swirl of billowing cloth. She had her medical scanner out and in motion before anyone could speak to her.

"What happened?" she demanded.

"I was hit from behind," Lucia said. "A mugger, I think. Mother Irfan, my head hurts."

"You have a concussion." Harenn removed a dermospray from her kit, racked in an ampule, and thumped it against Lucia's arm. "This will ease the pain and the dizziness. You should remain quiet for the rest of the evening and for tomorrow. Perhaps it would be best if you stayed the night here."

"Lars," Kendi said suddenly, "this is private business. Go back outside, please."

Lars drew down bushy blond eyebrows and looked ready to argue. Kendi, however, leveled him a hard look he had learned from Ara, and the younger man retreated without further discussion.

"Details, Lucia," Kendi said. "Start from the beginning."

"I—I'm not sure if—" she stammered.

"It's okay, Lucia," Ben said. "Go ahead and tell them."

Kendi glared at him. "You've been up to something behind my back."

"It was supposed to be a surprise," Ben said. "Tell him, Lucia."

Lucia did. Kendi listened, openmouthed, as she described breaking into the Day house, finding the file, discovering two dead bodies, and getting hit on the head.

"Everything becomes disjointed after that," she finished. "I remember trying to send an emergency message to Ben. The next thing I knew he was picking me up off the walkway."

"What if the Guardians do a DNA sweep?" Kendi asked. "Won't they find out you were there?"

"The suit and mask prevent DNA leavings," Lucia said. "Besides, DNA sweeps are ungodly expensive. The Guardians only use them in truly high-powered cases."

"Speaking of expensive," Harenn said, "where is the money sack? You said you found it."

Lucia looked around, as if she expected to find it on the floor beside the couch. "I don't know. I must have dropped it. Or the mugger took it."

"I'll go look for it," Ben said, heading for the door.

"Take Lars with you," Kendi called after him.

"So someone broke into the Days' house just before you did," Kendi said. "Whoever it was killed the Days, found the file about Ben, and started to delete it, but you showed up before they could finish the job. Do you think the killer was the person who mugged you?"

"I don't see how it could be," Lucia said. "I traveled quite a ways on the safety net before I came back up, and I didn't see anyone following me. I'm trained at spotting a tail, even at night, and I'm sure I would've noticed something. Besides, if the killer *did* mug me, why just hit me instead of kill me?"

Kendi rubbed his temples. "I don't know."

"Where's the disk?" Harenn asked.

Lucia fumbled in one pocket. A frightened look came over her face and she quickly checked her other pockets. "It's gone," she said.

"Oh, shit," Kendi groaned. "Why didn't you wipe the disk when you released the file?"

"Ben wanted the file," Lucia said. "He thought he could take them to the Guardians as proof."

"Proof of what?" Kendi asked.

"The blackmail plot. The markers on the file tell where it came from. Ben said he wanted to have a hold on the blackmailer, threaten to take the disk to the Guardians or the police unless they dropped the whole issue."

"Blackmailing the blackmailers," Kendi muttered. "Except Ben said he didn't want the Guardians involved."

"He doesn't," Lucia said. "But he said the blackmailers wouldn't know that."

Kendi gave a snort of admiration. "Sounds like something I'd do."

The front door opened and shut. "No sign of the sack," Ben reported. "Lars is still looking, but it's gone."

"Perhaps it was a simple robbery," Harenn said. "The

thief took the money and the disk without realizing what it is."

"It's possible," Lucia said.

"The *disk?*" Ben said, face pale. "The disk is gone too?"

Lucia's face reddened. "I'm afraid so."

"So there's a mugger out there who knows who I am?"

"Not necessarily," Lucia said. "It would take a certain amount of reading and interpretation to understand what the file means."

"Finn and Helen Day figured it out," Ben pointed out.

"I have a theory about that," Lucia said. She sat up with a slight wince and waved away Kendi's offer of help. "I'm feeling better."

"What's your theory?" Kendi asked.

"Finn Day has—had—contacts with Foxglove's Federalists, remember. I wonder if Foxglove used Finn and Helen to get access to the *Poltergeist* when we got back."

"What for?" Kendi said, puzzled.

"Trolling for random dirt. It isn't unheard of for politicians to dig around for scandal that might discredit their opponents. Ben is Senator Salman's grandson, and he spent considerable time on the *Poltergeist*. What if Ben did something scandalous and left a record of it on the ship? It would have been worth it to look around and find out."

"Seems like a real long shot to me," Kendi said. "It'd be expensive to arrange, for one thing."

"And Foxglove is poor?" Lucia said. "At any rate, it wouldn't surprise me in the slightest to learn that Mitchell Foxglove arranged for Finn Day—one of his secretaries, remember—to be hired at the shipyard. It's entirely possible Finn knew about the *Poltergeist* from his sister and put the idea to Foxglove himself. Helen had access to the ship, Finn had the computer knowledge. She sneaks him on board during the refit to look for dirt, and he finds gold. But instead of turning the information over to Foxglove like they're supposed to, they figure they can squeeze some money out of Ben with a little blackmail."

"So Foxglove found out about it and murdered them?" Ben said. "That's seems . . . extreme."

"This is Bellerophon's first gubernatorial election since it joined the Independence Confederation, and our first governor will be in a position to dictate policy and custom for centuries to come," Harenn said. "There is considerable power at stake, and the murder of two low-level workers does not strike me as at all extraordinary."

"But why kill them?" Kendi said. "If Foxglove—or whoever he hired—were caught, it would destroy his campaign. And they're his own people. It'd make more sense to discipline them or fire them."

"Not so," Harenn countered. "The information they possessed would only hurt Foxglove if it were released—Salman's popularity would increase if her grandson turned out to be Irfan's child. If Foxglove angered the Finns, they might release the information just to spite him. Foxglove is better off with them dead."

"So is Ched-Pirasku," Lucia added. "It's possible that Foxglove's Federalists uncovered the information but Ched-Pirasku's Populists worked to suppress it—for the same reasons."

"The women in this room are certainly bloodthirsty," Kendi remarked.

"The women in this room are realistic," Harenn corrected. "Do you think Salman is any less so?"

"She's my grandmother," Ben said.

"Has your grandmother ever been a wrinkled old lady who bakes blue cupcakes for the Awakening Festival and spoils her grandchildren on weekend visits?" Harenn said.

Ben snorted. "Hardly. She's been a Grandmother with the Children of Irfan for as long as I can remember. Her idea of a relaxing weekend was serving on only two committees instead of four. Sometimes I think Mom went so big on field work because Grandma was such a heavyweight at the monastery—it gave Mom a chance to do something Grandma wasn't involved with."

"So Salman is driven to succeed just like Foxglove and Ched-Pirasku," Harenn said. "Bloodthirsty or practical?"

"This is all speculation," Kendi said. "And it's too

complicated. I think someone mugged you, Lucia—possibly that girl you talked to—and took both the money and the disk. End of story."

"Someone should tell the authorities about the Days," Lucia said. "Anonymously. They live—lived—outside the monastery, so it'll have to be the police, not the Guardians."

"I will do so," Harenn said, rising.

Kendi noticed Ben was still looking pale. He put an arm around him. "The mugger will just throw the disk away, Ben. I promise. We don't have anything to worry about here. Really. Let's go to bed and forget about it."

They did. But Ben tossed for much of the night.

In the morning, Kendi woke with the feeling that he was forgetting something important. He sat up and looked down at Ben, who in the manner of insomniacs everywhere, had managed to fall asleep just before it was time to get up. His red hair was sleep-tousled, and the sheet had slipped down from his upper body, displaying smooth skin and hard muscle relaxed in sleep. The bruises from Kendi's rescue were already fading, thanks to Harenn's ministrations, and he wouldn't need the sling anymore. Kendi ran a dark finger along the underside of Ben's raspy jaw. Ben didn't stir, though his chest and stomach rose and fell with steady breathing. Kendi was going to have a child with this man. They were going to be parents. The idea filled him with—

Parents. Children. Ched-Hisak. *That's* what he had been forgetting. Ched-Hisak's children were Leaving today, and he and Ben were supposed to be there.

Kendi slid out of bed, wrapped a robe around himself, and headed for the bathroom. On the way he pressed an ear to the closed guest room door. Silence. Lucia must still be—

"She is fine," Harenn said behind him. Kendi jumped.

"I'm combat-trained, you know," he growled. "I could have killed you where you stand, woman, mother of my child or not."

"The male ego," Harenn remarked, "continues to be a mystery. I have already checked on Lucia, and she is fine."

"You went home last night, didn't you?"

"Of course. But now I have returned to visit my patient—and make her a decent breakfast. One of you two bachelors must one day learn to cook."

Kendi shook his head and wandered into the kitchen. He smelled toast, hot rice cereal, honey, and butter. Bedj-ka was sitting at the table, digging into a steaming bowl with a spoon. A data pad on the table in front of him showed a feed story about a boy who had gone missing on a solo nature hike. The boy was a few years older than Bedj-ka.

"Shouldn't you be in school?" Kendi asked.

Bedj-ka swallowed a mouthful of cereal. "They've shortened the school week because of money. We're supposed to study at home on the computer. I'm doing current events."

"Are you going to study all day?" Kendi rummaged through the cupboards.

"Mom'll make me," Bedj-ka said. "It's not fair. School gets canceled, but we have extra homework."

"Suffer, kid," Kendi said heartlessly, still searching the shelves. "When I was your age, things were a lot harder. We didn't have these sissy walkways and monorails to get to school. We had to swing from tree to tree on vines. In the rain. Against the wind. And we *liked* it."

"If you are looking for coffee," Harenn said behind him again, "we are out. The grocer also has none. Have some tea."

Kendi groaned. "I wanted coffee."

"Wow," Bedj-ka said around a mouthful of toast. "You *do* have it rough."

"Your son," Kendi said, "is turning into a smart aleck."

"He does not get it from *my* side of the family," Harenn said. "How did you sleep, Bedj-ka?"

Bedj-ka shrugged. "Okay, I guess. I had a rigid dream! I was racing flitcars through the woods. It was like riding a roller coaster. I was dodging through the trees and branches, and one time I almost crashed. When I woke up, I was shaky—way better than a sim-game."

"Good. Then you will not miss the sims while you are doing your homework today."

Bedj-ka turned morosely back to his cereal, and Kendi

took a a quick shower. Afterward, he was heading back to the bedroom to get dressed when he ran into Lucia in the hall. Her complexion was back to its usual olive coloring, and she managed a smile at him.

"I feel fine," she said, forestalling his question. "Physically, at any rate."

"Physically?"

"I'm still upset about losing the disk."

Kendi patted her shoulder. "I'm not worrying about it. You shouldn't either."

"I'll try." She sniffed the air. "Did Harenn come over and make breakfast?"

"How do you know it wasn't me?"

Lucia didn't deign to reply and disappeared into the bathroom. Kendi entered his own room, and Ben stirred, only half awake. Kendi slid back into bed next to him and gave his ear a long, languorous lick. Ben shuddered sleepily and opened blue eyes. Kendi ran his hand over Ben's warm chest and stomach.

"Once we have kids," he said, sliding his hand even lower, "you'll have to start sleeping in pajamas in case they walk in."

A pause. Then Ben whispered, "Don't start something you aren't willing to finish."

"How do you know I'm not willing?"

Kendi's hand moved under the sheet. Ben gasped, then gently pushed him away. "Not with Lucia and Harenn in the house."

"How did you know Harenn's here?"

"I smell rice cereal."

"Then we'll have to be quick and quiet," Kendi said roguishly. "Good practice for when we have kids in the house."

Some time later, Kendi was dressing, and Ben was rifling the messy closet, looking for his bathrobe. In the end, he gave up and pulled on a pair of shorts and an old shirt. His hair stuck out in all directions, giving him a rumpled, boyish look.

"Is that what you're wearing to the Leaving this afternoon?" Kendi said.

Ben's eyes widened. "I'd forgotten all about that. It's today?"

"At noon. I'd forgotten, too."

Harenn knocked on the door. "Even I cannot keep breakfast warm forever, gentlemen."

A few hours later, Kendi stood with Ben outside the home of Ched-Hisak's family. The house was larger than a human dwelling, and the corners were rounded. Other Ched-Balaar houses sat on the branches around them, connected by the ever-present walkways. The day was bright, sunny, and unseasonably warm. Ben and Kendi both wore short pants, sandals, and simple shirts in muted colors. Kendi's had a tear near the collar. Ben carried an enormous loaf of bread stuffed with fragrant herbs—Lucia's handiwork.

"So we don't do anything special or different," Kendi said.

"Right," said Ben.

"Are you completely sure?" Kendi asked.

"I've lived on Bellerophon all my life," Ben reminded him, "and I've heard about Leavings, even if I've never been to one. When Ched-Nel and Ched-Pek emerge from the den, act as if it's nothing special. Talk to them as if you've met them before. Ched-Hisak and Ched-Miran will have shown them images of us, so they'll know who we are. Remember, as far as we're concerned, they've always been around. And for heaven's sake, don't say the word *child*. Not here."

Kendi nodded. "I still feel like I should bring a present."

"*No!* That would make it seem like a special occasion."

"It *is* a special occasion."

"Not one we're supposed to draw attention to," Ben said. "We can bring food because that's for everyone, but we can't bring anything that's just for Ched-Nel and Ched-Pek."

"It still doesn't make sense," Kendi said.

"It makes perfect sense," Ben insisted. "The Ched-Balaar hide their children to keep them safe from predators or enemies. It's probably an evolutionary thing that turned into strict custom. Now that the kids are old enough to join society, we don't want to draw attention to the fact that the family can reproduce in case there are any other children still hidden away." He shook his head. "You're thinking too much like a human, Kendi."

"A true failing," Kendi said.

"And don't forget about their names when we're in their house."

"I'm not a total ignoramus," Kendi said. "I've lived on Bellerophon for a while, too, you know."

"Sorry," Ben said. "I just don't want to make a mistake. Let's go in."

Ben pressed his hand against the door and waited for the computer to announce them. Then the door jerked open, and they found themselves face-to-face with a female Ched-Balaar. Kendi blinked. The Ched-Balaar were much taller than humans, but this one was on a level with the two men. It felt distinctly strange to look one in the eyes without craning his neck.

"Kendi!" clattered the Ched-Balaar. "Ben! Come in!"

Ben recovered first. "Thank you, Nel," he said. "Nice to see you."

"We brought bread," Kendi said lamely.

Nel dipped her head in acknowledgment and ushered them inside.

The air inside was damp, just as it had been in the Ched-Balaar restaurant. A large room opened in the center of the house with smaller rooms branching off to the side, rather like a forest clearing with smaller glades scattered here and there. Dark green moss made a thick blanket on the floor. Comfortable-looking pillows in muted colors were the only furniture. About a dozen Ched-Balaar moved gracefully abut the room, many of them holding drinking troughs or food platters. Four Ched-Balaar, all wearing bright orange head cloths, played a variety of percussion instruments in intricate rhythms augmented by tooth chatter. Several other Ched-Balaar were dancing to the music, rearing up on their hind legs, bobbing their heads, and adding their own clatter to the drumming. A curved table off to one side held a variety of food, from fresh fruit and fried fish to steamed insects and poached slugs. Nel set the bread among the offerings.

"I'm glad you could come," she said. "It seems like

fewer and fewer humans visit Ched-Balaar homes these days."

"If Foxglove has his way," Kendi said, "we'll all live separate lives."

"That would indeed be a shame," chattered a new voice. Tumaar, Salman's running mate, dipped his head in greeting. "Our species have spent far too much time together on this planet to separate now, no matter what certain factions among us think."

"It's no fun to have a political discussion," Kendi remarked, "when you agree with everything the other person says."

"What also frightens me," Tumaar continued, "is the way Ched-Pirasku ignores the problems that Foxglove and his supporters drum. If Ched-Pirasku wins the election, the separatists will gain momentum—they will rally over their anger at losing the governorship, and Ched-Pirasku will refuse to stop them. He is too willing to compromise."

"You're drumming to the band, Tumaar," Kendi said.

Ben craned his neck, scanning the room. "I don't see Pek anywhere."

"Over there," Nel said. "Next to Father."

Pek was hanging back, sticking close to his father Hisak, who appeared to be deep in conversation with someone Kendi didn't recognize. Pek was the same height as his sister, with the same dun-colored fur and wide-spaced green eyes. It was interesting, Kendi mused, that custom allowed Nel to refer to Hisak as her father, but that he couldn't refer to her as his daughter. Not that human customs always made sense. Mention the word "menstruation," and most human males dove for cover.

"We should go over and say hello," Ben said pointedly. "Right, Kendi?"

"Oh! Right!" Kendi said, jolted out of his reverie. He let Ben lead him across the room. Pek raised his head and blinked at them with enormous green eyes.

"Hisak," Kendi said. "I haven't seen you since that argument with Putan."

"*Ched*-Putan," Hisak corrected. "She is no member of this household. But I am glad to see *your* presence."

"And Pek." Kendi turned to the younger Ched-Balaar and offered his palms. "Are you in good health?"

"I am," Pek said shyly, covering Kendi's palms with his own. "It's nice to see you, Ben."

Kendi's face warmed. It was a gaffe—Pek, who had only seen Ben and Kendi in images had gotten the two of them mixed up, thereby calling attention to the fact that they had never actually met. There was a tiny, embarrassed silence. Then Ben stepped in and nudged Kendi's palms aside, replacing them with his own under Pek's hands.

"Thank you, Pek," Ben said as if Pek had been addressing him all along. "It's good to see you, too."

Pek bobbed his head. The four of them made further conversation about the weather and the upcoming election, and the momentary awkwardness was smoothed over. After a while, Ben and Kendi excused themselves to visit the food table.

"Nice save," Kendi murmured to him.

"Second one this week," he said. "And I didn't sprain my shoulder this time. Hey! Bug salad!"

They ate and they mingled and even danced a little to the ever-present drumming. Nel and Pek, who would choose a second syllable for their names at a later date, did the same. Everyone acted as if there were nothing special about their presence, though Kendi had to force himself not to stare at the twins. They were so much shorter than the other Ched-Balaar and a bit ungainly. Still, there were differences between them. Nel moved easily among the partygoers while Pek stayed close to Hisak or his mother Miran. Kendi wondered what it must be like, living in seclusion, only being allowed to come outside at night, with only a handful of people even acknowledging your existence, and then suddenly being thrust into full-blown society. It would probably be like living a lifetime on the sims, only to have someone shut the game off.

Eventually, however, Kendi got used to the twins' presence, and in the end he decided a Leaving was actually pretty boring. It made sense not to draw attention to the youngest, least-experienced members of your herd, he supposed, and he guessed that Nel and Pek were enjoying their newfound freedom as full members of Ched-Balaar society, but it was a strain even for sociable Kendi to keep the conversation casual and light so that the two newcomers could join in as if they'd always been there.

After an hour or so, Kendi tracked down Ben, and they bid their farewells, taking care to include Nel and Pek without calling too much attention to the fact.

"We're leaving a Leaving," Kendi said after they exited. "So after a Leaving is over, is it a Left? Do you have the Right to be Left?"

"I'm not listening," Ben said, clapping his hands over his ears.

"You're just jealous you didn't think of it."

"Not listening."

"Hi, guys. What are we not listening to?"

Kendi pulled up short, and Ben took his hands down. Sejal Vajhur was standing in front of them.

"Sejal!" Kendi shouted, and embraced him. "You're back!"

"Your mom told us you were someplace secret," Ben said, giving him a quick hug as well. "God, it's good to see you. What have you been up to? What's been going on?"

"Lots," Sejal said in a voice that sounded much too serious for a young man of seventeen. "Let's go someplace and talk."

They went to a coffeehouse and ordered tea. When Kendi remarked on the strangeness of it, Ben shrugged. "Coffee's like gold these days," he said. "You want to stay in business, you offer tea."

The little shop was deserted except for the owner, who polished teacups and rearranged tea jars behind the count. The trio's booth lay in the back. Herbal scents hovered in the air, along with the smell of fresh-baked cookies. Sejal sat across from Ben and Kendi. He was a strikingly handsome young man, slender and wiry, with dark coloring and contrasting blue eyes that reminded Kendi of Keith. Kendi had, in fact, once suspected Sejal of being Keith's son. Wrongly, as it turned out.

"What's been going on?" Ben asked over a mug of raspberry tea.

"Senator Reza hired me to spy on Mitchell Foxglove in Othertown," Sejal said. "Undercover."

Has your grandmother ever been a wrinkled old lady who bakes blue cupcakes for the Awakening Festival?

"All life," Kendi breathed.

"How long have you been doing it?" Ben asked.

"A little more than three months. It started right around the time you guys left to find Harenn's kid."

"Why you?" Kendi asked.

"Didn't Ben tell you?" he said. "I talked to him in the Dream when you guys were up to your asses in some scam on SA Station."

Kendi shot Ben a glance. "He didn't say anything. Tell me what?"

In answer, there was a flicker. Kendi's mug of tea blinked from its place in front of him to a spot closer to Sejal. It took Kendi a moment to understand what had happened.

"I moved that, didn't I?" he said. "You can still possess people from the solid world."

"I'm not as good as I used to be," Sejal admitted. "The Despair, and all. And I don't flash on people's feelings much anymore. I can still make people feel things, though."

"Handy abilities for a spy," Ben said. "I hope you charged Grandma an arm and a leg."

"She'd pay with someone else's," Kendi muttered. "What did you find out, then?"

"Short version? Foxglove runs that place like his own private kingdom. He owns fucking *everyone*. Cops, fire, local newsfeeds, even the school board. I caught Senator Reza's speech during the whole Taper thing, and she was lying through her false teeth about getting votes in Othertown. I mean, there are rumors spreading around that when you identify yourself at the polls, his hackers will send a copy of your vote to his office. You don't vote for him, and you'll get a visit from the club 'em and cleave 'em committee."

"He can't do that," Kendi sputtered. "That's illegal. And impossible! Ben, he can't do that, can he?"

"Any system can be hacked," Ben said, "but there's no way *I'd* try it, and I've hacked the Unity."

"So fucking what?" Sejal said. "It only matters that everyone *thinks* he can do it. They're too scared to vote for anyone else. I'll be surprised if Senator Reza and Ched-Pirasku get more than six votes apiece from Othertown."

"Does Grandma need Othertown?"

Sejal shrugged. "Not my job to figure that out. Hell, Kendi, the votes he can't scare, he's been buying. He paid for his party's nomination with cold, hard free-marks. I've even seen him bribe individual citizens."

"Awful expensive way to run a campaign," Ben said. "Where's his money coming from?"

"That I couldn't find out. I didn't dare manipulate the real higher-ups in his campaign in case they suspected something. I stuck with secretaries and flunkies."

Secretaries. "Sejal, did you ever come across anyone named Finn Day? Or Helen Day?" Kendi asked.

"Nope. Why?"

"Just curious."

"I still want to know where his money's coming from," Ben said thoughtfully. "It sounds like he's spending money like water. Do you have proof of any of this, Sejal?"

"Nothing that would stand up in court," Sejal said. "Like I said, I had to be really careful. He's probably got sets of account books that would make a prosecutor juice his slacks, but I don't know enough about computers to access them."

"I might be able to find something out," Ben said, "but I'd have to get hold of one of his computers, first."

"I thought you didn't want to get involved," Kendi said.

Ben sat back. "I suppose I'm involved whether I want to be or not."

The ground rumbled. Kendi stared into the talltree forest, made some adjustments to the controls, and the gravity sled rose to a position about eight meters off the ground. The ground cover surrounding the talltrees trembled as if in fear. Martina grabbed Kendi's upper arm from behind.

"Are you sure they won't hurt us?" she asked.

"Positive," Kendi said. "I've done this dozens of times, and I'm still around to tell the tale."

"How many people have died doing this?" Keith asked.

"No one that I know."

"That's not very encouraging."

Kendi almost snapped that nothing could encourage Keith, but he bit back the words and peered into the shadows among the talltrees. Enormous forms moved in slow motion, and eventually the first irvinosaurus plodded into view. It was enormous, a house that had sprouted legs and a tail. Its little head rose high into the air, high enough to browse the lower branches of the talltrees. Tiny, wide-spaced eyes peered sharply about, and it had a single nostril in the center of its receding forehead. Its tail didn't drag the ground, but pointed straight backward and gave Kendi the impression it could smack a rear ambush with devastating accuracy. After a moment, a second, slightly smaller irvinosaur came into view, then a third and fourth. Three babies the size of Clydesdale horses were next, followed by more house-sized adults. Kendi adjusted the gravity sled down a meter and got a firmer grip on the tow rope tied to the front of the sled.

"Not the first one," he murmured. "They're all dumb as dishwater, but the alpha female always has a few more brain cells."

"Are you sure about this?" Keith asked, clearly awed. "I don't know if—"

"Oh, Keith," Martina said. "Give the morosity a rest, will you?"

"Morosity?" Keith said. "What the hell kind of word is—"

"Shush!" Kendi hissed. "They're getting closer."

The first irvinosaur was only a few meters away. For a moment it came straight at them, bearing down like half a dozen freight trains. Martina increased the pressure on Kendi's arm. Then the dinosaur seemed to notice them. It turned aside and passed them by so close that Kendi could have reached out and touched it. The animal smelled of decaying grass, manure, and musk. The second irvinosaur followed the first, passing the sled by.

"Now!" Kendi said. He and Martina leaped off the sled straight onto the dinosaur's back. Keith hesitated. "Hurry, Keith! I'm not going to tow you."

Keith jumped. He hit the irvinosaur's back and lost his footing. His feet went out from under him, and he fell, rolling, toward the animal's flank. Martina grabbed him. He got to his feet, shaken and staring.

"I can't believe I let you talk me into this," he wheezed. "I'm a fucking idiot."

Kendi hauled on the tow rope, and the gravity sled slid into a position behind them so they could get off later. "It's fun, Keith. You have to let yourself go sometimes. Figuratively, I mean."

Keith didn't answer. Kendi drove a small stake into the dinosaur's thick, pebbled hide and tied the tow rope to it. The gravity sled obediently followed. Kendi raised his hands and stretched. The dinosaur's back was so broad it had only a slight slope to it. Talltree trunks moved past at a slow, steady pace. He could feel the creature's huge muscles moving under his feet like boulders sliding around far below the earth. Behind came the rest of the herd, plodding steadily forward. Every so often, one of them gave a low, moaning call that the others answers. The sound vibrated Kendi's bones, and he felt a rush of exhilaration.

"Are you sure it won't hurt us?" Martina whispered.

"Positive," Kendi said. "It barely knows we're here. Hey, if a fly lands on your back, do you even notice?"

"It's just so . . . big. I can't imagine how much it weighs." She spread her arms wide and spun in place. "This is *marvelous*, Kendi. Breathtaking! A little slow, though."

Keith squatted down and ran his hands over the heavy skin at his feet. "Wow."

"Dinosaur riding is a big sport here," Kendi said. "We're trying the easy version."

"What's the hard version?" Martina asked.

"Smaller dinos who are more likely to notice you.

And for the *real* danger-mice—carnosaurs. People *have* died trying that one."

"Oh, god," Keith said.

Another round of moaning cycled through the herd. The sound traveled up Kendi's body in a low, almost delicious vibration. A flock of glider lizards slid overhead, squeaking like excited children. The herd plodding on as if the Weavers didn't exist.

"You mean people actually climb on a wild meateater?" Martina said. "All life!"

"Yeah. And people call *me* insane," Kendi said. "You'd never catch *me* trying to—"

"How can you do it?" Martina asked. "Is there a club or something?"

Kendi realized her eyes were sparkling. It made her look bewitchingly beautiful. "You can't be serious," he said. "You want to try—"

"I never imagined such things were possible before," Martina said. "Not even in the Dream. I want to try them, Kendi. I want to try *everything*. Riding a meateater—that would be a real slice of life!"

"Long as you don't let the life slice *you*," Kendi said.

"I'm serious, big brother," she said. "Look at me! All life, a month ago I was a slave, and now I'm riding a dinosaur! I'll have to work hard to top this!"

And she ran toward the dinosaur's neck.

"Martina!" Keith shouted. "What are you—"

"I want a better view, guys. Come on!" She reached the base of the creature's neck. It was as big around as a good-sized tree trunk, but Martina wrapped her arms and legs around it. With a wide grin, she shimmied upward, using her arms and thighs for purchase.

"Martina!" Kendi yelled.

The dinosaur didn't react at first. Then it brought its head around, trying to see what was going on. Martina laughed and clung tightly as the animal's neck swung and twisted beneath her. Kendi's heart leaped into his throat.

"Martina!" he yelled again. "Get down from there!"

The irvinosaur made a low, rumbling sound Kendi didn't like. Martina whooped one more time, then slid back down to the creature's back. She trotted back to her brothers, breathless and laughing.

"That was the greatest!" she said. "All life, you have to—"

"Martina," Kendi said with absolute calm, "move slowly toward the gravity sled. Now. Right now."

"Why? What's wrong?"

"Do it!" Keith hissed. He grabbed her arm. "Come on!"

"Why?" she repeated. "I don't see—oh."

The entire herd had come to a stop. Half a dozen dinosaurs, including the one the Weavers were riding, had bent their heads around the siblings like strangely animated trees. One or two were chewing cud. They blinked and stared, clearly uncertain about these strange creatures riding their lead male. Kendi swallowed. Irvinosaurs were stupid and slow to react, but if they decided the humans were a threat . . .

One of the herd let out a bellow that nearly blasted Kendi off his feet. The alpha female raised her head high in an aggressive posture. Her roar was echoed by the others.

"Run!" Kendi shouted.

Keith and Martina dove for the sled. The alpha brought her head down toward Kendi, and he leaped aside just before it crashed into the spot where had been standing. The male they were riding roared in pain, anger, or both. Kendi scrambled aboard the sled and kicked the tow rope loose. Another dinosaur raised its head.

"Hang on," he snapped, and punched one of the controls on the pedestal. The sled shot straight up. Kendi's stomach fell into his shoes, and the dinosaurs smeared into green-brown blurs.

"Watch it!" Martina yelped.

Kendi flicked another control, and the sled stopped. For a split second he was weightless, and his feet left the surface of the sled. His head brushed something, then he came back down on the sled again. Keith looked queasy. A talltree branch stretched into the forest only a few centimeters above their heads. Another split second and the sled would have crashed into it. Kendi's knees felt weak, and he sank slowly to a sitting position. The irvinosaurs continued to bellow below.

"All life," Kendi whispered.

Martina raised her arms and whooped. "That was great!" she yelled. "We are *gods!* Do you hear that, world? You can't touch me!"

"Martina?" Keith said. "You're scaring me."

"You've been acting like an old woman ever since Kendi freed us, Keith," she said. "Me, I want to live it up."

Kendi peered over the side of the gravity sled. The irvinosaur herd had moved on, leaving a trail of trampled undergrowth. "Let's go home and live it up there for a while," he said. "There's a staircase topside over that way."

Keith said he wanted to lie down, so they dropped the gravity sled off at the rental agency—Kendi caught Martina checking the place's message board for notices about dinosaur riding clubs—and trooped back to the house Keith and Martina shared. It was a small house and high up in its tree, where the branches were barely thick enough to support the platform. The house rocked perceptibly during strong winds. It had originally belonged to Ben, then to Ben and Kendi, then just to Ben again. Kendi had once observed that friends could update themselves on the status of his and Ben's relationship by checking local housing records. With Ben and Kendi now living in the house Ben had inherited from his mother, the little house had stood vacant until Keith and Martina's rescue from slavery. Kendi had offered to let them live with him and Ben, but both of them had refused.

"We can take care of ourselves," Martina had said. "Besides, I like the idea of living in my own, separate house."

Martina, still glowing from the ride, entered first, followed by her brothers. Keith went immediately into his room and shut the door. Martina checked the kitchen.

"I'm starved," she said. "Want some lunch? I make a mean macaroni and cheese."

"Sure," Kendi said. He sat down at the tiny kitchen table. The place was scrupulously clean. A window looked out over a long talltree branch. Gloomy sky sulked in the spaces between green leaves. "Will Keith want anything?"

"He hasn't been eating well lately," Martina admitted. She set a pot of water on the stove and took an onion from the refrigerator. "He's had a few good days since we got here, but they're getting few and far between."

"I know. I've been watching him." Kendi ran a fingertip over the tabletop. "I could pull some strings, get him into a counselor."

"He won't do it." Martina skinned the onion with deft movements and set to chopping. The sharp, sweet smell mingled with steam from the pot. "You can't make someone see a therapist if they don't want to. And anyway, getting him in would displace someone else, someone who was Silenced and who really *needs* a counselor."

"You don't think Keith should see someone?"

"No. I just think that other people—Silenced people—need it more."

She went back to chopping. Kendi watched her for a while. All life, she had grown. She had been barely ten years old at the slave auction that had broken their family into bits. Now she was a fully grown woman, able to cook and enter the Dream and ride a dinosaur.

"How was it for you?" he asked suddenly.

Chop, chop, chop. "How was what?"

"Slavery."

"I've told you that."

"No." Kendi crossed his ankle over his knee. "Not slavery to the SA Station cult. I mean before that. When you were a . . . a *regular* slave."

Martina smiled at him. She had a beautiful smile, Kendi decided, and a wave of affection flowed over him.

"Regular slave," she said. "I like that. I was only a regular slave for a little while, though. A history professor bought me to work in his house. He wasn't a bad guy, in his way. He didn't molest me or beat me or anything like that, and he let me read in his library when my work was done for the day. But when my Silence surfaced—I think I was twelve or thirteen—he sold me for the profit to a company that trains Silent slaves and resells them. I stayed with them for . . . six years? Seven? Anyway, they sold me to a law firm, and *they* eventually sold me to DrimCom. I worked for them until that weirdo cult kidnapped me a few months after the Despair. Overall, I had it pretty good. You hear stories about slaves being tortured or beaten or"—she lowered her voice and glanced toward Keith's bedroom door—"raped. But none of that happened to me. It took me a long time to get over being sold away from you guys and from Mom and Dad, but I eventually coped. No other choice, you know?"

She got chunks of cheddar and mozzarella cheese out of the refrigerator and started grating them. The cheeses made fluffy, pungent mounds next to the pale pile of onion.

"So how was slavery for you?" she continued. "You said you worked on a frog farm."

"I hated it," Kendi said. His stomach growled, and he wondered if he could swipe a piece of cheese. "No surprise, eh? I was a mucker, the lowest of the low. We worked right in the ponds, catching frogs, reconfiguring the shorelines, digging new water holes. It was hard, filthy work, and the managers were always looking for an excuse to crack their whips."

"But Mom was there." Martina poured flour, salt, oil, and other ingredients into a small machine. It whirred busily, and a small heap of elbow macaroni tumbled out the bottom like soft, misshapen snowflakes.

"Yeah. They put her in the kitchen. She snuck me and Pup extra food when she could."

"Pup?"

"Another boy my age. We became best friends after a while. Then a woman visited the farm. She was Silent, and she touched me. Pow! I thought she had socked me with a cattle prod. Mom turned out to be Silent, too, and Mistress Blanc—my owner—sold us for the profit. We were split up. I was lucky that the Children of Irfan bought me, but I never heard from Mom again." Kendi's throat grew thick and he cleared it hard. "Sorry. I've been looking for her and Dad ever since, but I've never gotten a lead."

"I'll help you look," Martina said. "If Mom and Dad are out there, we'll find them one day."

"I hope so."

"Hey, you found me and Keith." Martina dumped the macaroni into the water and counted to twenty. She drained it, mixed it with the cheese and onions, poured in a little milk, and popped the dish into the oven.

"Bake medium, ten minutes," she said to the computer, then sat next to Kendi at the table. "So was Pup just a friend or something more?"

"Just a friend," Kendi laughed. "I think I wanted something more from him, but I wasn't sure what it was. Too young yet. I don't think Pup was interested anyway. What about you? Did you ever pair up with anyone?"

Martina's eyes went flat. "Only once. He was sold away. I haven't really been looking since then. Some slaves grab whatever love or sex they can, but me—I didn't want to."

"Too much to lose," Kendi said quietly.

"Something like that."

They sat in silence until the computer chimed, announcing that the macaroni and cheese was done.

"Father Weaver, I'd like to ask a candid question, if I could," said Tel Brace.

"Shoot," Kendi said, leaning back in his office chair. The holograms of Ben, Gretchen, and himself were lined up on his desk. Kendi had deliberately set them so that they seemed to staring up at Tel Brace.

"Are you in negotiation with another game company?"

Kendi's eyes widened a tiny bit. "No!" he said a little too quickly. "I wouldn't do such a thing. It might upset the generous deal I have with you, Mr. Brace. I've just been really busy with Grandma's campaign and all and haven't had much of a chance to look at the agreement."

"Well, I'm glad to hear that." Brace managed a weak smile, and Kendi noticed a tiny line of sweat at his blond hairline.

"Speaking of the contract," Kendi said, "I had a question about one part. This clause states that you'll own the exclusive rights to use my image in any capacity. I'm not so sure about that one. The other—I mean, I've *heard* that other game companies don't run things that way. I need to appear in the game itself, obviously, and in ads for the game, but I might need to use my own image somewhere else once in a while, you know?"

"Well, maybe we can pare that back a little." Brace tapped his data pad, then beamed a change to Kendi's pad. "I like your data pad, by the way. New?"

"A gift," Kendi said.

"There. How's that? Game and ads—that's it."

"Better," Kendi said. "Where's my stylus? I can probably sign right—oops! You forgot to take out the word *exclusive.*"

"Sorry. Just strike it."

Kendi took out his stylus, touched the tip to the agreement, then paused. "When's the deadline for this, anyway?"

The sweat on Brace's forehead became more pronounced. "Er, it's not firm yet. We hope to start beta testing next year."

Kendi nodded, though inside he was grinning wide. Brace was lying through his keen, white teeth. Ben had spent a little time on the gaming boards and uncovered plenty of rumors that "Dream and Despair" was actually almost ready for beta testing now. That meant Hyper-Flight had made the enormous mistake of starting production on the game before all the contracts were signed. Kendi, Ben, and Gretchen were in a position to stall the release indefinitely and cost the company millions of freemarks.

"You know," Kendi said, toying thoughtfully with the stylus, "three percent royalty seems a little low. I know I'm not doing any of the actual writing, but it *is* my story. Ben did some research and found out that the—that other companies pay four percent."

"Only for really famous celebrities," Brace said. His eyes never left the stylus.

Kendi gave a self-deprecating laugh. "Sometimes I swear my name is a household word, Mr. Brace. But if HyperFlight doesn't want to do that, I can understand. Times are tough. You can take the agreement back and ask your bosses about it, I guess. I'll be out of town for a couple of months on the campaign trail, and maybe we can talk again when I get—"

"I think we can handle four percent," Brace said.

"And raise the other rate, too?" Kendi asked. "Five point five percent on every copy sold after the first two million? Though I read somewhere that the breakpoint for books is the *first* million. I don't suppose that—"

"Five point five after the first million," Brace said recklessly. "And we'll raise the advance to one point five million freemarks."

"And make the same offer to Ben and Gretchen."

"They're minor characters," Brace countered. "Half a million advance to each of them, royalties at two and two point five."

"Three quarters of a million to Gretchen. Ben stays at half."

"Done."

Kendi signed with a flourish. "Thank you, Mr. Brace. I'm sure Ben and Gretchen will sign without a problem."

Brace got up, shook Kendi's hand, and moved toward the door. He seemed to be in a daze. Kendi picked up Ben's hologram by the base and turned it over. The movement caught Brace's eye, and he turned in time to see Kendi scrape a tiny, translucent button off the bottom and crush it with his fingertips. Brace winced and his hand rose to his ear. At the last moment, he scratched his temple instead.

"Speck of dirt," Kendi said. "I look forward to playing this game when it comes out, Mr. Brace. Do you think I'll choose Gretchen or Ben as my love interest?"

"I really have no idea," Brace said in a faint voice. He left Kendi's office and quietly, carefully closed the door.

Jolanda Rondeau double-checked the pheromone tanks. Full. The motor on the ultralight purred like a contented lizzie-bat. Her mechanic made a final adjustment and gave Jolanda a thumbs-up.

"Thanks," Jolanda said, and put on her helmet. "Tell Frank I hope he's feeling better."

"Will do," the mechanic said.

Jolanda boarded her craft. The ultralight looked like the skeleton of a tiny airplane, one just big enough for a single pilot. Ahead of the craft stretched a fallen talltree trunk, which was so massive the top formed a nearly flat surface. The bark had been sanded off, and platforms hung off either side. At one end, the monstrous roots made a tangle that reached three stories above the trunk. A small hangar had been built there. At the other end, the branches had been cut off, leaving a long, smooth expanse that made a fine runway. The fallen tree left open a strip of open space that would let small aircraft slip unhindered into the sky.

Jolanda goosed the motor and started down the runway. To her left she caught sight of the mechanic. He was a dark-haired man with bland features. Jolanda had never seen him before, but it wasn't unusual to have a substitute mechanic now and then. She put him out of her mind and turned her attention to flying.

The takeoff was smooth, as it always was, and her stomach dropped as she grabbed fast altitude. Jolanda inhaled the crisp, clean-smelling air that rushed over her face. Below her, the tops of the talltrees made a green carpet that stretched all the way to the horizon. Jolanda loved it up here. She could pretend she was the only person in the entire world, with nothing but sunlight above and leaves below.

Jolanda checked the navigation computer and nosed around until she was pointed in the right direction. Then she tapped a button. Behind her, a thin, steady stream of mist jetted from the pheromone tanks. The pheromones would disperse and spread, keeping the more dangerous carnosaurs away from Treetown. Jolanda checked the tanks and went into a grid dispersal pattern. Once she had flown this route twice a week. Now she did it twice a month. The city couldn't afford any more than that. The irony was that tent cities had sprouted like mushrooms beneath the city, meaning more people walked the forest floor than ever. The inhabitants erected their shelters well away from the stomping grounds of the big herbivores, but the carnivores wandered more. Jolanda wondered how long it would be before a carnosaur chomped down some hapless homeless person.

The ultralight's motor cut out. Jolanda froze, then hit the restart. Nothing. A tinge of fear thrilled through her.

The ultralight went into a long, gliding dive. Jolanda hit the emergency anti-grav generator. A red light told her it was malfunctioning. The fear blew into full-blown panic. A scream tore itself from her throat as the ultralight skimmed over the trees and dropped down into the forest.

CHAPTER EIGHT

"You know who I want to slap? The guy who said that a crisis is an opportunity in disguise."

—Irfan Qasad

Applause thundered over Kendi as he left the platform. Lewa Tan followed. Several people in the school auditorium chanted, "Tapers! Tapers! Tapers!" Kendi turned to give them a wave and a grin. The noise swelled, and Kendi trotted backstage, where Wanda Petrie was bending over to pick up the stylus she had dropped. The grin dropped off Kendi's face as she straightened.

"Where now?" he asked wearily over the noise.

"Dellton," she said, naming a small city south of Treetown. "You're speaking at the military base there in an hour, so we have to get moving."

"We're always moving," Kendi muttered. Ignoring this remark, Petrie took him by the elbow and led him firmly to the exit where the flitcar was parked. Tan went outside ahead of them for a quick look around. A rectangle of late summer sunshine fell onto the floor, radiating golden heat. Tan gestured from the door, and Kendi ducked into the back seat of the waiting flitcar. Petrie and Tan climbed in beside him, and Tan went up front. Gretchen had the controls. Even after signing the lucrative sim-game contract, she had continued to show up for her job as bodyguard. No words of thanks or explanation—just a clear and quiet determination to keep Kendi safe.

Kendi watched the trees drop away, then merge into a blurry green carpet as Gretchen took them up to speed. Spring had melted into summer, but Kendi had barely noticed. It seemed like all his time was spent in the flitcar these days, rushing from one speaking engagement to the next, giving the same speech over and over until someone handed him a new one. The in-between times were spent in the studios making commercial announcements. Kendi'd had no idea that standing in front of a camera and giving a short speech could be so complicated. It took forever for the staff to choose the right clothes, the right makeup, the right lighting, the right *mood*, whatever that meant. And then the repetition. Say it this way. Now say that way. We need more energy, Father Kendi. We need better enunciation, Father Kendi. We need more warmth, Father Kendi. We need, we need, we need.

The sun shone down heavily on the emerald talltree leaves. Kendi missed the talltrees, missed walking among their cool, green depths, feeling calm and protected from the hot summer sunlight. Up here in the campaign's flitcar, everything was always hot and blue and gold. Even the flitcar's environmental controls couldn't keep the temperature completely even. Bright sunshine flooded the cabin with yellow heat and made Kendi's skin itch with discomfort. He knew it was a nonsensical complaint from a man who created a desert every time he entered the Dream, but the Outback was *meant* to be hot. Bellerophon was supposed to be cool and temperate. The natural order had been upset.

Fatigue pulled at Kendi's body and bones. He was always tired now. The speaking had turned out to be more strenuous than he had through. For the last three months, he had done nothing but speak and run, speak and run, speak and run. He had returned home every night only to fall into an instant, exhausted sleep. In the morning he was up before dawn, traveling for two or three hours to another round of speeches, more monotonous dinners of tasteless food, and endless flurries of handshaking before he could flee back home to Ben and Harenn. Harenn had finally convinced Kendi that she and Ben didn't mind if he spent the occasional night or two away from home, that nothing interesting was going to happen this early in the pregnancy. Kendi had finally agreed, but he never slept away from home for more than three nights in a row.

Sometimes it felt like *he* was running for office.

Petrie's data pad clattered to the floor of the flitcar.

She made an annoyed chirping noise. "First the stylus, now this. I can't seem to hold onto *anything* today."

She retrieved the pad and called up a newsfeed. Again. Kendi sighed. Petrie's data pad ran feed stories almost constantly, and the drone of the caster had become part of Kendi's daily life. A dinosaur farmer in Othertown supported Foxglove's expansion plans. The search continued for a woman who had gone down in an ultralight glider crash. Salman Reza's polls were up by three percent or down by two percent or up by four percent. Kendi wished the voters would make up their minds.

They arrived at the military base an hour later. Dellton was on the outskirts of the talltree forest that stretched across much of the continent, and the buildings were built on cleared ground. It was a military town, dependent on the base for most of its existence.

Petrie escorted Kendi to a small arena. Hundreds of human soldiers wearing the green and brown uniforms of the Bellerophon military occupied the bleachers. The Ched-Balaar soldiers wore green and brown head cloths and sat in neat rows on the ground, as was their custom. A handful of high-ranking officers had chairs or sitting areas on the speaking platform. Wanda Petrie made brief introductions. Kendi shook human hands, grasped Ched-Balaar palms, and completely forgot every single name.

A Ched-Balaar officer introduced Kendi, and the soldiers roared their approval as he took his usual position behind the usual podium. He smiled at them. Salman's position on increasing military spending made her very popular with the armed forces. This speech would be easy.

The sun poured down heat as he praised Salman Reza and urged their support. The words streamed out of him, but he barely heard them anymore. He made the right gestures, gave the right inflections, created the right mood. He dropped a joke here, told a poignant story there, and when it was over, the soldiers rose and shouted or clattered like rolling thunder. Then it was more handshaking, more palm-touching, and back into the flitcar with Tan and Petrie.

"Now where?" he asked.

"Home," Petrie said. "We're done for now."

"I've got news," Gretchen said from the front seat. Her data pad was open and text crawled across the holographic screen. "The High Court handed down its decision about the mining rights a few minutes ago."

Some of Kendi's exhaustion vanished. "And? Don't keep us in suspense, Gretchen."

"Would I do that?"

"Gretchen," Tan growled.

" 'The High Court made its final ruling today on Bellerophon's long-standing mining, farming, and tree harvesting restrictions,' " Gretchen read aloud. " 'In a four-to-three vote, the Court ruled to relax all three restrictions, effective immediately.' "

"All life," Kendi said.

" 'Gubernatorial candidate Mitchell Foxglove praised the ruling minutes after it was handed down. "This was the right decision for the right time," he said in a press conference on the steps of the High Court building. "All the people of Bellerophon will benefit this time, not just the Silent, as it was before the Despair." ' The man's a walking butt-crack."

"I assume that last sentence wasn't part of the quote," Petrie said in an icy voice.

"Ched-Pirasku?" Tan asked in her raspy voice.

"He's next. 'Opposing candidate Ched-Pirasku was more cautious. "I am sure everything will work out for the best," he said in a prepared statement. "I look forward to seeing the impact on our economy." ' The guy has the personality of a damp sponge. How he survives as a gubernatorial candidate, I'll never understand."

"What did they say about Senator Reza?" Petrie demanded.

"That she wasn't available for comment," Gretchen said. "She isn't even—oh, wait. This is coming from a feed owned by Foxglove. They probably didn't try very hard to reach her."

"Polls?" Petrie said. Her data pad was open.

Gretchen checked. "Latest one shows Foxglove on the rise to the tune of sixteen percentage points," she reported. "Salman dropped by eight. Except among the military."

"No," Petrie whispered. "God, she's in last place now. Gretchen, get us back to Treetown. Fast! This is a crisis."

Her pad chimed, and a hologram of Salman's head popped up. The flitcar took off.

"I heard," Petrie said, her lips tight. "We're already on our way."

"The bastard's leapfrogged right over me," Salman snapped. *"The mining companies are already taking applications, and so are the loggers. Treetown's going to be empty within a week, Wanda. Be ready for an all-nighter."*

"Not me," Kendi said. "The ruling sucks rocks and gravel, Grandma, but I'm so bushed I could sleep on a bed of nails. I need a break."

"Don't get too comfortable at home, my duck," Salman warned. *"We're going to need you even more if we want to catch up. Thank the wretched skies we have almost ten months before the election, or we'd be fucked."*

The hologram vanished, and Petrie shut her data pad with a snap. Her face was pale, and her lips were drawn tight over her teeth. Her eyes glittered above a sharp nose. "We can't allow her to lose," she said, half to herself. "We just can't."

Kendi patted her shoulder. "You look more upset than Grandma. Listen, Wanda, it's just one election. Grandma could always run again in five years if she doesn't—"

"No!" Petrie spat with so much vehemence that Tan reached for her sidearm. "She has to win *this* election, Kendi. No matter what, Senator Reza has to get the governor's chair."

"Hey, I want her to win, too," Kendi said, "but it's not life and death."

"Maybe not to you." Petrie pecked out every word. "If it weren't for the senator, I'd be . . . I'd be on the street. I had a dead-end job with a . . . a boss who made me miserable, and I couldn't afford to quit. Not after the Despair. And then I got sick, and my boss wouldn't pay the medical expenses. Then he fired me on top of everything."

"What kind of job did you have?"

But Petrie barreled on. "Senator Reza was speaking at the hospital when they discharged me. I still don't know where I got the courage, but I marched up to her and asked for a job. It startled her so much she said yes, and I ended up in her office pool. I worked sixty and seventy hours a week for her, I was so grateful, and she promoted me closer and closer to her." Petrie's eyes took on fire. "I've seen her at her best and at her worst. She yells and howls at her staff sometimes, but did you know she donated half a million freemarks to an orphanage run by the Church of Irfan?"

"No," Kendi said.

"Of course not," Petrie said. "It's because she won't tell anyone. It's PR gold, but the senator said she won't use it because it would be exploiting the kids. She wants what's best for them, and she wants what's best for Bellerophon. I won't let her lose this election, Kendi. Foxglove and Ched-Pirasku will have to dance a waltz on my grave first."

The heat in her voice made Kendi recoil for a moment. She sounded like a religious fanatic praising a prophet. "With you on her side," he said with newly learned diplomacy, "I don't see how she could lose."

Petrie spent the rest of the trip pecking at her data pad. Kendi half dozed in his seat and was jarred into wakefulness only when the flitcar landed next to the drawbridge. Gretchen, Tan, and Kendi got out while Petrie took the controls. She gave a curt farewell and took off.

Down beneath the trees, darkness was already falling. Tan lowered the drawbridge. Kendi caught sight of Grandmother Mee putting away her gardening tools in her house below theirs. He waved at her, and she returned the gesture. A pang of guilt touched him. He knew she was Silenced and lonely, but he hadn't spoken to her since the day the drawbridges had been installed. These days, the campaign ate up most of his time, and the rest was given over to Ben and Harenn. Bedj-ka, too, for that matter. Maybe he and Ben could invite Grandmother Mee up for dinner.

"If you two don't need me tonight," Gretchen said, "I'll head home."

Tan gave assent, and Gretchen trotted off toward the monorail station.

"Don't know how you do it," Tan rasped as the drawbridge ahead of her lowered itself.

"Do what?" Kendi said.

"Inspire people that way. Woman made three-quarters of a mil on that game. Between that and her future royalties, she could retire. But she still wants to guard you."

Kendi's face grew warm. "I think it keeps her busy. Takes her mind off being Silenced, you know?"

"I do know," Tan said grimly and stood aside so Kendi could enter the house.

The sound of many voices engaged in conversation met their ears. They encountered Lars sitting alone in the living room. He merely nodded as they passed. In the kitchen they found a lively group gathered around the table. Ben, Bedj-ka, Harenn, Martina, and Keith were playing a card game. Hands of holographic cards hovered in front of each player. Martina flicked one, and it fled to the discard pile. Bedj-ka brushed it with his finger and it rose to join his own hand. Lucia was at a counter mixing something in a bowl. Kendi stuck his finger into the mixture out of general principle, and Lucia rapped his knuckles with her spoon.

"Wash your hands first," she said. "How did the speech go?"

Kendi licked his finger. Salty and spicy, with a sour cream base. Had to be some kind of snack dip. "Fine. I'm wiped, though."

Tan leaned against the door jamb. "The High Court ruled the mining restrictions invalid."

"We heard," Harenn said. She had just started her second trimester and was showing. Ben said she was already fending off guerrilla attacks from total strangers who wanted to rub her stomach. Ben himself was looking more relaxed and happy than Kendi had seen him in a long time. No one had contacted them about the contents of the stolen disk in the past three months, and Ben had finally written it off as a random mugging, just as Kendi had.

"I assume Senator Reza is unhappy," Harenn added.

"Good guess." Kendi kissed Ben hello, then impulsively kissed Harenn's cheek as well. "Mom," he said. Harenn laughed. Her face was rounder these days.

"Ew!" Bedj-ka said, and discarded.

"Keep the comments to yourself, junior," Kendi said.

"Less talk, more play," Keith said. "I'm up ten points."

Lucia set the bowl of dip on the table, along with another bowl filled with deep-fried *ben-yai* leaves. Several hands went at once to the treats, and the crunching began. Kendi sat on the counter, surveying all these people in his home. Children would only increase the size of the crowd. But everyone here, with the exception of quiet Lars, was someone Kendi considered family. The idea of his and Ben's house becoming the hub of an extended family network filled him with a joy he couldn't describe.

"Did you have dinner?" Lucia asked. "I've noticed Petrie isn't big on keeping you fed."

"I can call Maureen's," Kendi said.

Lucia waved a hand at him. "Sit, mighty Father. We have leftover mickey spike pot roast and gravy. I baked bread this morning, and Ben didn't eat all the fruit salad, so I'd say you're good for a hot sandwich with gravy and a fruit cup."

"Your drippings gravy?" Kendi said. His mouth was watering.

"Of course."

"We must do something to keep this wondrous woman around," Kendi remarked to no one in particular. "Maybe we should—"

An alarm buzzed through the room. The talk fell silent as everyone looked around, trying to locate the source. Abruptly Ben bolted to his feet and ran from the kitchen. Kendi followed. He didn't recognize the sound, but the expression on Ben's face left no doubt that it was bad news.

Ben ran into his den and grabbed the star-shaped

cryo-unit from his desk. It was buzzing unhappily. Ben tapped at the controls, then glanced up at Kendi, face pale.

"What's wrong?" Kendi demanded.

"One of the embryos is degrading," Ben said. "It's going to die soon."

"All life," Kendi whispered. Implications flashed through his mind. The dying one was only a single embryo out of the ten left. Cryo-embryos degraded and died all the time, and it was a small miracle that these had survived so long. But Kendi knew all the embryos were important to Ben, that he wanted to give life to each one. To Ben, losing one of these embryos would be like losing a child.

"Is there anything we can do?" Kendi said.

"How much time is left?" Lucia asked behind him.

Ben checked the reading. He looked ready to cry. "An hour, maybe less."

"Then we'll have to hurry," she said briskly. "Harenn! Can you make the call? We need to run."

"On it," Harenn called from the kitchen.

Lucia grabbed Kendi by the arm and towed him toward the front door, gesturing for Ben to follow. "Move!" she said. "Quick!"

"Call who?" Kendi said, bewildered. "Run where?"

"The medical center," Lucia said. "There's only one way I know of to save that embryo."

Forty-five minutes later, Lucia lay draped in green on a medical table with Ben and Kendi standing beside her. Dr. McCall's plump fingers worked with quick efficiency, examining Lucia and readying the implantation equipment. The room was eerily quiet. A light on the cryo-unit flashed a frantic warning—Ben had silenced the buzzing alarm. Kendi swallowed. Last time they had visited this room, the atmosphere had been cheerful and optimistic. Now it was grim and filled with worry.

"I think we're ready," Dr. McCall said. She opened the cryo-unit with a hiss of escaping steam, plucked a frozen ampule from among the ten still contained inside, and inserted it into the implantation device. "Please relax, Ms. dePaolo. You'll feel a slight pressure but no pain."

Kendi, Ben, and Lucia linked hands without speaking. A moment later, Dr. McCall straightened and set the implantation syringe aside.

"Did . . . did it work?" Ben asked.

"I hope so," McCall said, in stark contrast to her more usual cheery manner. "Ms. dePaolo's menstrual cycle isn't in the ideal stage for embryonic implantation. The implantation itself came off just fine, but keeping it from miscarrying is a whole other matter. Ms. dePaolo, you'll need to stay here in the hospital for a few days so we can keep an eye on you."

"I understand, Doctor," she said. "But Irfan will protect this child. She won't let anything happen to it."

"We'll put you in a room where you can rest," McCall concluded. "Don't get out of that bed, not even to go to the bathroom. You just go right where you are, and the bed will take care of it."

An orderly wheeled Lucia's bed to a private room a few floors up. Kendi and Ben followed. So did Lewa Tan, who had been waiting in the hallway during the implantation procedure. Kendi tried to hide his nervousness and appear confident for Ben's sake. Ben's face had gone all over stony.

Once Lucia was installed in her room and the nurse repeated Dr. McCall's strict instructions about staying in bed at all costs, Ben sat next the bed and took Lucia's hand. The nurse had set the bed to recline so Lucia could sit almost upright. Kendi leaned against the dark window glass. No stars were visible outside. Tan was waiting in the hall again.

"Lucia," Ben said, "I'm glad you're doing this for us. Even if it's because of . . . what you know about me."

Lucia pushed long black hair off her forehead. The white blankets and sheets on the bed contrasted with the green hospital pajamas she wore. "What I know?"

"About my parents. You and your church venerate my . . . my mother and—"

"You think this is because I'm a member of the Church of Irfan?" Lucia said. Then she gave a gentle laugh. "Ben, you have it wrong. I do venerate Irfan. She

is wise, serene, and powerful, and everyone should rise
to her example. I do my best, and I often fail. But Ben—
I volunteered to be a surrogate mother before I knew
the truth. I would be in this hospital if your biological
mother had turned out to be a slave trader,
understood?"

Ben managed a smile. "Understood."

"Now," she said, "if you want to help me—"

"Name it," Kendi said.

"Go home and get my things—toiletries, underclothes.
Ask Harenn. She'll know what to send. And bring my
data pad. We left so quickly I didn't even snatch up
something to read."

Kendi slid his own pad out of his pocket. "Use mine
until we get back. It's the new one Petrie gave me.
You'll like it."

"Thank you," Lucia said, accepting it. She accessed
the newsfeeds with a tap, and a holographic newscaster
popped up.

"—*voiced her opposition to the decision,*" the caster said.
"*We go live to Treetown, where the Senator is speaking
from her campaign headquarters.*" The image switched to
Salman Reza, who was apparently already speaking.

"—*disagree with the High Court's decision, I nonetheless celebrate the numerous jobs it will create. A strong
economy also means we can keep a strong military for
our defense. Now that we no longer enjoy the protection
of the Independence Confederation, we need to defend
ourselves from potential enemies, and the time to prepare
is now.*"

The image switched back to the newscaster. "*Senator
Reza is currently trailing in the polls by a considerable
margin,*" he said. "*Mitchell Foxglove, who has champi-
oned mining rights for several years, is now leading the
race by ten points over Ched-Pirasku, who is in second.*"
The caster paused, then said, "*I've just received word
that Mitchell Foxglove is also speaking from his headquarters in Othertown. We go live.*"

Foxglove, silver-haired and handsome, appeared
above the data pad. "*My worthy opponent Senator Reza
is warmongering. Every time our hardworking taxpayers
make some money, she wants to turn it over to the mili-*

tary. Well I'm here to tell you that I think you should keep your money. Use it to feed and clothe your children and put a roof over their heads. My administration promised jobs, and we've delivered—even before we won the election. With your support we can continue the trend. We must never forget—"

Lucia shut the feed off. "I think I'll read for a bit," she said. "And then I'll pray. I'm truly tired of politics."

"Me, too," Kendi said with a heartfelt sigh. "I have the feeling Wanda's going to call me tomorrow with a brand-new schedule."

"Then you'd better go home and get some rest," Lucia said. "Out! I'll be fine until you come back in the morning with my things. The baby will be fine, so don't worry."

"It must be nice to have so much faith," Ben said on the way home. The gondola glided noiselessly through the dark branches, and it felt like they were floating in space. Tan had taken the one ahead of them at Kendi's request—he'd wanted some time alone with Ben. The late summer air was warm and sensual, sliding over the two of them like a satin breeze. Kendi put his arm around Ben's shoulders and inhaled the smell of leaves and flowers. He felt some of the tension leave Ben's muscles.

"We did everything we could," Kendi said. "So don't you go feeling guilty if it doesn't work out. It's not your fault the embryo degraded."

Ben leaned against him, and Kendi smelled his scent, familiar and foreign at the same time. He stroked Ben's sunset hair and Ben sighed.

"It'll be fine," Kendi said. "Just don't—holy shit!"

Ben bolted upright, wide-eyed. "What? What's wrong?"

"It just hit me—we're going to have *two* kids less than three months apart. They'll be practically twins!"

"Oh god. In all the rush, I didn't even think about that." Ben laughed. "Well, other parents get through multiple births, and they survive. We've got three months between them to prepare. And we've got a whole houseful of people to help us."

"Yeah. Yeah, you're right." Kendi rubbed his face with a slightly shaky hand. "But we're going to have to change a few plans, buy more baby things. All life, I don't know how much more drama I can stand tonight."

When they arrived back home, everyone demanded to know how things had gone. Ben made explanations.

"I'm glad it worked so far," Martina said with clear relief.

"Nothing's sure yet," Keith said morosely. "She could still—ow!"

"Time to go, dear brother," Martina said sweetly, hauling him toward the door. "We'll check with you in the morning, guys. Good night!"

"I will put together a bag for Lucia," Harenn said as they left, "and bring it to her first thing in the morning after Bedj-ka leaves for school. And speaking of which—it is time we went home as well. It is well past your bedtime, Bedj-ka."

"I'll be too tired to go to school in the morning," Bedj-ka said brightly. "It's almost midnight."

"You were the one who begged leave to stay up to hear the news," Harenn said, "and now you must accept the consequences of your choice. Come along."

Bedj-ka groaned theatrically, and Kendi laughed. "You can't get anything past your mother," he said, putting a hand on Bedj-ka's shoulder. His thumb brushed the back of the boy's neck above his shirt collar. "No point in even—"

The jolt smashed them both to their knees. Kendi knelt on the floor, gasping, until Ben recovered his wits and hauled him up with easy strength. Harenn let out a small cry and helped Bedj-ka to the sofa.

"What was that?" Bedj-ka said in a scared voice. "It felt like I touched an electric wire."

"Are you injured?" Harenn demanded.

"I don't think so."

"What happened?" Ben asked, alarmed. "Kendi, are you—?"

Kendi sank into a chair. "That was a Silent jolt," he said dazedly. "All life—Bedj-ka is Silent."

CHAPTER NINE

"We can't keep this a secret any longer."

—Daniel Vik

No one spoke for several moments. Then amazed babbles broke out from all quarters.

"That can't be. Bedj-ka lost his—"

"I'm Silent? But Matron said—"

"Look, I felt the damned *jolt* all the way down to my—"

"He had *dreams*."

This last remark came from Harenn. She didn't speak above a whisper, but she still managed to silence the room. Kendi dragged himself upright, and Ben gave him a belated hand.

"What dreams?" Ben asked.

Harenn helped Bedj-ka stand. "You have been telling me about your realistic dreams ever since Silent Acquisitions Station," she said to him. "It never occurred to me that you were showing symptoms of Silence."

"I . . . I didn't think of it either," Bedj-ka said in an awed voice. His brown eyes were large and round. "I mean, the Enclave—the people that bought me the first time—they said that realistic dreams were early signs of Silence, but—"

"This calls for a sit-down meeting," Kendi said abruptly. "Because I need a sit-down. And a drink. Beer?"

"We're out," Ben said. "Hops shortage. Tea?"

But Harenn produced a flask and handed it over. Kendi drank, and it burned all the way down. He sighed. Bedj-ka watched with open curiosity.

"Can I—?" he began.

"No," Harenn said.

"But I got jolted, too."

"You may have a cookie."

A few minutes later, they had reassembled in the living room with mugs of milk and a plate of Lucia's soft ginger cookies. Kendi was grateful Lars was currently stationed outside the house—he didn't feel like explaining anything.

"Let's start at the beginning," Kendi said. "Bedj-ka, you've been having realistic dreams?"

"For a while, yeah. It's like I'm really there, and when I wake up—"

"—it takes a minute to figure out that you're not still dreaming," Kendi finished. Bedj-ka nodded. "All life, we were staring at it all the time and never realized it."

"Perhaps it was a fluke," Harenn said.

In answer, Ben reached over and tapped Bedj-ka on the forearm. They both jumped.

"Not a fluke," Ben said.

"Ow!" Bedj-ka rubbed his arm. "Mom!"

"Have another cookie," Kendi said.

"It only happens the first time, my son," Harenn said. "And now you will be able to find Ben and Kendi much more easily once you enter the Dream."

Kendi sprang to his feet. "We have to tell someone. This is important. This is *big*. All life—a Silenced child who got his Silence back. This is—I can't even *say* how big this is."

"Why?" Bedj-ka asked.

"Because you may not be the only one," Kendi said. "What if *all* the Silenced are getting their Silence back?"

"Or what if it is only Bedj-ka?" Harenn said. "Choose your words with care, Kendi. You do not want to look the fool in public. Especially now."

"You're right, you're right." Kendi started to pace. "But who do we—"

"That noise!" Ben interrupted. "God, Kendi—that noise!"

Kendi paused in mid-step. "What noise?"

"The one we heard. In the Dream. When you were a dolphin. We never did figure out what it was. Do you think it's related?"

"Has to be," Kendi said, his excitement rising like a wave. "Ben, the Silenced are coming back! They're—"

"Stop!" Harenn barked. Kendi halted in midsentence. "You are making assumptions based on no evidence. Right now you only know you heard a strange sound in the Dream and that Bedj-ka reacts to the Silent touch. Nothing more."

Kendi started to object, then cut himself off. Harenn was correct. For a moment he had fallen back into his old patterns, creating planets from clouds of dust. He nodded, acknowledging the wisdom of Harenn's words.

"There's only one thing left to do," he said.

"What?" Ben asked, on cue.

Kendi reached into an end table and produced a dermospray. "Go hunting."

The gray plain lay flat and hard beneath Kendi's paws. He stood as high on his hind legs as he could, stretching long kangaroo ears until they quivered. Beside him, Ben cocked his head.

"What do you hear?" Ben whispered.

"Shush," Kendi snuffled. "I'm trying to—wait! Wait!"

~ . . . ~

"I heard that!" Ben said with hushed excitement. "I heard it! But just barely. What is it?"

"Children," Kendi said. His ears swivelled this way and that, trying to catch even the tiniest hint of the sound. "They're all so young, barely touching the Dream. I can't hear any adults. Hold on."

He leaped into the air and shrank, his form twisting and reshaping until he was flitting through the still air as a pale blue Australian ghost bat. Sounds that had lain in the background leaped into the foreground—Ben's quiet breathing, the soft flapping of Kendi's own wings, the rustle of Ben's clothing as he shifted position to look upward. The distant whispering babble of other Silent became an abrupt roar, like a dripping faucet bursting forth as a waterfall. Kendi's sharp ears, however, had no trouble sorting out the individual voices. It was like seeing the waterfall as a trillion drops of water instead of a single raging torrent. Kendi twisted through the empty sky, listening with every speck of power he possessed. The waterfall of sound rushed and splashed around him, a picture of sound in three dimensions.

Then he heard it. Scattered among the droplets of sound—

~ . . . ~

—were the newcomers. They were weak as newborn chicks, their presence shy and innocent. Children who touched the Dream without realizing what they held. Kendi's tiny heart pounded. It was a far cry from his hope of all Silent finding the Dream once again, but if Silenced children were regaining their Silence, it meant the Dream would once again be restored to its former self. Kendi's head swam with the possibilities. The Children of Irfan could restore themselves. The Independence Confederation might even re-form with Empress Kalii back on the throne. The children would grow up and enter the Dream. In a few decades, everything would be back to normal. In a hundred years, the Despair would be nothing but a chapter in history books that bored a new generation of schoolchildren.

Ben and Kendi's children would never know a universe without the Dream.

Kendi's heart soared, and he did a little backflip that almost cost him his equilibrium. He righted himself and flittered back down to Ben, who was waiting with ill-disguised impatience. Kendi exploded back into kangaroo form and landed with a thud that shook the ground.

"Children," he said, and went on to explain. Ben nodded, his face mostly impassive, though Kendi could see him tense with suppressed excitement.

"We can't make too much of this," Ben warned. "We don't know what it means yet."

"The hell we don't," Kendi shot back. "This is huge, Ben! The children are coming back. I remember what it felt like before the Despair, how new children felt when they were just touching the Dream, and these touches feel exactly the same."

"We should tell Grandma," Ben said. "She's still a Grandmother Adept with the Children, and she'll know what to do with this information."

Kangaroo Kendi made a whuffing snort. "I know what she'll do with it."

*   *   *

In her living room, Salman Reza set down the teacup with shaking hands. Kendi watched her from his position on the hovering sofa. Ben sat next to him. Keith and Martina were also present. Wanda Petrie perched on the edge of her chair.

"It's just the children," Salman said. "No new adults?"

Kendi shook his head. "Afraid not."

"Dammit." Salman looked hard at nothing for a long time, and Kendi realized she had been hoping this was a sign her own Silence was returning.

"Why are only the children coming in?" said Keith.

"It'll take some study, I'm sure," Martina said. "Maybe children are more resilient, and their brains were able to heal the damage caused by the Despair. Or maybe Silent children who were too young to be affected by the Despair are getting old enough to touch the Dream now. Silence is a genetic gift, so there's an entire generation of Silent babies being born who will be able to touch the Dream soon. Hell, in species that mature quickly, we'll have Silent back in the Dream within five or six years."

"You're absolutely sure about this," Salman said. "It's children in the Dream."

"One hundred percent sure," Kendi replied firmly. "Ben and I stayed in the Dream for several hours last night to make sure, and I noticed the sounds got a little louder. We persuaded Keith and Martina to check this morning, and they heard it as well."

"It's true," Martina said with a nod. "I would never have found it on my own, but once Kendi showed me what to look for, it almost slapped me in the face." Keith added a wordless nod of his own.

"The children are coming back, Grandma," Kendi finished. "No doubt about it."

"Who else knows?" Petrie asked intently.

"The people sitting in this room," Ben said. "And Harenn and Bedj-ka. Harenn's at the medical center with Lucia, but we asked her not to mention it. She's keeping Bedj-ka home from school for now so he doesn't accidentally tell someone there."

"That's a relief," Wanda said. "We need to decide

how best to break this. God, Senator—this is just what we need to raise your polls."

"Raise her polls?" Ben said. "What do you mean?"

Petrie smiled at him with neat white teeth. "If your grandmother is the one to break the news that the Dream is returning to normal, Ben, what do you think it'll do for her popularity? This is a godsend!"

"But it has nothing to do with the issues surrounding the election," Ben protested.

"Of course not. But issues aside, elections are nothing more than popularity contests." Petrie's eyes sparkled. "We can promote her as the senator who restored the Dream. The voters will eat it up!"

"Even though it was Kendi who figured it out," Keith said.

Petrie brushed this aside. "Kendi works for her campaign, so it's the same thing."

"Why did you sense it and no one else, Kendi?" Salman asked, changing the subject.

Kendi shrugged. "I've always been good at sensing Silent and tracking people in the Dream. The Despair didn't change that. Other Silent will probably start to notice the kids, though. Within a couple of weeks, I should think."

"Give me two days, Senator," Petrie said, all but glowing with fervor. "That'll let us double-check the information and set up a proper news conference. In a few months, you'll be sitting in the governor's seat."

"Do it," Salman said. "Let's show Foxglove and Ched-Pirasku how to run a real campaign."

Salman swore everyone to secrecy one more time before she let them leave. Her expression was so serious, Kendi half expected her to ask for pricked fingers and dripping blood, though he kept the comment to himself. Wanda Petrie's training in evidence.

Keith and Martina headed toward the monastery— "Some of us have to work for a living," Keith said— while Ben and Kendi took Salman's flitcar to the medical center to check on Lucia. Gretchen, who had remained on outdoor guard duty during the meeting, piloted while

Tan rode shotgun. Kendi sat in the back seat with Ben, trying to assimilate everything that was going on. So much so fast! Kendi had just signed a lucrative sim-game contract based on his life during the Despair, he and Ben were going to be fathers of two children—assuming Lucia didn't lose this one—and now the Silent were re-entering the Dream. Kendi felt restless, like a lion in a cage. He didn't want to be riding in this flitcar high above the trees. He wanted to be running through the streets, his feet pounding the boards and making the balconies tremble like the mickey spikes. Ben touched his hand and squeezed it, reading his mood and knowing the cause. Kendi gave him a wan smile but felt a little better.

When they arrived at the medical center, they found a small crowd of people in Lucia's room. She lay propped up in bed amid a veritable forest of flowers, balloons, and stuffed animals. Several dozen photographs and holograms covered every inch of wall space, and someone had set up a small altar in the corner. From it, a figurine of Irfan Qasad gazed serenely about the room.

"What the hell?" Kendi said.

A tall, dark man with silvering hair the same color as Lucia's stepped forward with outstretched hand. "Father Kendi Weaver! I've been wanting to meet you for a long time! But does my daughter arrange an introduction? Does she let me meet the great man whose baby she will bear? Or does she let her poor old father languish in—"

"Dad!" Lucia protested from the bed. "Don't let him bully you, Kendi. He'll talk until your ears fall off if you let him."

"Someone who can outtalk Kendi," Ben said. "Pretty impressive."

"You must be Ben Rymar," said a nearby woman who resembled a heavier, slightly tired version of Lucia. She leaned in to kiss his cheek. "I suppose this makes you my son-in-law, in a way. I should be happy—it's better than no son-in-law at all."

"Hey!" called a young man from one corner. "What do I look like? Pastrami on rye?"

"You married my oldest," Lucia's mother replied primly. "It's different when it's your youngest."

"Mom!" Lucia warned.

"Do you know all these people, Ms. dePaolo?" Tan demanded from the doorway.

"They're all family," Lucia said. "They're fine." Gretchen and Tan withdrew to the hallway, looking grateful for the chance to escape.

Introductions went around. The only names Kendi remembered were Alberto and Julia, Lucia's parents. The rest were a tangle of brothers, sisters, and cousins, all with the same glossy black hair, olive skin, and brown eyes. They sat on the floor, leaned against the walls, and perched on the edge of Lucia's bed.

"The nurse tried to throw us all out, if you can believe that," Alberto said. "Imagine! We're her *family*, and they try to throw us out on the streets like yesterday's trash."

"You are a little loud, Dad," Lucia pointed out.

"Loud with love," he said, and kissed her loudly on the top of the head. "The best healing there is!"

"Dr. McCall says the baby is just fine, by the way," Lucia said. "I'm allowed out of bed now, but the doctor wants to keep me here for another day just to be sure."

Kendi exhaled heavily, and he felt a load of tension drain from him. Ben looked even more relieved.

"So tell me more about my new grandchild," Julia said.

"Grandchild?" Kendi said.

"Of course!" Julia said. "My daughter is going to give birth to it. That makes it my grandchild, and don't you dare forget it."

"You have six grandchildren, Mom," Lucia said.

"Which doesn't make this one any less precious," Julia said firmly. "But I want to know where this baby came from."

"I hope I don't need to explain *that* to you," Alberto said, squeezing Julia's arm.

She made a playful slap at him. "You know what I mean. Lucia says it isn't her place to tell, so that means someone else has to."

A moment of silence fell over the room, and every

eye turned toward Kendi and Ben. Kendi's glance went irresistibly to the altar. Irfan looked serenely back at him. In one hand she bore a scroll, symbol of communication. Her other hand was raised in a beckoning gesture. A DNA matrix wound around the arm. Kendi realized the silence was stretching out a bit too long.

Finally Ben spoke. "My mo—" his voice cracked, and he cleared his throat. "My mother found these embryos on an abandoned ship several hundred light years from Bellerophon. She took one for her own—me—and gave the others to Grandfather Melthine at the monastery. He and my mother died during the Despair, so I sort of kept the others. Genetically they're my brothers and sisters, but Kendi and I want to raise them as our children. Silent babies don't survive in artificial wombs, so Lucia agreed to help us."

"The bright lady has blessed our family," said a cousin. What was her name? Franca? Francesca. It was Francesca. "Will you be raising the child in the precepts of the Church of Irfan, Father Kendi?"

Kendi blinked. "We . . . we haven't thought that far ahead."

"But you must," she insisted. "Irfan looks after all children, but the Silent ones are her special province, and they must come to bosom of the Church, especially now that Vik has destroyed the Dream."

"Vik?" Ben said. "But Padric Sufur was the one who—"

"The evil Vik worked his will through Sufur," Francesca said. "There is no doubt. Vik taints us all, Mr. Rymar. His evil is everywhere, and we must work hard to stamp it out. That is why we fight poverty and homelessness in the name of the Church—the poor and homeless are more susceptible to Vik's wicked—"

"Thank you, Francesca," Lucia said. "We all serve the Church in our own way. I've chosen this one." She rubbed her stomach. "I think I need to rest now."

"Everyone out," Alberto ordered. "She needs her rest. Out!"

Everyone duly filed out of the room, though each person paused to give Lucia a kiss or a hug. Ben and Kendi were the last.

"Thank you for coming," Lucia said when they were alone. "I know my family can be a bit . . . overwhelming, but they mean well."

"I suppose they should be part of the child's life," Kendi said. "I hadn't thought of that. Harenn has only Bedj-ka, but in your case . . ."

"I have an entire clan," Lucia finished with a small smile.

"What about the religious side?" Ben said. "Everything happened so fast that we didn't have time to talk about it."

"Do you object to the child being raised by the precepts of Irfan?" Lucia asked. Her hand went to the Irfan figurine around her neck.

"I hadn't thought about it either way," Ben admitted. "It's just . . ." He lowered his voice. "They worship my *mother*. And Irfan is also this child's mother. Isn't that just a little . . . strange?"

" 'The universe is stranger than the Dream,' " Lucia said. "Irfan's precepts and teachings are fine rules to live by, Ben. She teaches us to love and tolerate one another while we seek inner strength and serenity."

"They're good teachings," Ben said. "And I don't object to them. I just don't know how to go about it."

"I will handle that," Lucia said. "Besides, we are not one of the more extreme sects of the Church, no matter what Francesca might sound like."

"Let's go, Ben," Kendi said. "She does need to rest."

They found Lucia's family just down the hallway in a small waiting area that smelled of stale donuts. They were arguing heatedly about something. Kendi gave Ben a look. Gretchen and Tan pointedly kept their distance.

"I don't see how she can go through with it," Francesca was saying. "Not without a guarantee from the fathers that the child will be raised properly in the Church. It scares me that they might grow up ignorant of Irfan's precepts."

"It's their decision," said someone Kendi couldn't see. "Lucia is just the vessel, not the mother."

The sound of a slap. "Ow! What was that for?"

"You say such terrible things!" came Julia's aghast voice. "Of *course* Lucia's the mother, just as Mother Ara was Ben's mother. And we can't force anyone to embrace the Church. Irfan would frown on such a thing. But we can still—"

"Father Kendi!" Alberto said, suddenly noticing him standing in the doorway. Julia cut herself off. "Come in, come in."

"We were just heading home," Kendi said, "now that we know Lucia and the baby are all right."

"Good, good," Alberto said. "We will be seeing much more of each other, eh? Now that you two are the fathers of Lucia's child."

"This is getting more complicated by the second," Ben said when they were out of earshot. "How are we going to handle this? I hadn't even occurred to me that Lucia's family might want to get involved with our child. Children."

Kendi shrugged. "Legally they have no claim, so it'll be completely up to us how involved they are. We can work it out as we go, but I'm thinking the more babysitters we have on tap, the better."

Ben laughed, but it sounded a bit forced.

They exited the medical center and walked a ways in silence, Tan and Gretchen following a bit behind. It was still cloudy outside, and the light lay heavy with gloom beneath the trees. Kendi smelled rain coming. After a while they passed a playground on a wide platform. A trio of children were jumping rope, and they chanted with every jump.

Miss Irfan married Danny, and Danny went insane.
He stole her wealth and children, he ruined her good name.
He ran away to Othertown and tried to start a war.
He met up with some Silent and killed them by the score.
How many Silent did Dan Vik kill? One, two, three,
  four . . .

Kendi looked at them as he passed. He had heard the rhyme a thousand times but hadn't really paid close attention to it until now. A little gory. He supposed that's what made it attractive to children.

"Do you think I'm evil?" Ben asked abruptly. "Or that I'll go insane?"

"What?" Kendi started. "No! Why on earth would you think such a thing?"

Ben shrugged. "Daniel Vik was my father, and like those kids said, he went insane."

"Not all historians agree with that assessment," Kendi said. "And anyway, you're you. Not Daniel Vik and not Irfan Qasad. Ben Rymar."

"Insanity is sometimes inherited," Ben insisted.

"No risk factors showed up on the genetic scans," Kendi said. "Did your doctor ever say anything?"

"No," Ben admitted.

"There you go."

"It's still creepy," Ben said gloomily. "My dad was a genocidal maniac, and my mother was a saint, and they both died a thousand years ago."

"It's probably for the best that they're dead," Kendi said. "I mean, imagine what it would be like for me if they were still alive."

"For you?"

"Sure. Irfan Qasad as my mother-in-law. I'd *never* get the house clean enough for her to visit."

This time Ben's laugh was real. In the middle of it, Kendi's data pad beeped, and a message flashed across his ocular implant.

"Whoops," Kendi said. "I forgot—we were supposed to meet Keith for some male bonding time today."

"Who's we?" Ben said.

"I made the invitation on both our behalf," Kendi said, "and then forgot to tell you about it. Can you come? Please? I'm trying to bring Keith out of his blue funk. We're going to take part in an ancient Australian Aborigine ritual."

"What ritual would that be?" Ben asked warily.

"Drinking our lunch. Come on."

Kendi told Tan and Gretchen what was going on, and the women continued following the two men. The four of them made their way across several walkways, down a pair of staircases, and along a public promenade. Multiple shops, stores, and restaurants were stacked on top of one another in the trees, connected by lifts and stairs. Several of the shops were boarded up, and only a handful of humans and Ched-Balaar browsed among the open ones. Panhandlers sat among the dead, damp leaves that littered the walkways, begging from passersby in dull, monotonous voices. Eventually, Kendi caught sight of Keith, who was wandering aimlessly back and forth on a narrow rope-and-plank bridge between two balconies. His hands were in his pockets. Every few moments he glanced at his fingernails, checking the time. Kendi called his name and waved, but Keith continued pacing.

"He can't hear me," Kendi said, heading for the bridge.

"Funny. Everyone else did," Ben grumbled.

Keith had his back to them and had reached the other side of the bridge. Kendi trotted ahead of Ben to catch up to his brother. He was halfway across the bridge when a shower of wood chips cascaded over him, and he smelled something burning. A terrible cracking noise groaned above him. Kendi glanced up and saw a branch the size of a support beam rushing toward him. Then something hit him, and he was flying through the air. He landed hard. All the air burst from his lungs, and his head smacked something solid. A tremendous crash tore the air. Several people screamed, and the noise mingled with panicked Ched-Balaar hooting. Kendi lay stunned for a moment, then sat up.

He was lying on the platform he had been trying to reach. Behind him lay a torn bridge and a stomach-turning drop. Gretchen was stretched out at the rim of the platform. The lower half of her body hung over the edge, and she was clawing at the remaining boards in an attempt to regain solid planking. Her face was pale. Kendi scrambled over to help her, trying to ignore the pounding in his head. He seized her arm and helped her up.

"Are you all right?" he demanded.

"I'm fine," she said. "You?"

"My head's going to ring for a while, but I'll survive. What happened?"

"That." Gretchen pointed up. A bare spot in the talltree above showed where the branch had broken off. It had fallen onto the bridge and demolished it. A raw stump showed pale wood. Kendi looked down and saw the wreckage of a second bridge. Far below, he could just make out the branch lying on the forest floor. From here it looked like a twig.

"I saw the branch start to go," Gretchen continued, "and shoved you. It almost got me."

"Kendi!" Keith said behind him. "God, are you—?"

"I'm fine. We're fine." Kendi scrambled to his feet, his heart suddenly pounding hard. "All life! Where's Ben? And Lewa?"

"You're welcome," Gretchen said.

Kendi caught sight of Ben and Tan on the other side of the bridge. He waved at them and activated his earpiece.

"I'm all right," he said before either of them could answer. "Gretchen saved me."

"I'll give her a raise," Tan said. *"Wait right there. We've already called the Guardians."*

"I can't breathe," Ben said. *"God, are you* sure *you're all right, Kendi? When that branch fell—"*

"Don't go all panicky, Ben," Kendi said. "Gretchen said she'd protect me, and she did. Everything's fine."

"Not until I get over there, it isn't."

Ben and Tan circled around on another bridge and arrived on Kendi's platform at about the same time the Guardians did. A mixed crowd gathered in the meantime, but fortunately no one seemed to have been hurt. The lower bridge had been unoccupied when the branch hit. Keith stared over the edge into the hole as if transfixed. Kendi had a sudden fear that Keith was planning to jump, and he pulled Keith away.

"We don't want another accident," he muttered.

"Why do you have wood chips in your hair?" Keith asked.

"Father Kendi?" It was a Ched-Balaar who wore a blue head cloth on her head and a silver medallion around her neck. Silver for Guardians. "I'm Inspector Ched-Theree. If you and your companions could answer some questions?"

Kendi went off with her alone except for Lewa Tan, who refused to leave his side. Gretchen stayed with Ben. Ched-Theree's first question, of course, was "What hap-

pened?" Kendi explained events as best he could remember, and it was during the retelling that he
remembered the chips falling on him from above.

"Our technicians are inspecting the branch and keeping me updated by vocal transmission," Ched-Theree
clattered. "They are nowhere near finished, but they tell
me even a novice could see this event was planned. Preliminary examination leads them to think some sort of
directional incendiary device cut through the branch."

"An explosive?" Kendi said.

Ched-Theree ducked her head in acknowledgment.
"One whose force went entirely inward, toward the
wood. This rendered the explosion nearly silent so you
would not hear it and be warned."

"All life."

"Furthermore," Ched-Theree continued, pressing a
hand to the side of her head and listening, "the explosive
was set of by remote control, not a timer. In other
words, your potential killer was watching while it happened." She paused. "Father Kendi, who knew you
would be in this place at this time?"

Kendi's mouth was dry. "I'm not sure. Me. Ben.
Keith. Maybe my sister Martina, if Keith told her.
Lewa Tan and Gretchen knew, but I only mentioned
it to them just before we headed over. They couldn't
have told anyone in time for them to set up a . . . a
trap like this."

"We will, of course, speak with Mr. Rymar and
Brother Keith," Ched-Theree said.

"It wasn't them," Kendi said hotly.

"They may have spoken to someone about your meeting, Father Kendi," Ched-Theree said. "And we must
speak with all those involved in any case. They may have
seen something important."

"Right." Kendi rubbed a tired hand across his face.

"The Guardians have been reading the death threats
you forward to us," Ched-Theree continued. "Our psy-
chologists have so far informed us that the senders are
ultimately harmless, though we shall certainly look at them
more closely. Do you have other enemies, Father?"

"A long list, I'm afraid," Kendi said ruefully. "I've
stolen slaves from half the slavers in this part of the

galaxy. I'm sure they'd love to see me squashed under something heavy. And I've been campaigning for Senator Reza lately, so one of her enemies might want to see me dead. More recently a bunch of us really pissed off a whole truckload of people at Silent Acquisitions when we destroyed one of their pet projects. Maybe they hired an assassin."

"We can narrow the field," Tan said, "by taking into account who knew you'd be on that bridge at that particular time. When did you contact Keith to set up the meeting time?"

"Two days ago," Kendi said. "I sent him a text message and he replied the same way. Ben keeps my messages scrambled better than a chef's eggs, though, so I can't imagine anyone would have intercepted my mail."

"Whom did you tell you were meeting your brother?" Ched-Theree asked again. "Please consider carefully."

Kendi thought. "No one I haven't already mentioned. I didn't even write it on my calendar—just set my message program to remind me of it in case I forgot, which I did."

Ched-Theree had Kendi go over the events leading up to the attack twice more before Kendi finally begged off, pleading hunger and fatigue.

"Very well," Ched-Theree said. "I will give you my contact codes. If you remember anything, anything at all, let me know immediately, even if it is the middle of the night."

To this Kendi agreed. He turned to leave—

—and found himself facing a phalanx of reporters. "Father Kendi, can you comment on what happened here today?" "Father Kendi, was this an assassination attempt?" "Father Kendi, what impact do you think this will have on Senator Reza's foundering campaign?" "Father Kendi—" "Father Kendi—" "Father Kendi—"

Kendi blinked at them. He had been concentrating so hard on his report to Ched-Theree that he hadn't even noticed their arrival. A holographic "Keep Out—Guardian Scene" border hastily erected by the uniformed Guardians had kept them out of Kendi's face, but now they were blocking the only bridge leading away from the crime scene.

"Father Kendi has no comment for you vultures," Tan bellowed. "Now move, it or I'll move you!"

Gretchen, Keith, and Ben appeared, released by their own inquisitive inspectors, and they joined with Tan to form a wedge that plowed through the crowd with Kendi in the middle. Free-floating microphones buzzed and flitted around his head as the reporters continued calling out questions.

"Father Kendi, who wants to kill you?" "Father Kendi, was this more than just an accident?" "Father Kendi, can you comment on the recent lifting of the mining restrictions?" "Father Kendi—" "Father Kendi—" "Father Kendi—"

Kendi felt his shoulder and neck muscles tighten like screws. He didn't need this right now. He wanted to shout at them to leave him alone, to stop taking his picture and quit their questions. But he said nothing, forcing himself to move at Tan's pace. Twice she shoved aside a reporter who refused to give ground. Gretchen, meanwhile, tripped a human and elbowed a Ched-Balaar hard in the ribs. Ben raised a fist to one man, who shied away when he saw the thick muscle in Ben's upper arm.

Finally they broke free of the crowd. They trotted across a bridge with the reporters in hot pursuit. Once Kendi reached the other side, Tan turned and blocked the end of the bridge. She drew her pistol.

"Go the fuck away," she growled.

"You won't shoot us," one of the front-runners said.

In answer, Tan aimed at one of the four support ropes holding up the bridge. There was a flash of light, and the rope thumped to the wood like a dead snake. The bridge swayed. Tan aimed at a second rope. As one, the reporters turned and fled.

"Nice," Keith said.

"Let's move," Tan said.

"You wouldn't have cut the bridge out from under them," Ben said.

Tan shrugged. "The safety net beneath would catch them. One or two would have broken something, I'm sure. Would've been fun to see."

They made it back home without further incident.

Harenn was waiting for them, and she gave Kendi an uncharacteristic hug.

"The story has already flooded the newsfeeds," she said. "I am glad to see you well."

"Someone got the whole thing on holo," Bedj-ka reported. "It was rigid! Gretchen shoved you aside just like an action hero!"

"Wait until the sim-game comes out, kid," Gretchen said. "I get to be a fighter *and* a lover."

"Someone got it on holo?" Kendi asked. "Who?"

"Some woman who happened to be taking images of her kids," Bedj-ka said. "It was—"

"Can you show it to me?" Kendi said. "It might have a clue."

This hadn't occurred to Bedj-ka. He scampered over to the coffee table and snatched up his data pad like a wriggling puppy that had just discovered a way to please its master. A few taps brought up a newsfeed hologram.

The image was wobbly, clearly amateur. Two human children, age four or five, both blond with green eyes, waved at a camera. Kendi saw himself in the background starting to cross the bridge. Gretchen came a few paces behind. Keith stood on the other side with his back to Kendi and his hands in his pockets. The little boy reached behind his sister's head and made a rude gesture. A female voice from behind the camera admonished him. Kendi reached the halfway point of the bridge, and a flash of light flared from the talltree just above and behind him. Gretchen glanced upward and flung herself forward at Kendi, who was just noticing the shower of wood chips. The heavy branch above was already falling. Gretchen connected, and both she and Kendi went flying. Kendi landed on the platform beyond the bridge just as the branch crashed like a falling giant onto the bridge. It plunged downward out of sight without even slowing. The safety net beneath was ripped to shreds like an old spiderweb. Screams erupted all around the shopping area. Gretchen was lying with the lower half her body on the bridge as it collapsed, and she scrabbled madly at the platform to avoid following the branch down to the forest floor. Kendi turned, looking dazed, saw Gretchen, and pulled her to safety. The holo ended. A newscaster appeared and went into a report about a monk who had gone missing and left a suicide note. The Guardians were searching for the body. Kendi switched it off.

"We have to send that recording to Inspector Ched-Theree," Ben said. "If she hasn't seen it already."

Kendi reset the recording and watched it again. This time he scanned the crowd, looking for familiar faces. The boy and girl, unfortunately, were much in the way, and once the tree branch fell, the view became even more wobbly as the woman behind the camera became agitated. Maybe the Guardians would see something. He sent a copy to Inspector Ched-Theree and watched the holo one more time. And once more. Then one more time again.

Eventually Ben and Harenn dragged him away and forced him to eat something. Keith had gone home. Tan announced that she wanted to look at the recording and absconded with the data pad after shooting Ben a pointed look. Ben plunked down on the sofa next to Kendi, who raised his hands.

"I surrender," he said.

"Surrender?"

"Lewa wants you to distract me from staring at the holo too much. I'm no match for the pair of you, so I surrender." He rolled his head. "And I'm getting a crick in my neck. That, in case you missed it, was a hint."

Ben gave a lopsided grin and reached around to massage Kendi's neck with warm hands. "Let the Guardians and the police handle this one," he said. "It's their job, not yours. Lewa, Gretchen, and I will keep you safe, all right?"

His hands moved lower over Kendi's back, and Kendi felt his muscles turning to butter. "All right. But wouldn't it be better to do this where I could lie down?"

In the bedroom, Ben continued working on Kendi's tense body. He groaned under Ben's talented hands and felt his worries ease. Other people could handle the problems. He didn't have to solve everything personally. Maybe just for today he could let everything slide, and in the morning everything would look better.

*   *   *

In the morning, Wanda Petrie stormed into the house before Ben and Kendi could even finish breakfast. Her clothes were wrinkled, and her hair looked windblown, as if she had flown in through a hurricane.

"It wasn't her fault," she burst out. "God, she didn't even *know*."

"Who didn't know what?" Kendi asked. Tension snapped his muscles taut again. "Wanda, calm down. You aren't making sense."

"Have some tea," Ben said, emptying the morning pot into a clean cup. "It's raspberry."

"Thank you." Petrie gulped down a mouthful and visibly composed herself. "Foxglove is going to break the news this afternoon. It turns out . . . turns out . . . god, I can't even say it."

"What, for heaven's sake?" Kendi said. "Just blurt it out."

"One of the senator's primary contributors has connections with a known crime syndicate," Petrie said. Her eyes were rimmed with red. "It's as if she's been taking money from gangsters. God, we had no idea. None!"

"Shit," Ben said. "Grandma knows *crooks*?"

"That's the whole point, Ben—she *didn't* know. Do you think if we had any inkling that we'd've taken the contribution? But it's too late."

"Who is it?" Kendi asked.

"A man named Willen Yaraye. He's been brought up on charges of racketeering, embezzlement, money laundering, and half a dozen other 'enterprises.' We've been up all night trying to deal with it. I had to get away for a while and found myself at your doorstep." She pulled a handkerchief from her pocket and wiped her face with it. "There isn't really anything the two of you can do, I'm afraid. I'm sorry to have bothered you."

"We needed to know," Kendi said, "and you needed to unload. Look, this Yaraye bloke has only been charged. He may not be guilty."

"Oh, he's guilty all right." Petrie blew her nose. "The senator used her connections to get information on the prosecution's case, and there's no doubt. It'll be a long, nasty trial, and you may be sure that the senator will be dragged through it. There's already talk of investigating her campaign as a money laundering organization."

"Has it been used that way?" Kendi asked. "The truth, please."

Petrie shook her head. "Not that I know of. Yaraye made his donations, ate at several fund-raising dinners, attended a few parties, and that was the end of the senator's involvement with him. In retrospect I think he was using her to make connections with other government officials. God, this is a disaster!"

"What about the news about Silent children coming back into the Dream?" Ben asked. "Once Grandma reveals that, no one'll even remember something as petty as a crooked donor."

"We've talked about that," Petrie said. "And the senator thinks the same way. That's why she's decided to break the news today instead of tomorrow. We aren't fully prepared, but we've no other choice." She sighed and gave Ben a wan smile. "And if that doesn't restore her, I suppose I still have a trick or two left."

"How did you learn all this publicity stuff, anyway?" Kendi asked curiously. "Bellerophon hasn't had a gubernatorial election since it joined the Independence Confederation."

"Research," she said succinctly. "Lots and lots of research. And I seem to have a talent for publicity. I love doing it. Or I did."

Ben patted her hand. "It'll be fine. The Silent children will wipe out everyone's objections, you watch."

"They'd better. Otherwise we're sunk. And I can't let her lose. I *won't* let her lose." Petrie drained her cup and rose. "Thanks for listening, gentlemen. Watch the feeds today. We're going to make history."

And she left. Kendi flung himself backward against his chair. "What a start to the day. If I ever complain about being bored, I want you to slap me hard."

"Want to go over to Grandma's house to watch the feeds?" Ben said. "It'll be more interesting. Lewa will like it—more guards over there."

Kendi shrugged. "Sure. Do you think there'll be food involved? The cupboards are empty again."

*   *   *

Sister Reeta Gerrold checked her fingernail for the time, swore, and tried to hurry. It would be the third time this week if she were late, and although there was no way she could be fired, it wasn't fair to the others coming off-shift. She rounded a corner and came to a halt. The double-wide walkway over to the monastery's main communication building was crammed with demonstrators, both human and Ched-Balaar. Signs bobbed up and down. CHED-PIRASKU #1! CHED-BALAAR SUPPORT CHED-PIRASKU! ONE PLANET, ONE PEOPLE! IRFAN CALLED FOR MODERATION!

"Shit," she said. "How am I going to get through all that?"

At the forefront of the demonstration stood a dark-haired man. He was leading a chant for the humans while the Ched-Balaar in the crowd provided percussion. Reeta made an exasperated noise. She had to get in to work. As one of the few Silent Children left, she helped keep the monastery afloat, if only barely. Now these idiots were—

Something thumped against the back of her neck. Reeta turned and caught a glimpse of a dark-haired woman before the drug took effect and the political chants faded into darkness.

Salman's house was a beehive when Kendi and Ben arrived with Tan and Gretchen in tow. People rushed in and out carrying packages and data pads. A harried-looking house servant showed them in, and Salman immediately set them to work assembling "personal" messages to send the other campaign donors.

"You'll be earning your lunch," she said. "And don't stray too far, Kendi Weaver. I'll need you close by as my confirmation when I make my speech this evening about the children. Petrie will brief you on what to say."

Kendi almost made a smart remark, then changed his mind. Salman's face was lined and heavy, as if the earth itself were dragging at her. Rather than add to her tension, he merely smiled and nodded.

Once she was out of earshot, Ben said, "Sorry. I should've realized it wouldn't be interesting in a good way."

"I'll collect later," Kendi said wryly.

The house was filled with noise. Data pads chimed, people chattered, and Ched-Balaar clattered. Servants dashed around handing out snacks and drinks. Kendi found a quiet corner where he and Ben could work on Salman's messages. A few hours later, two servants set up a food table. Everyone filled plates or trenchers, depending upon species, but none of them paused in their working to eat. Kendi alternated computer work with bites of sandwich.

"He is on now," Ched-Tumaar announced. Kendi turned in time to see a giant hologram of Mitchell Foxglove pop up in the center of the enormous living room. The noise stopped and everyone watched. Kendi swallowed a bite of bread and ham.

"It has come to my attention," Foxglove said, *"that a human named Willen Yaraye has been arrested on several charges relating to organized crime. This in itself is a remarkable event—Bellerophon was not known for its organized crime before the Despair. But more remarkable still is the fact that this alleged criminal has donated hundreds of thousands of freemarks to the campaign of my worthy opponent, Senator Salman Reza."*

Across the room, Salman closed her eyes, then opened them and set her mouth hard.

"I want it known here and now," Foxglove continued, *"that the charges against Mr. Yaraye have not yet been proven, and I would not in any way want the fact that he donated heavily to Senator Reza to besmirch her campaign. The charges may be mistaken or false, and even if they are true, it doesn't necessarily follow that the senator knew anything about his alleged criminal dealings. After all, it takes a lot of time to run a major campaign, and Senator Reza couldn't possibly follow everything that happens right under her nose."*

"Bastard," spat Petrie. "He's damning the senator with praise. He knows the media will crucify her while his mealymouthed words make him sound like he tried to stop them."

"Shush!" Salman said.

"However, I don't come before you today with nothing but bad news," Foxglove said with a wide smile. *"I have great and wonderful news as well. I'm sure everyone will be happy to hear that—yes, it's absolutely true—that Silent children are once again entering the Dream."*

CHAPTER TEN

"Cooking may be chemistry, but it's no fun to eat a chemistry experiment."

—Irfan Qasad

The house was absolutely still. No one moved, or even breathed. Then a roar crashed through the room as everyone talked, clattered, hooted, and chattered at once. Kendi swore. Ben stared with open mouth. Petrie gesticulated madly at Ched-Tumaar and shouted something incoherent. Tan and Gretchen watched from the walls, looking unhappy.

"QUIET!"

Everyone froze again. Salman stood tall and terrible in the middle of the room, her face a thunderhead. The hologram of Foxglove continued to speak, though the sound had been muted.

"How did he find out?" Salman demanded. *"How*?"

No one answered. The room remained frozen like a stage tableau. Kendi swallowed. It didn't take a political analyst to figure out that Salman's plan to distract the public from her criminal donor lay in ruins. If Salman publicly claimed that she also had known about children reentering the Dream, it would look like desperate whining. Salman would have to answer to Foxglove's charges on her own, with nothing to back her up.

The silence continued. Finally Salman sank down into a chair and covered her face with her hands. The tableau broke, and everyone started talking again. Petrie snatched up a data pad and pecked madly at it. Ben crossed the room and knelt by his grandmother's chair with her hand in his. Kendi was struck at how alike they looked. It wasn't so much a physical resemblance as a similarity in posture and expression. They both resembled Ara.

After a while, Salman gave a heavy sigh. Ben released her hand, and she stood up with a resolute look on her face. "Conference!" she said. "Top five in my office."

Petrie, Ched-Tumaar, Yin May, and two other people Kendi didn't recognize followed Salman into her office. They shut the door. In the living room, various hushed conversations continued. Ben came back to Kendi.

"We should probably get out of the way," he said. "I'm sure she'll call soon and have some speaking engagements for you."

"Let's go," Kendi agreed.

No one spoke on the monorail ride home. Kendi wore sunglasses and a hat to remain more anonymous, though Gretchen and Tan remained vigilant. Their eyes darted about without stopping, examining this human, that Ched-Balaar. Kendi stared out the window at the blur of leaves and branches that currently resembled his life. Lucia was pregnant, he had discovered Silent children reentering the Dream, a scandal had broken within Salman's campaign, and Mitchell Foxglove had somehow managed to usurp her possession of Kendi's secret.

Kendi tapped long fingers on his knee. How *had* Foxglove learned about that? Modesty aside, Kendi had never met another Silent who could sense and track people in the Dream nearly as well as Kendi himself could. That didn't mean one didn't exist, but in the post-Despair Dream? He doubted it. Kendi himself would have sensed such a person. Besides, Foxglove was publicly against the mixing of Silent and non-Silent and had no Silent working for him. That meant Foxglove had gotten his information from a different source. So, who had known?

Kendi himself, of course. Martina and Keith. Ben. Harenn and Bedj-ka. Salman. Wanda Petrie. And various people within Salman's campaign circle. A lot of people, come to that, but no one who would blab. No one who—

Kendi sat up straight. It was obvious—Foxglove had planted a spy inside Salman's campaign. But who was it? Kendi grimaced. That was a question more easily answered by Salman herself. Kendi only knew a few of the people who worked for her. She and her Top Five were in a better position to ferret something out. He would have to send her a message—if she hadn't already come up with the idea herself.

When they arrived home, Harenn was waiting for them. Her middle was well-rounded these days, and the sight always made Kendi's heart swell with fatherly anticipation. Was the baby a boy or a girl? Would it look a lot like Ben? What would the baby's personality be? Would Kendi be able to cope with the pressures of parenthood? One way or another, he was going to find out. Twice over—Lucia was there as well, though she wasn't showing, of course. Her face wore a solemn look.

"We saw Foxglove's speech," she said. "Council of war?"

"Council of war," Kendi agreed.

They gathered around the kitchen table. Lucia took up her usual position at the counter, busily chopping sharp-smelling herbs she had bought that morning. When Harenn asked her to sit down, she shook her head. Cooking, she claimed, helped her to think better.

"And I want you to know," she added, "that I don't intend to do this full-time for a huge household. Ben and Kendi are going to take lessons."

"From who?" Kendi asked, trying to imagine the logistics behind enrolling in a cooking class with bodyguards and a full schedule of speeches.

"From me." Her gleaming knife whacked the stems off a bunch of greens. "Which means you'll pay *very* close attention."

"What do we need to talk about?" Ben asked. "Best to go about it methodically."

"Two issues," Kendi said. "Who's trying to kill me, and who's the spy in Grandma's campaign."

"Spy?" Harenn asked.

Kendi quickly outlined his thinking. Harenn pursed her lips. "I am not entirely sure of your reasoning. A great many people knew this so-called secret, Kendi, and it is likely that someone accidentally revealed it."

"I thought about that," Kendi agreed. "But there's

another factor—why was *Foxglove* the one to get the information? If one of us had said something by accident, it's way more likely the information would've reached a reporter before it reached Foxglove. And what reporter wouldn't kill to break *that* story?"

"True," Harenn said, drawing out the word. "But I remain skeptical."

"We also have no idea who killed Finn and Helen Day," Lucia said, "or if their deaths are related to everything else that's going on."

Kendi drummed his fingers some more. "All my instincts say there's a connection here. We're just not seeing it."

"The fact is," Ben said, "we just don't have enough information. We have no idea who murdered the Days. Just about anyone could be a spy in Grandma's campaign. And lots of people would love to see Kendi dead."

"Oh, thank you."

Lucia got out a loaf of bread, a bowl of butter, two tomatoes, and a wedge of cheese. Her knife went back to work.

"What do all these elements have in common?" Harenn asked. "A single common vector would—"

"Who are the Days?" Tan rasped.

Silence. Lucia's knife stopped moving. Kendi bit his lip. He had gotten so used to Tan and Gretchen following him around that he had completely forgotten that they didn't know about Lucia's illicit visit to the Days' house and what she had found there.

"Are the Days connected with the attack on Lucia?" Tan continued. "Lars told me about that, but he didn't have details."

"You're holding out on us, Kendi," Gretchen said. "Come on—give. We might be able to help."

Kendi glanced at Ben. His lips were set in a hard line, and he shook his head the tiniest bit possible—*No way can you tell them.* Kendi grimaced—*We have to tell them something.* Ben spread his hands—*Just the minimum, then.* Who needed the Dream when you had private body language?

"The Days were the blackmailers," Kendi said. "Ben

and Lucia tracked them down and learned that Finn Day had a connection to Foxglove and the Federalists. Lucia . . . paid them a visit."

"Broke in, you mean," Gretchen said.

"She found the file the Days were threatening us with," Kendi said. "She also found their corpses."

"Murdered," Tan said.

"The bodies were still warm," Lucia said. She finished slicing tomatoes and went to work on the bread with a serrated knife. "I think the killer was trying to access their computer. I came in and frightened him or her away without realizing it. I downloaded the file, saw the bodies, and fled. On the way home I was accosted by a beggar. A few minutes later, someone hit me over the head and took the disk with the file on it. We were afraid the blackmail would start up again, but three months have gone by, and we haven't heard a thing. The mugger probably doesn't know what was on the disk or can't understand the information. At any rate, we believe we're safe."

"Unless the killer was the one who hit you," Gretchen said.

Lucia blinked. Kendi stared at her.

"It would've been easy enough for the person to wait outside the Days' house," Gretchen continued. "In fact, it would make sense. The killer wanted something from that computer. Lucia may have scared the person into getting the hell out of the house, but a smart guy would hang around and wait for you to leave because he still needs that file. He—I'm gonna assume it's a he—sneaks back into the house, discovers the file is gone, and figures you have it. He runs after you, coshes you, and takes the disk."

"But how would he know where to find me?" Lucia objected. "The beggar girl delayed me, but not for long. By the time the killer got in and out of the house, I would have been well away. I was almost back at Ben and Kendi's house when I was mugged, in fact. The killer couldn't possibly have followed me."

"You're assuming," Tan rasped, "that the killer didn't know where you were going."

"How could he know that?" Ben said.

"He would know where to go," Harenn spoke up, "if he recognized Lucia."

Kendi's blood chilled. "The Days' killer is someone we know," he said. "All life!"

"This theory doesn't hold up," Ben objected. "The file is only valuable to me or to someone who might want to blackmail me, and no one has contacted us about it. Why go through all that trouble to steal a file and then not use it?"

"I don't know," Tan admitted. "But you have to consider that possibility."

Ben dropped his head into his hands. "The blackmail might start up again, then. God."

Kendi leveled Tan a harsh look. He wanted to hit her. It had taken weeks to persuade Ben that the file was gone, that no one was going to blackmail them or reveal the secret of his parentage, that he could sleep at night without worrying. Tan had raked it all up again.

"Ben," she said as gently as her raspy voice would allow, "you can tell me what's in the file. I'm not going to judge you, and the information might give us a clue to—"

"No."

"Ben—"

"I said *no*," Ben snarled. "And if you ask again, you're *fired*, got that?"

Tan's mouth hardened into a thin line. She nodded without answering.

"I think," Lucia said, "that all this is worth investigating again. Kendi, if you like, I could put together a little team to start some spying. I believe it would be interesting to watch some of Mitchell Foxglove's people. Gretchen is good at surveillance, for example." She put a large griddle on the stove to heat and set to spreading bread slices with thick, yellow butter.

"I have a job," Gretchen objected.

"We can add it to your job description," Kendi said lightly, "and hire another bodyguard to pick up the slack. Who else were you thinking about for a team, Lucia?"

"The Vajhurs," Lucia replied. "We know them, and we know they can keep quiet. Prasad and Vidya have worked for us before, and Sejal's . . . talent at possession would be a big asset. Katsu is also trustworthy. And I'm sure they can use the money."

"I'm thinking we'll find a way to charge this one to Grandma," Kendi mused aloud.

"It won't even be difficult work," Lucia said. "We can set up remote spider cameras and set them to alert us whenever someone enters or leaves Foxglove's house. That way, the Vajhurs can monitor everything from home. No danger of getting caught."

"What can I do?" Ben said. "I'm not going to sit at home all day doing nothing."

"Use your computer," Lucia said. "See if you can hack into Foxglove's records."

Ben thought about that. "It'd be a challenge," he said at last. "Foxglove will be heavily guarded and encrypted."

Lucia put together buttery sandwiches of tomatoes and herb-sprinkled cheese and dropped them sizzling on the hot griddle. "We never did discuss common vectors in all these events. What are they?"

"Kendi, for one," Ben said. "He's the target of the killer, he's involved in the blackmailing, and he's working for Grandma's campaign."

"That also makes Senator Salman a vector," Tan said. "Kendi, the target, works for her campaign, which may have a spy in it."

"This leaves out the blackmail," Harenn said.

"It may be an attempt to discredit Kendi and render him useless to the senator," Tan replied.

"I don't like it," Kendi said. "If they want to discredit me, why strike at Ben? He's the primary blackmail victim, not me."

"The campaign itself is a vector," Gretchen said. "Kendi-the-target works for it. Ben-the-blackmail-guy is the grandson of the senator, and Finn-and-Leona-Day-the-corpses had connections to Mitchell Foxglove." She scratched her nose. "Sounds to me like someone is trying to disrupt the campaign."

"But not just Grandma's campaign," Ben said. "If the blackmail attempt may have been an attempt to hurt

Grandma by hurting me, but the Days' deaths *benefit* her and hurt Mitchell Foxglove."

"So someone's trying to disrupt *both* campaigns?" Kendi said.

"That would point to Ched-Pirasku." Lucia slid a spatula under each sandwich and gave it an expert flip. The kitchen smelled of toasted bread, hot cheese, and baking herbs. "He benefits if the Federalists and the Tapers—Unionists—lose."

"A possibility," Ben said. "Should we watch Ched-Pirasku, too?"

"Maybe," Kendi said. "But only if Foxglove doesn't pan out. I still think it's him."

Lucia brought to the table a platter piled high with crispy grilled sandwiches filled with soft cheese, aromatic herbs, and juicy tomatoes. Everyone dug in with appreciative moans. Bedj-ka appeared from Ben's office, where he had been playing sim-games, snatched a sandwich, and vanished back into the office again. Harenn, who solemnly maintained the most dangerous place to stand was between a pregnant woman and a plate of hot food, ate two sandwiches and started on a third while the group discussed approaches. Tan refused to get involved in the surveillance except as it might relate to the safety of Ben, Kendi, and Harenn.

"And to Lucia's safety, come to that," Tan finished. "I'll definitely have to put more staff on this one."

"Doing our bit to improve the economy," Kendi observed wryly.

"And increase the Silent population," Ben added with his mouth full. Lucia gave him a playful slap on the top of the head.

They outlined plans and options. Kendi called the Vajhurs, who were happy to accept the surveillance job, and Harenn went to work on a schedule. A few minutes later she put her stylus down.

"I should not bother with this until I have had a chance to speak with Sejal," she said. "He spied on Foxglove's campaign, after all, and is more likely to know who we should be watching."

"We're not watching Foxglove himself?" Kendi asked.

"The media keep a close eye on him, which restricts his movements," Harenn said. "Foxglove's lackeys are the ones who will lead us to anything illicit."

"Attention! Attention!" said the computer. "Wanda Petrie is calling for Father Kendi Weaver."

Kendi accepted the call, and Petrie's face appeared on the kitchen wall. She looked even more tired and frazzled than before.

"I have a new speaking schedule for you," she said. *"Check your messages for the details, but it starts in three days."*

"Good," said Lucia. "Three days' worth of cooking lessons before you disappear again."

"The Senator is giving a press conference at four," Petrie said, *"if you're interested in watching."*

"Is she going to answer to the charges?" Ben asked.

"Certainly not!" Petrie said, aghast. *"That would be tantamount to admitting guilt at this stage. In a couple of days we will address that problem in public, when we have more information and some of the crisis has calmed down, but not until then. In the meantime—"*

"Don't talk to any reporters," Kendi said. "I know."

"When do you want us to start watching Foxglove's people?" Gretchen asked after Petrie signed off.

"As soon as Harenn finishes that schedule," Kendi said. "What are you writing, Lucia?"

"A shopping list," she said. "You and Ben are cooking me breakfast tomorrow morning."

Kendi stared at the recipe text floating above the new data pad Petrie had given him. Outside, the sun had risen, tree lizards were chirping, and birds were singing. A fire extinguisher sat conspicuously on the cupboard. Ben's idea, not Lucia's. Ben himself stood in the corner, looking like a deer ready to flee a forest fire.

"Are you sure about this?" Kendi asked. "I'm warning you—I couldn't even get a kitchen job as a slave. My mother was a cook, and she tried twice to get me out of mucking ponds, but I was so horrible in the kitchen that the manager put me right back outside again."

"You can read directions, can't you?" Lucia said.

"Yes."

"And you can do as they say, right?"

"Yeah."

"Then you can do it. Cooking is nothing more than following a recipe and caring whether or not it comes out. So. The recipe says beat two eggs in a large bowl with a fork."

Kendi picked up an egg and cracked it so hard against the cupboard that it squelched into a yellow shambles. Lucia didn't move to help him clean it up. Once he had taken care of the mess, he cracked a second egg more carefully, and it dropped neatly into the bowl. He followed with one more. Lucia nodded approval. Kendi scrambled the eggs with a fork.

"How long do I do this?" he asked.

"Read the recipe," she said.

" 'Beat until fluffy,' " he read, and checked the bowl. "Looks fluffy to me."

"What comes next, then? Ben, don't you leave. There is ham in the refrigerator. Check the recipe database to see how you should prepare it for breakfast."

Kendi, meanwhile, got out the milk and started to pour some into the bowl. Lucia caught him by the wrist before he could begin.

"What are you doing?" she demanded.

"The recipe calls for milk," he said.

"How much?"

"I can measure it by eye," he protested.

Lucia wordlessly handed _him_ a measuring cup and watched while he poured the correct amount and emptied it into the bowl.

"Seems stupid to pour twice," he grumbled.

"You are not pouring twice. You are measuring once and pouring once."

She watched while he also measured out flour, salt, sugar, and baking powder. While he stirred the mixture with a wire whisk, Lucia turned to Ben, who had put a frying pan on the stove with a bit of butter in the bottom. It was melting into a golden puddle.

"Very good," she said. "And the right heat. Set the

ham on the cutting board and slice it as thick as you want it. Don't look at the slice—keep your eye on the part that remains, and you'll be more even."

"Just for the record," Ben said, "I'm not a *bad* cook. I just hate cooking."

"Perhaps because you associate it with being alone in the kitchen doing something boring," Lucia said. "If you and Kendi cook together, it'll become a family event and therefore more interesting."

"Maybe," Ben said dubiously, "but what about—"

Lucia's hand shot out and caught Kendi's wrist again. He was holding a spice container over the bowl of pale pancake batter. "What are you doing *now*?"

"Just adding some cinnamon," he said plaintively. "My mother always put cinnamon in our pancakes."

Lucia removed the container from Kendi's hand and set it firmly aside. "I think this is why you always fail at cooking," she said. "You make changes in the recipe before you understand what you're doing. It's perfectly fine to tinker with a recipe, but *only* after you know how the original works. Never, ever change a recipe until you've tried it once or twice as it's written. Besides"—she held up the spice container—"this is chili powder, not cinnamon."

Under Lucia's gimlet eye, Kendi heated the griddle and poured spoonfuls of batter into a light coating of sizzling oil. Ben, meanwhile, dropped thick slices of ham into the frying pan. The kitchen began to smell of salty meat and hot pancakes. While they were cooking, Kendi tried to turn away, but Lucia stopped him.

"Don't leave the stove."

"But they'll be a while," Kendi said. "I just wanted to check my messages real quick."

"Another reason why your earlier attempts went wrong," Lucia said. "Let me guess—you get engrossed in something else and only remember your meal when the smoke alarm goes off."

"That's the way of it," Ben said. "One time he put a loaf of store-bought bread dough in the oven and left it there for seven hours. It was a crust brick all the way through."

"That was just one time!" Kendi protested.

"And then there was the molasses cookie crisis," Ben said, "and the donut disaster and the spaghetti—"

"All right, all right."

"You're burning," Lucia pointed out.

The first batch had turned black. Kendi thought the pancakes might still be salvageable, but Lucia ordered him to pitch them and start over.

"A hint of burned taste ruins everything," she said.

The second batch came out golden-brown and fragrant. Ben finished frying ham while Kendi started a third batch and Lucia set the table. In the end they sat down to a delicious breakfast of crispy pancakes, sweet syrup, and rich ham.

"A fine meal," Lucia said. "The nice thing about cooking is that the reward is usually immediate and delicious."

"I hear that," Kendi said, waving his fork.

"And we have just enough time," she added, checking her fingernail.

"Time for what?" Ben asked warily.

"To start a batch of bread for lunch."

Over the next three days, Lucia taught the two men how to make bread, pasta, simple sauces, fried chicklizard, mickey-spike stew, roasted potatoes, stuffing, cookies, and more. To relieve the surplus of food, they fed Tan, Gretchen, Lars, Harenn, and Bedj-ka. One day Ben invited Mother Mee up for lunch. She accepted with pleasure and gave them a few recipes of her own. Even Gretchen grudgingly admitted that the food was "more or less edible."

"I'm better at this than I ever thought I could be," Kendi admitted as they put the last of the dishes away late on the third day. "Thanks to an inspired teacher. How about you, Ben?"

"I don't loathe it," he said. "Though I'll admit to a mild dislike."

Harenn, meanwhile, set up a twenty-four-hour surveillance schedule on Foxglove's campaign. It wasn't difficult—the cameras did most of the work, and Gretchen and the Vajhurs could keep an eye on the monitors from their own data pads. Ben worked on finding a way into

Foxglove's personal and financial records. Tan, Lars, and a few others continued rotated guard duty on Kendi, Ben, Harenn, and Lucia.

More time passed, and the winter rains began. Salman's campaign dragged in a dismal third place, and the dreary weather mirrored everyone's morale. The trial of Willen Yaraye began, and the prosecutors dragged Salman into it, forcing her to testify. She swore that she knew nothing of his criminal connections, but the media portrayed this as an appalling ignorance rather than an innocent mistake—especially in Othertown, where the few feeds Foxglove didn't own were trying to curry his favor—and Salman's poll scores dropped even further.

Despite the depression hovering over Salman's campaign, Bellerophon itself enjoyed a lift of spirit. The news that children were once again entering the Dream stormed across the planet, bringing hope to thousands. The news spread through the Dream as well, and Kendi could feel the excitement when he walked there. Bedjka transferred to school at the monastery, where he took classes in meditation and memory training in a special accelerated series of courses designed to ready him for Dream communication work as soon as he was old enough. He took to the exercises as if he had been born to them, and Harenn bragged of his progress to anyone who would listen.

No adults among the Silenced found their way back into the Dream, whether they were human, Ched-Balaar, or members of other species. Dream experts set forth a great number of theories about this, most of which followed Martina's reasoning—that children's brains were more resilient, able to weather the Despair better than their elders. Foxglove, of course, referred to "his" discovery at every opportunity on the campaign trail, and his popularity soared even higher.

Ben, meanwhile, continued poking around with his computer system. Although he wasn't able to hack into Foxglove's records, he did discover through other sources that Foxglove was wealthier than anyone imagined because he owned most of the mines surrounding Othertown. The situation tugged at Kendi's instincts, even if he couldn't put his finger on what was wrong. Not that he had much time to ruminate, with the endless rounds of speeches, fund-raisers, and rallies. Fewer and fewer people showed up as the months wore on, and it got harder and harder for Kendi to muster up the energy to keep speaking.

There was no word about the missing file, and Kendi was relieved to see Ben able to sleep through the night again, though he still occasionally came out of the Dream with cuts and scratches on his hands. He brushed aside Kendi's questions about them, saying they were side effects of "stress relief."

Harenn entered her third trimester, and Lucia entered her second. Harenn's movements were slower and more deliberate as her middle grew larger and heavier. Regular checkups showed the fetus was developing perfectly, with no complications, and the baby was expected to arrive right on time—a few weeks before the election, as it happened.

"I am not sure which event is more momentous," she said from the rocking chair Ben had installed in the nursery. "The gubernatorial election or this baby's birth."

"Depends on whose household you're in," Kendi said. He aimed his data pad at the wall and thumbed it. The walls swirled into a talltree forest setting, complete with smiling, child-sized dinosaurs roaming among happy flowers and grinning bushes. He frowned and thumbed the data pad again. The forest disappeared and an ocean scene washed over the walls in its place. Fish and merfolk danced among waving kelp, pausing to wave at Kendi and Harenn every now and then. Bubbles made smiley faces. Kendi made another frown and aimed the data pad at the wall.

"Just choose one," Harenn said. "The child will not care."

"I want it to be perfect," Kendi objected, gesturing at the offending room. Two cribs awaited occupants. Two dressers were filled to bursting with baby clothes, and the shelves beneath the changing table bulged with baby supplies. More shelves were filled with playthings, ranging from simple stuffed toys to interactive holographic animal playmates that adjusted themselves to meet the child's stage of development. Outside, the sun had set, and dark shadows pooled under the talltree branches.

"The main thing is that you love the child and pay lots of attention to it," Harenn said. "Everything else is secondary. Ah—it's moving."

Kendi set down the pad and knelt next to the chair with his hand on Harenn's stomach. He felt the movement beneath his palm.

"Hi, Baby," he said as he always did. "I'm your Da."

"Bedj-ka is becoming more and more impatient," Harenn said. "He wants very much to be an older brother."

"We'll have to remind him of that when he's a teenager and complains about getting stuck babysitting." Kendi grinned.

The baby stopped moving. Kendi stood up and surveyed the walls. "All right. We'll go with the underwater theme."

Ben poked his head into the room. "Hey you guys—Gretchen's here."

"What? Isn't she on surveillance duty?" Kendi said.

"She said she left early because she has big news, but she won't spill until we're all there. Hurry up!"

"Help me out of this chair," Harenn said. "Medical science may have overcome many of the discomforts associated with pregnancy, but the laws of physics haven't changed one bit."

Kendi gave her a hand, and they headed for the living room. Kendi's curiosity was piqued. Still, he kept his excitement in check. They had had false alarms before, and this was probably one of them.

One look at Gretchen changed his mind. She was pacing about the living like a nervous blond lion, a mixture of excitement and agitation playing across her square-cut face. Ben was sitting on the edge of the sofa beside Tan.

"All right, Gretch," Kendi said. "We're here. What's going on?"

"I was following Foxglove up close and personal instead of using the spider-cams," she began. "I saw him go into the house he uses in Treetown, and there weren't any reporters around. A while later, he snuck out the back door by himself. Not even a bodyguard. He was wearing a rain hat and sunglasses, and I only knew it was him because I recognized the way he walks."

"Cut to the chase," Tan said. "Some of us are old."

"Right." Gretchen took a deep breath. "He took the monorail and a gondola to a little house near the border of Treetown and the monastery. He went inside. I climbed up a level and watched from there. About half an hour later, this woman came out."

She tapped her data pad and conjured up the image of a Ched-Balaar.

"She looked familiar, but I couldn't quite place her, so I did a computer search. Ben's face-recognition software turned up an ID image. She's a judicial clerk at the High Court."

"So?" Kendi said.

"So?" Gretchen's tone was incredulous. "Don't you see what this means? It means Foxglove has connections with someone at the High Court who probably knew what the mining rights decision was going to be several days before it was officially handed down."

"In other words, he knew how the Court voted before the decision was made public," Kendi said. "Which is why he bought all those mining companies when he did. He *knew* they'd be worth billions."

"It's the source of all that money," Gretchen said, "and how he managed to buy Othertown in everything but name."

"It's not enough evidence to bring any kind of charges," Ben mused. "Though Grandma can probably use it. Did you get any images of him going into the house?"

"Yeah." Gretchen grimaced. "But he was in disguise, and you can't really tell it's him. Won't hold up. But now that we know where to search, we can *find* evidence."

"Nice work," Tan rasped. "I don't suppose you got any footage of Foxglove leaving the house? Maybe he's recognizable."

"Not really," she said. "Here, I'll show you." She tapped the data pad, and the scene with the holographic house sped up. The house's door popped open, and Gretchen returned the image to normal speed. A human in a rain hat and a long coat emerged, turned to speak briefly with a barely visible figure in the doorway, and walked away.

"See?" Gretchen said. "You can't tell for sure that—"

Ben leaped out of his chair. "Back that thing up! Back it *up*!"

"Ben?" Kendi said. "What's wrong?"

In answer he snatched the pad away from a startled Gretchen and reset the image to the beginning. Again Foxglove emerged from the house in his rain hat. Ben froze the hologram, then zoomed in and enlarged it. His lips were drawn into a tight line.

"Ben, what—?" Kendi began.

"Shut up," Ben snapped. "I just have to—oh. Oh my god."

He set the pad on the coffee table and backed away as if it were a bomb. Kendi and the others turned to look. Harenn and Tan looked puzzled. Kendi gasped. The display showed the image of an old man, hawk-nosed and white-haired.

"It can't be," Kendi whispered. "What the hell is he doing here?"

"Who is it?" Tan demanded. "I don't recognize—"

"It's Padric Sufur," Ben said. "The bastard who killed my mother."

CHAPTER ELEVEN

"Enemies, like lovers, always eventually meet."
—Daniel Vik

No one spoke for a long time. Finally Gretchen said, "That's what he looks like? I've never seen him before."

"I'd recognize him with my eyes shut," Ben said in a cold and terrible voice that speared Kendi with alarm. "Gretchen, what's the address? Where can we find him?"

"All right, all right," Kendi said. "We aren't going to do anything just yet."

Ben's jaw tightened so hard it looked like granite. He sat on the sofa, rigid as a statue with an explosive inside. Kendi swallowed and turned back to the hologram. It was definitely Padric Sufur.

Kendi had never actually met Sufur. Neither had Ben. But some time after Ara's death, Ben had dug around the computer systems and produced several images of him. He hadn't said why, and Kendi, still caught in the throes of his own grief, hadn't pressed for details. He had simply assumed Ben had wanted to put a face to the name.

Padric was one of the wealthiest—perhaps even *the* wealthiest—being in the known galaxy. He had funded a laboratory that used the genes of Sejal's father Prasad to produce twisted Silent children. Their Silence had been as powerful as their bodies had been monstrous, and when they came into their full power, they set out to destroy the Dream forever. This was as Sufur had wanted it. In his view, the Dream was the chief source of warfare, allowing commanders to communicate with their troops over interplanetary distances. Destroying the Dream would be the same as destroying war. Unfortunately, Sufur had been unaware that destroying the Dream would also create a backlash that would, over time, destroy all sentient life everywhere.

When Sufur's destructive children attacked the Dream, the first thing they had done was remove every Silent in the universe from the Dream. A great many went insane at the separation. Large numbers had committed suicide out of despair. Kendi had almost been one of them, but Ben and Harenn had gotten to him in time.

They had not gotten to Ara. Ben had discovered her broken body on the forest floor, shattered from the leap she had taken off her own balcony.

The Vajhur family, meanwhile, had managed to put the twisted children's bodies into stasis chambers, effectively snatching them out of the Dream before they could fully destroy it. The stasis chambers currently lay on the ocean floor on the planet Rust, forgotten by everyone except the Vajhur family, Kendi, and Ben. The team of geneticists that had created the children for Padric Sufur were either dead or fled. Padric Sufur himself had been nowhere near Rust during the Despair and had escaped unscathed but for the loss of his Silence. Kendi knew Sufur numbered among the Silenced because Kendi had personally scoured the Dream for the man's presence and found not a single trace.

Now, however, he was apparently living on Bellerophon. Kendi rubbed his chin, feeling oddly calm. Ara had been both mentor and mother to Kendi, and by all rights Kendi should be the one rushing out the door to confront Sufur—or worse. Instead he felt perfectly in control, his mind cool and calculating. Why had Sufur come to Treetown? What possible business could he have here? And why was he consorting with Mitchell Foxglove?

"Let's blow the lid off him," Gretchen said. "Call the Guardians, call the police, call the feeds. They'll be all over him. Or I can take him out. One shot's all I need."

"Stand in line," Tan said without a trace of irony or humor, and Kendi remembered that Sufur's plan had Silenced both Tan and Gretchen.

"No," Kendi said. "We aren't going to kill him."

"Why the hell not?" Gretchen demanded.

"We need to learn what he's up to," Kendi said. "Look, I hate him as much as you do—"

Gretchen rose to a terrible height. Her face was red beneath yellow hair. "How the *fuck* can you say that to me, Weaver? *You* can still reach the Dream. *You* kept your career. *You* are still Silent. Sufur took everything away from me. Every*fucking*thing I had—my Silence, my job, my friends. I don't care how many game contracts you arrange because you feel guilty, you don't have the right to hate him as much as I do. You *never* have the right. I want Sufur dead. I want to watch him squirm and shit blood at my feet before I crush his throat, and I want to record it so I can watch it over and over again and laugh my fucking head off while everyone I know pisses on his grave."

Gretchen's face had turned blotchy. Her entire body vibrated like a violin string, and her tirade all but pushed Kendi into his chair. Kendi firmed his jaw. She was being insubordinate, rash, and stubborn.

She was also right. Kendi couldn't imagine what it must be like to lose his Silence and loved ones both. A twinge of the guilt Gretchen had mentioned pinched at him.

"I'm not denying you the right to be . . . *angry* isn't a strong enough word, I think," Kendi said quietly. "And I agree that Sufur is a filthy animal that needs to be put down. Maybe even we—you—will be the one to do it. But he's here on Bellerophon for a reason, and I can't imagine it's to help the Children of Irfan. The last time Sufur had a plan, he nearly destroyed all life everywhere. We need to find out what he's trying to pull."

"If we kill him," Ben said in that same chilly voice, "his plan will die, too."

"Not necessarily," Harenn said, speaking for the first time. "He may have people who can carry it out after his death. I have to say that in comparison to you three, I have lost almost nothing to Sufur, but I am no stranger to loss and anger. I understand your need to see him pay for his crimes, but I must also agree with Kendi. More people on Bellerophon have reason to hate Sufur than on any other known planet—except, perhaps, the

Ched-Balaar homeworld—and it would be foolish in the extreme for him to come here without a very pressing purpose. We must uncover it."

"And then what?" Gretchen said.

"And then you can see to his punishment," Harenn said. "I will not stand in your way. I will also point out, however, that it may be more satisfying to see him punished while he lives. If he dies, his punishment is short-lived. If you leave him alive, there are any number of ways to make him regret what he has done."

Kendi remembered the revenge Harenn had taken on her ex-husband, the man who had sold Bedj-ka into slavery, and he shuddered.

"Point," Tan growled.

"Maybe we should just tell everyone that he's here," Gretchen said. "See how long before someone gets lucky."

"Be impossible for him to operate here," Tan said. "Too many people watching."

"No!" Kendi said. "If we do that, Sufur will just disappear. Now that we know where he is, we can keep an eye on him, figure out what he's up to. Harenn, let's change the surveillance schedule and have Sufur watched around the clock."

"As you wish."

"The rest of you keep *quiet* about this," Kendi warned. "Not one word, not a hint to anyone."

"I don't need to talk to him to see him dead," Gretchen said.

Ben stared out into the night, hard and unmoving as a rock. Kendi stepped out onto the balcony, uncertain and a bit frightened. He hadn't seen Ben this worked up since Ara's death.

The winter air was damp and chilly, and Kendi could see his breath. Only a few night animals made faint calls to each other. Most of the dinosaurs had migrated to warmer climates, the plant eaters taking the lead with the meat eaters following close behind. The holiday season would arrive soon, beginning with Three Drink Night, after which came Ghost Eve and the Drum and Tooth Revel. Irfan's Birthday came next. Kendi didn't much feel like celebrating, though a relentless cheer seemed to have swept up everyone else in Treetown. There was even talk of adding a new holiday to commemorate Mitchell Foxglove's announcement that children were returning to the Dream. Kendi ground his teeth at the thought. History would record the event as Foxglove's triumph instead of as a theft. Kendi didn't want or need any more fame, but he hated the idea of the truth going unrecorded. For an irrational moment he wondered if history had maligned Daniel Vik just as it was exalting Mitchell Foxglove.

Kendi laid a tentative hand on Ben's shoulder. Ben didn't react. Kendi hugged him from behind, but it was like embracing a stone.

"Talk to me, Ben," Kendi said. "You shouldn't keep it in."

Ben remained silent.

"You're angry with me." Kendi sighed. "Ben, the thought of you wanting to kill someone scares me. You've never done it."

"And how would you know that?" Ben said in a strangely gentle voice.

A familiar anger flared. Kendi knew what Ben meant. There were a lot of things Kendi didn't know about Ben because their relationship had been stormy for years, with Ben coming and going from Kendi's life like an ocean wave. But Kendi had never once initiated a breakup. Ben's capriciousness, not Kendi's, had put holes in their time together, and for him to intimate the apart times were Kendi's fault . . .

Kendi gritted his teeth and bit back sharp words. Ben rarely started arguments—he said small things calculated to anger Kendi and get *him* to start the fight, leaving Ben blameless. It was one of the things about Ben that annoyed the hell out of Kendi and served as a sharp reminder that no one, even someone you loved, was perfect. The only way to deal with this trick was not to rise to the bait, a skill Kendi had only recently learned.

"Look, Ben," he said quietly, "no matter how much Sufur deserves it, no matter how justified your anger is, the law would still count it a murder if you killed him. I'm ready to party on his tombstone, but I'm also terrified the police will take you away from me—from our kids. Please promise me you won't do anything. I can't lose you like—like I lost—"

He stopped, unsure if he should go so far as to mention Ara's name. But Ben had clearly understood. There was a long pause. Their breaths mingled in white puffs. And then Kendi felt Ben's body slacken. He sagged back against Kendi, who sank to the balcony under Ben's weight. He managed to control the slump, and they both ended up on the cold planks. Kendi braced himself against the wall of the house. Ben lay like a rag doll against Kendi's chest, his legs sprawled brokenly on the wood. His body shuddered noiselessly. It took Kendi a moment to understand that he was crying. Kendi wrapped his arms around Ben and held him while he wept.

"The bastard killed her," Ben said in a thick, harsh voice. "He killed my *mother*. I *hate* him, Kendi. I want him *dead*. Why is he alive when she's dead?"

Kendi didn't give an answer, knew Ben didn't want one. He rocked Ben like a child until Ben grew still and calm. At last Ben sat up and wiped his nose on his sleeve.

"I'm freezing," he said.

"How about some tea?" Kendi said. "Or maybe a beer. I think Lucia found some."

They rose stiffly. Ben put a heavy arm around Kendi's shoulders. "Thanks," he whispered. "And I promise."

Back in the house, they found Harenn, Gretchen, and Tan in the living room. The sharp smell of strong alcohol hung in the air, and several empty and half-empty bottles and glasses littered the coffee table.

"If we can't kill him," Tan said in an uncharacteristically bright voice, "we can at least get drunk."

"So who's going to guard us?" Kendi asked, more out of curiosity than uncertainty.

"Who the fuck cares?" Gretchen said. "I've saved your ass—what? Three times? Four? Save it yourself for once."

"You aren't drinking, are you?" Ben said to Harenn.

"Certainly not," Harenn said. "I wanted to plan our next steps, but—"

"Lighten up, Hare," Gretchen slurred. "A few hours won't make a difference."

"I was thinking," Ben said, picking up a glass and sniffing at it, "of trying to hit Sufur's computer trail. Since I know his home address, I can track quite a lot. He must have utilities and net hookups, and the ones connected to that address will have whatever name Sufur is using on them. Once I have that information, I can track down more records—his buying habits, what bank he uses, and so on. It might tell us what he's up to."

"I'll search around the Dream," Kendi said, "see if there are any rumors about him there. But first I'm going to go see him."

"What?" Gretchen said. "You just said not to confront him."

"I didn't say *confront*," Kendi replied. "I said *see*. I need to look at him with my own eyes. He tried to kill me, too, you know."

"I'm going with you," Ben said. "Don't try to talk me out of it—it won't work, and I'm stronger than you are."

"All right," Kendi said. "But you're it. No bodyguards. It's dark out anyway—no one'll see us."

"Unless they have night-vision equipment," Tan said. "Oh, just go. I'm too drunk to do you any good. You die, though, your estate still pays me."

They did take the precaution of wearing low rain hats and anonymous slickers as simple disguises. Outside, the damp winter air was still chilly but no rain fell. Kendi and Ben made their way over dark walkways toward the Treetown address Gretchen had given them. The neighborhood was quiet and middle-class, though very few outdoor lights offered to illuminate the way, and the two men slipped from small pools of light into long lakes of shadow. Sufur's house was the highest in a small cluster of homes stacked up against the talltree trunk. A lattice of staircases gave access. Lights glowed behind Sufur's curtains. Kendi picked a vantage point on a public balcony and watched it intently.

"Now what?" Ben asked.

Kendi shrugged. "I just needed to see the place." He paused. "It doesn't look like a monster's house."

"It looks like the kind of place a little old lady would

live in," Ben said. "Like Grandmother Mee." He took
a deep breath. "I want to throw rocks through his windows. Or maybe a grenade."

"Me, too. But that wouldn't tell us what—hold it!"

A figure on a small electric scooter buzzed toward the
bottom of the staircase lattice. In the dim light of a
lonely street lamp, Kendi could make out the name
"Maureen's" emblazoned on the figure's jacket. He dismounted and started up the stairs toward Sufur's house.

"Come on!" Kendi said, and ran down the walkway
toward the delivery boy without looking to see if Ben
was following. They reached the boy before he was quite
halfway up the steps.

"Excuse me," Kendi said. "Hey!"

The delivery boy turned. He was carrying a food
warmer, and he looked distinctly nervous at seeing two
grown men dashing up the stairs toward him. "Look, I
don't carry cash, okay? You want the food, you can—"

"We don't want the food," Kendi said a little breath-
lessly. "But you're delivering to that house there, right?"
He pointed at Sufur's house.

"Yeah," the boy said. "So?"

"So the guy who lives there is a friend of ours," Kendi
said. "Listen, can you help us play a little joke on him?
He won't be expecting us to deliver his supper. I'll give
you fifty freemarks if you let me and my friend borrow
your jacket and do the delivery for you."

The money, Kendi knew, was probably more than the
kid made in three days. "You're on," he said, and
handed over both the jacket and the food warmer. "I
need those back. Maureen's will charge me if I come
back without them."

"No problem," Kendi said. "Here—you can take my
rain slicker as collateral."

A moment later, Kendi and Ben were mounting the
stairs, Kendi wearing the delivery boy's jacket and Ben
carrying the food warmer.

"What are you doing?" Ben hissed.

"Just getting a look," Kendi whispered back, his calm
voice belying a pounding heart. "To make sure it's really
him. Are you going to be all right?"

Ben paused, lifted the lid of the food warmer, and rummaged around inside. "Now I will be," he said, closing the warmer.

"What did you do?" Kendi asked.

"I spat in his *ben-yai* leaves."

Kendi gave a choked laugh and knocked at the door. "Delivery from Maureen's," he said, knowing the house computer would relay his words to the occupants. His heart continued to beat fast, and his mouth went dry. Abruptly the door opened, and Kendi was staring at Padric Sufur. The man's face was lean, largely unlined, and hawklike, with a long nose and thin lips. His body was equally lean, with long limbs and hands. He wore a heavily quilted comfort suit. With a sudden rush of anger, Kendi wanted to reach out and snap the man's neck. It would be so easy. The brittle old bones would break under his hands with a satisfying *crunch*, and Kendi would be able to watch the man squirm and shit himself on the floor. Beside him, Kendi felt Ben tense, and he knew Ben was thinking the same thing.

"I prefer to pay in cash," Sufur said. "No prints. I assume that's all right?"

"Yeah," Kendi said shortly. "No problem. I don't have change, though."

Kendi collected the handful of bills Sufur gave him. Their hands touched at the transfer. No Silent jolt. Sufur's skin was warm and dry, and Kendi felt nausea at the contact. Sufur hissed at the touch and yanked his hand back. He accepted the food packets Ben handed him from the warmer, thanked them curtly, and slammed the door.

"It was really him," Ben said in a gravelly voice.

"Yeah. Let's get out of here before it starts raining again."

They returned the jacket and food warmer to the delivery boy, who was waiting below with his scooter, and headed wordlessly for home.

Jak Peer, delivery boy, climbed onto his scooter and hit the starter. This was shaping up to be a seriously weird night. He suspected that the guys who had asked to make the delivery for him were crooked somehow, but fifty freemarks was fifty freemarks, and he'd have been stupid to refuse it.

The scooter didn't start. The misty rain intensified and Jak tried again. The scooter still didn't respond. Jak wiped cold water from his face in exasperation. Now what? Had those two weirdos had anything to do with it? He touched his pocket. The weirdo's freemarks were a gift from Irfan, and he wondered how best to use it. Jak Peer didn't see himself as a delivery boy for the rest of his life, no sir. He had been an Initiate at the monastery with dreams of becoming the youngest Grandfather Adept in history. The Despair had changed all that, Silenced him and crushed his Dream to dust. Now he had to find a new dream, and maybe fifty freemarks would let him buy one. The mining restrictions had been lifted. Perhaps he could use the money to travel to Othertown and get a job there. Mining would pay a hell of a lot better than delivering steamed slugs and *bey-yai* leaves.

One more try. The scooter's engine clicked twice and remained still. Jak made an exasperated noise.

"Having some trouble?"

The speaker was a woman wearing a rain slicker. Jak saw a few locks of dark hair peeping out from under the hood. He had been so intent on the scooter and his thoughts that he hadn't heard her approach.

"It won't start," he said. "And I'm not any kind of mech."

"Let me take a look," she said. "I know a few things."

"Thanks," Jak said, grateful. He dismounted and held the scooter upright while she took out a small flashlight and peered at the motor.

"Major sucking to be a delivery boy in this weather," she said.

"You know it," Jak said. "The good stuff never lasts, either."

"Here's your trouble." The woman did something Jak couldn't see. "Try it now."

Jak hit the starter, and the motor sprang to life. "Perfect!" he said. "Hey, thanks a—"

Something thumped against the side of his neck. Jak

managed a gasp before the drug hit, and he fell into wet unconsciousness.

"Okay, I'm watching," Kendi said. On the sofa next to him sat Martina. They were at her house, the one she and Keith rented from Ben and Kendi. It was a week later, and the rains had begun in earnest. Sheets of cold water washed down the windows, and the damp got into everything. Kendi wore heavy sweaters, and Martina was keeping the heat cranked up, but he still felt chilly and vaguely wet. The weather also put a damper on all the campaigns—open-air speeches were impossible, and few people braved the weather to attend the indoor ones, so most of Kendi's activity was limited to commercials and newsfeed interviews, and that could be done close to home.

Martina lounged on the sofa, her brown eyes wide and on the edge of her usual mirth. Then she abruptly shifted posture, becoming stiffer and more upright. She put both hands on her knees in a gesture Kendi recognized immediately. It both chilled and excited him.

"All life!" he said. "Ben?"

"It's me. Can you believe it?" It was Martina's voice, but Ben's inflections. "We've been working on this for a while now." Martina-Ben got up and strode around the tiny room. "This is weird. Her body moves different from mine. And I can smell perfume."

"Wait until you wear an alien's body," Kendi said. "I kept tripping over my own feet the first time I possessed a Ched-Balaar. Why didn't you tell me about this?"

"We wanted to surprise you. You kept saying how you wanted me and Martina to get closer. And we have."

"Okay, that would be an 'ew' sort of thing," Kendi said. "What about Keith? Could you possess him, too?"

Martina-Ben shrugged. "He didn't want to try it. He's kind of hard to talk with, you know?"

"I know," Kendi sighed.

Martina-Ben sat back down. "And that's not all. Hold on." A shudder, and Martina looked blankly at Kendi for a moment. Then she regained her composure. "Ta da!" she said in her own voice.

"That's great, Sis." Kendi said, impulsively grabbing her hand. It was then he noticed the red scar running up the inside of her forearm. "What the hell is that?"

"Nothing," Martina said, and pulled her hand away. "It's fine."

"It can't be nothing," he said. "That must've hurt like a ballyhoo. What did you do—go carnosaur riding?"

He had meant it as a joke, but the startled look on Martina's face told him he had hit the mark right off.

"All life," he said. "You *did*."

"It was just a little fun," Martina said defensively. "Only the little ones hang around during the winter, and they're not very dangerous if you know what you're doing. I made a little mistake, that's all."

Anger seized Kendi. "How the hell did you learn what to do?"

"I found a club. It's called the Wild Dinosaur Rodeo. Look, we take all the appropriate precautions."

"Precautions?" Kendi echoed in disbelief. "*Precautions?* How about this for a precaution—stay the hell away from wild carnosaurs!"

"It's my life," Martina flared back. "You're my brother, not my father. Or my owner."

Kendi was seized with an urge to slap her. How could she endanger herself like that, especially after everything he had gone through to rescue her? After he had worried for fifteen years that she was already dead? But he forced himself to calm down. She was right about one thing—he hadn't rescued her from slavery in order to dictate her—

A presence brushed his mind, and suddenly Kendi was hungry. Ravenous. Starving. He'd been feeling a little peckish before, but now he felt ready to run down a dinosaur and tear into it with his bare teeth. As quickly as the sensation came, it vanished. A wave of tender sentimentality flooded him. Martina, his baby sister, so lost and abused for so many years, and now she was right here on the sofa next to him. He shouldn't feel angry at her. He should to apologize, beg her forgiveness, ask for—

~*All right, Ben,*~ he thought. ~*So you can whisper, too.*~

~I'm getting pretty good,~ came Ben's mental voice. *~Though I haven't tried it with a non-Silent yet.~*

Martina deduced what was going on by the shifting expressions on Kendi's face. "He did it, huh?"

"He did it," Kendi said. "And now he can stop." Manipulating people's emotions from the Dream—whispering—had never been one of Kendi's talents, and it always made him feel a little creepy.

~I'll come out,~ Ben said. *~See you in a second.~*

The presence vanished from Kendi's mind. A moment later, Ben emerged from Martina's bedroom, twirling his dermospray like a short baton. Kendi shook off the remnants of false emotion and gave Ben a congratulatory hug, his anger at Martina forgotten.

"The Children of Irfan are going to want you more than ever now," he said.

"Forget it," Ben said. "I've worked freelance all my life, and I'm not going to tie myself down with their rules and regulations."

"That sounds strange coming from you, Ben," Martina said from the couch. "I would expect to hear that from Kendi."

"Kendi's no good unless he has rules to break," Ben said. "I avoid the rules altogether."

"What's going on?" said a sleepy voice. Keith stood in his bedroom doorway, looking rumpled. "You guys are being really noisy."

"Ben and I were showing off for Kendi," Martina said. "Enjoy your nap? You must be getting pretty good at them by now."

"Was that sarcasm?" Keith said. "I'm not awake enough for sarcasm."

"Keith," Kendi said gently, "sleeping all the time is a sign of depression. Look, I can get you in to see a counselor. Or maybe the two of us can talk about . . . stuff. I don't have a degree in psych, but I can listen. And maybe you can—"

"I'm not depressed," Keith interrupted with a hint of steel. "I'm tired all the time because the Children are keeping me so busy in the Dream I barely have time to piss. In the last week, three people have quit or just disappeared, and I have to help cover for them. This is the first day off I've had in almost two weeks. Pardon me if I want to sleep late."

"It's after lunch," Martina said in a quiet voice. "A little late for late."

There was a long pause. Then Keith said, "What's there to eat?"

"Kendi and Ben brought a whole lot of stuff," Martina said. "We put it in the refrigerator. There's ravioli, herb bread, some kind of salad. And cheesecake. You have to try the cheesecake. One bite and your depre— your *grouchiness* will disappear like a bad dream."

"I'm not grouchy," Keith growled, and stomped into the kitchen. A second later, he squawked, "What the fuck?"

"Sorry!" Kendi called. "Lars is here. Should've warned you. Lars, you know my brother Keith, right?"

"We know each other," Keith called back. "Still scared the shit out of me. Fuck." The refrigerator door opened, then slammed shut.

"He's like this all the time," Martina murmured. "Either sleeping or complaining. I'm starting to invent reasons to get out of the house so I don't have to listen to him."

"We'll keep working on him," Kendi murmured back. "Not much else we can do. We can't *force* him to see a counselor."

"I don't know," Martina grumbled. "I have a cricket bat around here somewhere."

Keith came back into the living room with a reheated plate of food. The rich herb and tomato smells would have set Kendi's mouth to watering if he hadn't just eaten. Lucia's cooking lessons were paying off. Neither Kendi nor Ben would ever be chefs, but they were no longer dependent on ordering out every day and had managed to cut their food bills by more than half. And ever since Kendi had come up with a . . . creative new use for cheesecake batter, Ben had become much more receptive to spending extra time in the kitchen.

"So what's on the schedule for Three Drink Night?" Ben asked. "It's just next week, you know."

"Three Drink Night?" Keith asked around a mouthful of bread. "What's that?"

"Don't you pay attention?" Martina said, gesturing at the living room. "I've been decorating."

She had. Three large candles stood next to three silvery goblets on the coffee table. Three sketches of Irfan—done by Martina herself—hung on the wall next to a small shelf with three new books on it. Three talltree withes hung over the entrance to the hallway.

"It's a party holiday," Kendi said. "You do everything in threes—eating, drinking, gambling, and . . . um . . ."

"Sex?" Martina supplied. "Must be hard on the guys."

"It's a Ched-Balaar holiday," Kendi laughed. "Things are a little different for them."

"Mom usually threw a party," Ben said. "I think . . . I think I'd like to throw one, too. If Lewa will let us, that is."

"Grandma's throwing one," Kendi said. "I'll have to put in an appearance."

"Then we'll throw a little one here as well," Martina said. "Just for an hour or something. That'll make three parties."

"I like that," Ben said with enthusiasm. "We start here, go to Grandma's, and end up at our house."

They discussed plans for almost an hour. Keith volunteered little, though his eating may have interfered. At least, Kendi observed, his appetite seemed unaffected by his mood.

After a while, the rain lightened noticeably, and the gray sky visible through the window showed a few cracks of blue.

"We should get home," Kendi said, rising. "This break in the rain won't last long."

Keith set his plate aside and brushed crumbs from his shirt. "I'll go with you. After that meal, I'm suddenly in the mood for a brisk walk."

They collected Lars from his waiting post in the kitchen, donned rain slickers, and headed out. The late afternoon air was chilly and damp but clean-smelling. Water glistened and dripped from every talltree leaf, pattering lightly on Kendi's slicker. The foursome made their way over the walkways and staircases. Pedestrian traffic was light, and their footsteps thumped over the boards like muffled drumbeats. Lars walked just ahead of Kendi, eyes alert.

They were halfway to their destination when Kendi felt a sting on the back of his neck beneath his slicker. He slapped at it and spun around with an oath. Keith, walking behind him, had also turned.

"What the hell was that?" Keith said, looking over his shoulder. "I thought I saw—"

Kendi collapsed to the boardwalk. Ben blinked down at him, uncomprehending. Lars shoved Ben aside and dropped to his knees. He rolled Kendi over, revealing a thin trickle of blood that flowed from the back of Kendi's neck. Face set, Lars pulled a small metal dart from the wound, then yanked a kit from his under his slicker. Belated fear thrilled through Ben.

"What's wrong with him?" Ben demanded. He tapped his earpiece. "Emergency! I need a medical emergency team right away!"

"We're tracking your signal, sir," said a calm voice in his ear. *"A team is on the way. What's your emergency?"*

"It's Kendi," Ben said tersely. "He collapsed. He's unconscious. I think it's poison."

Lars, meanwhile, opened the kit and produced a dermospray and a small suction unit. He ripped Kendi's slicker off, pressed the suction unit to the wound, and set the dermospray against the skin beside it. The dermospray thumped and the suction unit clamped itself to Kendi's neck.

"Is he breathing?" asked the voice.

"I think so," Ben said. "Yes. But it's fast and shallow, and he's sweating. Our bodyguard is giving him something. A broad-spectrum antidote."

Lars took out a medical scanner and touched it to the suction unit. It beeped once, and text scrolled down the display. Ben read over his shoulder, surprised at how calm he felt. It was as if he were floating in a quiet pool of water, watching everything happen to someone else. A crowd was gathering, but Ben was too busy reading to notice.

"The first aid kit found polydithalocide in the wound," he reported. "Oh, god. That's a neurotoxin."

Lars put another ampule in the hypospray and thumped it against Kendi's neck.

"The rescue team is almost there, sir," the voice said. *"You should see them now."*

"They're here!" Keith said, pointing upward and waving his arms. "Hey! Over this way!"

An ambulance dropped from the sky like a stone and landed a few yards away. The backblast blew through Ben's hair and sent a shower of water over everything. Two paramedics were on the ground before the ambulance had fully landed. They gave Kendi a quick examination and bundled him onto a hovering stretcher while a third paramedic asked questions. Ben answered as best he could, but Kendi's ashen face and slack body were a terrifying distraction. Ben climbed into the ambulance behind the stretcher, leaving Lars and Keith on the walkway with the crowd. Several people in the crowd had cameras and other recording devices. Ben turned his back on them as the paramedics slammed the double doors.

The ride to the medical center was horrible for all that it was short. Ben pressed himself against the side of the ambulance while the paramedics worked on Kendi. They slapped IVs on his hands, and the tubules burrowed into his skin like worms. One medic injected more drugs. Then a shrill alarm sounded. Kendi's heart had stopped.

Ben stuffed a fist into his mouth to keep from crying out and distracting the medical team. The first paramedic, a blond man, slapped a patch on Kendi's chest—they had already cut his shirt off—and jabbed at one of the medical scanners. Kendi twitched, then lay still. The alarm continued to shrill. The paramedic jabbed the scanner again. Kendi twitched, but didn't respond further. Another paramedic slipped a breathing tube into Kendi's mouth, and it slid down his trachea like a long snake. Oxygen hissed. Ben watched, feeling cold, alone, and helpless. The paramedics ignored him and gave each other tense, terse orders.

Please, Ben pleaded. *Oh god—please don't let him die. I can't lose him. Please, please wake up, Kendi. I can't lose you like I lost Mom.*

The blond paramedic slapped the scanner again.

Kendi twitched once and lay still. Ben wanted to lie down and die. Ben's children—their children—would grow up without their Da. They would never know him, never play with him, never take family trips or run through the park with him. And neither would Ben.

The scanner beeped once, then twice, and a third time. It took Ben a moment to realize it was Kendi's heartbeat. His legs went weak, and he slid to the floor. The paramedics continued their work. Why was it taking so long to get to the medical center? They should be there by—

The ambulance landed, and the paramedics whisked Kendi's hovering stretcher into the emergency room. Ben hurried to follow, but an orderly blocked his way.

"I know you're worried, Mr. Rymar," she said, "but you need to give us room to work on him. The moment we have news, we'll let you know. Do you have anyone you can call?"

Slowly Ben nodded. He turned and walked like a zombie into the waiting area, which was just off the main doors. A scattering of other worried-looking humans sat in worn chairs or paced about. The room smelled like floor polish and stale fried food.

A commotion at the main entrance caught his attention, and Ben turned to see what was going on. A bunch of people crowded the entrance, trying to push past a trio of security guards that barred their way. Cameras beeped wildly, and a dozen voices shouted questions.

"Mr. Rymar, can you tell us what happened?" "Mr. Rymar, can you confirm that Father Kendi is dead?" "Mr. Rymar, was this an accident or an attempt at murder?" "Mr. Rymar—" "Mr. Rymar—" "Mr. Rymar—"

Ben fled. He shoved open the nearest door and stumbled into the hallway beyond. The door swung shut, cutting off the noise. It was too much. He couldn't handle it. Already, he knew, pictures and holograms and live reports were cramming the feeds, feeding the relentless, hungry maw of a nosy public. The weight of it all pressed him down with a terrible weight, and he suddenly felt dizzy. He sank to the cold floor, put his head between his knees, and tried to slow his breathing. After several breaths, he sank into a stupor, staring at the white tiles without thinking. It was a blessed blankness.

A hand touched his shoulder. "Ben?"

He looked up to see Lucia kneeling beside him. Harenn, Keith, Martina, and Bedj-ka stood beside her. He hadn't even heard them come in.

"Is there news?" he croaked. His mouth was so dry he could barely move his tongue.

"None yet," Lucia said. "Keith called us, and we came right over."

"I want to be with him, Harenn," Ben said. "I should be there."

"I know." Lucia put an arm around him, and he noticed her newly rounded stomach. "The orderly said we can wait in that empty patient room over there. Can you stand up?"

Ben found he could. The group filed into the room. Lucia and Harenn sat on the bed while the others crowded along the wall. No one spoke. Ben started to take the only chair, then found he was too restless to sit.

"You probably want to know what happened," Ben said.

"Lars and Keith filled us in," Martina said. "You don't need to talk about it if you don't want to."

"His heart stopped for a while," Ben said dully. "But they got it started again. Now they're doing other stuff to him, but I don't know what."

"Polydithalocide poisoning is treatable," Harenn said. "And Lars acted quickly. I am confident Kendi will be fine."

Ben tried to find hope in her words, but his mind kept shutting down. Bedj-ka, standing in the corner, was clearly fighting tears.

"The reporters were real assholes," Keith growled. "A pack of vultures hanging around the—"

"Okay, Keith," Martina interrupted. "We don't need to dwell on that."

"He's my fucking *brother*," Keith snarled. "I'll dwell on whatever I—"

"Mr. Rymar?" A man in a white coat stood in the doorway. "I'm Dr. Ridge."

Ben's heart jumped. "How is he?" he demanded, wanting and not wanting to hear the answer.

"He's going to live," Dr. Ridge said, and a universal breath of relief sighed through the room. "It was touchy for a while, no question, but he'll recover. The rain slicker prevented the dart from penetrating completely, and he only got a partial dose of the toxin. Still, Father Kendi wouldn't have made it if your bodyguard hadn't administered those antidotes. You can thank him more than me."

"I will," Ben said. His throat was thick. "Is Kendi awake? Can I see him?"

"We're transferring him to intensive care upstairs," Dr. Ridge said. "He's still unconscious but should wake up soon. You can see him when he does. He'll be very weak and will have to spend several days with us."

Ben thanked Dr. Ridge and accepted embraces from everyone in the room, including Bedj-ka. Almost everyone was wiping surreptitious tears from their eyes. Upstairs at the intensive care ward, the nurse on duty firmly refused anyone who wasn't family to enter.

"Mr. Rymar and no one else," she said. "Those are the rules."

"I'll stay here in the waiting room in case Ben needs me," Martina said. "The rest of you should go home, especially the pregnant ladies. You need your rest."

"I will need to speak with you first, Mr. Rymar," said a new voice. It was Inspector Ched-Theree, her blue cloth tied neatly around her head and her silver medallion around her neck. She looked incongruous, standing in a low-ceilinged hallway designed for humans. The Ched-Balaar's medical needs were vastly different from human ones, and they had a different medical center. "This was a clear attempt at murder, and I have many questions to ask."

Ben swallowed. In all the stress and excitement, he had completely forgotten about that. Anger kindled inside him and overshadowed the fear. The bastard who had done this would pay. Ben wouldn't rest until he had his hands around the asshole's throat. If only he knew who had—

The thought struck him with absolute clarity. *Sufur. It has to be Padric Sufur.*

"I have already spoken to Father Kendi's brother and to the bodyguard," Ched-Theree was saying. "Now I will need your statement, Mr. Rymar. Perhaps we could sit in the waiting area."

"Do you wish that we stay, Ben?" Harenn asked.

"No," Ben said, forcing the anger back. "Martina was right—you should go home. I'll be fine with Martina."

The others left. Martina, Ben, and Ched-Theree retired to a small waiting room, where the inspector had Ben go through the events. Unfortunately, Ben had been walking just in front of Kendi and hadn't noticed much.

"And then he just collapsed," Ben finished. "I didn't see anyone who could have done it."

"Did you notice any movement?" Ched-Theree persisted. "Anyone acting in the least bit strange?"

I saw Padric Sufur, Ben thought, *in a house. Walking free and unmolested.* But he didn't want to tell Ched-Theree this. He shook his head. "I didn't see a thing. I was mostly looking at Kendi. Did Keith see anyone?"

"He says he only saw a flash of movement just before Father Kendi collapsed," Ched-Theree said. "The bodyguard gave us the dart he pulled from the wound. The alloy carried a tiny magnetic charge, which seems to indicate it was propelled rather than thrown by hand or blown from a pipe. We will analyze the data more thoroughly for further clues, of course."

A nurse poked his head into the room. "Mr. Rymar, Father Kendi is awake."

"We can finish at another time," Ched-Theree said. "Gratitude."

Ben barely heard. He hurried to follow the nurse into Kendi's room. The lighting was dim. Kendi lay faceup on a hospital bed surrounded by medical equipment. Sensor patches were stuck on his head, arms, and chest. The equipment made soft beeps and whirrs.

"Only five minutes, please," the nurse said. "He needs to rest." And he left.

Ben sat next to the bed and took Kendi's hand. It was

cool and dry. Kendi turned his head and gave Ben a weak smile.

"Still here," he whispered. "Wow."

Ben's throat thickened. "You just *stay* here, mister. I'm not going swimming in the Dream by myself."

"The Real People . . . spoke to me," Kendi said in a halting voice. "They said . . . we have to repopulate the Dream and I . . . I have to help. So I came back . . . even though it was . . . cold. I was cold."

"Are you cold now?" Ben asked uncertainly. "I can probably find the temperature control on the blanket and—"

"Not cold now. Tired."

"I'll go," Ben said. "You sleep. And we'll find the bastards who did this."

He started to rise, but Kendi squeezed his hand with surprising strength. "Promise."

"That we'll get them?" Ben asked. "You're damned right I—"

"No. Promise you'll . . . let the police do it. Don't . . . go after Sufur."

Ben gasped. "How do you know it was Sufur? Did you see him?"

"Didn't see anyone. I just know . . . how you think. Promise me. *Promise.*"

The effort was costing Kendi a great deal, and Ben couldn't bring himself to refuse. "I promise."

Kendi released Ben's hand and fell instantly asleep. Ben looked down at him for a long time. All right. He couldn't go after Sufur directly, but damned if he was going to sit and do nothing. He kissed Kendi's forehead and tiptoed out of the room.

The next day, Kendi was much improved and could sit up unaided. The day after that, he was trying to climb out of bed. After three days he was complaining to anyone who would listen about how bored he was. After six days he tried to leave the hospital and was physically stopped by Gretchen and Tan, who were standing guard outside his room. After eight days, the doctor pronounced Kendi in perfect health and ready to go home. Ben guided the hoverchair to the main entrance, and

Kendi all but leaped for the door. Outside, an enormous crowd of reporters were standing in the rain, held back by a line of police officers. They shouted incoherent questions when the doors opened. Kendi gave them a brief wave before Tan hustled him into the flitcar.

"Praise the Dream," he sighed as the car door shut. Gretchen took the pilot's chair and her takeoff was smooth. "I have to say that rainy air never smelled so good. It's *fresh* air."

"Three Drink Night is tomorrow," Ben reminded him as they flew home. "Lucia's been cooking up a storm. Are you up for a party?"

"You bet!" Kendi said with enthusiasm. "I've been sitting on my bum for so long it's gotten flat." He ran his hand up Ben's leg. "There are lots of other things I've missed, too."

"Keep it for home, please," Tan said from the front seat.

"Tell him your surprise, Ben," Gretchen added. "Maybe it'll distract him."

"Surprise?" Kendi said, curiosity piqued. "You got me a present?"

Ben gave a strange grin that conveyed both pleasure and severity. "Sort of. I found out a few things about Padric Sufur."

Kendi's mood shifted from ebullient to wary. "Like what?"

"With you in the hospital, I had a lot of time to hack around," Ben said. "I finally managed to access a few of Sufur's accounts. He's operating under the name Patrick Sulfur—original—and he has all the utilities and network accounts you'd expect. I'm not up to hacking banks, thanks, but he pays his bills in advance and buys some pretty expensive groceries. His messages are too deeply encrypted for me to crack—yet—but I've been able to tell he's communicating a lot with *somebody*. And we haven't bugged his house."

"Why not?" Kendi asked.

"He's always home. Lucia scrounged up some distance listening devices, and we tried to listen through the walls, but he's insulated his house, and we couldn't hear a thing. We're keeping an eye on the place, but it's barely worth it because he rarely goes outside. That makes it hard to plant bugs in there. Besides, if he's insulated the house, he's probably also set up detectors and scramblers."

"Okay," Kendi said. "I'm assuming there's more."

"Martina and I started sniffing around the Dream, too," Ben said. "We learned something really interesting. We would have picked it up earlier pre-Despair, but these days it takes news quite a while to get—"

"What did you *learn*?" Kendi demanded. "No babbling."

"Sorry." Ben took a deep breath. "We found out that Silent Acquisitions was in bankruptcy. When we freed all those Silent slaves and destroyed the Collection last year, we destroyed Silent Acquisitions. Except at the last minute they found a buyer. Guess who?"

Adrenaline thrilled through Kendi's veins. "Sufur."

"Sufur knew the Despair was coming because he arranged it," Ben said. "Turns out he managed to set himself up so his own fortune would remain untouched, and he has the buying power to be a savior. He owns a majority of stock in Silent Acquisitions now."

"All life," Kendi said in awe.

"Now we just have to figure out why he tried to kill you," Ben said.

"Ben," Kendi said, "this is going to sound really strange coming from me, but—aren't you jumping to conclusions?"

"He shows up on Bellerophon at the same time the attempts on your life begin," Ben said. "That's opportunity. You foiled his plan to destroy the Dream. That's motive."

"We haven't seen means," Kendi said. "Did the Vajhurs say they saw him leave the house when I was darted?"

"No, but he probably hired someone."

"He could have," Kendi said, "but I'm still thinking Foxglove is involved."

"Why?" Ben said. "You're no threat to him anymore. Grandma's polls are at an all-time low. I know Petrie was hoping there'd be some kind of martyr effect with you being attacked and all, but it never happened. Grandma's credibility is shot, thanks to that gangster, and Ched-Pirasku is too boring to put up a good fight. It would be stupid of Foxglove to try and kill you now. If he got caught, it would ruin his chances of winning an election he's already got locked down."

"I'm just saying we should keep an open mind," Kendi said. "Sufur's high on my list, but he isn't the *only* one I'm looking at."

"Who else do you have in mind besides Foxglove and Sufur?" Gretchen asked.

"Um . . . well . . ."

"That's what I thought," Gretchen said.

The rest of the ride was silent. Gray rain washed over the windows, and below Kendi could see golden glimmers of lights set out on balconies in groups of three. He tried to summon up some holiday spirit, but it was hard. In addition to everything else, this would be the first Three Drink Night since Ara had died.

They arrived home to a houseful of delicious kitchen smells. Lucia emerged from the kitchen holding a wooden spoon and gave Kendi a welcome-home hug. Her abdomen pressed against his like a small basketball. Harenn sat on the couch with her feet up, both hands on the mound of her stomach.

"The cow gives you welcome," she said.

Kendi laughed. "You're not a cow. You're a beautiful woman."

"Flatterer. I feel like something that washed up on a beach and could not flop back into the water."

"It won't be long," Ben said. "Can I bring you anything?"

"A bigger bladder."

Kendi leaned down to kiss her cheek, something he would never have considered doing even a year ago. "We deeply appreciate everything you're doing, Harenn. Every moment."

"You may prove your devotion by bringing me three glasses of eggnog."

"I'll get them," Ben said with a laugh, and went into the kitchen. He emerged a moment later with four small glasses on a tray. Brown nutmeg floated on the white-gold nog. "The fourth one's for me," he said. "I have to check my messages. I'll be right back."

"Bedj-ka is playing sims in your office," Harenn said. "But his time is up, so you may kick him off."

"Got it." He left.

"How do *you* feel, Kendi?" Harenn asked.

"Perfect," Kendi said. "I could run wind-sprints. If it weren't raining outside, I probably would, just to get my blood moving again."

"You won't be running anywhere," Tan said. "You're staying under lock and key until the police catch whoever's trying to kill you."

Kendi sighed. "I figured as much. It may be for my own good, but—"

A cry came from Ben's study, followed by the sound of breaking glass. Kendi darted out of the living room and got there first. He found Ben standing in the room with Bedj-ka. The glass of eggnog had shattered on the hardwood floor. Both of Ben's hands were over his mouth, and his blue eyes were filled with horror. Bedj-ka was pale.

"What's wrong?" Kendi demanded as Tan, Gretchen, and Lucia crowded into the hallway behind him.

Ben pointed at the data pad on his desk. The floating display showed a text story from a newsfeed. The headline read, SALMAN REZA'S GRANDSON REVEALED AS SON OF IRFAN.

CHAPTER TWELVE

"A secret dies when it's revealed."

—Irfan Qasad

Senator Salman Reza set her teacup on the coffee table with a firm *clack*. A composite hologram of her grand-children—Ben, Tress, and Zayim—wobbled slightly. "So it's true."

"Yeah." Ben was sitting on her sofa next to Kendi, his hands clasped tightly between his knees. Harenn and Lucia had chairs of their own. Wanda Petrie steepled her fingertips on a loveseat. Tan and Gretchen stood guard at either entrance to the room. "Grandma, I don't know what to do. I need your help."

"You're the biological son of Irfan Qasad and Daniel Vik," Salman said. "No hoax. No joke."

"The truth is the truth," Kendi said. "It doesn't change when you repeat it."

"I'm just trying to get my mind around the concept," Salman said. "My god, Ben—this is . . . this is . . . I don't *know* what this is."

"A miracle," Lucia said. "People are already pointing out that the news about Ben has come out right at the time young Silent are reentering the Dream. How can that be a coincidence? Ben and these children Harenn and I are carrying—true Children of Irfan—are arriving to lead us out of the Despair and into a new age of peace and prosperity."

Harenn clasped her hands protectively over her heavy abdomen. "I will not allow my child to be exploited by the Church of Irfan, Lucia."

"Exploited?" Lucia said with uncustomary heat. "Is that how you see my church? As a bunch of exploitative fanatics? Never mind how many orphans we clothe and feed, never mind how many people we shelter and guide. We are exploitative fanatics because we do these things in the name of spirituality." Her voice rose. "I am also carrying a child of Irfan. Do you think I want *my* baby to be exploited?"

"I did not mean to imply any such thing," Harenn said. "But I fear there will be many people who want to get their hands on our children, and not all of them work for the good of society."

"I am not—"

"Please," Salman interrupted. "Please. This is no time for arguing, my loves. We need to figure out what to do."

"The newsfeeds are carrying nothing but stories about Ben," Kendi said. He waved his data pad. "My public mailbox is so full of requests and demands for interviews that it's run out of memory, and the Council of Irfan has been ringing us without stop. It's only a matter of time before someone ferrets out our home address. The neighbors knew not to tell people—they didn't want strangers sniffing around the neighborhood anymore than we did—but now . . ."

"I'm not talking to the Children or the feeds," Ben said. "I'm not talking to *anybody*. They don't own me."

"You don't have to talk to anyone you don't want to, Ben," Petrie said. "But do you understand what this means for thousands—millions—of people? Not everyone reveres Irfan Qasad as a goddess—"

"Human incarnation of the divine," Lucia corrected.

"—but they do view her as a symbol of hope and power. Your presence would bring hope and happiness to a great many people."

"And boost the senator's polls?" Tan said evenly.

"Yes," Petrie said blandly. "Yes, it would."

"You want me to endorse your campaign, don't you?" Ben said tiredly.

Salman leaned forward in her chair. Behind her, the orange lizards chirped softly in their cage. "I'm going to lose the election, Ben. I imagine my polls have increased a bit with this news—"

"Eleven percent," Petrie said, tapping at her data pad.

"—but it won't be enough to carry me through unless you specifically endorse me."

"Didn't take her long to go from stunned to shrewd, did it?" Gretchen said sotto voce to Tan.

"I don't know, Grandma," Ben said. "I think you're the best candidate for the job, and I'm not saying that just because you're my grandmother, but I . . . I'm not good at public speaking. It makes me sick just thinking about it. I don't want to be a celebrity."

"You are one whether you want it or not, my duck," Salman said gently. "The genie is out of the bottle, and we can't put it back in." She sighed. "You were hoping that I somehow could make it go away because I'm a senator. I don't have that power, love. I wish I did, because I don't like seeing you upset or in pain. I want to see you a happy father with his new children—my great-grandchildren. And you can be. Just because you're famous doesn't mean you can't be happy, too."

"You could move off-planet," Gretchen pointed out. "There are lots of places where no one would recognize you."

"Bellerophon is my home," Ben said. "I've never lived anywhere else. I don't want to leave."

"Then help me make it a better place," Salman said earnestly. "Not only that—if I were in the governor's office, I'd be in a better position to run interference for you and the children. All of them."

There was a long pause. At last, Ben said in a barely audible voice, "All right."

Salman and Petrie both sagged slightly in equal relief. "Thank you," Salman said. "Ben, you've just made history in this room."

Kendi set his own data pad on the coffee table next to the grandchildren hologram. "What I want to know," he said, "is who dropped the news? Lots of people knew about the young Silent reentering the Dream, and I don't think we'll ever trace that leak, but only four people knew about Ben's family—me, Lucia, Harenn, and Ben. And we didn't tell *anyone*."

"It must have been whoever stole that disk from Lucia," Tan said. "There's no other explanation."

"We've gone over that before," Kendi said. "And it still doesn't make sense. The Days were almost certainly working for Foxglove when they found that medical file, but it's also highly likely that they didn't have Foxglove's permission to blackmail Ben—too much potential damage to his campaign if anyone found out. The information about Ben would only hurt Foxglove. He must have ordered the Days killed so they wouldn't leak the info and destroy his chances. Either his operative stole the disk from Lucia, or it really was a random theft."

"If it was a random theft," Lucia said, "and the thief was the news leak, all this would have happened long ago."

"Remember how we decided the mugger was someone who knew where Lucia was headed?" Harenn said. "I still think it a sound theory."

"Except how would the person have known where Lucia was going?" Kendi objected. He picked up the hologram of Ben and his cousins and toyed with the base. "It's all tangled up."

"It seems a paradox," Harenn agreed. "It would appear Salman's enemies stole the information, but they are also the least likely people to reveal it. Either the person who killed the Days was also the person who attacked Lucia—in which case the information should not have come out because it would hurt Foxglove—or the two events were unrelated—in which case the information should not have come out at all or should have come out long ago."

"Yeah," Kendi said, still playing with the hologram base. "It's as if someone . . . someone knew . . ." There was a *click* inside Kendi's head, and a cold finger slid down his spine. Moving with great care, he set the hologram back on the table next to his data pad. His brand-new data pad. Slowly, unwillingly, he turned on the sofa and faced Wanda Petrie in her loveseat.

"It was you," he said.

Petrie stared at him. "I don't know what you mean."

"The data pad you gave me is bugged," Kendi said with icy calm. "Just like the hologram Tel Brace gave me for that stupid game. The day you first visited our house was the day Ben told me about his parentage, and the data pad you gave me was sitting right there on the table. You heard every goddam word. You knew about the plan to break into the Days' house because you over-heard Ben and Lucia talking about it while I was at the Taper rally *and I had left my pad at home.* You ran down to the Days' house ahead of Lucia, broke into the house, and killed them with a neuro-pistol." He turned to Tan. "Don't people who fire neuro-pistols get tempo-rary palsy in their trigger hand for a few days afterward?"

Tan nodded grimly. "Especially when it's set high enough to kill."

"And Magic Wanda over there was dropping things left and right at the speeches just after the Days were killed," Gretchen said. "I remember that."

"This is—" Petrie began.

"You were trying to find the file about Ben on their house computer when Lucia showed up and scared you off," Kendi interrupted. "You wanted that file bad, and you knew Lucia would go back to our house after she finished with the Days' computer, so you hid and waited. Once she got close enough, you hit her and stole the disk."

"Ridiculous," Petrie said. Her face and voice were perfectly calm. "Why would I do such a thing, Kendi? Listen to what you're saying."

"You were all but frothing at the mouth that day in the flitcar when Grandma's polls really started to slide," Kendi continued relentlessly. "You said you'd do any-thing to ensure she won the election. What exactly was that awful job Grandma rescued you from? The one where your boss wouldn't pay for medical procedures? The one you clearly didn't want to talk about? Tan here has police contacts. Perhaps she could find out, if you don't want to tell us."

"She was a sex worker," Salman said quietly. "I knew that when I hired her. One of Wanda's clients . . . hurt her, and her employer refused to pay for the healing. Then he fired her because he said the incident was her fault. The sex industry lost a worker, and I gained a publicist."

"A fanatic publicist," Harenn spat.

"It wasn't like that," Petrie said. Her voice was tremulous. "I didn't want to hurt anyone. But the senator *has* to win. Ched-Pirasku is weak, and Foxglove is a lying, cheating son of a bitch."

"He was the client who hurt you, wasn't he?" Kendi said with a flash of insight. "You aren't so much committed to seeing Grandma win as to seeing *him* lose."

The statement cracked the last of Petrie's calm. "You don't know what it was like," she cried. "Watching his polls climb higher and higher because of his lying and cheating and scheming. Seeing his smug face on the feeds every goddammed day. Standing by as he breaks the news of children reentering the Dream. I killed the Days, yes—but they were filthy extortionists distracting Kendi from his work for the senator. Thousands of lives will change for the better with the senator in office. The Days just didn't measure up to her purpose."

"Oh, god," Salman said. Her face had gone a bit green.

"I only wanted what was best for *you*, Senator," Petrie pleaded. "You have to understand—I didn't want to hurt Ben. I *like* Ben. That was why I didn't release the information about Irfan right away. If you could have won without it all being made public, I would have quietly erased the disk, and no one else would have needed to know. But now—" She waved an agitated hand. "The scandal about Yaraye's campaign contributions and the loss of your chance to break the news about the Dream destroyed everything. I waited, hoping for something else to come along, another opportunity. But nothing did. We're too close to election day now. So I sent the file to all the major—" She halted, took a moment to get herself under control, and drew herself upright. "Well. Now you know. I can't say I'm sorry. Ben has agreed to endorse the senator, and that gives the campaign another chance."

Kendi was so angry it was all he could do to stop himself from leaping across the coffee table and smashing Petrie across the face. Ben had turned to stone on the sofa beside him. Harenn and Lucia looked like someone had kicked them both in the stomach. Gretchen and Tan wore tight, wrathful expressions.

"I'm going to do two things," Salman said in the silence that followed. "First, I'm terminating your employment with malice, Wanda. Second, I'm calling the police."

"You wouldn't," Petrie said, aghast. "Not after everything I've done for you."

"Watch me."

"Think of the scandal," Petrie said quickly. "The scandal of having a killer on your staff, as one of your most trusted advisors. I don't think even Irfan's son could counter that."

Another long silence. Salman's lined face was rigid and immobile. At last she said, "Ben, I'll leave it up to you."

"That's unfair," Kendi said. "If he tells you to call the police, he's ruining your campaign. If he tells you not to, he lets a killer go free."

"Let Ben say that," Salman said. "He can also choose not to decide."

Ben sat immobile as a pile of rock. Kendi couldn't even see him breathing. Then he said in slow, careful words, "I hate you, Petrie. I think I hate you almost as much as I hate Padric Sufur. But I'm committed to seeing Grandma win the governorship. Lewa, do you have access to personal trackers?"

"Only the best," Tan said.

"Good. Can you implant Petrie with one?"

Tan nodded.

"Do it. Petrie, you can roam free until the end of the campaign. After it's over and everything has calmed down, we're coming to get you, and you're going to prison for what you've done."

Petrie opened her mouth to protest, then shut it again and nodded once. Lewa Tan took her firmly by the arm and led her from the room.

"There's more going on than just that," Kendi said. "We've also learned that Padric Sufur is on Bellerophon."

Salman started so violently that she kicked the coffee table and upset the teacup. The delicate china broke, and tea gushed over the table. Lucia quickly mopped it up with a linen napkin while Salman recovered herself.

"Explain," she said in a hoarse voice. Her face was white as milk, and her hands trembled.

Kendi did, finishing with, "We decided we shouldn't confront him or report him to the authorities until we can figure out what his plan is. The Vajhurs are keeping watch on his house, but so far nothing's happened."

"Everything is moving so fast," Salman lamented. "I can't keep up. Young Silent reentering the Dream, Ben's heritage, attempts on your life, Kendi, and now Padric Sufur. After this, being governor will be easy."

"An ancient curse commands the recipient to live in interesting times," Harenn said. "I believe we have long passed *interesting* and gone straight into *enthralling*."

"I think Sufur is the one behind the attempts on Kendi's life," Ben said.

"Why is that?" Salman asked.

"Here we go," Gretchen muttered.

"Kendi stopped Sufur's plan to destroy the Dream," Ben said. "He probably figures Kendi might stop him again, so he's trying to make sure it doesn't happen."

"Except," Salman said, holding up a finger, "that stopping Sufur was a team effort. The entire Vajhur family was involved, as were you yourself, Ben. Sufur has to be aware of this. Why would he single out Kendi? What do the police think?"

"They're still mystified," Kendi admitted. "Ched-Theree says the charge used to cut the tree branch didn't give them anything traceable, and they went over the holo-vid that woman made pixie by pixie. No clues. As far as the poisoning goes, Ched-Theree said the dart is one used for hunting glider lizards, and the sporting goods stores carry thousands of them. The military kept polydithalocide in its arsenal until fifty-some years ago, when it was outlawed, but there are still stores of the stuff around. The police are checking with the military bases to see if any of the stuff has gone missing, but it's slow work."

"I'll see if I can speed things up a bit," Salman said grimly. "The military *likes* me. I have to apologize, Kendi—I should have been more involved with all this."

"You've been a little busy," Kendi said wryly.

"So what do we do about Ben?" Lucia asked.

"First we need to have independent confirmation of his identity," Salman said. "If you can give us a little blood, Ben, we can get it checked so you don't go out there without hard evidence to back you up."

"Go out there?" Ben said.

Salman nodded. "I'll have Yin May set up a press conference. For this evening, if possible."

Ben swallowed hard, and Kendi put an arm around him. His entire body was humming like a high-tension wire.

"I'll be right there with you, love," Kendi said. "You'll do great."

"Long as I don't throw up in front of everyone," Ben said tightly.

Ben did throw up. Twice, in fact. Kendi stood outside the auditorium bathroom, waiting for him. At last he emerged, his fair skin still pale, but his expression determined. Without a word they made their way to the dimly lit backstage area. It smelled of old cloth and dust. Harenn, Lucia, Salman, and various campaign functionaries awaited them. A rumble of voices indicated the audience was filled to capacity. On the stage was a wooden podium, standing like a leader in front of a small army of chairs.

"Not exactly how we were planning to spend Three Drink Night," Kendi said to him.

"Is your ocular implant showing the speech text?" asked a technician.

Ben nodded. "I'm ready," he said, and only Kendi knew he was shaking.

"Let's go, then," Salman said, and strode onto the stage. Immediate applause thundered through the auditorium. Two assistants escorted Harenn and Lucia to chairs behind her and helped them sit as Salman took the podium.

"My fellow citizens of Bellerophon," Salman said, voice booming through the chamber, "today you received some news that struck like a thunderbolt. I'm here to tell you that I was as stunned as everyone else. My grandson, Benjamin Rymar, went to great lengths to keep this information private. He didn't even tell his own family. Recent events, however, have changed that, and I have arranged for him to speak with you for a short time. May I introduce my grandson, Benjamin Rymar."

Ben didn't move. Kendi gave him a nudge, and he took a hesitant step forward. Then he stopped. The auditorium had fallen silent. Salman shot an expectant look backstage. Ben took another faltering step forward, and then another. Kendi put a gentle hand on the small of his back.

"I'm right here," he murmured. "I love you, and I know you're strong enough to do this. Give 'em hell, Rymar."

Ben snorted, then cleared his throat and strode onto the stage. The explosion of noise that greeted him vibrated the entire building. In homes, offices, restaurants, bars, and schools across the planet, citizens of Bellerophon, both human and Ched-Balaar, crowded around holographic displays and held their breath. The conference was being broadcast live on every single feed. There was no other news, no other entertainment. Just Ben. Kendi was glad there was no way for Ben to see that. One auditorium full of roaring humans and hooting Ched-Balaar was more than enough.

Salman yielded the podium to Ben, who took it with obvious trepidation. True to his promise, Kendi stood right behind him. Salman had said Kendi's presence would make Ben look less credible, but Kendi had refused to surrender the spot, and Ben hadn't disagreed. Every human and Ched-Balaar in the auditorium was on his or her feet, shouting, clapping, waving, and clattering. Ben blinked at them and swallowed hard. Kendi wondered if he was going to throw up a third time. Then Ben held up a hand. It took several moments for the crowd to calm down.

"Good eve—" Ben's voice cracked, and he cleared his throat. "Good evening. Irfan Qasad said, 'The greater your knowledge, the lesser your risk.' I think that after tonight, there won't be any risks left."

The crowd roared with laughter. A small smile played across Ben's face, and he visibly relaxed. And when the laughter died down, he turned and nodded a dismissal to Kendi. Kendi was so startled it took him a moment to realize what Ben wanted. Suppressing a proud grin of his own, Kendi took a seat next to Salman behind the podium.

"First I'll break the suspense," Ben said, reading from the text that scrolled across his optical implant. "Irfan Qasad, the first human to enter the Dream, is indeed my biological mother, and Daniel Vik is my biological father."

Another roar burst through the auditorium. The reporters in the front row—given this prime spot because they were the most respected of their kind on the planet—leaped to their feet and shouted questions. Ben stopped speaking until they quieted.

"I have submitted my DNA to several different laboratories for independent confirmation," he said. "The information is widely available, and you can download the files from the net at the address now appearing on the feed display.

"I know you're wondering how this is possible. The answer is that I'm not completely sure. I can only tell you what I know. My mother—the woman who gave birth to me and raised me—was a Mother Adept with the Children of Irfan. Almost thirty years ago, her team found a derelict ship orbiting a gas giant."

He went on to explain how Ara found the embryos and how she had elected to give birth to Ben. Ben's words were calm and measured, even serene. The audience stayed quiet throughout, riveted now. Kendi's heart swelled with pride.

"It is also true," Ben continued, "that the babies carried by Harenn Mashib and Lucia dePaolo are from the same group of embryos. Genetically they're my siblings, but to me and my husband Father Kendi Weaver, they will be sons and daughters."

Murmurs rippled through the crowd at this. Ben waited a moment, then continued. "I learned of my genetic heritage only a few months ago, and I had hoped to keep the information private. However, the news got out, and my family and I have to live with the consequences. I know a lot of people are looking to me to be some sort of savior, as someone who will bring peace and prosperity to Bellerophon. I can understand that sentiment. The Despair hit Bellerophon hard, harder than most places. People are hungry and homeless. But I'm not a savior. I may be the son of Irfan Qasad, but when it comes down to it, I'm really just Ben Rymar, a guy who's good with computers and who's a little nervous about becoming a father.

"I know that people are saying that I'm some sort of . . . avatar, here to lead the people of Bellerophon to some great destiny—or just back into the prosperity we knew before the Despair. I'm afraid that those people are going to be disappointed. The people who can bring prosperity back to Bellerophon are the ones watching this broadcast, the people who walk the solid world and the Silent who walk the Dream. You have the power, not me or my family. Irfan Qasad is part of everyone, not just me. Her legacy touches everyone on this planet.

"As for me, my mother was Mother Adept Araceil Rymar do Salman Reza. She gave birth to me, raised me, loved me. Irfan Qasad is to me as she is to you—a wise, serene woman who lived a very long time ago." Ben paused. "I'll take a few questions."

The auditorium exploded into noise again, and it was some time before the audience calmed down enough for the front-row reporters to make themselves heard.

"Mr. Rymar," said a dark-haired man, "what went through your mind when you found out about your heritage?"

Kendi gave an inward sigh. The feeds couldn't seem to get away from *How did you feel when* questions.

"I was as stunned as you were when you heard about it," Ben said. "Well, maybe a little more than stunned. It's not the kind of news you ever expect to get."

Another reporter asked, "Mr. Rymar, what impact does this have on your relationship with Father Kendi Weaver?"

Ben pretended to think about this one. Kendi, however, knew that backstage certain members of Salman's staff were coming up with answers and feeding them into Ben's optical implant, just as they had done for Ben's speech. The delay was to give the team time to upload the text.

"I love Father Kendi deeply," Ben said. "He was a little startled, too, but it hasn't changed our feelings for each other."

The questions continued. "Why did you choose Ms. Mashib and Ms. dePaolo to carry your children?"

"They volunteered," Ben said. "Both of them are close family friends, and Father Kendi and I were thrilled when they agreed to it."

"Mr. Rymar, are you planning to join the Children of Irfan?"

"No. I have Father Kendi and the two expected babies. That's enough children in one household."

More laughter. Then a young Ched-Balaar reporter gestured for Ben's attention. He was relatively new and inexperienced, and Salman's staff had granted him a front-row seat in exchange for his promise to ask one particular question.

"Mr. Rymar," he clattered, "which candidate do you support for the governorship?"

"Senator Reza," Ben replied. "And I'm not saying that just because she's my grandmother. She's simply the best candidate for the position. Senator Reza and the Tapers have my complete, unhesitating support."

Another murmur rippled through the auditorium. Ben spoke—read—at greater length about Salman's strengths and merits while Salman herself looked modest in the chair behind him. Ben answered a few more questions, then took his leave amid a standing ovation. Next, Kendi took the podium to make a short speech and take questions, followed by Harenn, Lucia, and last of all, Salman herself. She carefully avoided mentioning her campaign—an election speech would make it look as if she had somehow orchestrated the revelation of Ben's parentage—and talked instead about the pride she felt toward her family and how she hoped the citizens of Bellerophon would allow Ben and his children to keep their privacy. And then it was over. A waiting flitcar, one large enough to transport a small platoon, whisked them away from the auditorium and back to Salman's house. The place bustled with people.

"Your polls have climbed thirty-two percent, Senator," Yin May reported the moment everyone entered. "You're in the lead by two points!"

A small cheer went up, and Salman kissed Ben on the cheek. He flushed, and Kendi laughed.

"We can't expect that to last, of course," Salman said. "But praise Irfan—I'm back in the race!"

Much later that night, Kendi and Ben arrived home. Tan and Gretchen climbed out of the flitcar first to establish a safe perimeter and lower the drawbridge. Ben started to get out, but Kendi stopped him and went first. Ben grimaced. Would the rest of his life be like this—always looking out for danger? He fervently hoped not. Maybe all the fuss would die down after the election and people got used to him.

Kendi finally gestured for him to emerge. Ben obeyed, and the flitcar rushed back into the sky. Before the four of them could go inside the house, however, a familiar voice called out of the damp darkness.

"Mr. Rymar! Mr. Rymar! Please wait!"

Ben recognized Grandmother Mee. Gretchen and Tan tensed as the old woman limped toward them. Kendi nudged Ben toward the door, but Ben refused to move. He wasn't going to live his entire life mistrusting everyone.

"It's all right," Ben said quietly. "I'll talk to her." He raised his voice. "Hello, Grandmother."

Grandmother Mee halted a few feet from the drawbridge. Her wrinkled face was uncertain, even a little frightened. "It's true?" she whispered. "Your mother is really . . . her?"

"Yes," Ben said. "It's true."

"And to think," she said incredulously, "that I've been in your house. Eaten your food. I didn't know. I'm sorry." And to Ben's horror, she started to kneel. He reached down and stopped her.

"Don't do that," he said in a harsh, choked voice. "I'm the same person I was yesterday."

"How can you say such a thing?" she asked, and there were tears in her words. "Irfan was your *mother*. You can save us just as she saved her people."

"I can't save anyone," Ben said. "I'm just me."

Grandmother Mee hesitated, then said in a quavering voice, "Can you . . . can you give me my Silence back?"

Ben felt his heart twist and break. The desperate hope that shone on her face slashed like a razor, and he wanted to run from it, hide himself away. "I wish I could," he said softly. "But I can't. I'm sorry."

The hope died from her face. Grandmother Mee nodded once and started to leave. At the last minute she turned back and grabbed Ben's hand. She kissed it once. Her lips were soft, like butterfly wings.

"Help us," she said. "Please." And Ben knew he would have to try.

The next few weeks were a whirl of activity. Everyone wanted a piece of Ben. He was offered houses, flitcars, cash, sex, and the chance to endorse any number of products. Organizations dedicated to charity wanted him for speaking engagements. Organizations dedicated to Irfan begged him to perform services, weddings, and funerals, or simply bless their church building. Every day the feeds carried a dozen stories about Ben—his daily activities, a history of his childhood, interviews with people who had known him. Sil and Hazid transformed themselves into a loving uncle and aunt who remembered being proud of Ben when he was child. Hazid even billed himself as Ben's surrogate father figure until an angry call from Kendi threatened legal action if he didn't knock it off. The spotlight also fell on Tress and Zayim, but not as often. HyperFlight Games put out a hastily altered version of Dream and Despair, one in which Ben was given an expanded role, and the game flashed through two million copies on its first day.

And then there were the offerings.

It didn't take long for the general public to learn where Ben lived—too many people knew—and every day crowds of humans and Ched-Balaar made pilgrimages to the house. Tan kept the drawbridges stubbornly raised, and Ben and Kendi were forced to use a flitcar anytime they wanted to go somewhere. At night, candles and lanterns left by well-wishers made a ring of light around the house, and the dawn always revealed piles

of offerings—food, wine, flowers, clothing, musical instruments, holograms of dead loved ones, live bluelizards
in tiny cages, and more. After the stuff began to pile up,
Lucia suggested that Ben donate the gifts to the Church
of Irfan, a solution Ben readily accepted. Eventually, he
had a small outbuilding built near one of the drawbridges, and two representatives of the Church remained
on duty to direct traffic and accept the offerings on Ben's
behalf. There were never fewer than a hundred people
on the balconies and walkways around the house, and
at least once a day, someone tried to find a way across
the drawbridges. Reluctantly, Ben and Kendi started
searching for another house, one with more privacy.
Within moments of their first inquiries, two different
wealthy people offered up estates—free. Ben politely
declined.

The news also carried through the Dream, and Ben
found himself approached more and more often when
he walked there. Fortunately, he was able to refuse contact more readily in the Dream than in public.

The Children of Irfan tried to contact Ben almost
daily with offers of membership. These Ben steadfastly
ignored. Kendi wondered if Ben still blamed the Children for sending Ara away on long missions when he
was a child. Ben was never rude to the Children, but he
did remain pointedly aloof.

"They're desperate for you to join," he told Ben one
day. "The Council of Irfan called me into their chambers
and asked if I knew of any way to persuade you. I think
they would have ordered me to persuade you, if the idea
weren't so patently ridiculous."

"Tell them you can't persuade me," Ben said with a
shrug. "No one can. I'm not going to tie myself to them
or anyone else."

"They've even created a new position for you," Kendi
said. "The Offspring."

Ben's laugh was like a bell. "Oh no! Is that a joke?
Would my correspondence come from the Office of the
Offspring? When I'm on holiday, would they say 'The
Offspring's off'?"

"You could take longevity treatments and people
would say 'Offspring's eternal,' " Kendi said with a laugh

of his own. "But seriously—they want you bad. It's not only because you'd be a big boost to them financially—"

"How?" Ben interrupted. "I can only carry so many messages through the Dream every day."

"You'd bring in grants and investors and universal interest," Kendi said. "Especially once Dream communication is up and running again. More Silent will come from other planets to join the Children if you're in the club. And you'd be an enormous boost to morale."

"You're taking their side?" Ben said.

"Nope. Just telling you what they told me. Far as I'm concerned, they have me. They don't need you, too."

In addition to the social changes, the Rymar-Weaver house itself also underwent a transformation. Tan oversaw the installation of cameras, monitors, and one-way windows that would allow people to see out but not in. Harenn, Bedj-ka, and Lucia—all of whom had bodyguards of their own—found it harder to come and go, and ended up spending most of their time in Ben and Kendi's house. Ben himself was not allowed to go anywhere without at least two bodyguards.

Kendi, meanwhile, found himself in Ben's shadow instead of the other way around. It felt distinctly strange. Kendi hadn't realized how much he'd grown used to the spotlight until it shone on someone else. And the strain was showing on Ben. He did relatively few public appearances—most of them were political speeches for Salman or festive functions like appearing as grand marshal in Treetown's Ghost Night parade—but they were still a strain. He always threw up at least once before any such function, though he told Kendi that once he was on stage or in front of the camera, he was fine. Still, he lost weight, and Kendi worried.

Harenn, meanwhile, grew larger and larger, until her due date was only seven days away, meaning she could go into labor at any time.

"And how I look forward to that," she grumbled one day from her customary place on the sofa. Through the one-way windows, Kendi could see the usual little crowd of people who stared across the gap created by the raised drawbridges. "I have not slept a full night in so long, I have forgotten what it is like."

"Did you get this big when you had me?" Bedj-ka asked.

"Almost," Harenn said. "And you were a much quieter child. This one kicks and punches and performs backflips."

"Mom said the same thing about me," Ben said with a laugh.

The computer announced a visitor. Tan checked the monitors, answered the door, and escorted Nick Dallay into the room. He was a dark-haired, middle-aged man engaged in a running battle with his waistline. This week he was looking trim, though Kendi had seen him expand like a balloon during a holiday. Privately, Kendi assumed he must have five or six sets of clothes in different sizes. Despite this, he had a sharp mind and was the head of the legal team Ben and Kendi had hired to handle the legal affairs that seemed to explode into their lives with annoying regularity of late.

"Hey, Nick," Kendi said. "Who's suing us this week?"

Nick's face remained serious, and Kendi, who had been joking, gave an inward sigh. It was always something.

"What's going on now?" Ben asked. "More charges of fraud over my true identity? Liability junk? No wait—I've been secretly persuading little old ladies to give me their pension funds."

"I wish it were that simple," Dallay said. "This one's . . . this one's bad."

Kendi tensed. "How bad? What is it?"

"The Church of Irfan is suing you," Dallay said. "They want custody of your children."

CHAPTER THIRTEEN

"The greater the joy, the worse the despair."
—Daniel Vik

The main conference room of Dallay, Muskin, and Kared was furnished with dark talltree wood, a handwoven rug with blue designs on it, and padded conference chairs around a long table. Kendi sat between Ben and Harenn, trying to keep his temper under control.

"Explain their case," he said tightly to Nick Dallay, who sat on the other side of the table next to Ched-Muskin, a distinguished-looking Ched-Balaar with silver-gray fur and a neat head scarf in muted green.

"The Church of Irfan has legal jurisdiction over all orphans," Dallay said. "Their lawyers claim that the embryos Mother Ara found should have been immediately turned over to the Church, and the Church is now suing for its rightful custody."

"Custody over what, exactly?" Ben asked.

"The remaining embryos and the babies Ms. Mashib and Ms. dePaolo carry."

"That's stupid!" Kendi burst out. "How can they call that a case? The babies have parents—Ben and me and Lucia and Harenn. They aren't orphans."

"They're claiming that because the Church should have had custody of the embryos, it is by extension granted custody of the . . . young people," Ched-Muskin clattered, unwilling to say the word *baby*.

"Never!" Harenn spat. "I will not lose a second child. They will have to kill me first."

"Exactly what does the law say about the status of unborn embryos?" Ben asked.

"It's murky," Dallay sighed. "Decided case by case. And that's what the Church is basing their arguments on. If the embryos are considered living children but have no parents of record—and in this case we know the parents are definitely deceased—they must be classified as orphans and handed over to the Church. If the embryos are considered property, they are salvage and rightly belong to the Children of Irfan, since Mother Ara found them while on a Child mission. That would mean Mr. Rymar, however unwittingly, stole them, and they must be returned."

"What a crock of shit!" Kendi exploded. "I can't believe you would—"

"I didn't say I agreed with them, Father," Dallay said. "These are just their arguments. We have our own side—that the embryos and the babies have a living relative in Mr. Rymar, and his custody overrides the Church's, that the Children were clearly uninterested in the embryos and failed to claim them after Grandfather Melthine's death, and that it would be cruel and unfair to separate these children from their parents."

"I do not suppose," Ched-Muskin said, "that you filed any adoption papers on behalf of the young ones?"

Ben shook his head. "It didn't even cross my mind. God, do you think they have a chance of winning?"

"We argued for a dismissal, of course," Dallay said, "but the judge denied it. We could have pushed for a jury trial, but we would, in all likelihood, have Ched-Balaar on the jury, and they would be likely to decide hastily on a case involving a taboo subject like children. The same would go for a Ched-Balaar judge. We moved for a simple hearing before a human judge, and we got it. That's the good news."

"And the bad?" Kendi asked.

"Because Ms. Mashib is due at any moment, the Church moved for a speedy trial and got it," Ched-Muskin said. "This means we have less time to prepare, and you may be certain the opposition has been preparing since Mr. Rymar's first press conference."

"Wait a moment," Harenn said. "You said that if the embryos are classified as property, they are salvage and should be returned to the Children of Irfan. The Church cannot sue Ben for harm suffered by the Children of

Irfan. The Church can only sue Ben for harm he has done to the *Church*. All we need do is persuade a judge to call the embryos property, and the Church no longer has a case."

"Normally this would be true," Dallay said. "Except the Church is affiliated with the Children. The Council of Irfan has granted the Church the power to sue in their name."

"*Grandmother Pyori* is behind this?" Kendi sputtered. "I can't believe it!"

Ben said, "So what can we—"

The door opened and Lucia entered. She was entering her third trimester, and her steps were slow and measured.

"Lucia!" Kendi said. "Where have you been? And what the hell do you mean by—"

"I had nothing to do with the lawsuit," Lucia replied in her usual calm, serene tones. "You know me better than that, Kendi. I have been talking with people in my Church, trying to find out what *they* mean by all this."

"That was unwise," Ched-Muskin said. "You are involved in this lawsuit, and anything you said could be used in court."

"I have recordings of it all," Lucia said. "And I was careful to say as little as possible. Do you want to hear what I learned?"

"Go," Ben said tightly.

"The Church is divided. Many members see this for what it is—a chance to grab power and prestige through Irfan's progeny. A fair number want nothing to do with Ben or the babies because they are also the children of the evil Daniel Vik. Grandfather Ched-Jubil is the head of the Church, and he also serves on the Council of Irfan. He is the primary proponent of the lawsuit, and he persuaded Grandmother Adept Pyori."

Kendi started to speak, then shot a glance at Dallay and Ched-Muskin and shut his mouth. The legal team probably wouldn't sanction what he wanted to do next, so he kept it to himself.

"What's the next step, then?" Ben asked.

"The first is for me to ask an official question," Dallay

said. "Do you wish to accede to the Church's demand that you relinquish custody of your unborn children and the embryos?"

"No!" said everyone in the room at once.

"In anticipation of your answer," Ched-Muskin said, "we have begun preparing a defense. This includes readying each of you to enter the witness cage and testify. The hearings begin in four days, so the sooner we begin, the better."

Kendi strode through the wide corridors of the Marissa Rid Building, which housed the main administrative offices for high-level Children of Irfan. In his days as an Initiate and a Brother, he had secretly found the place intimidating, with its perfectly polished floors, stone sculptures, and oil paintings of wise-looking Grandparent Adepts. After the Despair, however, he had spent a great deal of time here, and the building had lost its awe factor. The place also had a shabby air these days. The floors hadn't been waxed in quite some time, and several statues were missing, perhaps sold. The windows showed grime.

Kendi strode through a set of double doors, past the Sister who tried to bar his way, and straight into the office of Grandmother Adept Pyori. The Grandmother Adept *looked* like a grandmother—white-haired, wrinkled, and slightly plump. She closed watery blue eyes as Kendi slammed the doors behind him. He didn't make the traditional fingertips-to-forehead salute.

"I was wondering when you would come," Pyori said.

"What's going on, Grandmother?" Kendi growled. "I want to hear it from you. No lawyers, no judges. Just you."

"Liza," Pyori said, addressing her computer, "are any recording devices present in this room?"

"There are none," the computer replied.

"You'll pardon if I don't take your word for it," Kendi said. "I've been burned by this before." He took a scanner from the pocket of his tunic, checked for himself, and nodded. "This monastery owes me *everything*, Pyori. Every. Goddammed. Thing. Why are you doing this?"

Pyori got up and went to the window, which showed only gray rain. It struck Kendi as a prosaic gesture. Everyone, it seemed, stared out a window when they had to talk about something difficult.

"Ched-Jubil's arguments are well-reasoned," she began, "but they—"

"They're bullshit," Kendi interrupted. "The Church didn't care one shred about those babies until they turned out to be—"

"If you want me to explain, you need to be silent," Pyori snapped back. Kendi ground his teeth and obeyed. "As I was saying, Ched-Jubil's arguments did not convince me entirely, though they convinced half the Council. The other Councilors believe Ched-Jubil is motivated by self-interest and greed."

"Leaving yours the tie-breaking vote," Kendi said softly. "So what do *you* believe?"

Pyori continued to stare out the window, refusing to meet his gaze. "We're bankrupt, Kendi. Our few working Silent can't keep us solvent anymore. Next week we have to announce we're terminating all our remaining lay employees and that we can no longer pay stipends to the Children. We've gained a lot of new Initiates now that the younglings are entering the Dream, but they won't be ready for communication work for a few years yet."

"The government won't bail you out?" Kendi said, shocked to the core. "What about a loan? The Children have been the center of Bellerophon's commerce since the founding."

"We've asked," Pyori said. "Mitchell Foxglove opposes the idea, and he's talked a lot of Senators into agreeing with him. They've stalled the legislation for so long, it won't do us any good. Bellerophon has its mines and tree farms now."

Kendi stared. It didn't seem possible. The Children had always been wealthy, able to scatter a fleet of slipships across the galaxy and pay outrageous prices to set Silent slaves free. Kendi had spent their money like water. Now Pyori was telling him the well had run dry.

Other issues, however, took precedence. "I hope you

aren't looking for sympathy from me," he said. "Right now I'm waffling between loathing and disgust. What would Irfan say about this?"

Pyori's body shuddered at his words, as if they were physical blows. "I don't want to hurt you and Ben," she said. "But . . . if the Church or the monastery had custody of Irfan's true children, we could attract the interest of off-planet investors, something we can't do in our current position. The media attention can also be milked for cash. I know it sounds coldhearted. Perhaps it is. But it will save thousands and thousands of families from homelessness and hunger."

"At the price of destroying mine," Kendi spat.

Pyori said nothing. Kendi turned and left.

His Eminence Judge Nutan Prakash called the court to order, and everyone sat. The audience portion of the courtroom was nearly empty—Prakash had barred the feeds. Kendi, Ben, Harenn, and Lucia sat with Ched-Muskin and Nick Dallay at the defendant's table. Ched-Jubil crouched alone behind the plaintiff's. Kendi's heart pounded, and his hands were slick with sweat. On a table in front of the bench sat the star-shaped cryo-unit, lights winking with machinelike serenity.

"I'd like to remind counsel that this is a hearing, not a trial," Prakash said. "I don't want grandstanding or powerful oratory. I know the basic facts of the case, so you don't need to explain them to me. Let's keep it straightforward and simple. Grandfather Ched-Jubil, I understand you are representing the Church?"

"I am, Eminence," Ched-Jubil said. He was big, even for a Ched-Balaar, and possessed a silky-looking, night-black coat of fur.

"Then state your case."

Ched-Jubil rose. Kendi flicked a glance at him, then stared carefully forward. If he looked at Ched-Jubil for any length of time, he got so angry he felt he would erupt like a boiling geyser.

"Your Eminence," Ched-Jubil clattered, "the Church of Irfan is rightly and legally awarded custody of any orphaned children on Bellerophon."

Kendi snuck a startled glance at Ched-Jubil. He had

actually used the word *children*. Of course, it would have been hard to argue this case using circumlocution. Ched-Jubil went on to explain the Church's arguments as Dallay had outlined them to Kendi and Ben three days ago. Beside Kendi, Ben sat still as a statue. Harenn and Lucia shifted now and again, trying to find comfortable positions in their chairs. Would the children they carried come home to him and Ben? Or would they end up wards of the Church? If that happened, who would be their parents? Who would take care of them and play with them and love them? Kendi swallowed to keep his throat from closing.

Prakash's face remained impassive during Ched-Jubil's speech, and Kendi would have given his Silence to know what the judge was thinking. At last Ched-Jubil finished, and Prakash motioned at Dallay.

"Counselor," Prakash said. "It's your turn."

"Your Eminence," Dallay began, "although the defense respects Ched-Jubil's careful arguments, we maintain they are without merit. We move for a dismissal."

"Denied," Prakash intoned, as Dallay had said he would. "Continue, Counselor."

"Eminence, the babies Ms. Mashib and Ms. dePaolo carry can hardly be called property. Slavery has never been legal on Bellerophon. This means they must be classified as children. You can see with your own eyes that they have mothers, and later we will produce documents that prove Mr. Rymar and Father Kendi are their fathers of record. Mr. Rymar is also related to the children. He is their brother, and there are hundreds of legal precedences granting custody of children to relatives other than parents.

"My colleague has also argued that the embryos are stolen property. Ched-Jubil is obviously trying to preserve the log and eat the grubs inside. Either the embryos are children, or they are property. However, I will answer his arguments. If the embryos are children, they should go to their nearest living relative—Mr. Rymar. If the embryos are property, they clearly qualify as a case of laches and abandonment of property. Legal precedence clearly states that valueless property which is lost or stolen, and then somehow increases in value, cannot be held up as valuable to the original owner just because the new owner has found value for it.

"In other words, Eminence, the embryos had no intrinsic value to the Children of Irfan for a long time. Grandfather Melthine made no secret of this fact. Just because Mr. Rymar and Father Kendi discovered the embryos' value after Mr. Rymar removed them from Grandfather Melthine's home doesn't mean the law can treat them as if they had *always* been valuable and desirable. Because the Children of Irfan and the Church didn't bother to try to get the embryos back before they were discovered to be Irfan's issue, they relinquished all right to them. They can't claim to have a right to them now."

Dallay paused meaningfully. "The case is clear, your Eminence. Once again, I must move for dismissal."

"Denied," Prakash said, and Kendi let out a breath he didn't realize he'd been holding. It had been a slim hope, but a hope nonetheless. "Ched-Jubil, call your first witness."

The hearing continued. Ched-Jubil called up legal experts, medical experts, Church officials, and members of the Council of Irfan. Dallay cross-examined. Sometimes he managed to discredit them, sometimes not. Prakash stayed true to his word and cut several of the longer-winded witnesses off. By the end of the business day, Ched-Jubil had not presented his closing arguments, and Prakash declared a recess until the morning.

The moment Kendi, Ben, Harenn, and Lucia got home, a small crowd descended upon them. Keith, Martina, Bedj-ka, and Salman all talked at once, demanding to know how it went. Gretchen and Tan watched in the background.

"The transcripts aren't available yet," Salman said over the noise, "and we haven't heard a thing."

"I need a shower," Ben said, and strode for the bathroom. "I feel filthy."

"Oh dear," Martina said. "It didn't go well?"

Feeling suddenly exhausted, Kendi sank to the sofa. "It's hard to tell. Right now Ched-Jubil is having his say, so yeah, things look bad."

"He's an asshole," Bedj-ka said.

"Language," Harenn said, but the rebuke was half-hearted.

"You have a lot of public support," Salman said, patting his hand. "That probably doesn't make you feel any better, but it's true nonetheless."

"I've had it with the public, Grandma," Kendi said, feeling every iota of gravity pull at muscle and bone. "I'm sick of being in the public eye. I'm sick of the whole thing. I just want to enjoy being a dad, but I'm worried and scared all the time."

"Welcome to my world," Keith grumbled, but no one paid attention.

Ched-Jubil spent the rest of the following day with witnesses and further arguments. At last, with perhaps an hour to go, he made his final statement. He said nothing new, and Kendi spent his time trying unsuccessfully reading the judge's face. The third day belonged to Dallay. He stood straight and tall before the bench and called his first witness, a legal expert on medical law. Several other witnesses took the stand as well before Dallay finally called Lucia, followed by Harenn, who seemed to fill the witness cage with her enormous belly.

On the fourth day, Dallay called Kendi to the stand, and finally Ben. Two more experts testified, and Dallay gave his closing arguments.

"I can't find any way to make it clearer, Eminence," Dallay finished. "We have proven beyond the tiniest shadow of a doubt that the babies and the embryos belong with their parents Benjamin Rymar, Kendi Weaver, Harenn Mashib, and Lucia dePaolo. Thank you."

Dallay sat down, and Prakash spent several moments looking at his data pad. Kendi held his breath again.

"I will have my decision in the morning," Prakash said in a flat voice. "Adjourned."

Neither Kendi nor Ben slept well that night. Kendi barely managed a light doze filled with dreams of crying children being ripped from his arms. And then he couldn't find Ben anywhere. He was alone in the Dream, trapped in dolphin form and trying to swim in water thick and heavy as gelatin. He woke alone, with the covers twisted around his body. Outside, dim light filtered through the talltree leaves. Ben was sitting on the floor with his back against the wall. Dark circles made heavy rings under his eyes, and his hair was dull and lackluster as a dying sun.

"I don't know if I can go, Ken," he said thickly. "I can't even stand up. The judge is going to take away our kids, I know it. I won't have anything left."

Kendi sat on the floor next to him. "You'll have me. No judge can take me away."

The mood was somber as everyone took their seats in the courtroom. Prakash looked out across the bench, his face impassive. The silent, stuffy courtroom was filled to capacity—the feeds were allowed access for a decision. Martina, Keith, Bedj-ka, and Salman were all present. Harenn was looking particularly uncomfortable in her defendant's chair, but she waved away offers of food or drink. Kendi was so tense, he felt he would snap in two. An ice-cold hand—Ben's—stole into his and squeezed.

"This was no easy decision," Prakash said. "Even after a thousand years of debate, we can't easily classify human issue as property or as a sentient life, and so we move on a case-by-case basis. I'm not going to summarize the arguments again or my reasoning—you can read them in the transcripts." He took a deep breath, and Kendi thought his heart would stop. "The court finds that the Irfan embryos are and have always been the property of the Children of Irfan, and it grants that organization immediate ownership. The children carried by Harenn Mashib and Lucia dePaolo were implanted illegally and without the permission of their owners. The court therefore declares them orphans and awards custody to the Church of Irfan. So be it."

The courtroom erupted in a storm of voices. Judge Prakash exited quickly. Kendi stared at the empty bench, stunned. His mind refused to work. With a few words, one man had brought down Kendi's entire world. The children—*his* children—would be taken away from him. From his family. His whole body felt cold, and his hand hurt. Kendi looked down. Ben was squeezing so hard both their knuckles were white.

"Ben, that hurts," Kendi said over the noise, and Ben

let go. His face was devoid of all expression, but his body was trembling.

"Bastard!" Lucia shouted after the judge.

"We'll appeal," Dallay said. "It's not over yet." But Kendi barely heard. He watched Ched-Jubil exit the courtroom through a side door with the cryo-unit, and he had never wanted to kill anyone as much as he wanted to kill that single Ched-Balaar.

The reporters, meanwhile, formed themselves into a seething mass, but the bailiffs kept them away from the defendant's table.

"We have to get out of here," Harenn said. Her brown face was pale. "Now. It's broken."

"The case?" Kendi said stupidly.

"My water," Harenn said. "I am in labor."

An officer of the court followed them to the medical center. A small platoon of police officers worked hard to keep the reporters out, and Harenn was given a private birthing room for greater security. Tan and Gretchen stood outside the door. The officer of the court, a short blond woman, tried to enter, but Harenn ordered her out.

"I will not allow the thief who steals my child to watch the birth," she barked, and Tan firmly escorted the woman away. Ben watched her go, hating her, hating Prakash, hating the entire damned world. This was supposed to be a joyous occasion, the birth of his first child. He wanted to wrap his fingers around Petrie's neck and squeeze until her eyes popped out. She had destroyed his family to get her petty revenge against Foxglove.

Lucia took a seat near the bed. The birthing room was meant to be cozy, with a warm wood floor, armchairs, bright curtains at the windows, and flowers on the shelves. A pair of nurses prepped Harenn by helping her into a hospital robe and affixing a small blue patch to her forehead.

"This will prevent the contractions from feeling painful," the first nurse explained. "Dr. McCall will be in shortly to see you."

Kendi took up a position on the side of the bed opposite Lucia. Ben trembled. He felt like he was going to be sick. He felt like he was going to fly apart. He felt like he was going to die. He glanced at the door and wondered what would happen if he grabbed the baby after it was born and fled. As if he'd get more than ten steps outside the medical center without tripping over a reporter.

"How do you feel?" Kendi asked.

"Physically I feel perfectly fine," Harenn said. "You may guess about the rest."

"I can't believe the judge ruled against us," Lucia said, rubbing her hands over her belly. "How could he be so cruel? I feel like Irfan has deserted us."

"Your Church would say it's Irfan's will," Kendi snapped. Then he exhaled hard. "I'm sorry, Lucia. That just popped out."

"I want nothing more to do with them," Lucia said. "Never again."

Harenn sucked in a gentle breath.

"What's wrong?" Kendi asked.

"Just a contraction," Harenn said. "A small one. It will be three or four hours yet."

"Perhaps I should judge that," said Dr. McCall from the doorway. "How long have you been having contractions, Ms. Mashib?"

"Since early this morning," Harenn said. "I did not want to miss the trial, however."

McCall's round face hardened. "I heard about the ruling. It was an abomination." She ran a scanner over Harenn's abdomen. "You're dilated to three centimeters already. Moving along quickly."

"Bedj-ka's birth was the same," Harenn said.

"I'm guessing you'll be able to start pushing in about three and a half hours," McCall said. "I'll check back."

A silence fell over the room when she left. Ben could barely breathe. It was as if the gravity in the room had doubled, grinding him to the floor. He looked at Harenn. Soon she would give birth to the child he had been awaiting for months—years. He remembered being a child and pretending the embryos were sleeping playmates, boys and girls who would understand him and like him for who he was. He remembered the joy he had felt when Kendi had agreed to raise children with him and the surprised elation when Harenn and Lucia had unexpectedly volunteered to carry two of the babies to term. All that joy turned to crushing despair.

"Why?" he whispered. "Why are they doing this to us?"

Kendi moved toward the door. "I have to get out of here," he said. "I have to go."

Ben couldn't even summon the energy to ask where Kendi was going. He leaned against the windowsill and watched Harenn, trying to disconnect himself. The baby was going to live somewhere else. It wasn't his anymore. He wouldn't ever hold it. No diapers to change, no midnight feedings, no screaming, no tantrums, no silly noises, no first steps, no first day of school, no—

Just no.

The minutes dragged by, and Harenn's contractions came closer and closer. Kendi didn't return, and Ben's calls to him went unanswered. He was probably hiding, waiting until it was over so he wouldn't have to watch. Ben wished he could do the same—hide his head and not look until it was all over. He wanted to resent Kendi abandoning him and the others like this, but that would take too much energy. Whenever Ben left the birthing room, he saw the officer of the court sitting in a waiting room up the hallway. One time he stopped and spoke to her.

"Do you enjoy stealing children?" he asked.

She didn't answer. Ben noticed a diaper bag full of baby supplies on the floor next to her, and the rage he had been holding back suddenly boiled out of him in an unstoppable flow.

"You're a bitch," he snarled at her. "A child-stealing, family-wrecking, fascist bitch. What kind of filthy, putrid person could steal a *baby* from its rightful family?"

The woman didn't move, though her jaw trembled slightly. A muted holo-display in the corner showed an image of a reporter talking in front of the courthouse. Ben didn't have to guess the story he was covering.

"I hope they pay you good money for ruining my life and the life of my child," Ben said relentlessly. "You're not even good enough to rot in hell."

A hand touched his arm. "Ben," Gretchen said in an uncharacteristically gentle tone, "why don't you come away? She's just doing her job. If it weren't her, it'd be someone else."

"Slavers say the same thing," Ben snapped.

"Dr. McCall says Harenn is ready to push," Gretchen said. "Come on. You'll miss it."

Ben spat on the floor near the officer's feet and strode from the room. He thought he heard a small choked sob behind him, but didn't pause to find out for sure.

In the birthing room, Dr. McCall was already in position to receive the baby. Ben quickly ran his hands under the sterilizer's red light and stood beside her. Harenn lay on the bed holding Lucia's hand, her face screwed up in concentration. Kendi was nowhere to be seen.

"And *push*," McCall said.

Harenn let out a soft sigh as a ripple crossed her bare abdomen.

"Good!" McCall said. "I can see the top of the baby's head."

Ben wanted to be excited, tried to be. Failed.

"Is Kendi out there?" Lucia asked. "He's going to miss the birth."

"I'm here," Kendi said, striding into the room. He carried his data pad with him.

"Where have you been?" Harenn panted.

"Busy," Kendi said with a weak smile. "Is the cow ready?"

"The cow was ready a month ago," Harenn said.

"Push," McCall said. "And *push!* . . . Here it comes!" A moment later, Dr. McCall held up a bloody, slippery baby. It cried angrily. "It's a boy!"

"I want to hold him," Harenn said. "Before they take him away."

"Are you sure?" McCall said. "It'll only make it—"

"Give him to her," Kendi ordered. Tears stood in his eyes, and Ben realized his own eyes were wet. McCall wrapped the baby in a blanket and handed him to Harenn. Ben, Kendi, and Lucia gathered around to see. The baby calmed down once he was in Harenn's arms, and he opened his eyes. They were blue, like Ben's. A faint fuzz of blond hair covered his head.

"His name is Evan," Ben said around the lump in his throat. "Evan Weaver."

"Don't," Lucia choked. "Don't name him. It'll only make it worse when—"

"I'm afraid I have to take the baby now," said the officer of the court from the doorway. "By order of the—"

"No," Kendi said, barring her way. "You won't take Evan anywhere. He's our son, and he will stay with us."

"I'm sorry, Father Weaver," the woman said. "I don't want to do this, believe me, but—"

"I have legal documents from the Children of Irfan," Kendi interrupted. He brandished the data pad and brought up a text file. "The Council has granted Ben and Harenn and me permanent adoptive custody of Evan. The same goes for Lucia's baby and the embryos."

Hope exploded through Ben. "What? When?"

"Just now," Kendi said. "I spent the last three hours arranging it."

"I need to see those," the woman said, taking the pad from Kendi. She read for a moment, then wrinkled her forehead. "This isn't official yet. It says Mr. Rymar has to sign the attached agreement."

"What is it?" Ben asked. "I'll sign it, whatever it is."

Kendi faced him. "I'm sorry, Ben. It was the best I could do."

"Sorry?" Ben echoed. Dread stole over him. "What do you mean? What's it say?"

"The Council agreed to make the Church grant us custody," Kendi said. "But only if you join the Children of Irfan as the Offspring."

"Oh god." Ben backed away. Behind him, Evan started to cry again.

"I used every bit of influence I have," Kendi said. "Grandmother Pyori said her main concern—her *only* concern—is to save the Children from bankruptcy. She said you can do that just as easily as the babies can. It was either them or you."

"A deal with the devil," Ben said.

"Or Daniel Vik," Lucia said.

"The Children are not the devil," Kendi said. "But it is a lifetime contract."

Ben hesitated less than a second. He pressed his thumb to the data pad in the officer's hand. It beeped once in acknowledgment.

"The babies are yours, Mr. Rymar," the officer said. "I'm glad." And she left before anyone could respond. Ben felt a momentary twinge of guilt about the things he had said to her. Then he turned to watch Harenn nurse his son, and his heart overflowed.

"Whoozawiddiewuddyden? Whoozabigboy?"

Kendi poked his head into the nursery. Gretchen was leaning over the crib, making faces and cooing at Evan. It was one of the few times when no one was holding the baby. For the last three days, Evan had been steadily passed from one person to the next, barely set down long enough for diaper changes. Ben, Harenn, and Kendi held him the most, of course, but Lucia, Bedjka, Martina, and even Keith had all taken their turns. Mysteriously, Evan always ended up in the hands of his fathers when his diaper needed changing, but Kendi didn't mind. Not yet, anyway.

"Amazing how babies soften even the most hardened adult into putty," Kendi remarked.

Gretchen ignored him. "Wuzzawuzzabigboy," she said. "Whoozerauntiegretchenden?"

Kendi joined her at the crib. Evan stared up at both of them with enormous blue eyes and a solemn face that came straight out of the holograms and pictures Kendi had seen of Ben as a baby. It seemed both strange and completely natural to have this baby in his life, this infant that carried Kendi's own childhood name. Unlike adults friends and family, Evan never left. He was always somewhere in the house, and he always needed something—a diaper change, feeding, burping, cuddling. It had only been three days, and already the entire house revolved around him. Kendi found himself willing to do nothing but stare at Evan for hours on end. It was weird. But he liked it.

"We can't really say he looks like you, Kendi," said Keith, also entering the room.

Kendi put his dark hand on the fair skin of Evan's forehead. "Nope. He looks like his daddy. I'll just have to make sure he *acts* like me."

"So how many people have been asking for publicity photos of this kid?" Keith asked.

"Only every single reporter on every single feed. They can get stuffed, far as I'm concerned."

"What's the latest on the move to the new house?" Gretchen asked.

"We're hoping for next month," Kendi said, still looking down at Evan. "It'll be spring by then, and the rains will have stopped."

"What's the place like?" Keith said. "I haven't seen it."

Kendi picked Evan up. He smelled like sweet powder. His skin had lost most of its blotchiness, and he seemed more alert. "It's bigger," Kendi said. "On the outskirts of Treetown. There's enough room for Harenn, Bedj-ka, Lucia, and a whole bunch of kids. It's also the only house in the entire talltree, so we'll have a lot more privacy."

Keith whistled. "Sounds expensive."

"It is, but Salman's realtor—we hired her—says we'll get a nice price on the current house. Apparently the fact that Ben lives here is going to spark a bidding war. We haven't even listed yet, and she's already getting offers."

"Nice," Keith said.

"And we got a royalty check from HyperFlight last week. Thanks to Ben, Dream and Despair has already sold four million copies both here and off-planet. HyperFlight can't crank them out fast enough."

"Don't I know it," Gretchen said. "I'm set for years."

"So we're doing fine." He wanted to ask how Keith was doing but swallowed the words. Keith would get angry. Martina would let him know if they needed anything.

The computer announced a visitor. Kendi carried Evan into the living room in time to see Ben admit his uncle Hazid, aunt Sil, and cousins Tress and Zayim. Kendi tried not to grimace. Evan, who had dozed off, stirred restlessly in Kendi's arms.

"Those security guards outside are gangsters," Sil complained before she even had her coat off. "They wanted to *search* me. Imagine! And why don't you get rid of those . . . gawkers around your house? I don't know how I'll stand the strain of them staring at me every time I come to visit."

"Hello, Sil," Kendi said. "Nice to see you. Something to drink? Water? Tea?" *Hemlock?*

"I want to see him," Tress said, holding out her arms to take the sleeping Evan from Kendi, who handed him over warily. "So you're the little guy that's causing all this fuss. Yes, you are. Yes, you *are*."

"Oh, brother." Zayim plopped down on the sofa. "It's just a baby, sis."

"He's your cousin," Tress said. "God, he looks just like Ben. He's so *cute*."

Kendi warmed toward Tress against his will. Anyone who found his son cute got automatic brownie points.

"Where's everyone else?" Hazid asked, also taking a seat.

"Harenn and Lucia are napping," Ben told him. "Bedj-ka's in school at the monastery. Martina's out doing her level best to restore the economy by shopping until she drops. Either that or she's riding dinosaurs again."

"I don't want to hear about that," Kendi said.

"Has Mother been by to visit yet?" Sil said.

"Yesterday, briefly," Kendi said. "She's enormously busy now that her polls have jumped. Me, I can't wait until the whole stupid thing is over."

"We saw your speech, Ben," Tress said, and Kendi remembered that they hadn't spoken to Ben's extended family since the revelation. "I've gotten letters from total strangers asking what it's like to be related to you. How come you didn't tell us?"

"I didn't tell anybody," Ben said. "I didn't even tell Kendi for almost a month after I found out."

"Reporters have been asking to interview me," Tress added, "but your publicity team said to turn them down for now."

"It's a control thing until the election's over," Ben said.

Tress chucked Evan under the chin. "I don't mind. I'm not much of an interview person."

"I am," Zayim grumbled. "Some of them have offered me money, and I'm not exactly flush these days."

The last sentence was a none-too-subtle hint, but Kendi happened to know that Salman had already given Tress and Zayim generous stipends in return for their media silence, so he pretended not to have heard.

"So what's it like being the famous Offspring?" Hazid asked.

Ben grimaced. "I haven't met with the Council of Irfan to discuss it yet. They can contact *me* if they want to talk. Right now, I have a baby to take care of."

"If you need another babysitter, let me know," Tress said. "He's such a sweetie. How many times does he get up at night?"

"Only twice," Ben said. "It's not as hard taking care of him as I thought it would be. Of course, we have lots of people involved."

"Wait until you have two and three and ten and eleven," Sil sniffed. "I can't imagine having that many children. Tress and Zayim were plenty enough, and then Ara kept leaving you with me."

"Mother," Tress warned. "Remember what we said about counting to five before you said anything?"

"Who wants tea?" Kendi said loudly. "I'll put a kettle on."

While the water was boiling, Ben showed everyone the nursery, which was stocked with enough toys, clothes, and supplies for ten Evans.

"A lot of it we got for free," Ben said. "Companies and stuff who want my endorsement. We keep what we need and give the rest to charity."

"To the Church?" Zayim asked.

"No. There are other children's charities."

Tress laid the sleeping Evan in his crib. "Are you angry at the Children?"

"Very," Ben said, face set. "They put me through hell, and then made me work for them."

"I don't blame you," Tress said. "Still, I've heard

they've already gotten a couple of investors from off-planet to help in the bailout. You know, a lot of Silenced monks lost their homes when the Children slashed stipends. The dormitories are filled to overflowing—entire families living in one room. If you hadn't agreed to be Offspring, they would have had to close even the dorms and throw all those people out onto the walkways. You helped a lot of people, Ben."

"Maybe," Ben said. "But only because they put a gun to my head."

They visited a bit longer before bidding formal goodbyes. Tress, the last one out, hung back.

"Let me know if I can help," she said softly to both Kendi and Ben. "Either with the baby or other things. Just don't let Mom and Dad and Zayim know. They're still mad at me for apologizing to you at Grandma's."

And then she was gone.

The Dream was definitely noisier. Kendi's kangaroo ears easily picked up more background whispering, and the place just *felt* more populated. The young Silent weren't actually in the Dream yet, but they were touching it, dreaming about it with breathtaking realism, sensing something in the air. Kendi remembered his early days when his Silence stirred, though he hadn't know what it was. All he knew was that at night it felt like the world was holding its breath, and if Kendi could just say the right thing or do the right dance or turn the right corner, Something Amazing would transport him to a new world, one far away from the frog farm that enslaved him.

Before him, Outback sand and rock lay baking beneath the hot golden sun, even though it was night in the solid world. Kendi felt restless and uneasy. He shifted his weight, stirring the sandy soil with his tail. It was probably just normal nerves. So much had been going on lately, and he hadn't had time to sit still and sort it all out. No wonder he felt uneasy.

Kendi closed his eyes and stretched out his mind, sniffing, seeking, listening. He found Bedj-ka. The boy's mind felt focused, and Kendi guessed he was meditating. A bit more searching turned up Ben, whose mind was filled with both strain and contentment. Ben had been holding Evan when Kendi dropped into his customary meditative pose, but Kendi couldn't sense Evan's mind yet. Kendi sighed. Evan's gene scans said he was Silent, of course, and Kendi should have been able to find at least a trace of him in the Dream. But Kendi felt nothing. There were a number of explanations for this. The Despair had impaired Kendi's tracking ability. Evan was only a few days old. Kendi's current edginess made it hard to concentrate. Still Kendi worried. He wanted Evan to be Silent, and he dreaded how the world would react if he turned out to be like Ben was for so long—genetically Silent but unable to enter the Dream. Sejal had pulled Ben into the Dream, awakening his full Silence. Perhaps Sejal could do the same for—

Kendi shook his head. He was getting way ahead of himself. Evan wasn't even a week old, and already Kendi was worrying about his future. Did all fathers do this?

The unease increased. Kendi opened his eyes and leaped into the air as a falcon. He turned and dove and swooped, trying to let the exhilaration of flight through the hot updrafts sweep away the stress.

It got only worse. Kendi's wings shook, and he tumbled briefly before righting himself. Thoroughly unnerved, he forced himself to land and change into a dingo. Kendi sat for a few moments in an attempt to calm down, then he got up and paced. All the hair on his body rose, prickling his skin. His breath came in short, quick pants. He had to run, had to get away, get *out*.

Kendi closed his eyes again and tried to summon up his concentration. *If it is in my best interest and in the best interest of all life everywhere,* he thought, *let me . . . let . . .*

He couldn't concentrate. The hot sun burned like a bonfire, and pure, unadulterated fear tucked Kendi's tail between his legs. Kendi changed into a brown-and-white desert skink. The lizard form was much smaller, allowing Kendi to dart under a rock, where he felt slightly more secure. He summoned his concentration.

If it is in my best interest and in the best interest of all life everywhere, he thought again, *let me leave the Dream.*

There was a *wrench*, and he was standing in the corner of his and Ben's bedroom with his red spear under his knee. Ben and Harenn were sitting on the bed. Harenn was nursing Evan. Kendi had expected his tension to dissipate once he left the Dream, but it only grew worse. His heart beat an unpleasant cacophony inside his chest, and his mouth was dry. He almost lost his balance while removing his spear because his hands shook so badly.

The motion caught Ben and Harenn's attention. Ben noticed the expression on his face and immediately stood up. "What's wrong?"

"We have to get out of the house," Kendi said hoarsely. "Now! Grab Evan's diaper bag and run. *RUN!*"

Harenn clutched Evan to her chest and ran without hesitation. Ben sprinted after her, pausing only to snatch the diaper bag from the nursery as he passed by. Kendi followed, shouting for Lucia, Bedj-ka, Tan, and Gretchen. Bedj-ka tried to ask what was going on, but Ben grabbed his arm and hauled the boy bodily toward the front door. Tan didn't waste time asking what was going on and instead activated her earpiece and shouted orders to the outdoor guards. Lucia, also used to field work, hurried as quickly as she could, but her heavy body slowed her down. Kendi and Gretchen stopped to help her. Every nerve in Kendi's body shrieked at him to hurry, move, *run*, but he stayed with Lucia.

"Carry-chair," Gretchen said at last. "Quick!"

Kendi grasped the inside of his own elbow and with his free hand grabbed for Gretchen's. She did the same for him, forming a square of flesh and bone for Lucia to sit on. The moment she sat down, they hoisted her up and fled out the door.

Outside, Tan had lowered one of the drawbridges. The security people were forcing the usual group of gawkers back to a safe distance. Fortunately, the night was chilly, and the crowd was thin. Harenn, still clutching Evan, stood with Ben and Bedj-ka, surrounded by four more guards. Lars was one of them. Kendi and Gretchen carried Lucia over and set her down. Tan hurried up, face flushed.

"I've called the Guardians," she said. "They're on the way. What's this all about? Did you see something?"

Kendi shook his head. Now that they were outside, his tension and fear had evaporated like water on a hot rock. He couldn't for the life of him think what had scared him so badly.

"I don't know," he said. "I was in the Dream, and suddenly I had to get everyone out the house. I don't know why—I just did. Now . . . now it all seems kind of stupid."

"Something must have set you off," Tan said. "We'll do a full sweep of the house before we—"

The explosion knocked them off their feet.

CHAPTER FOURTEEN

"Work for me. You'll like it. I promise."
—Irfan Qasad

Fiery debris rained down from the sky and struck the walkways with thuds and clunks. The humans and Ched-Balaar who had managed to keep their feet fled in a screaming stampede. Evan's thin, frightened wail rose above the noise. Barely aware of what he was doing, Kendi got halfway to his feet and flung himself on top of Harenn, who had curled herself protectively around the crying baby. Out of the corner of his eye, he saw Ben sheltering Lucia. Something hit Kendi's back with a stab of pain and bounced away. He stayed where he was. The smell of burning wood and scorched wet leaves filled the air. After a time, Kendi slowly raised his head. The house was on fire. The nursery and main bedroom were a wreck.

"Is everyone all right?" he demanded, getting to his feet.

The group shakily stood up on the wooden walkway past the drawbridge. Harenn, still clutching the screaming Evan, looked desperately around. "Where's Bedj-ka? Bedj-ka!"

"I'm here, Mom," said the boy. His face was pale, and he was bleeding from a cut on his cheek but otherwise seemed fine. A quick check among the others revealed a few bruises and minor cuts, including one on Kendi's back, but no serious injuries.

"How did you know that was going to happen?" Ben asked.

"I didn't know it was going to be a bomb," Kendi said, a little awed. "I just knew we had to get out."

The fire squad arrived and had the fire out in short

order. The police provided crowd control and handed out blankets to the Rymar-Weaver household to ward off the chill. Evan finally quieted. Inspector Ched-Theree also arrived and set about taking statements.

"We have an entire team looking into this," she said. "It seems reasonable that the same people are responsible for this and for the other attempts on your life, especially since the tree branch was also severed with an detonation device. Unfortunately, the clues are few. A forensic team will examine the house in careful detail, and they may have something to tell us in a few hours."

"What I'd like to know," Tan said, her raspy voice even more hoarse than usual, "is how a bomb got past our security measures. Got chemical sniffers to watch for explosives. Should have spotted a bomb right away. Who planted it, and how did it get there?"

"Who has access to your home?" Ched-Theree asked.

"These days?" Ben said. "Only family and close friends."

"There's Ben and me," Kendi said, ticking off his fingers, "Harenn, Bedj-ka, Lucia, Grandma—Senator Reza—my brother Keith and sister Martina, Ben's aunt Sil and uncle Hazid, and his cousins Tress and Zayim. And the security people."

"Would any of them want to kill you?" Ched-Theree said.

"We don't get along well with Ben's aunt, uncle, and cousins," Kendi said, "but I don't think they want him dead. Ben?"

"Tress and I get along fine these days," Ben said, pulling his blanket tighter around himself and Evan. "Sil still whines, and Zayim and Hazid are complete jerks, but killers? No."

"When was the last time each of these people was in your house?" Ched-Theree asked.

"They were all here today," Kendi said. "Except for Grand—Senator Reza. She visited the day after we brought Evan home from the hospital."

"The explosive had to be planted within the last week," Tan said. "We do a complete security sweep of the house every seven days—"

"You do?" Kendi said, surprised.

"Standard," Tan said. "We turned up nothing. Has anything new come up on the other attacks? Might give us a clue."

Ched-Theree dipped her head. "Indeed. Thanks to Senator Reza's expediting, I learned that a military research laboratory near Othertown was keeping a small supply of polydithalocide for study. It was recently stolen. We are working with the military to solve the theft. I also learned that the medical center took extensive scans of Father Kendi's dart wound, and we took a very close look at the angle of entry. It may point us toward the place occupied by the attacker. We must first finish here, however."

"Why are we standing outside?" Gretchen demanded. "It's not safe for all of you to be standing around in the open like a herd of mickey spikes. Someone with a rifle might take potshots."

"Grandma's," Ben said. "We should be safe there."

A quick phone call followed by an equally quick flitcar ride, and they were securely ensconced behind the walls of Salman Reza's enormous home. Salman herself showed them to guest rooms.

"Make yourselves at home, my poor ducks," she said. "Wash up and then come downstairs for tea and sympathy."

After quick showers to wash off soot and grime, Kendi, Ben, and the others wrapped themselves in thick bathrobes and gathered in Salman's living room. Evan was asleep on Ben's lap, apparently none the worse for wear. A generous array of foods that impressed even Lucia was spread across the coffee table, along with steaming mugs of herbal tea. Kendi's stomach growled with previously unnoticed hunger, and he wolfed down most of a ham sandwich without really tasting it. Then he took Evan so Ben could eat. The baby made a warm bundle in his lap. Kendi looked down at his sleeping face, and a lump the size of an apple grew in his throat. His son, this little baby, had almost died. Kendi's hands started to shake. He himself had come close to death any number of times, but the possibility of Evan coming to harm unnerved him. He stole a glance at Lucia's round belly. Would it be like this for all their children?

"Perhaps we should hold a council of war," Salman said. "That's what this has become, after all—a war."

"But who are we at war against?" Lucia sipped her tea. "We don't know who our enemy is."

"Or exactly who the *target* is," Gretchen said. "The first two attacks were clearly made against Kendi, but the bomb could have been for any one of us. Most likely are Kendi or Ben, but it could also have been meant for—sorry, it has to be said—meant for Evan. He's a child of Irfan just like Benny-boy there."

"The question to ask is *Who benefits?*" Tan said. She got up to pace the floor. "If Kendi died, who would benefit? Same for Ben and for Evan."

"Foxglove," Kendi said. "Before Ben's revelation, my endorsement was keeping Grandma's campaign going. The branch and the dart both happened prerevelation. After the revelation, Ben—and Evan—became dangerous to Foxglove as well. Look at the change in tactics. The branch and the dart would hurt only me. The bomb would take out all three of us. Foxglove benefits."

"As would Ched-Pirasku," Harenn pointed out.

"Ched-Theree said the polydithalocide in that dart probably came from a military base near Othertown," Lucia said. "That may point toward Mitchell Foxglove."

"I still think Sufur has a hand in this," Ben growled. "We can't discount his presence here."

Kendi said, "Maybe we should—"

"Excuse me, Senator," said a black-clad servant in the doorway "Inspector Ched-Theree is here. Shall I show her in?"

Salman gave assent, and Ched-Theree joined them, sitting on the floor next to the sofa. Her blue head cloth was limp and sweaty-looking, and her silver Guardian's medallion was dark with soot. Salman offered her tea, but she refused politely.

"We have preliminary findings," she said. "The forensic crew scanned the site and found traces of a chemical explosive. The common name for it is Trip-Slap, and it is quite rare and expensive."

"Chemical explosive?" Gretchen said. "Why didn't the sniffers catch it coming in?"

"Trip-Slap is short for 'triple slap,'" Ched-Theree

chattered. "It involves three chemicals. The first is a buffer solution which is, by itself, not dangerous. The second is a stable chemical held in the buffer solution as a suspension. The third chemical is an enzyme. It breaks down the stable chemical, which then reacts with the buffer solution to create a liquid so volatile that simple ambient vibrations cause it to explode."

"How did the attacker manage to get it inside the house, then?" Kendi asked.

"The first two chemicals were probably placed together in a container. Then whoever built the explosive dropped a second container containing the enzyme into the mix. When the container dissolved, it released the enzyme and transformed the entire jar into an explosive."

"How long would it take to dissolve the enzyme container?" Ben asked. "That might tell us when it was planted in our house."

"That we do not yet know," Ched-Theree said. "It will require painstaking scans to uncover such microscopic shards. Pray to Irfan that it does not rain within the next few days."

"You still haven't told us how the bomb got past the sniffers," Tan said.

"None of the chemicals are volatile by themselves, so sensors that sniff for explosives miss them entirely. All three chemicals are also extremely expensive and difficult to manufacture. As a result, the manufacturers of chemical sniffers rarely include them in the sniffer's database." Ched-Theree lifted a hand to fiddle with one end of her head scarf. "Perhaps after this incident, they will do so."

"If the chemicals are expensive, the attacker has to be wealthy," Ben said with a pointed look at Kendi. Evan stirred on his lap.

"It would seem so," Ched-Theree said. "This does narrow the field of suspects."

"Do you have suspects?" Kendi asked.

"We have leads," Ched-Theree said, then lowered her head and gave Kendi a hard stare. "Is there anyone *you* suspect? Someone you have not yet mentioned? Perhaps because it only recently occurred to you?"

Kendi shook his head. "Sorry. No one."

"What of you, Inspector Tan?" Ched-Theree asked. "Is there anyone you suspect?"

"No," she said.

"A pity," Ched-Theree said. "I will continue my investigation. Meanwhile, do not travel anywhere alone. It would be a terrible thing if you were to disappear as well."

"As well?" Harenn said.

"You have not heard the news?" Ched-Theree said in exaggerated surprise. "I suppose it is understandable. The lawsuit and the election and becoming new parents have doubtless been a distraction."

"What are you talking about?" Kendi said sharply.

"Well over a dozen people have disappeared in the past few months. We have recovered no bodies and received no ransom notes. They simply disappeared. The only thing all of them have in common is Silence. In fact, exactly half of the victims are Silent, and the other half are Silenced. We cannot help but wonder about a connection."

Kendi suddenly remembered reading about disappearances on the feeds—the girl on the hiking trip, the Silent monk who hadn't come home, the people Keith had said stopped coming to work. He should have noticed, should have spotted it, but he had been so busy with everything else. Besides, Bellerophon was supposed to be *safe*, a haven. Who would have thought Silent were in danger here?

A silence had fallen around the room. Finally Salman said, "A connection sounds worth investigating, Inspector. If anything comes to any of us, we'll let you know."

A clear dismissal. Ched-Theree dipped her head once and left, this time without pausing. A great deal of the room's tension left with her.

"Do we tell her?" Ben asked, voicing Kendi's thoughts.

"It seems stupid not to," Lucia pointed out. "The police and Guardians can do a much better job watching Sufur than the Vajhurs."

"They'd arrest him," Kendi said flatly. "This isn't the first time Sufur's been to Bellerophon, remember. The first time he showed up, he persuaded Sejal to take part in his project—unknowingly on Sejal's part, I might add—and he helped a spy escape. Technically he didn't break any laws, but—"

"Last I looked, helping a spy escape is breaking the law," Tan asked.

"The man in question was spying on the Empire of Human Unity," Kendi said. "That isn't illegal on Bellerophon. But I know the Guardians and the police would like to talk to Sufur at great length. If we tell them he's here, they'll arrest him, and we'll lose any chance of finding out what he's up to."

"And the Guardians won't be able to figure it out?" Gretchen said sardonically. "If they arrest him, they'll get access to his computer and communication records and anything else in his house."

"Not if he's smart, they won't," Ben said. "And Sufur is pretty smart. It's not hard to set up a self-destruct virus that'll clean-wipe your system if you say the word. I'd do it."

"We may be able to persuade the Guardians to watch him," Harenn said.

"And we may not," Kendi said. "They're an unknown."

"There has to be a connection between Sufur's presence and the disappearing people," Salman pointed out. "He owns Silent Acquisitions, and they've kidnapped people before."

"But why would they kidnap both Silent and Silenced?" Ben asked. "The Silenced would be useless to Silent Acquisitions."

"Perhaps he's only kidnapping Silent and the other disappearances are coincidence?" Lucia said.

Kendi shook his head. "We're still flailing around in the dark. I think the best course is to keep watching Sufur and wait for something to break. Something always does, if you're patient."

"You are counseling patience?" Harenn said. "This is a new thing."

"I'm getting really tired of that," Kendi said, suddenly snappish. "Yeah, I was headstrong for a long time, but

Ara's death hit me fucking hard, so now and again I *think*. Is that such a big deal?"

"Apologies," Harenn murmured.

Kendi took a deep breath. "Anyway. We need to keep Sufur to ourselves for a while. Once we know what he's up to, we'll turn the whole thing over to the Guardians."

His tone made it clear that it wasn't a question, and even Salman accepted his words with a nod.

Ben flung open the meeting room door and strode inside. The startled Councilors gathered around the central table leaped to their feet, including the Ched-Balaar. Ben didn't pause, but his heart was pounding in his throat, and he could still taste the bile from the last time he had thrown up. He strode to the foot of the table—Grandmother Adept Pyori stood at the head—and placed his palms flat on the surface.

"I'm here," he growled. "Let's get started."

The Councilors stared. Ben stared back. It was the first time he had met with them, the first time he had set foot on monastery property since he had accepted the role of Offspring, and the Council was clearly uncertain. Ben began to feel uncertain himself. These people were powerful. They ran the monastery and had direct influence on both local and planetary government. Most of them outranked even Grandma. Then he saw that most of the Council was looking at him with awed expressions. He caught sight of Ched-Jubil, and his resolved stiffened.

"Well?" he said. "The Offspring is a busy man."

The Councilors turned as one to Grandmother Pyori. She cleared her throat. "Why don't we all sit down?"

What would Kendi do? Ben thought of a sudden. He folded his arms. "I prefer to stand. Keeps the meeting short."

Pyori closed her eyes for a moment. "Ben—"

"That's Mr. Rymar."

"We're starting on an angry note," Pyori said. "I don't think we want—"

"Want?" Ben said, anger overcoming his earlier apprehension. "*Want?* Since when have the Children cared about what I might *want?* You tried to take my children away from me, and now you've forced me to join an organization I've . . . I've . . ." He tried to pause, but the words burst out of him. ". . . an organization I've *despised* for my entire life. You took away my mother, you tried to take away my children, and now you're trying to take away my life. Let's get one thing straight right now, *Grandmother*—I may have joined your filthy organization, and you may have my thumbprint on a contract, but you'll never have my cooperation. Don't talk to me about what I *want*, Pyori."

"*Grandmother* Pyori," Ched-Jubil corrected in shock. "Offspring or not, you do not have the right to—"

"And if that child-molesting Ched-Balaar slaver ever speaks in my presence again," Ben snarled, "I'll cram his head up his own ass."

"Ched-Jubil," Pyori said gently, "your presence causes the Offspring understandable distress. Perhaps there are other duties you could attend to right now?"

Ched-Jubil started to protest, then caught a glimpse of the stony expression on Pyori's face. He ducked his head and withdrew without another word.

"Thank you," Ben said, slightly mollified.

"I always said that lawsuit was a foolish idea," clattered a Ched-Balaar Councilor quietly.

"Please sit down," Pyori said in the same gentle voice. "I'm an old lady with tired feet, but I don't feel comfortable sitting in . . . in your presence, Offspring, if you remain standing."

Reluctantly Ben took a seat at the table. The rest of the Council followed suit, with the humans in chairs and the Ched-Balaar on floor cushions. Counting Pyori, there were six of them—three human and three Ched-Balaar. The humans were dressed in formal brown robes trimmed with blue silk while the Ched-Balaar wore brown head cloths, also edged in blue. All the Councilors wore rings of indigo fluorite to indicate their rank as Grandparents. Only Pyori's ring carried the amethyst that gave her rank as Grandmother Adept, and her robe was embroidered with gold thread.

The echoing, wood-walled room seemed too large and too stark for this small group to meet in. Ben recalled when there had been nine Councilors, four of which were from species other than human and Ched-Balaar. He also recalled that when Melthine had been Head of Council, the meetings had been held in the Dream. The Despair, however, had taken the lives of several Councilors and Silenced the rest, including Grandmother Pyori. Ben wondered how much distress Ched-Jubil felt at being Silenced. He hoped it was a lot.

"Ben—Mr. Rymar," Pyori said once everyone was seated, "I apologize for every moment of distress the Children caused you and your family, and I am, in fact, prepared to release you from your contract."

Hubbub broke out in the room. The human Councilors leaped to their feet, their protests joining the hoots and clatters of the Ched-Balaar. Pyori picked up an elaborately twisted walking stick set with an enormous amethyst at the nob and thumped it hard on the floor. The talk died down. The humans sat again, stiff with tension.

Ben eyed her warily. "What's the catch, Grandmother?"

"No catch," she said, "except that before you decide, you hear me out." She continued before Ben could reply. "Mr. Rymar, you know that your discovery has touched off a storm all around Bellerophon—throughout the universe, really. I have to admit that I feel . . . awed standing here, in the same room, with Irfan's own son. I think the rest of the Council feel the same way."

Nods and head-ducks of assent all around the table followed this last statement.

"I never wanted your awe," Ben said.

"You have it just the same." Pyori leaned on the walking stick. "Mr. Rymar, because of your presence, we—the Children—have been able to attract three off-planet investors to help bail us out of bankruptcy. We can now remain solvent long enough to survive until this new generation of Silent is able to begin courier work. As a result, we can pay our people again.

"I don't want to force you to work with us, Mr. Rymar. You said you've hated us your entire life because you see us as the people who sent your mother away from you when you were a child, and lately because we tried take your own children away from you.

You may not believe it, but it tore my heart to let Ched-Jubil file his lawsuit. I was faced with the terrible choice of preserving one family or rescuing hundreds."

She tapped a control on her data pad, and a series of holograms popped up in the center of the table. A thin, ragged child tried to warm his hands in front of a meager fire. A Ched-Balaar whose ribs showed through her fur rummaged in a garbage heap for food. A human mother held the hands of two small children as they stood in a long, long line at a soup kitchen. A shaky town of tents and crude lean-tos stretched out across the forest floor, the people looking hopeless and afraid. Ben swallowed hard. Every night he slept in a fine, soft bed. His and Kendi's house had been nearly destroyed, but there was no question about whether or not they and Evan would have food to eat and a warm place to sleep. He had given plenty of money to charities, but he had never walked through the downbelow tents or visited the bread lines. In all the fuss over the election and his revelation, he had forgotten how bad it had become for some people. For many people.

"Some of our Silenced brethren have left us to work new trades in Othertown's mines and on the farms," Pyori continued, "but many have remained in Treetown, barely surviving. Infant mortality rates have soared. People—children—die of simple viruses and bacterial infections because there is no money for medical care. But thanks to your presence, we can once again provide food, housing, and medicine to these families. We can put them to work, give them their lives back."

Pyori nodded, and the Ched-Balaar Grandfather sitting closest to Ben set a data pad and a small box on the table in front of him.

"Mr. Rymar, I've signed an agreement that releases you from your obligation to the Children of Irfan. It also states that you and Father Kendi will keep permanent adoptive custody of the babies and the embryos. All you have to do is sign."

"What's in the box?" Ben asked.

"Open it," Pyori said in that same, relentlessly gentle voice.

Ben did so. Light glinted off a gold ring set with a

circle of seven small stones—ruby, topaz, amber, emerald, lapis lazuli, fluorite, and amethyst. One stone for each rank of Child. It was beautiful, and its symbolism was clear.

"It's up to you," Pyori said, "whether you want the agreement or the ring."

Ben stared at the ring. After a long time, he set it down and picked up the data pad. Pyori bit her lip. Ben pressed his thumb to the pad. The agreement erased itself. Then he picked the ring back up and put it on. Every Councilor sighed.

"Thank you, Mr. Rymar," Pyori said.

"Call me Ben," he said. "So. What's this Offspring business going to be about?"

Kendi-the-bat flitted restlessly through the Dream. His keen ears picked up whispers, tiny threads of the minds around him. Many were familiar—Ben, Bedj-ka, Keith, Martina, even Harenn and Lucia, who weren't Silent but whose minds were familiar enough to him that he could sense them without even trying. Now, however, he was looking for something he had never touched before. He was looking for a sensation.

Before the Despair, Kendi had been a tracker nonpareil. He had, for example, been the first Silent to sense Sejal's strange talent at work in the Dream, and he had managed to pinpoint his location to a single city on a single planet. Pretty good, considering he'd had an entire universe of Silent minds to sift through. Nowadays, however, his hold on the Dream was weaker, and it was harder to find people. Last night something had told him to flee his own house, and Kendi suspected his subconscious had picked up something his conscious had missed. Now he was flitting through the Dream trying to see if he could figure out what it was.

A stark round moon outlined the sand and rocks of the Outback in hard silver below Kendi, and the desert air was cold beneath his wings. Faint whispers coursed on the still air, and Kendi concentrated hard, trying to separate out each one. The phenomenon had to be local to Bellerophon, so he worked at tuning out the noise that came from other planets and star systems. His mind automatically rearranged the Outback to reflect this, soundlessly warping the landscape into a box canyon that encompassed Bellerophon and deadened the sounds from everywhere else. Kendi fluttered back and forth across the canyon in a criss-cross pattern, listening, smelling, even tasting. Every rock and stone, every leaf and stem on the stubborn plant life was a mind on Bellerophon, and he did his best to check—

Kendi caught a strange double echo that immediately faded as he moved away. He flipped around and back-tracked, flittering left and right, until he caught the sound again. It was the voice of someone in the Dream whispering to someone in the solid world, and the whisperer was whispering from outside the canyon. The mind on the receiving end felt familiar to Kendi, but he couldn't place who it was—the whisperer was changing the person's thought patterns and interfering with Kendi's impaired ability to recognize who it was.

Kendi, however, had the whisperer's own unique sound in his ears. He flew up out of the canyon and followed the little thread of noise. His tiny heart beat quickly—this was important, he knew it. After a few moments, he came to the edge of his Outback. Past the boundary of his turf, the sandy soil melded into a posh office, complete with enormous desk, thick carpet, and huge windows that looked out over a landscape of sky-scrapers. Cheery sunlight beamed across the room, hurting Kendi's night-sensitive eyes. Sitting in the executive chair behind the desk was a dark-haired man Kendi didn't recognize. The man's eyes were shut and his lips were moving. Whispering.

Kendi changed shape in midflight, shifting into his falcon body, and flashed across the boundary into the office. The man instantly sensed the intrusion into his turf and his eyes popped open. Kendi changed shape again and thudded onto the desk as a full-grown kangaroo. The man leaped backward, shoving his rolling chair away from the desk.

"Who the hell are—" Kendi began, but the man whipped an ugly-looking pistol from under his suit jacket. He fired, but Kendi was already moving. He leaped straight up and came down, aiming for the man's lap. The bullet struck the wall and exploded, leaving a hole the size of Kendi's head. The man twisted out of the chair with an agility that would be impossible in the solid world. He rolled away and came up firing. Kendi flipped back into bat form and twisted away. The shots shattered the window behind him with an ear-ripping crash. Kendi dodged and flittered like mad. Psychosomatic carryover would force his solid-world body to duplicate any injury he sustained in the Dream, including his own death. Kendi was at a further disadvantage because he was limited to animal shapes in the Dream, meaning he could conjure up weapons of his own, but he couldn't use them. He was also on this man's turf, making it difficult to change the environment as a method of attack.

The man bolted from the office and fled into a newly appeared corridor outside the double doors. Kendi twisted around again to give chase. The doors tried to slam shut, and Kendi turned sideways, skimming through just before they crashed together. He had to keep his quarry off-balance and not allow him enough time to gather his concentration and leave the Dream.

The man was already halfway up the corridor, heading for a bank of elevators. His gun was nowhere to be seen. Kendi dropped back into kangaroo form and bounded ahead. He had almost caught up to the other Silent by the time the man reached the elevator bank. One set of doors was already open. Kendi gave a desperate leap. Before he could land on the other Silent's back, the man whipped around, pistol back in his hand. He fired. Something slammed into Kendi's leg and knocked him backward. Fiery pain tore at him. Kendi heard the elevator doors close and a moment later, the office vanished, leaving a flat, gray plain in its place. The other Silent had left the Dream.

Kendi tried to get to his feet, but every movement caused him intense pain. Finally, he forced himself to take a deep breath and concentrate. *If it be in my best interest and in the best interest of all life everywhere,* he thought, *let me leave the Dream.*

He was lying on the floor, with plush carpeting under his cheek. Pain throbbed hot in his left leg. His short, red spear, the one that he stood his knee on like a peg leg, lay to one side. Kendi managed to sit up, hissing at the pain the movement cost him. A bloody hole had opened in his upper thigh, and blood ran down his leg. He wondered how Salman would react to him bleeding on her guest room rug.

"Muldoon," Kendi said through gritted teeth. "Tell Harenn I need her to bring her med-kit. Now!"

"Acknowledged," said the computer.

Harenn hurried into the room a moment later, med-kit in hand. She stopped the bleeding, disinfected the wound, and gave him a shot of painkillers before asking him what had happened. He explained in short, terse sentences.

"You have no idea who he was whispering to?" Harenn asked when he finished.

"I couldn't tell," Kendi admitted. "It was someone I know, but that's a lot of people. I didn't recognize the whisperer, either."

Harenn helped him up onto the bed so she could affix a heal splint to his leg. "How do you know that what he was doing is connected to you?"

"Because he ran like hell when he saw me," Kendi said. "If he was innocent, why run? Why shoot at me?"

"True." Harenn fastened the splint around his upper thigh. "What is the next step, then?"

"I'll have to keep hunting for this guy in the Dream." Kendi sighed as the heal splint took full effect and the last of his pain faded. "And keep watching for someone who wants to kill me. Have you seen Ben?"

Harenn shook her head. "He hasn't come back from his meeting with the Council of Irfan yet."

"That should have been over a long time ago." Kendi stood up gingerly and tapped his earpiece. "Ben?"

Pause, then, *"I'm here, Kendi. What's going on?"*

"Where are you?"

"At our old house. I'm just . . . I'm okay."

"You don't sound okay," Kendi said, heading for the door. "What's wrong? Who's guarding you?"

Another pause. *"It'd be easier to talk about it in person, I think. Meet me down here."*

*   *   *

Cold rain clattered off Kendi's rain poncho as he approached the ruin of his and Ben's house with Gretchen just behind him. The place was a ruined mess. Blackened beams poked upward like broken fingers, and the remaining walls leaned drunkenly. He found Ben standing near one of the drawbridges and staring with melancholy eyes at the wreck.

"Ben?" Kendi said. "It's raining. What are you doing here?"

"I needed to get something," Ben said in a distracted tone. "Closure, maybe. This was my mother's house. Then I lived here, and I was looking forward to raising our kids here. Now it's gone."

"Everything changes," Kendi observed philosophically. "It's the only constant in the universe."

"I suppose."

"You're not here alone are you?" Gretchen demanded. "Who's guarding you?"

"I came by myself because I wanted to see this by myself," Ben replied. "No one knew I'd be here, so it's safe."

"Ben, it's never safe anymore," Gretchen said.

Ben looked at the wreckage again. "Ain't it the truth?"

"How did your meeting with the Council go?" Kendi asked.

Ben told him. Kendi blinked with surprise. "So you're sticking with them."

"Yeah. It'll help a lot of people who need it. Why are you wearing a heal splint?"

Kendi told him. Ben's mouth fell open. "He tried to *kill* you?"

"Maybe. He may have been just trying to scare me. In any case, we have to find him."

"How's your downstairs neighbor?" Gretchen said, changing the subject. "I never heard if she was hurt in the explosion or not."

"I talked to Grandmother Mee just now," Ben said. "There was some minor damage to her house, but she wasn't hurt. She's trying to sell the place, says she can't afford to keep it up anymore."

"Where's she going to go?" Kendi asked.

"I guess she's moving in with her son. He doesn't have room for a garden, though. It's sad."

"Yeah." They stared at the wreckage a while longer, then Kendi led Ben back to the flitcar.

CHAPTER FIFTEEN

"A celebrity is a person who's known for being well-known."

—Daniel Vik

Over the next two weeks, Kendi spent every spare moment in the Dream fruitlessly looking for the whisperer. His spare moments weren't many. Evan took up a great deal of his time. The baby was strangely hypnotic. Every so often Kendi would shake himself and discover he had spent nearly an hour just staring at him. It didn't seem to matter what Evan was doing—waving his fists, trying to put a finger in his mouth, sleeping. It was all good.

He was also forced to deal with the house. The explosion had destroyed the nursery, demolished the master bedroom, and badly damaged the rest of the house, causing the building inspector to condemn the entire structure. Sorting out the insurance claims took up yet more time. In the end, Ben had directed Nick Dallay to handle it, but he and Kendi still had to approve offers, read paperwork, and sign forms.

A bonded moving crew, carefully checked by both Salman's people and by Lewa Tan, took over the task of packing and moving the Weaver-Rymar household's surviving possessions to the new house, though for simplicity's sake, everyone was staying with Salman until the election. Even though Kendi wasn't directly involved in the move, he lost more time to answering questions and dealing with small crises that arose.

Kendi tried to hook other Children of Irfan to searching the Dream for the strange Silent who whispered from an office, but without success. Every moment the monks spent hunting was a moment they weren't ferrying messages. Every moment they weren't ferrying messages was a moment the monastery earned no revenue, and at the moment, revenue ruled supreme. In the end, only Keith and Martina spent time with the search, and they turned up nothing.

Ben, of course, was even busier. His face appeared on the feeds almost constantly, whether he was making campaign speeches and commercials, appearing at public functions, or just caught on camera. Spurious, often pernicious headlines about him grew like poison ivy. OFFSPRING CAUGHT IN HOTEL SEX SCANDAL! OFFSPRING CHECKS INTO RECOVERY PROGRAM! OFFSPRING ADMITS DOUBT ABOUT PARENTAGE! OFFSPRING GIVES IN TO VIK SIDE OF NATURE, THREATENS SHOOTING SPREE. The monastery and the law offices of Dallay, Muskin, and Kared made tidy sums by suing the more libelous feeds. The publishers usually paid up and went right back to writing more fake stories—anything with Ben's name or face on it was a guaranteed sell.

In addition to the feed publicity came marketeers. Offers to name toys, games, food, even a flitcar after him poured in. Ben universally turned them down.

Another type of offer plagued Ben as well, this one from women. Hundreds of female humans—and a few female Ched-Balaar—offered themselves as surrogate mothers for the remaining embryos. These Ben also turned down, but not without a shudder.

"It's like they're offering to climb into bed with me," he told Kendi one day, "only much more . . . much more intimate, if you know what I mean."

Salman's initial burst of popularity wore off somewhat, but Foxglove's dropped considerably, leaving Salman just ahead of Ched-Pirasku and his Populist party. The election was now a week away. Between that and caring for Evan, Ben and Kendi barely slept. They got even less sleep when Lucia woke them up in the middle of the night and announced it was time to go to the medical center. Harenn said she would stay with Evan while Gretchen and Tan got the flitcar. Kendi and Ben spent the subsequent ride sending frantic messages canceling various appearances.

* * *

Lucia's mother Julia and her cousin Francesca were waiting at the medical center entrance, as was a man in the blue robe and clerical collar that marked a priest from the Church of Irfan. Ben closed his eyes and wrestled back a spurt of ire. Even though he had performed countless blessings and rituals for various parishes within the Church of Irfan, he hadn't managed to give up his final shreds of anger toward the organization and its members.

"You want me and Tan to shove them aside, boss?" Gretchen asked.

"Don't you dare," Lucia hissed back. "Mom! I didn't expect to see you here." Her usually serene voice took on a note of frost. "Or you, Francesca."

"Lucia," said Francesca. "I'm glad you're well."

"Of course I'm here," Julia put in. Her words echoed off the hard tile floors of the medical center lobby. "I was at the birth of all my grandchildren."

"And I came with Friar Pallin," Francesca put in. "He's here to perform the birth blessing."

"How *thoughtful* of you to bring him," Lucia said. "You just think of *everything*."

"*Someone* has to think of what's best for the child," Francesca purred.

"Odd. I never considered you much of a thinker," Lucia replied.

"Lucia!" Julia said, aghast.

Before anyone could react further, Friar Pallin knelt before Ben, effectively ending the conversation. The friar was balding, a bit pudgy, and possessed of an enormous nose. Ben looked down at him and sighed. When his career as the Offspring began, he had refused this gesture and told people to stand, but after a while it became easier just to give them a "blessing" and move on. He brushed the priest's head with his fingertips, and the man rose.

"Thank you, blessed one," Pallin said in a startlingly rich, deep voice that sounded like it belonged to a feed newscaster. "I've longed to meet you ever since . . . since your presence was revealed to us. Lucia has been a parishioner of mine all her life, and I never dreamed she would bear . . ."

"Speaking of which," Kendi interrupted, "we should probably get into a room instead of standing in the lobby."

A nurse was already heading toward them with a hoverchair. Less than a minute later, they were in a private suite of rooms. The place smelled of hospital antiseptic despite the wood floors and cheery curtains over dark windows. Ben felt a stab a déjà vu. Lucia moved carefully from hoverchair to bed, then gave a groan and ran a hand over her ripe, round abdomen.

"How fast are they coming?" asked the nurse.

"About every twenty minutes," Lucia said, adjusting the sheet.

"We have time, then," said the nurse. "I've already sent for Dr. McCall. She should be here soon." She turned to the crowd of people. "Anyone who isn't an immediate relative of the baby needs to leave. You can visit one at a time once she's settled."

Julia, Francesca, and Friar Pallin left with obvious reluctance. As with Evan's birth, Tan and Gretchen took up positions guarding the door while Ben and Kendi gathered around Lucia. Only Harenn was missing—she was at Salman's house with Evan and Bedj-ka.

"Do you want your mother here?" Kendi asked. "We can bring her in."

Another contraction swept over Lucia, but the pain patch on her forehead kept it from being painful. "Maybe in a bit." She bit her lip. "I've barely spoken to her these last few months. Ever since . . . the lawsuit. I don't think she supported it, but she never told me she opposed it, either."

"What about Francesca?" Ben asked.

"She was a supporter," Lucia growled. "I think she was secretly hoping to be implanted with one of the other embryos, or even being granted custody of Evan or this baby. I don't want her in here."

"Suits me," Kendi said. "How do you feel about Friar Pallin and the blessing?"

Lucia looked torn. "Let him in," she said finally. "But only for the blessing."

Ben took Lucia's hand. "Whatever you want. Mom."

"Dad."

They all laughed. Ben couldn't help comparing this birth to Evan's. He felt far more relaxed and also eager. This baby, his next son or daughter, would go home with him, Kendi, and Lucia, no matter what. It was a relief and a pleasure to look forward to it. He caught Kendi's eye and knew he was thinking the same thing.

Dr. McCall arrived, checked Lucia, proclaimed her fine, and left again. Julia bustled in and out, fetching ice chips, offering to rub Lucia's shoulders, and asking if Ben or Kendi needed anything. Francesca and Friar Pallin stayed in the waiting room.

Eventually, as the sun rose on a fine spring day, Dr. McCall told Lucia to push. Half an hour later, she placed a healthy, wailing baby girl in Lucia's arms. Julia wiped tears from her eyes as Ben and Kendi gathered around the head of the bed. Ben felt his insides melt like butter as he looked down at his daughter's patently unhappy face. She waved tiny fists, and her eyes were screwed shut as she screamed her displeasure at this new world.

"Her name is Araceil," Ben said, and his voice caught. Kendi nodded his solemn agreement. Lucia gave Ara her breast, and the baby calmed down to nurse.

"Did I hear a cry?" said Father Pallin from the doorway. Francesca was trying to peer over his shoulder. "Is everything fine?"

"Come in, both of you," Lucia said, the birth thawing her a little toward her cousin. "You can give the blessing, Friar."

Friar Pallin approached the bed. With one hand he beat a slow rhythm on a small drum that hung from his shoulder. Francesca followed with a ritual rattle that she shook at every step. Pallin held his hand over Ara's head. Julia watched, a wide smile on her face.

Without pausing his drumming, Pallin pulled a small stone from the recesses of his robe. He slipped it into Ara's blanket. "We ask for the blessings of the world on this child," he said. Then he took out a water shaker and sprinkled a few drops of water on Ara's head. "We ask for the blessings of the sky on this child." He scattered a pinch of dust from Bellerophon's moon over Ara's body. "We ask for the blessings of the stars on this child. Great Lady Irfan, we ask for your blessings, your protection, and your inspiration. Let this child grow and flourish and be free of the taint . . . the taint of . . ."

"The taint of Vik," Ben said in a flat voice. "Her biological father and mine." Francesca gasped, and Julia's smile faltered.

"The taint of Vik," Pallin finished. He leaned down and gingerly kissed the top of Ara's head. "May she be hale and happy until the end of days."

"Thank you, Friar," Kendi said.

"I never thought I'd give Irfan's blessing to one of her own children," Pallin admitted.

"Aren't you going to name a spirit parent?" Francesca asked.

"That's not necessary, Friar," Lucia said quickly.

"But Lucia!" Julia interjected. "The baby needs a—"

"Ara has three parents already," Lucia responded. "Four, if you count Harenn. She doesn't need more."

"As you like," Pallin said, and withdrew.

"What was that for?" Francesca demanded. "Why didn't you name one?"

Ara finished nursing. Lucia burped her, and she fell asleep before Lucia could bring the baby down from her shoulder.

"I'm too tired to say clever things," Lucia said, "so I'll be direct. The only reason you came here was because you were hoping to be named spirit mother. But I know where you stood on the lawsuit, Francesca. You can leave now."

"Lucia!" Julia said, shocked. "She's your cousin!"

"Did you point that out to Francesca when she said she supported the Church's lawsuit, Mother? Leave, Francesca, and be grateful I allowed you to look at this blessed child for as long I did."

Francesca looked ready to protest, then apparently changed her mind and marched out.

"Lucia," Julia said. "Can't you just—"

"No, Mother," Lucia replied. "I can't."

"I want to hold her," Ben said, holding out his arms. Lucia handed Ara up to him. Ben looked down at his daughter's sleeping face and felt a fine peace.

"I hope she does that a lot," Kendi said beside him. "Evan hogs enough attention for three."

"Just like his da," Ben said.

Sister Gretchen Beyer kicked off her shoes and leaned back on the sofa with a heavy sigh of relief. Kendi and Ben were safely back home from the hospital, Harenn was with them, and Lucia was being guarded by someone else. She wiggled her toes and considered the merits of a long, hot bath. These days it seemed like she was either on guard duty with Ben and Kendi or watching images of Padric Sufur's house on a monitor, but this was a good thing. Every waking moment was full of work, giving her no time to think. Tan had finally ordered her away.

"Burned-out bodyguards make mistakes," Tan had said. "Go home. I don't want to see you for the next two days."

Gretchen closed her eyes and let her body sink further into the supremely comfortable sofa, unwilling to think about what two days of leisure would mean. Leisure gave her time to think about . . . things. The Despair. Being Silenced.

Padric Sufur.

Every night before she went to sleep, she saw his hawklike face. In the mornings she usually got five Sufur-free minutes before he surfaced in her mind like a shark shooting up from the depths. She loathed Sufur with a power that both surprised and exhilarated her. It was good to know hatred could run so deep.

Knowing where he lived was the worst part. She knew exactly where to find the bastard. She knew where he ate and slept and breathed and shit. But she couldn't do anything about it. The only thing that made it bearable was the knowledge that he would eventually pay. Gretchen intended to make sure of that.

"Attention! Attention!" said the computer. "An unknown visitor is requesting entry."

Gretchen opened her eyes, surprised. She never got visitors. "Sergio, tell the visitor to identify him- or herself."

Pause. "The visitor wishes to deliver a singing telegram."

"What?" Gretchen crossed her little living room to the door and peered through the one-way peephole. She saw the distorted image of a blond man in a formal black tunic. He was holding a bunch of brightly colored balloons. "Who are you?" she said through the door.

"Delivery, ma'am," the man called back, his voice somewhat muffled. "From Father Kendi Weaver."

Gretchen's eyes narrowed with suspicion. She wouldn't put it above Kendi to send her some kind of joke delivery, one that would spray whipped cream or silly snakes in her face. Still, she was intrigued. Maybe it was a belated thank-you gift for the lifesaving. She opened the door.

The man had a companion who hadn't been visible through the peephole. She had dark hair and eyes. "Sister Gretchen?" the man said, looking down at a little card tied to the balloon strings.

"That's me."

"My assistant and I have a song for you." The man whipped out a pitch pipe and blew a note. The woman hummed it.

Gretchen glanced uneasily up and down the hallway. "Uh, not out here," she said. "Come on in."

The pair followed Gretchen into the living room. She turned to face them. "Okay, what's this all about?"

"It's all in the song, ma'am," the man replied. "Oh—these are for you." He handed her the balloons. Gretchen had just grasped the strings when a flash of movement caught the corner of her eye. Her reflexes, honed by years of field work for the Children of Irfan and weeks of bodyguard duty for Kendi, snapped her other arm up. The motion knocked the dermospray out of the woman's hand. Gretchen instantly released the balloons. They bumbled against the ceiling, and Gretchen dropped to the floor. The man's roundhouse swing swished through empty air. Gretchen lashed out with her foot as she went down, catching the man in the knee. He screamed. The woman pulled a pistol from her pocket. Gretchen rolled to her feet. The woman fired and Gretchen dove. The pistol burned a circle in the

wall, and Gretchen smelled scorched wood. She landed
near the coffee table and shoved it desperately toward
the woman, who easily twisted out of the way. The man
snatched up the dermospray while the woman leaped
toward Gretchen. Gretchen tried to dodge, but the
woman landed full on top of her. The two of them rolled
across the floor. Pain exploded against Gretchen's ear as
the woman landed a punch. Gretchen sank her fist into
the woman's midriff. The breath rushed out of her, and
Gretchen shoved her aside. She was just in time to catch
the man's wrist as he tried to press the dermospray
against her neck. Gretchen gritted her teeth and tried to
push his hand away, but he was strong. The dermospray
crept closer and closer. Gretchen's hand trembled, and
she shoved with all her strength. The dermospray moved
away. Out of nowhere another hand clamped around the
man's and rammed the spray downward. The last thing
Gretchen saw was the triumphant look on the dark-
haired woman's face.

Kendi and Ben stood in the hastily assembled nursery
on the top floor of Salman's house. Ara was now one
day old, and she was asleep in her crib, just as Evan
slept in his. Their mothers slumbered as well. The nursery walls were simple wood—no one had had time to
construct an animated scene—and the room smelled
sweetly of baby powder. The sun was setting, leaving
only three days before the election. Downstairs, the
house was filled with frantic people doing frenzied work,
but up here, everything was quiet. Kendi enjoyed every
second, especially because he knew that at any moment
the fragile peace would be shattered by a new crisis,
one that could range from a campaign upheaval to a
dirty diaper.

"This is so strange," Ben said, looking down first at
Ara, then at Evan. "They're here. And they'll be here
for the rest of their lives."

"Grandma's already arranged trust funds for their education," Kendi said.

"How did we live without them?" Ben asked.

"The trust funds?"

Ben dinged Kendi's ear. "The babies."

"Babies," Kendi repeated, rubbing his ear. "All life, I'm a father. Twice."

"I keep expecting Ara to have dark hair, like Mom," Ben said, laying a gentle hand on her head. "But she's going to be a redhead like me."

"Evan's going to be blond," Kendi said. "Irfan had brown hair, didn't she?"

"That's how she's always shown," Ben replied. "Danny Vik had blond hair, though. Maybe their hair will darken when they get older." He leaned on the edge of Ara's crib. "What do you think they'll be when they grow up?"

"Silent," Kendi said with a grin. "That's about all we can predict."

"Still fun to speculate, though. Maybe one of them will like computers. I can show Ara how to circumnavigate a trench trap and hack into a six-nine-p-fiver database."

"Most fathers want to teach their kids how to play football or cricket."

"Or ride dinosaurs like their Aunt Martina?"

Kendi shuddered. "Don't remind me. She goes out two, three times a week these days."

"What kind does she ride?"

"I've stopped asking. Scares the piss out of me, whatever she answers."

Evan stirred in his sleep and made small meeping noises. Both Ben and Kendi snapped to attention. Evan settled back down again, and they relaxed.

"We should probably leave," Kendi said. "Let them sleep."

"Yeah." Ben didn't move. "Probably."

"Your pardon," Yin May said from the doorway. "Senator Reza would like to see both of you downstairs."

The inevitable crisis. Kendi sighed. "What is it this time?" he asked as they headed for the stairs. "Alien invasion?"

"It would be easier for her to tell you," May said. His face was tight. Kendi tried not to tense up and failed.

Downstairs they found everyone swarming around like termites in a broken mound. Salman was talking urgently to her running mate, Ched-Tumaar. A muted newsfeed showed a life-sized holo of a Ched-Balaar newscaster.

"What's going on, Grandma?" Ben asked.

Salman's face was tight. "Wanda Petrie's been arrested for murder."

"All life," Kendi breathed. "Oh shit."

"It becomes worse," Ched-Tumaar said. "The person who—"

"It's coming on!" someone shouted. The room went quiet and everyone turned to the newsfeed, which was no longer muted.

"—ator Mitchell Foxglove," said the newscaster.

Mitchell Foxglove appeared on the feed. *"It is my sad duty,"* he said, *"to bring this to the world's attention. As many of you know, several months ago two people named Finn Day and Helen Day were murdered in their home. The crime distressed me beyond measure; the Finns were friends of mine, and I swore their killer would not go unpunished. However, the monastery Guardians were unable to find the killer."*

"Getting his jabs in about the monastery," Salman muttered. She put on a coat. "Just do it, you bastard."

"Thanks to a generous private donor, I was able to hire a private team of forensic specialists to perform a DNA sweep of the house. It took several months to process the results, but the team finally uncovered one set of DNA that we couldn't explain. The Guardians have arrested Wanda Petrie, publicist for Senator Salman Reza's campaign, and charged her with first-degree murder."

A murmur went through the room, quickly shushed. Foxglove paused, as if he knew his viewers were gasping in horror.

"Where are you going, Grandma?" Ben asked.

"Press conference," she said, already heading for the door with Yin May in tow. "For damage control. Stay here, my ducks, and don't talk to anyone."

"It saddens me that Senator Reza has now twice seen fit to involve criminals in her campaign," Foxglove continued. *"She accepted donations from racketeer Willen Yaraye and now one of her staff is accused of murder. She surrounds herself with crooks and killers, then dares*

to run for governor. I urge all honest citizens of Bellero-phon to—"

"Shut him up," Kendi barked, and the feed muted. "Now what?"

"The senator will give a counterstatement," said Ched-Tumaar. "She will point out that Wanda Petrie was fired many weeks ago and that we were unaware of any criminal activity."

"Will that do any good?" Ben asked as the various campaign workers went back to their tasks.

Ched-Tumaar dipped his head. "I doubt it. This will hurt us much. Three days come between now and the election. That leaves no time for the news of Wanda Petrie to grow old and die among the voters."

Foxglove vanished, and the feed showed a hologram of a restrained Wanda Petrie being led away by two human Guardians. She was trying unsuccessfully to hide her face.

"How long does it take to do a DNA sweep?" Kendi said suddenly.

"About a week to sweep the house," Ben said. "Another five or six weeks to sort and process all the DNA, maybe another two weeks to correlate the result and produce a list of people."

"So a little over eight weeks," Kendi said. "But Wanda killed the Days several months ago. It was before Evan was born."

"So?" Ben said.

Ched-Tumaar clacked his teeth in a wordless exclamation. "Mitchell Foxglove must have had the results of the DNA sweep weeks ago," he said. "He kept them to himself until this moment because he knew releasing them now would hurt our campaign the most."

"In other words," Kendi growled, "he let a murderer walk free to aid his own campaign."

"So did Grandma," Ben said.

"Yeah, but we were going to turn Wanda in after Grandma was elected."

"In other words," Ben said, "we let a murderer walk free to aid Grandma's campaign."

"Maybe so," Kendi said, "but we didn't . . . we weren't . . . ." He trailed off.

"Yeah," Ben said quietly. "You know, I'm really tired of politics."

Kendi sighed. "So am I."

The next three days were spent in a frenzy of activity. Both Ben and Kendi made as many appearances as they could squeeze in. It was rough going. Everywhere they went, reporters asked for comments about Petrie. Kendi kept his answers short and scripted and tried not to look like he was operating on less than an hour's sleep. He hated being away from Evan and Ara, but he consoled himself with the thought that it was only three days.

Unfortunately, his and Ben's efforts seemed to have little effect. Salman's polls dropped sharply, and even Ben's power as the Offspring couldn't seem to raise them to their original levels. Wanda Petrie, meanwhile, stayed in her jail cell and refused to speak to anyone, even her own lawyer.

On the day of the election, Foxglove and Ched-Pirasku were leading the polls, but Salman made a close enough second that the feed analysts declared it anybody's race. Salman announced the time for speech-making was over. She rented the same gymnasium that Foxglove had blacked out, thereby creating the "Taper" nickname for the Unionists. The place was crowded with Salman supporters, most of them high-level campaign workers, volunteers, and other celebrities who had, like Ben and Kendi, endorsed Salman's campaign. Kendi looked around at the crowd of humans and Ched-Balaar that formed a chattering, talking mass on the auditorium floor. Holographic signs silently shouted slogans. IRFAN CHOSE SALMAN! SALMAN SAVES THE FORESTS! SALMAN KEEPS US SAFE! Giant feeds projected on the walls and as freestanding holograms stood ready to report the latest exit polls. The voting itself had only opened a few hours ago, too early for projections. An undercurrent of expectation and hope threaded through the crowd.

Off to one side, Ben cradled Evan in one thick arm as he talked to Keith and another human Kendi didn't recognize. Lucia stood nearby with baby Ara. Reporters were everywhere, but they'd had to agree not to broadcast pictures of the infants before Salman's team would grant them entry. Salman herself was talking to Yin May, while Ched-Tumaar browsed through the enormous buffet. A young man was chatting up Martina by the drink bar, and Kendi made a mental note to find out who he was. Bedj-ka sat on the floor in the corner playing some kind of miniature holographic game with a pair of children his own age. Tan had taken up a post by the main doors. Kendi looked up at the stage, remembering how much had happened since he had stood in the audience with Gretchen and watched Salman declare her candidacy.

Speaking of Gretchen . . . he thought, and scanned the room. Gretchen was nowhere in sight. That struck Kendi as strange. In the past few months, Gretchen had spent more time on duty than off, and it seemed unlikely she'd absent herself today. Kendi trotted over to Tan to ask about it.

"No idea," Tan rasped. "She was supposed to be on today, but didn't show up. No one else could come in, so we're short."

"Gretchen didn't show up?" Kendi said, uneasy. "That's not like her. She may be abrasive, even bitchy, but she's always reliable."

Tan tapped her earpiece. "Gretchen Beyer." Long pause. "No answer. I can leave a message if I want, but I already did."

Kendi's unease blossomed into heavy worry. "I don't like it, Lewa. Ched-Theree said a whole bunch of Silent and Silenced have disappeared."

"Oh god." Tan looked worried herself. "I should have wondered if something was up, but I've been so busy coordinating with Senator Salman's—anyway. We should check her house."

"Let's go," Kendi said. "I'll get Ben and—"

"By *we*, I meant *not you*, Kendi. It could be dangerous."

"Gretchen's saved my ass more times than I can count, Lewa," Kendi said. "Besides, you said you were shorthanded today. Who are you going to spare?"

"The Guardians can—"

"The Guardians can't do anything until at least a day has passed," Kendi interrupted. "By then it may be too late." He tapped his earpiece. "Ben, Gretchen's missing. We need to go look for her."

"Kendi," Tan warned.

"I'm pulling rank, Lewa," Kendi said. "I'm going, and it's your job to keep me safe. So you better start planning."

Ben, meanwhile, handed Evan over to Harenn and hurried over as quickly as he could without attracting undue attention from the reporters. Keith came with him.

"What's this about Gretchen missing?" Ben demanded.

Kendi was already moving for the door. "I'll explain on the way. Come on."

"It's not safe," Tan said, catching his arm.

"I'll come, too," Keith interjected. "That'll make two guards."

Tan looked ready to protest further, but Kendi pulled away from her and headed out the door. Tan slapped her earpiece.

"Lars!" she barked. "Meet us out back with the flitcar. Now!"

Outside, the afternoon sun was shining. Lizards chirruped in the talltree branches, and spring flowers made merry rainbows in planters and boxes on balconies and window ledges. The walkways threading into the talltree forest around the gymnasium were busy with people, many of whom walked with one hand pressed to an ear as they listened to the feeds. A silver flitcar hovered just outside the gymnasium doors. Tan made sure the way was clear, then rushed Kendi and Ben into the vehicle with Keith close behind. Once the door was shut, Lars took them straight up. Kendi gave him Gretchen's address.

"I want to go on record as saying this is an incredibly stupid idea," Tan growled. "And that if anything happens to either of you, it isn't my fault."

"Noted." Kendi grinned, feeling strangely exuberant. He was still worried about Gretchen, but it also felt good to be out there and doing something instead of giving speeches and letting people shepherd him around.

Gretchen lived in an apartment building near the

boundary of the monastery and Treetown. On the flight, Keith dropped into a sullen silence. Ben stared out the window, obviously worried. The ever-present feed announced that early polls showed Foxglove with a two-percent lead over Ched-Pirasku. Salman trailed in a distant third place.

The apartment building resembled the beehive structure near the site where Ben and Kendi had made the blackmail dropoff, though this building was in better repair. Lars landed the flitcar on the roof, which poked up above the talltree. He left the flitcar running as Tan, Ben, Kendi, and finally Keith got out and dashed toward the stairway door. They clattered down the echoing stairwell to the fifth floor, where Gretchen had her apartment.

The corridor was a little dingy, and the wooden floor hadn't been swept in a while. Tan moved ahead of the group to Gretchen's door. She pressed her ear to it and listened, then pressed her thumb to the doorplate. From inside, Kendi heard the muffled sound of the computer announcing Tan's presence. No response. Tan pressed her thumb again, then knocked. Still nothing. Kendi shifted from foot to foot, his nerves rubbing raw. Gretchen might be inside, hurt or unconscious or even dead, and Tan was taking unreasonable precautions. He finally shouldered her aside and tried the door. It was unlocked. Before Tan could protest, Kendi burst into the apartment. Tan and the others boiled in behind him.

The living room was a total mess. Furniture lay askew, carpets were rumpled, and a broken coffee table scattered splintery shards across the floor. A circular scorch mark scarred one wall.

"A struggle," Kendi said.

"No kidding," Ben said.

"We need to call the Guardians. Don't touch anything." Tan tapped her earpiece.

Keith advanced cautiously into the room and disappeared into the kitchen. He reemerged a moment later. "No one's there."

"We should check the bedroom in case she's . . . unconscious," Ben said. He didn't mention the word *dead*, but Kendi heard it nonetheless. Kendi dashed down the short hallway to the bedroom with Keith right behind him. On the way he checked the bathroom. Empty.

In contrast to the living room, Gretchen's bedroom was perfectly tidy. Bed made, closet door closed, curtains drawn. Kendi dropped to the floor and checked under the bed. Nothing. A flicker of movement caught the corner of his eye. He flung himself sideways just in time to avoid the knife. The blade hit the floor with a *thunk*. Adrenaline singing in every vein, Kendi rolled to his feet. Keith yanked the knife free and brandished it at him.

"Keith!" Kendi said. "What the hell—?"

Keith lunged. Kendi twisted aside and collided with the side of the bed. He lost his balance and fell flat on his back on the mattress. A silent snarl twisted Keith's face. Part of Kendi's mind noticed that Keith's eyes had a glazed look. Then Keith leaped forward, bringing the knife down. Kendi flung up his forearm and blocked Keith's wrist. He stared at the knife pointed at his throat.

"You son of a bitch," Keith hissed. The knife quivered. "You and your Outback bullshit. You're going to join the Real People real soon and there's no way you can stop—"

"Help!" Kendi yelled. "Ben! Lewa!"

Keith shoved the knife downward with surprising strength. Kendi felt a pinprick as the point pierced the skin above his jugular vein. He struggled to push Keith's hand away, gained a centimeter, lost it.

And then Keith vanished. Kendi heard a crash and a cry of pain. He got to his feet and saw Tan pressing Keith face-first against the wall. His right hand still was still clutching the knife, but Ben was beating his wrist against the wood. Three blows, and the knife clattered to the ground. Tan used her body to keep Keith pinned and pulled out a set of wrist restraints. In one swift movement, she got his hands behind him, closed the silvery bands around his wrists, and activated the restraints. The bands stuck together with a firm *click*.

"What the fuck is going on?" Tan demanded.

"Are you all right?" Ben asked. "You're bleeding."

Kendi checked his neck. A streak of blood smeared his hand. "Just a scratch."

"I'll *kill* you, Outback boy!" Keith snarled at the wall.

"Shut up," Tan snapped.

"Why did he attack you?" Ben asked. "Where'd he get the knife?"

"The kitchen, I think," Kendi said. "As for why . . ." Kendi stared at Keith as several thoughts came together. "All life, we've been idiots! Ben, we have to get into the Dream. Now!"

"Kill you!" Keith howled. Tan rapped his head against the wall.

"What are you talking about?" Ben asked.

"Do you have your dermospray with you?" Kendi rummaged around in his pockets and found his own. "We don't have much time."

"For what?" Ben demanded, producing his own dermospray. "You don't even have your spear."

"I don't *need* it," Kendi said. "It's just easier if I have it. Lewa, keep an eye on Keith. We're going in."

"But—"

"This will go faster if you quit talking to me," Kendi said. He lay down on the recently rumpled bed and *thumped* the dermospray against his arm. Ben shrugged and lay down next to him to do the same. Kendi closed his eyes. It was hard to relax at first. The adrenaline from the fight hadn't worn off yet, and he was tense. It also felt strange not to be leaning on his spear. But eventually years of practice took over, aided by the drug. Colors swirled behind his eyelids, and he found himself in kangaroo form on the flat, empty plain of the Dream. Whispers swirled around him. A moment later, Ben flicked into view, his rapid appearance creating momentary distortions in the air and ground.

"What's this about?" Ben asked.

"Shush!" Kendi said, and stretched to his full height, listening hard. "This way!"

He bounded off, leaving Ben with little choice but to follow. Kendi dashed over the flat, gray ground as fast as he could, knowing that in the Dream, Ben could keep up with him on foot. Moments later, he crossed a boundary, and both men found themselves in a plush office that overlooked a skyscraper skyline. The strange Silent Kendi had chased several weeks ago sat in his executive chair, eyes shut in concentration. They popped open when Ben and Kendi appeared on his turf. Kendi didn't hesitate. He leaped over the desk and landed with his full weight on the man.

The man yelped with pain and surprise as the chair went over backward. Kendi shifted shape into a camel. His great split hooves pinned the man's shoulders to the carpeted floor. Kendi felt the man's bones creak, and the man cried out in pain. With his hind legs, Kendi kicked the chair backward out of the way, and it crashed against the rear wall.

"You were whispering to my brother," Kendi snarled at him. Thick camel spittle spattered the man's face. "You took advantage of the fact that he was suffering from depression and that his mind had been damaged from the time he spent on Silent Acquisitions Station. You whispered to him, made his depression worse, made him attack me, and *I want to know why*."

The man shut his eyes. Kendi bit the top of his head and ripped out a hank of dark hair. The man screamed. Kendi spat out the bloody hunk of scalp.

"No concentrating," he said. "And no leaving the Dream. Ben! Can you keep watch and make sure the son of a bitch doesn't disappear?"

"Not a problem."

Kendi glared down at the man. "Explain what's going on."

"Fuck you."

Before Kendi could respond, a small sledgehammer popped into Ben's hand. With a sickening *crack* he broke the man's little finger. The man howled in agony. Kendi gasped and shot Ben a startled glance. Ben's attention, however, remained riveted on the man's contorted face. Kendi recovered his composure. They could talk about it later. Right now they had to extract information. The man continued to yowl like a kicked cat. Kendi leaned down and snorted saliva into his mouth. The yowls turned into spits and sputters.

"Let me tell you what I already do know," Kendi said.

"Maybe it'll loosen you up. Keith was—or you were—behind all the attacks on me from the beginning. I was too stupid to see it because it never occurred to me to suspect him. Keith knew I was going to meet him at the shopping center, and Keith knew I would cross that particular walkway. The amateur hologram showed him with his hand in his pocket because *he* was detonating the device that severed the branch.

"When that didn't work, you got him to try the poisoned dart. He oh-so-casually volunteered to walk me home from his house after the rain cleared up, then let the bodyguards get ahead so he'd have a clear shot from behind me. I even saw him move, but I thought he was looking for the culprit.

"After that, you got him to plant the pieces of the bomb. He was right there in the nursery just before it exploded. In fact, Keith was the *only* person who was on the scene for all three murder attempts. You were whispering to him the night of the explosion, telling him to start the detonation process. Except I was in the Dream, and my subconscious picked up on what you were doing. I must have known even then it was Keith, but I didn't want to face it. So my subconscious mind scared me out of the house. It should have been obvious what was happening. What I want to know is *why.*"

"Who do you work for?" Ben interjected. "Tell, or I'll break your thumb."

The man's face contorted as he struggled with his dilemma. Blood ran from his scalp where Kendi had torn out the hair. Ben raised his hammer, and the man flinched. So did Kendi, though he tried to hide it. He had never seen Ben bloodthirsty before.

"All right!" the man said. "I work for Silent Acquisitions."

"Of course you do," Kendi sighed. "SA would be in a perfect position to know that Keith's mind is weak and that you could whisper him into doing things he would normally never do."

"You're also working for Padric Sufur," Ben growled. The man nodded.

"Can I say 'I told you so' now?" Ben asked.

"Save it for later," Kendi said. He shifted back into

kangaroo shape and sat on the man's chest. It made for easier conversation. "Why does Sufur want me dead?"

"Isn't it obvious?" the man spat. "He wants to make sure Reza loses the election. You—and the Offspring—keep giving her chances to win."

"And Sufur wants Foxglove to win," Kendi said. "He's funding Foxglove, isn't he? It's where Foxglove got the money to take over Othertown's mining corporations and everything else he's snapped up."

"He's funding Ched-Pirasku, too," the man said. "It doesn't matter to him who wins as long as Salman Reza loses."

"Why?" Kendi demanded. "What's so important about Salman Reza?"

"I don't know," the man said, and Kendi knew it was the truth—lies were impossible in the Dream.

"Is Sufur the one behind the missing people?" Ben asked.

The man remained silent.

"Trouble remembering?" Kendi said. "Let me remind you how the story goes. A whole bunch of good Bellerophon citizens have turned up missing, and all of them are either Silent or Silenced. Including our friend Gretchen Beyer. What do you know about her?"

"I don't know any Gretchen Beyer."

"That doesn't answer my main question. Why is SA making people disappear?"

The man shifted beneath Kendi's heavy hind feet. "Look, SA *owns* me. When Mr. Sufur says 'jump,' I jump. You think I liked manipulating your brother? His mind is so sad, and I had to make it worse."

"My heart is bleeding like your head," Kendi said.

"Do you know who Padric Sufur *is*?" Ben said. "He's the guy who touched off the Despair."

"He owns me," the man repeated quietly. "I have to do as he says."

"What's he planning?" Kendi persisted. "What's he want that Salman could stop?"

"Do you honestly think he'd tell me?" the man replied. "A slave?"

"Where's your body?" Ben asked abruptly.

"Back on SA Station. Look, I can barely breathe."

Kendi stepped off the man's body. "Get out. Go home." The man closed his eyes and vanished. The office went with him, leaving behind the flat, gray plain.

"Why did you do that?" Ben said. "The bastard tried to kill you. He tried to kill Ara and Evan, for god's sake."

"And what should we have done, Ben?" Kendi asked tiredly. "He's thousands of light-years away. Did you want to kill him like you smashed his finger?"

"He tried to *kill* us, Ken. He turned your *brother* into a puppet."

Kendi rubbed his forepaws together. "Since when did you become an advocate of torture?"

"Since someone tried to kill my son," Ben spat. "God, Kendi—it isn't like I really hurt him. The psychosomatic carryover will probably give him a sprained finger. Why is this such a problem with you?"

"The problem is that this isn't like you," Kendi said. "I'd expect this kind of thing of Harenn or Gretchen. Maybe even Tan. But not you."

"You don't think I'm strong enough to torture someone?"

"I didn't think you were weak enough to have to," Kendi said simply.

Ben spun around. He was still holding the sledgehammer, and his fingers were white around the handle. After a long moment, he let go. It vanished before it hit the ground. Kendi let out a long, heavy breath.

"What do we do now?" Ben asked without turning around.

"We take care of Keith," Kendi said, and let go of the Dream.

"So what happened?" Tan demanded when Kendi and Ben sat up. Keith sat on a chair, his hands still fastened behind him. His head drooped, and his eyes were shut.

"We saw a man about a plan," Kendi said, and gave a short explanation. Keith didn't react to any of it. "We should take Keith to the medical center," Kendi finished. "He needs a lot of help. And we should call—"

"The Guardians?" Tan said. "They're on their way."

"Then we should get Keith out of here before they

can ask awkward questions about him," Kendi said. "He needs a therapist, not a jail cell."

They took the unresisting Keith up to the flitcar, explained to Lars what was going on, and went back down to the apartment. Two human Guardians were just arriving. Kendi, Ben, and Tan answered their questions about Gretchen, carefully leaving out any mention of Keith's presence in the apartment. Kendi, however, couldn't keep his mind off his brother, and it was hard to concentrate. Ben seemed restless as well.

After the Guardians were finished, Kendi boarded the flitcar with Ben and Tan. Keith, on the seat beside him, seemed nearly catatonic. Ben stared grimly out the window. Tan conversed with Lars in a low voice. Kendi squeezed Keith's hand, but his brother didn't respond. Kendi's mind ran in a hundred different directions. He didn't know what to worry about most—Keith's condition, Gretchen's disappearance, or Padric Sufur's plan. That the latter two were connected, Kendi didn't doubt. But why would anyone kidnap Silenced people? And why was Sufur going to such lengths to ensure that Salman lost the election?

It struck him that Foxglove had mentioned a "generous private donor" whose funds had allowed him to hire the private forensics team and finger Petrie. That donor must have been Sufur. Kendi clenched a fist. Salman needed to know what he and Ben had learned. But would it do any good? The election was already in progress, and they had to get Keith to the medical center.

This actually turned out to be easier than Kendi anticipated. The staff took one look at Kendi and Ben—the famous Father and the blessed Offspring—and whisked Keith into a private room. A psychologist named Dr. Lev Mayfield arrived shortly thereafter, and Kendi was able to explain what had happened to Keith, who was now almost completely unresponsive.

"We won't be pressing charges," Kendi said. "And I'm hoping to keep things confidential."

"We keep all our patients confidential," Mayfield said reassuringly. "I'll see to his care personally, Father."

"I'll come and visit as soon as I can, Keith," Kendi said, squeezing his brother's hand again. Still no response. Kendi choked down a surge of anger, and he kept control with difficulty as he and Ben left.

Back in the flitcar, Ben said, "Do we tell Grandma about this?"

"What would be the point?" Kendi checked his fingernail for the time. "The election ends in less than an hour. Even if we had proof of what we know, and even if we went public with the information, it wouldn't help." He rubbed a hand over his face. "All life, what a day. I don't even know how the returns are going."

"It's close," Tan reported from the front seat. Text scrolled by on her data pad's holographic display. "Exit polls are showing Foxglove in first place with thirty-six percent of the votes. Ched-Pirasku and Senator Reza are tied for second place with thirty-two percent each. It's going to be *really* close."

A small image beside the text showed long lines of humans, Ched-Balaar, and a sprinkling of other races at various electoral polls. Then it switched to a montage of the candidates. Foxglove opening a new mine. Salman speaking to the military. Ched-Pirasku giving rides to human children on his back.

"So where do we go now?" Ben asked. "Lars is just circling Treetown."

Kendi set his mouth. "We need to go see Padric Sufur."

The day was drawing to a close as they approached Sufur's little house. The talltrees exuded long shadows, and a chill suffused the air. A dinosaur roared far below, and the noise was answered in the distance. Mating season. Kendi thanked all life that the dinosaur rodeo club closed down at this time of year. Even the most hardened rider stayed out of the way of male dinosaurs in full rut. Tan trailed Kendi and Ben, looking nervous. She had tried to talk Kendi out of this course of action, but Kendi had turned a deaf ear, as had Ben. The windows of the other little houses around Sufur's glowed with yellow light. Sufur's house, however, was dark.

They were climbing the stairs to his front door when a voice spoke in Kendi's earpiece. *"Kendi? What the hell are you doing?"*

Sejal. Kendi had forgotten that the Vajhur family was keeping remote watch on Sufur's home. He tapped his earpiece.

"It's okay, Sejal," Kendi said as they reached the top of the steps. "Just keep watching."

The door opened before either of the two men could knock. Padric Sufur stood in the doorway. Ben was white-lipped, and his body radiated tension. Kendi felt the same way. Tan appeared impassive until Kendi noticed she was rubbing her thumb and forefinger together fast enough to start a fire from the friction.

"I was wondering when you'd show up," Sufur said. "You may as well come in." He turned and went back inside without bothering to see if they were following. Kendi strode in after the old man with Ben and Tan in tow.

The inside of Sufur's house smelled stale, as if the windows hadn't been opened in months. Everything was perfectly tidy, however. A small part of Kendi noticed that although there were several holograms and pictures of nonhumans scattered about the simply decorated living room, there were no mirrors. A desk with a computer terminal occupied one corner.

Sufur, clad in a long white robe that made him resemble the ghost of a scarecrow, took a seat in an easy chair near the window. He didn't look like a man who had engineered the deaths of millions. "Sit. I won't be offering refreshment, so don't ask."

"I don't take food from filth," Ben spat, and remained standing.

Sufur nodded, as if Ben were commenting on the weather. "The Offspring. I've been watching the reports about you with some interest, young man. Which will win out, do you think—the supposed nobility of Irfan Qasad or the psychotic treachery of Daniel Vik? I'm betting on the treachery."

"Fuck you," Ben said.

"How nicely you prove my point." Sufur crossed his legs. "How much do you know? You can speak freely—these walls are insulated against listening devices, and any recording devices you may be carrying were disabled when you crossed my threshold."

"You've been financing both Ched-Pirasku's and Mitchell Foxglove's campaigns," Kendi growled. "You tried to have me—and then Ben—killed because our support helped Salman overcome all the scandals you engineered for her. Did you have your pet Silent whisper to Petrie, too? Is that why she killed the Days like Keith tried to kill me?"

"The Days embodied the worst of human greed," Sufur said. "They had become a detriment to Foxglove's campaign. A pity Petrie turned out to be thief as well as murderer when she stole that disk. *I* would never have revealed your secret, Ben, or exploited your heritage for personal gain. I don't count myself as cruel."

"You must have a different dictionary from us poor folk," Tan rasped from her position by the door.

"What about the people you're kidnapping?" Kendi demanded. "Where are they? What have you done with them?"

"They'll fulfill their destinies," Sufur said. "Helping me end the pointless struggle that makes up humanity."

"If you hate humanity so much," Ben said, "why don't you just jump off a balcony and end it all? One less human in the world."

"Because I'm a philanthropist," Sufur replied, voice mild. "You're young, you don't understand. To be human is to be miserable. We exist only to make war and rape and kill and prey on one another. Don't you find it interesting, Father Kendi, that your brother was so easily whispered into killing you? Whispers can't create thought or emotion. They only amplify what already exists. Your own brother resents the fact that you went free while he remained a slave, that you had your mother for a short time after he lost her. That a fellow human sodomized him and left you unmolested. Deep down, your own brother wants you dead, even though you rescued him from slavery. Human gratitude at work."

Kendi took a step forward, teeth clenched, but Tan put a hand on his shoulder from behind.

"Do you know how many sentient species have no concept of falsehood?" Padric continued as if Kendi hadn't moved. "Seventy-nine. And how many have no concept of murder? Ninety-seven. Humans don't number among them. As such, we deserve extinction."

"You don't have the right to judge anyone," Kendi said through clenched teeth.

"But I do. I spent my childhood in a concentration camp. I was rescued by some people—you would call them aliens—who became dear to me. They brought me to adulthood. They showed me how vile and violent humans are, how caring and compassionate other species are. I am a human who sees humans from an outsider's point of view. It makes me uniquely qualified to judge."

"So you want to kill all humans?" Ben asked in disbelief.

"I want to help them. I want to stop the warring and the fighting and everything associated with it."

"By destroying the Dream," Kendi said.

"Armies communicate through the Dream. Dictators give orders through the Dream. Without them, war ends. After the Despair, I wept from relief because I thought I had won, that war would end forever. Later I wept because I realized I had lost. The Dream still lived, even though I could no longer touch it. War will return. I have to stop it. For your sake and for the sake of all humans everywhere."

"Children are reentering the Dream," Kendi said. "More and more of them every day. You can't possibly think you'll stop them all."

"Of course not," Sufur said. "There are too many. The Ched-Balaar alone will repopulate the Dream in less than a decade. But I came to realize that interplanetary warfare among humans is a human problem. If we remove humans from the Dream, the species will be better off."

"That's what you're trying to do?" Kendi said. "Remove all humans from the Dream? You're insane."

"History may paint me that way," Sufur agreed. "I wonder if the same thing happened to Daniel Vik."

"How can you possibly remove all human Silent from the Dream?" Kendi said before Ben could respond.

"With the help of the Children of Irfan." Sufur gazed out the window. By now the room was so dark, Kendi could barely see him. "Thanks to the Despair, the vast majority of all human Silent are now concentrated in two places—Silent Acquisitions Station and—"

"Bellerophon," Kendi breathed.

"You yourself helped with that, Father Kendi," Sufur told him. "How many Silent did you bring here after the Despair? Fifteen? Twenty? Including Sejal and his sister Katsu and that boy Bedj-ka. And your own children, of course."

Ben charged like a raging bull. He reached Sufur's chair, and energy cracked through the air. Ben fell gasping to the floor. Kendi and Tan were beside him in an instant.

"Warning!" said a computer voice. "Persisted hostile activity will result in use of deadly force."

"You call yourself a philanthropist?" Kendi yelled.

"I'm also a realist, Father Kendi," Sufur said. "I'm just as violent as the next human being."

Ben sat up with Tan and Kendi's help. "I'll show you violence, Sufur," he gasped. "I'll rip your head off and listen to you blab about violence."

"You would be unwise to kill me," Sufur said mildly. "I transmit a regular coded message to . . . certain people. If they fail to hear from me, they have orders to terminate certain other people."

"Let's get out of here," Tan said. "We can't do anything more."

"What are you *planning*, Sufur?" Kendi snapped.

"It doesn't matter," Sufur replied in that infuriatingly mild tone. A soft tone chimed. Sufur tapped the arm of his chair and checked the readout that appeared there. "Ah. I see the election returns are in. I imagine your next step will be to inform the press and the police about my presence. I feel I should warn you that the governor-elect owes me a great many favors, and since I'm only vaguely implicated in any crimes on this planet, I can assure you that I will spend no time in jail."

"Who won?" Kendi demanded.

But Sufur stared out the window as if he hadn't heard. Tan made a sharp gesture, and Kendi nodded. They helped Ben limp outside. Kendi shot Sufur a final poisonous glance before Tan shut the door. Once in the fresh night air, Ben seemed to regain his equilibrium, and he shook off further help.

"I'm all right," he said. "But he's going to die, Kendi. No one in the universe deserves death more than he does."

His icy tone made Kendi shiver. "Ben, you promised me you wouldn't do anything stupid."

Ben stared wordlessly at him for a moment, then he ran down to the flitcar and jumped inside. Kendi and Tan followed. Once the door was shut and Lars was powering up the engines, Tan called up a newsfeed.

"Well?" Kendi asked.

"Final returns are in," Tan reported flatly. "Our new governor is Ched-Pirasku."

Ben closed his eyes. Kendi slumped back in his seat. It felt as if he had been punched in the stomach. All that work and heartache for nothing.

~Father Kendi.~

Kendi bolted upright. "Who the hell—?"

~Father Kendi, can you hear me?~ The mental voice felt familiar, but it took Kendi a moment to place it. It was the Silent slave who had whispered to Keith.

"What do you want?" he said.

"Who are you talking to?" Ben asked.

~I need to speak to you, Father. In the Dream.~

CHAPTER SIXTEEN

"I forget my successes every day and dream of my failures every night."

—Irfan Qasad

The feed hologram of Salman Reza showed an old woman with a sad but determined expression. She was still in the auditorium with her supporters and election workers. Kendi turned up the volume on the data pad while Ben rummaged around the guest bedroom, looking for his dermospray.

"Almost a thousand years ago," Salman said, *"Irfan Qasad left her position as our planet's first governor. On that day she said, 'The people have clearly decided someone else is more fit for the job.' I bow to her wisdom. I have spoken with Ched-Pirasku and congratulated him on becoming Bellerophon's first governor in over two hundred years. I also offered to meet with him as soon as possible to heal the divisions of the campaign and the contest the three of us just finished."*

Ben, who had found his dermospray, reached over and turned the volume back down with an angry tap. "She's going to be upset that we weren't there."

"Nothing for it," Kendi said. "We have more important things to do. You find that dermospray?"

"Yeah. Let's just get this over with."

With quick, jerky movements, Ben lay down on the bed, injected the drug, and closed his eyes. Kendi watched him worriedly. Ben's face was as cold and hard as ice, and there was murder in his every move. Kendi didn't blame Ben. Kendi himself would have given a lot to watch Sufur writhe on a spit. But the thought of gentle, quiet Ben killing Sufur turned his blood to ice.

Was there any other way to make Sufur pay for his crimes? The police and the Guardians wouldn't touch him. But perhaps Sufur had been bluffing about that. Ched-Pirasku had been Silenced by the Despair, and it was a good bet that he hadn't known Sufur was funding his campaign. On the other hand, the knowledge that Sufur had helped Ched-Pirasku win the governorship would create a scandal, perhaps even a recall. Kendi grew a little excited. Perhaps this would be a way to get Salman into the governor's mansion after all. Revealing that Sufur had been involved in both Foxglove's and Ched-Pirasku's campaigns would destroy both of their political careers, leaving only Salman left to take the governorship.

Then Kendi deflated. Getting proof was a major stumbling block. Kendi had no doubt that Sufur's involvement had been carefully obscured behind a dozen veils. It might take years to dig up solid evidence, and by then Ched-Pirasku would be too firmly entrenched for a recall. Still, it was a possibility to explore.

~Father Kendi, are you coming soon?~ whispered the Silent voice.

Kendi shook his head and thumped the dermospray against his arm. The whole idea of meeting this Silent again made him wary, but he couldn't turn down the chance. At least Ben would be there. Kendi hoped he wouldn't conjure up another sledgehammer.

Colors swirled and some time later, falcon Kendi was circling in the dry air of his hot, sun-drenched Outback. Far below, his sharp eyes picked out Ben in his explorer's outfit. Kendi dove down to land on a nearby rock. Without speaking, he cast out his mind and felt the presence of the other Silent.

~Approach,~ he thought. *~We meet on my turf or not at all.~*

The dark-haired Silent appeared in a splash of Dream energy. For a moment he wore a business suit. Then the suit flickered into a loincloth. The man, Kendi noticed with some satisfaction, wasn't built for such attire. He had a noticeable gut, and his pasty skin was hairless as a child's. Ben, looking handsome in his brown khakis, flashed Kendi a half grin. The man flushed, and Kendi clacked his beak. Here on his own turf, Kendi was the more powerful Silent. The lack of clothing reminded the other man of this fact, and also kept him off-balance in case he tried anything stupid.

"We're here," Kendi said. "Talk. Start with your name."

"Uh, I'm Frank. Frank Kowalski." The tear in his scalp had scabbed over, creating a dark blotch on his head. He wore a heavy bandage on the finger Ben had smashed.

"What do you want, Frank?" Ben said. "Out with it."

"I thought about what you said about Silent Acquisitions and Padric Sufur," he said. "I started . . . you know . . . asking around and looking at stuff. Uh, I guess . . . I mean . . ."

"Today, Frank," Kendi said. "I'm a busy bird."

"You were right about Mr. Sufur," Frank said. "He has . . . he has plans for Bellerophon. For the Silent on Bellerophon. Salman Reza would have gotten in the way."

"How, Frank?" Kendi said. "You're beating around the bush."

Frank wiped sweat from his face with one hand. "You have to promise me something, first."

"Promise what?" Kendi said.

"You have to promise you won't tell anyone where you got this information. I'll be . . . punished if Mr. Sufur finds out I talked to you. You have to swear on Irfan herself, or I'll leave right now."

Kendi raised his right wing. "I swear by Irfan herself."

"And the Offspring?" Frank said, turning to Ben.

"I swear on my mother's grave," he said without a trace of irony.

"All right." Frank took a deep breath. "Mr. Sufur is behind the disappearances of those Silent and Silenced, just like you suspected. It's part of a project he calls the Silent Corridor."

"What's it for?" Ben asked.

"Remember how you guys wiped out the Collection? It bankrupted the company and—"

"—and allowed Sufur to buy it," Kendi finished. "I *know*. Where is this going, Frank?"

"I'm trying to tell you. Mr. Sufur decided that SA needed to get out of the communication business entirely and go back to what it had been founded on—the slave trade. He reminded the board that Bellerophon now has the highest concentration of working Silent in the galaxy. With so many in one place, it would be easy to grab them and ship them back to SA Station."

"Why not just invade?" Kendi said. "Take over like Ormand Clearwater did when he invaded back in Irfan's time."

"Invade with what?" Frank sat gingerly on the ground, wincing as his nearly bare backside came into contact with the hot, uneven earth. "We don't have an army anymore, or much of a fleet. SA can barely afford to keep the air on, let alone pay a military. Mr. Sufur's plan was a lot cheaper, especially since the profit margin on Silent slaves is so high these days."

"What does this have to do with my grandmother?" Ben asked.

"SA's people have been snatching up Silent, putting them into cryo-sleep and bringing them up into a small cargo satellite in orbit around Bellerophon. The satellite used to belong to Mitchell Foxglove, but Sufur bought it from him. Once there are enough Silent on board to justify the trip, they're shuttled out to a ship hidden in the Bellerophon system. When that ship is full, it'll take the cargo back to SA Station for sale. Mr. Sufur's Silent Corridor. Right now the Corridor is feasible because Bellerophon has dismantled a lot of its military, including its fleet of ships. Senator Reza planned to increase military spending, which would mean more ships patrolling the sector. The Corridor would be discovered. So Mr. Sufur had to be sure Senator Reza lost the election."

Kendi thought for a moment. "This doesn't match what Su—what we've learned elsewhere, Frank. Sufur wants to end the human presence in the Dream, not sell Silent slaves to increase it. And why would SA kidnap Silenced humans? They're worthless."

"Mr. Sufur lied to the board. His real plan . . . his real plan is something else."

"What is it, Frank?" Ben said in a dangerous voice.

"Mr. Sufur has ordered the kidnapping of one Silenced human for every Silent one." Frank wiped more sweat from his face. "He told the board they were decoys. He said too many people would figure out what was going on if only Silent disappeared, so they'd have to snatch up extra people. And the whole thing *is* a decoy—for Silent Acquisitions.''

The knowledge slammed into Kendi like a gravity beam. His skin prickled and his feathers rose. "No," he whispered. "All life."

"What?" Ben said. "What's the decoy about?"

"He's planning to trick Silent Acquisitions," Kendi said. "Gretchen and all the others like her will show up positive on a gene test for Silence. They appear on SA Station, go under the auctioneer's hammer, and no one's the wiser. A few weeks of . . . creative coercion and drug therapy will ensure the Silenced themselves don't say anything about their real condition, and the new owners won't figure it out until it's too late. Meanwhile, Sufur still has the *real* human Silent locked away somewhere."

"And he can do with them whatever he likes," Ben finished. "Oh god."

"He isn't going to kill them, if that's what you're thinking," Frank said. "He's going to arrange an 'accident' in the cryo-chambers. All the Silent will come out of cryo-sleep with irreversible brain damage from improper thawing. They won't be Silent anymore, and they can still be sold as general laborers to recoup costs."

"This doesn't make complete sense," Ben said. "The people who buy fake Silent will raise a fuss when they figure out they've been tricked, and the scheme will lose money."

"He never wanted to make money," Frank said. His shoulders were turning faintly pink. "He'll be able to make two or three trips down the Corridor before anyone at Silent Acquisitions figures out what's going on, and by then he'll have grabbed most of the Silent humans left on Bellerophon. He bails out of SA, the company takes the blame, and Sufur moves on to another scheme. Look, can you conjure me a shirt or something? I'm frying."

Kendi considered denying the request, then settled his feathers in an avian shrug. The man had answered every question so far, and Kendi saw no need for continued discomfort. There was a slight shift of energy, and Frank was wearing a khaki explorer outfit similar to Ben's.

"Thanks," Frank said.

"We'll have to stop him and his Corridor," Ben said. "What are the coordinates for the cargo satellite and the ship?"

"That I don't know," Frank said. "I couldn't find out. Mr. Sufur has other Silent besides me who run messages back to SA Station, and he uses one of them to keep track of the ship and the satellite."

"Why are you telling us all this now?" Kendi asked. "Before, you were ready to kill us."

"I didn't want to kill you," Frank said. "I just wanted to get away. When we . . . talked that other time, though, you started me thinking, and I did some asking around, and that's when I found out what was really going on. It scares me, you know? If Mr. Sufur is going to give all those Silent other brain damage, I figure he'll . . . he'll . . ."

"He'll do the same to you," Kendi finished. "And here I thought you just wanted to do the right thing."

Frank just shrugged.

"So why don't you tell lots of other people?" Ben said. "Spread the word all through the Dream?"

Frank looked horrified. "Do you know what Mr. Sufur would do to me then? Brain damage would be a vacation. I only told you two because you promised to keep quiet about me. Don't forget you swore!"

"All right, all right," Kendi said. "Untwist your knickers. Maybe Ben and I can leak the information instead."

"I wouldn't," Frank told him. "Mr. Sufur has a whole shipful of hostages. If he thinks you're on to him, he'll just space the people he's captured."

"So how do we stop Sufur?" Ben said. "We can't get him arrested. We can't confront him with what we know. We can't find the ship."

Kendi clacked his beak again, this time with sudden inspiration. "Impersonation!"

"What?"

"You—or more likely, I—could pretend to be one of Sufur's pet Silent. If Frank here can show me who to talk to back on SA Station, I could relay a message

cancelling the entire program. We'll have to word it
carefully to avoid the whole 'can't lie' problem, but we'll
figure something out. After that, we grab Sufur and
make him tell us where the satellite and ship are. Hell,
once we get into his house, we might be able to trace
its location using Sufur's own communications equipment. And then—"

"Whoa, whoa," Frank said, holding up a hand. "You
can't just knock on a Silent back on SA Station and start
yakking away. Every time Mr. Sufur gives me messages
for Silent Acquisitions, he starts with a rotating logarithmic code generated by his computer. One of the computers back on SA Station has the same program, and the
Silent who receives the message first checks the code. If
the one I give him doesn't match the one Mr. Sufur
gives me, the communiqué is ignored."

"Oh, great," Ben sighed.

"It gets worse," Frank continued. "Mr. Sufur sends a
regular signal out to both the ship and the cargo satellite.
If they don't hear from him, they're supposed to space
the Silenced and run for it with the Silent."

"He contacts 'certain people,' " Ben muttered. "God."

"We need to get our hands on that logarithm program," Kendi said.

Frank stood up. "My drugs are wearing off. I have
to go."

"Tell me how to contact the Silent on SA Station
first," Kendi said. "Give me the pattern."

"The one who's usually on duty is named Marina Feldan," Frank told him. "Female, late thirties, brown
hair, brown eyes, heart-shaped face, average build."
He continued to speak, and Kendi listened carefully,
letting the pattern grow. Despite appearances, Frank
wasn't actually speaking—he was transmitting his
thoughts directly into Kendi's brain using the Dream
as a conduit. Kendi's mind chose to visualize the process as a man talking to a falcon in the Australian
Outback. Kendi "heard" Frank's thoughts as words because that was how Kendi's mind interpreted what was
going on. After a few moments, something clicked in
Kendi's head, and he knew he could find this Marina
Feldan on his own.

"Got it," he said.

"Then I'm gone," Frank said.

"Hold it." Kendi fluttered a wing. "Before you go, I want to know something—are you leaving anything out about Sufur's plan? Is there anything you're holding back?"

Frank took a deep breath. "No."

"All right. You better go."

"Just remember that you swore not to tell anyone," Frank said.

"We won't," Ben said.

Frank vanished messily, leaving heavy distortion in his wake. Kendi shuddered. The ripples tore at his Outback, and he could feel them washing over him like liquid nausea. It took several moments for the Dream to settle down.

"Sloppy," Ben said with disapproval.

"I don't like it," Kendi said.

"Me, either. He needs to practice leaving without—"

"That's not what I meant," Kendi said. "I don't like Sufur's plan. It feels like I'm missing something about it."

"Frank couldn't lie to us," Ben said doubtfully. "Except by omission. And your last question took care of that."

"I know. But the whole thing sounds . . . wrong to me." Kendi clacked his beak. "Let's get out of here. I want hands again."

Harenn tucked the soft yellow blanket more firmly around little Evan. Ben looked down at him. Evan breathed with his whole chest and stomach, and it was strangely compelling to watch. Ara slept in her own crib nearby, tiny limbs sprawled in four different directions. Although Evan preferred being wrapped snugly, his sister fussed and cried if her blankets were tight, and she protested being put into a sling. Only a few days old and she already had a personality different from her brother's. Ben marveled at that. He seemed to marvel a lot lately.

"So what is the next step?" Harenn asked.

"I have to access Sufur's computer," Ben said.

"At two o'clock in the morning?" Harenn said.

"Best time for it. The Vajhurs report that Sufur's lights always go out between eleven and midnight, so he'll be asleep. Lucia and I'll break in, and I'll swipe the logarithm generator and the coordinates for both the ship and the satellite. Kendi will get into the Dream and send a fake message to SA Station telling them to halt the Corridor program, and we'll sic the Guardians on the ship. All very simple."

"All Kendi's plans sound simple," Harenn said. "But they have a way of getting out of hand. Do you think Gretchen is all right?"

"Our informant says Sufur is keeping her and the others alive for the moment," Ben said, grimacing beneath a stab of worry. "But we have to move fast."

"At least tell me Lucia has a spare suit for you."

"Right here," Lucia said from the doorway. Her tone was bright, and Ben shot a worried glance at the babies. Both of them, however, had just had their second night feeding, and a thunderclap wouldn't have woken them up.

"Ready to go?" Lucia asked. She was wearing her own camouflage outfit and holding a second one out to Ben. He accepted it and pulled the suit on over his regular clothes.

"How's the loser party doing downstairs?" he asked.

"Winding down," Lucia said. "Ched-Tumaar left a couple hours ago, and Salman went to bed not long after that. Everyone else is getting maudlin over single malt."

"It isn't fair," Ben said, fastening the front of the suit. "Grandma should have won. *Would* have won, if Sufur hadn't interfered." A bubble of anger burst over him and suddenly he was seething. "I *hate* him, Lucia. Maybe we'd be better off if we just—"

"Don't," Lucia said, pressing a finger to his lips. "I would love to see him dead, too, but I would hate to see you in prison. Ara and Evan need their father. We're taking a big enough risk as it is."

Ben set his jaw, tried to swallow his anger. "I know. I'll keep myself under control."

He and Lucia slipped out of the makeshift nursery and crept down the hallway toward the rear of Salman's house. Up here the house was quiet, the lights mostly off. They passed Salman's room, and for a moment Ben felt like a teenager sneaking out after his mother had gone to bed. They reached a rarely used guest bathroom and set the lights to a dim glow. Lucia pulled a rope ladder from the towel cabinet.

"A little low-tech, isn't it?" Ben said.

"No-tangle static rope, ultralight polymer rungs, gravity hooks to hold it in place," Lucia said, opening the window and flinging the object in question over the sill. "Seems fairly high-tech to me. Put up your hood, and shift your suit to shadow."

Ben obeyed. His camo-suit swirled into a non-pattern of gray and black. Cool, spring air wafted through the open window from the darkness beyond as Lucia boosted herself feetfirst through the window.

"It feels wonderful to move normally again," she said, and vanished out the window.

Ben counted to ten, then swung his legs over the sill. His feet, clad in soft-soled shoes, found the rungs by touch, and he quickly climbed past the first story to the platform below, where Lucia waited. Night animals chirped and peeped in the tree around them, and a dinosaur grunted in the forest far below. The platform ran all the way around Salman's house and only yesterday would have been patrolled by bodyguards. Salman, however, had decreed that ex-candidates didn't need much in the way of special protection and had given most of her guards the night off. Kendi was supposed to keep Lars and Tan busy. Exactly how, Ben didn't know, but he trusted Kendi to come up with something.

Lucia jerked the ladder, and it dropped silently into her arms. They trotted to the corner of the house, where a midsized talltree branch stretched away into the night above them. Lucia flung the top of the ladder upward while keeping hold of the bottom. It rushed upward like a finger stabbing the dark and thumped softly against the branch. Lucia yanked hard, but the ladder stayed put. With a nod to Ben, she scurried upward. Ben followed, and a moment later he was standing on the talltree branch. Balancing carefully on the rough bark, they made their way to the trunk and used the ladder again to clamber down to the bridge that connected Salman's house to the other talltrees in the neighborhood. Ben kept a nervous eye out. The guards weren't exactly their enemies, but they'd definitely try to keep Ben and Lucia from going out alone. Everyone seemed to be inside the house, though, and Ben felt a little foolish at the elaborate precautions they had taken to avoid notice.

Once they were far enough away from the house, the couple changed their suits into a drab green (Ben) and a boring brown (Lucia). They dashed down to the monorail station, boarded a deserted train, and rode in silence to a stop not far from Padric Sufur's house. By now it was almost four thirty. A quick run brought them to Sufur's house. The entire neighborhood remained dark and quiet as they crept up the stairs leading to his platform. Lucia halted and took out a small scanner before they reached the top. Ben stared at the house and felt a sudden urge to charge into it and beat Sufur bloody. No more shattered statues—this time he could take the real man apart, bone by bone. The power of the emotion rocked him, and he trembled like a tree in an earthquake.

He tried to focus on Ara and Evan, on how much they needed their father. Kendi had been right—it wasn't up to Ben to mete out justice to Sufur.

The hell it isn't, he thought. *He killed Mom. My kids will never know her because of him.*

Ben stood there, caught between conflicting impulses. Lucia's scanner beeped.

"No external security measures that I can find," Lucia whispered, jarring him back. "In fact . . ." She crept to the top stair, edged close to the house, and ran the scanner over one of the windows next to the front door. "We're lucky. The alarm system doesn't seem to be active. He must have forgotten to set it before he went to bed."

"Yeah," Ben said warily. "Lucky. You know what my mom used to say? 'Luck means you get to choose your own casket.' "

"Do you want to leave?"

Ben thought about it. "No. We need his computer."

Lucia took Ben around to the house's back door,

where she pulled a lead from the data pad clipped to her belt and plugged it into a flat rubber square the size of a postage stamp. She pressed the rubber square over the thumb plate by the front door. Lights flickered busily on her data pad.

"What's that for?" Ben whispered.

"Lockpick. It picks up latent prints left by the last person to thumb the plate and uses them to re-create an acceptable print. The lock should open in—" There was a click, and Lucia cautiously pushed the door open. A whiff of cooked sausage drifted out. The darkness gaped like a pit. Ben stared into it. A monster lived in there. A monster who ate sausages for supper and slept in a fine bed.

"Mask," Lucia said, pulling hers up over her face. Ben copied her. He didn't like the suit. It seemed like he could feel his skin flakes gathering beneath the fabric and skittering around like dust mites trying to escape. Lucia moved to enter the house, but Ben made a snap decision. He grabbed her wrist.

"You stay out here and keep watch," Ben said.

"But—"

"Stay out here, Lucia," Ben said in a low, icy voice. "If I make a mistake, there's no reason for both of us to get caught."

Lucia looked at him for a moment, then nodded. Ben took a deep breath and entered the house.

Lucia dePaolo watched Ben go, not at all certain she had made the right decision. It was hard for her to refuse Ben anything. He was the son of Irfan, and although constant contact with him had proved to her that he was an ordinary man, she still felt the occasional thrill of awe. And she had borne his child. Irfan's child. Vik's child.

Lucia's hand went to her neck, automatically feeling for the figurine of Irfan she had worn as long as she could remember. It was no longer there. She had removed it the day she had learned about the lawsuit. Lucia no longer prayed to Irfan twice each day and had disabled the timer that reminded her to do so. But she hadn't gotten rid of her personal altar to Irfan either.

Irfan was still a serene, wise, and powerful woman, still an incarnation of the divine. But her Church . . . her Church had tried to take Lucia's child away. That she could not forgive.

Lucia hadn't spoken to her mother since Ara's birth. They hadn't exactly argued when they parted. Mother had simply kissed the top of baby Ara's head, touched Lucia's cheek as she had done since Lucia was a child, and left the hospital. The family hadn't tried to visit Lucia, hadn't even called. True, the birth had only been a few days ago, and they knew Lucia had plenty of help with Ara. But there seemed to be a chill in their silence.

Maybe Lucia was reading too much into it. The Church had been absent from her life for only a few months, and she was used to her family's loud, near-constant presence. The lack boomed through the silent days like a thunderstorm. Once it swept through, things would go back to normal, except that Lucia would never set foot in a Church building again. That made her sad.

The house in front of her remained silent. Night lizards chittered in the trees, and a few early insects buzzed about. Lucia kept a watchful eye out, but the neighborhood slept, completely oblivious to the presence of Padric Sufur and to the people breaking into his house. In the darkness it seemed like Lucia could see the faces of Finn and Helen Day. She started to say a prayer to Irfan about their souls, stopped herself, then finished it anyway. The Days, whatever their crimes, should have their path to the afterlife cleared. Lucia doubted she would say anything if Padric Sufur were to die.

An alarm whooped inside the dark house. Lucia jumped as sirens sounded in the distance as if in answer. Ben burst out the door, data pad in his hand. The sirens grew louder.

"Run!" Ben snapped, and Lucia obeyed. They fled down the stairs and along the walkway. Lucia's mouth was dry, and her heart was pounding. What had gone wrong? Ahead of them, Lucia saw a police scooter zipping toward them on the walkway, lights whirling like angry whirlwinds. Ben leaped over the railing, and Lucia dove after him. They both landed on the safety net underneath. It stretched like a spiderweb but didn't break.

The scooter zipped past them overhead. Ben and Lucia skittered along the stretchy strands until they came to a walkway intersection. Ben reached up and grabbed the edge of the walkway, hauling himself back onto the boards by sheer strength. A moment later, he reached down and hauled Lucia up like she weighed nothing at all. Lucia felt the power in his arms and upper body. For a moment she felt a little flushed, and she fully understood the attraction Kendi had for Ben. Then they were running down the dark walkways again. Behind them, police lights converged on Sufur's house like wasps dive-bombing an invader.

They found a shadowy stairwell and ducked into it to catch their breaths. Lucia pulled off her mask and changed her suit from swirls of gray and black into its simple, nondescript brown. Ben's suit shifted into drab green as he removed his own mask. Lucia took Ben's hand and leaned her head against his shoulder as they moved unhurriedly away, a couple out for a very late stroll. Lucia's heart beat like a triphammer.

Serene must you ever remain, she told herself. *Serene, serene, serene.*

Her heart slowed, and the police lights and noises faded in the distance. Lucia released Ben's hand. They passed under a rare streetlight, and Lucia saw his face. It was set in a grim mask.

"What happened in the house?" she demanded.

"Not here," he said. "Home." And he refused to say anything more.

The darkness was freezing. Gretchen Beyer shivered and tried to reach for the covers. Her hands wouldn't respond. She tried again and managed a twitch. The cold was so bad, it felt as if her bones would shatter like brittle icicles. With a small groan, she wrenched her eyes open. A translucent barrier curved just above her nose. Disorientation made her head swim, and her teeth began to chatter. Where the hell was she? The last thing she remembered was . . .

Her apartment. The man and the woman. The fight. The dermospray. A spurt of adrenaline cleared her head and gave her energy enough to press her hands against the plastic. It came to her that she was lying in a cryo-unit, a coffin-sized tube designed to put the inhabitant into frozen hibernation. By all rights, she should be asleep. So why—?

She pushed, and the lid opened, giving her the answer. The unit hadn't been closed completely and therefore, hadn't activated properly. The bone-cracking cold made her entire body shiver like a spring leaf in a blizzard. Gretchen gathered herself and forced her shuddering muscles to half roll, half heave her out of the tube. She flopped unceremoniously onto hard ceramic. The floor was probably cool, but to Gretchen's half-frozen body, it felt deliciously warm. She pushed herself to hands and knees and managed a look at her surroundings.

She was in some kind of cargo hold. Plain gray walls stretched up to an equally plain ceiling. Five other coffin-like cryo-units were lined up on the floor, taking up most of the space. Gretchen was kneeling next to one of them, and it exuded a wonderful warmth. Gretchen clung to it, a baby huddled against a mother's breast, until she stopped shivering. She stood up and noticed for the first time she was barefoot and dressed in a white jumpsuit she had never seen before. Clearly the dark-haired woman and the blond man had brought her here, but why? And where was "here"?

A quick check told Gretchen the other five units were occupied. She thought about waking the other people—victims just as she herself was—but decided against it until she knew more about what was going on. She padded noiselessly over to the windowless door and pressed her thumb against the plate. To her surprise, it slid smoothly open. Her kidnappers must not have expected anyone to wake up and try the door.

The gray corridor beyond was lined with doors but otherwise empty. More cargo holds? Gretchen eased down the hallway, heart pounding at the back of her throat. She needed to find a weapon, or maybe a communicator. Her earpiece was gone, of course, even if it had enough range to reach anyone. Gretchen's stomach tightened. This place felt like a ship, or maybe a space station. If that was the case, she could be light-years away from help.

Story of my life, she thought. *Okay, girl—keep moving. You can't be the only person on board.*

The corridor ended at a larger doorway, which opened at Gretchen's command. The space beyond boasted a set of elevator doors, and a ladder that led upward through a hole in the ceiling. Letters marched across the elevator: LEVEL 3 SAT 7395-A5-11. A tiny bit of relief touched Gretchen. She was on board a satellite, probably in orbit around Bellerophon. Worse than being on the ground, better than being on a slipship. If she could find a shuttle, or a way to call for help—

The elevator doors slid open. Gretchen leaped for the ladder and scuttled upward. The rungs bit into her bare soles like hard fingers. Human conversation floated up to her from below.

". . . recheck the units and then transfer everything to the ship within the hour." Gretchen recognized the voice of the dark-haired woman. "Then we hit slip."

"Shit. How are we supposed to keep to that schedule?" It was a male voice, not one Gretchen could identify. "We've been pulling double shifts for three days now, and I'm sick of hanging out on the stupid satellite with nothing to do but work."

"Welcome to life at Silent Acquisitions," the woman said. "We love our job."

"I just better be loving my bonus on this one. I haven't seen my wife in—"

The voices cut off as the door slid shut. A chill slid down Gretchen's spine. Silent Acquisitions. Padric Sufur. God *damn* it! She should have killed him, no matter what Kendi said.

Grimly she climbed the ladder. If she was on level three, and the emergency ladder only went up, the satellite was a small one with only two more levels above her. Experience told her the command center of the satellite was probably on the first level. She hurried as best she could, but her muscles were still twitchy from the aborted cryo-sleep. In her mind, she saw her captors checking the cargo bay and noticing her cryo-chamber was empty. Any moment they'd raise the alarm. Her lungs worked hard in her chest as she passed the second level and finally reached the first, emerging into the clevator bay. The double doors leading out of the area had actual windows in them. Trying to keep her breathing under control, Gretchen sidled over to the exit doors and stood with her back flat against the wall next to them. The only sound was the soft hum of the ventilation system. A line of exertion sweat prickled her hairline. First she had been too cold, now she was too hot. Holding her breath, Gretchen eased an eye around the edge of the window until she could peek into the room beyond.

It was a large, round chamber ringed with workstations. A man sat at one of them. His back was turned, but even from behind Gretchen recognized the blond man who had delivered the balloons. Gretchen's thoughts raced. The other two would probably discover her absence in a few seconds. She had to act now.

Gretchen thumbed the plate, and the doors slid open. The blond man didn't look up from his board. Gretchen rushed across the room at him.

"That was fast," the man said, tapping at the panel before him. "Or did you forget something?" He spun his chair and saw Gretchen charging him. "Oh, sh—"

Her fist drove straight into his midriff, cutting off the expletive. She followed with a hard left to his jaw. The pain in her hand was mitigated by the satisfying *crack* the blow made as it connected. He keeled over and spilled groaning out of the chair, just as an alarm blasted through the room. Gretchen ran back to the doors and slammed her hand against the plate.

"Lock!" she shouted, and the plate turned red, indicating obedience. The idiots hadn't bothered to program the satellite's systems to respond only to authorized personnel, probably because they hadn't figured anyone would escape the cryo-chambers. Their mistake, her advantage. Gretchen sped around the outer ring of workstations, scanning each one. Where the hell was the communications board? The alarm continued to blare. She got almost all the way around the outer wall before she found it not far from where the blond man wretched on the floor. Gretchen kicked him.

Someone pounded at the doors. Gretchen wasted five precious seconds orienting herself to the unfamiliar comm board. She slapped a control and was gratified to see the panels spring to life with blue and green lights.

Glass shattered. "Get away from there!" shouted the dark-haired woman through the broken window.

Gretchen found the regulator, spun it to the emergency frequency, and tapped the control to open the channel. "Emergency!" she barked. "I need help. I'm on board satellite number—" What the hell was the number? It was on the elevator door. She fumbled before her Silent memory training took over and the number popped into her head. "Number seven three niner—"

The panel exploded in a shower of sparks. Gretchen leaped backward and spun around. The dark-haired woman was aiming a portable gravity beam at the board, presumably the same one she had used to shatter the window. She aimed it straight at Gretchen. Before Gretchen could react, a green beam slammed into her. Gretchen flew backward, crashed into the wall, and slid to the floor. Her entire body went numb, but she retained consciousness. The blond man staggered to his feet and stumbled over to her. Blood streamed from a split lip. Gretchen tried to move, but her body refused to respond. She felt consciousness slipping away.

"Bitch." The man spat blood. "I'll feed you through the meat grinder."

He drew back his fist, but Gretchen was already out.

CHAPTER SEVENTEEN

"Nothing destroys a relationship faster than suspicion."
—Daniel Vik

Ara fussed and cried in Kendi's arms. Kendi rocked her in the chair, trying to calm her down. She refused a bottle. She didn't need changing. She spat out a pacifier. Kendi rocked and rocked and hummed a desperate little tune. The sound of Ara crying unnerved Kendi. Was something worse wrong with her? Was she getting sick? Maybe he should wake Harenn.

In his own crib across the room, Evan slumbered peacefully, completely oblivious to his sister's cries and his Da's distress. Kendi wondered if Ara fussed because she could sense Kendi's restlessness. The wrongness of Sufur's plan tugged at him. Originally Sufur had wanted to remove all Silent from the Dream and destroy it. Now, it seemed, he had scaled back a little and contented himself with trying to remove just the human Silent from the Dream. He was going to do it by getting all the human Silent in one place and damaging their Silence so they couldn't enter the Dream.

That was the problem. Bellerophon and SA Station had a lot of human Silent, but nowhere near *all* of them. Even if Sufur waved a magic wand and all the Silent on Bellerophon and SA Station dropped dead, there were enough human Silent scattered around the galaxy to replenish the population. And then there were people like Vidya and Prasad Vajhur, people who weren't Silent themselves but who produced Silent children. They didn't seem to be on Sufur's little list.

Then there was the problem of execution. Every kidnapping, every trip up to the cargo satellite, every transfer to the hidden slipship was a chance to get caught. Sure, the hostage situation kept Kendi's mouth shut, but all it would take is one innocent witness to a kidnapping or a single suspicious neighbor to call the police, and the authorities would slam Sufur to the ground before they even knew the hostages existed. A few people—including Gretchen—would die, but Sufur's main plan would sink like a leaky ship. Sufur had to know that. So what was Kendi missing? Maybe Ben and Lucia would turn up a clue at Sufur's home.

Ara continued to fuss. Kendi rocked and worried. A thousand things could go wrong with Ben and Lucia. The police might catch and arrest them. Sufur might wake up and catch them. The information they sought might not be stored on Sufur's computer. Ben might not be able to hack in. Lucia might—

A noise in the hallway halted his line of thinking. He got to his feet just as Ben and Lucia entered the nursery with the rope ladder. Relief washed over him.

"What's wrong with her?" Ben asked, holding out his arms. Kendi handed Ara over, and her cries instantly stopped.

"Sounds like she just wanted her daddy," Kendi said. "How did it go?"

"I'm not sure," Lucia said. "Ben won't say."

Kendi tensed. "What's going on? What happened?"

Ben took Ara to the rocking chair, sat, and stared down at Ara's face. "I didn't get it. The codes, the program—none of it. And he's . . . Sufur is . . ."

"What?" Kendi said, resisting the urge to grab Ben by the shoulders and shake him. "Sufur is what?"

"Dead," Ben said flatly.

Icy chills slid over Kendi's skin. "What do you mean he's dead?"

"I mean," Ben said, "that he's *dead*."

"That isn't very—"

"Ben," Lucia interrupted gently, "please start from the beginning. Tell us what happened."

Ben started to rock. Ara sighed once and fell asleep. "It was weird. I went into Sufur's house to find his computer. I remember seeing it when we visited him, so I knew right where to go. I was trying to be real quiet, you know? I turned on my data pad to give myself a little light, and I looked around. His computer was right there in the living room. I listened for a minute and didn't hear anything, but the house smelled funny. Sausage from the kitchen, but a sort-of sewer smell, too. I thought Sufur had maybe used the bathroom a little while ago or something, and that made me nervous—what if he hadn't fallen back to sleep yet? So I tried to work fast.

"His computer had a standard setup, and I was able to find my way around his system pretty quick. Parts of it were secured with expensive and powerful programs— I expected that—so I connected my data pad to the machine and uploaded a few programs of my own. Sufur probably thought his security was pretty good, but I've hacked government computers inside the Empire of Human Unity. Sufur's stuff was almost . . . cute by comparison."

"Only you," Kendi said, "would describe security protocols as *cute*."

"Shush," Lucia said. "Go on, Ben."

"I started nosing around the secure part of computer's drive," Ben said. "I found the logarithm generator pretty quick, along with the files containing the coordinates of the ship and the satellite. I also saw a manifest list of thirty people—fifteen Silent and fifteen Silenced—being stored in cryo-sleep aboard the ship. Six more people are on the satellite, and they're going to be transferred soon. One of them . . . one of them is Gretchen."

Kendi set his jaw. "We'll get her back, then."

"Maybe," Ben said. "At any rate, I figured it would be best to download the codes the program had created, erase them from Sufur's computer, and then disable the logarithm program entirely. Sufur wouldn't be able to communicate with SA Station or with the ship. Or rather, he would, but they would assume it was some kind of trick because he couldn't give them the clearance code."

"Right," Kendi said. "That's all according to plan."

"Except for one problem. I called up the logarithmic generator, but the computer was slow. The sewer smell was really strong now, and I couldn't figure out where it was coming from, and it seemed really strange that it wasn't going away. So while the computer was working, I looked around the room a little more. You remember that chair Sufur sat in when we visited before? It was still half-facing the window, so I couldn't really see into it, and now that I was paying attention to it, I could tell the sewer smell was coming from that direction. I went over to the chair, trying to stay really quiet, and that was when I saw him."

"Sufur," Lucia said.

"Yeah. He was just sitting there in the chair. His mouth was hanging open like he was surprised. There was a circle burned in the middle of his chest. The sewer smell must have been because his bladder had let go." Ben continued to stare down at Ara. "I didn't understand what I was looking at. I kept thinking it was some kind of joke—a dummy or a hologram set out to fool burglars or something. I reached out and touched him. That was when the alarm went off." Ben sighed. "I don't know what I was thinking. He'd shocked me when I just got near him that last time. I guess I figured with him being already dead, the defense system wouldn't kick in. But he must have had a proximity alarm set to go off in case anyone touched him. Anyway, the police were coming. I grabbed my data pad and ran for it. Lucia and I barely managed to get away. And here we are— screwed. The whole house is a major crime scene now. We'll never get in there."

"Shit," Kendi said.

"Yeah," Ben said.

"Who killed him?" Lucia asked.

Ben shrugged, but carefully, so as not to disturb Ara. "We should call the Vajhurs. The killer should have shown up on the surveillance cameras."

"I'm stupid," Kendi said, and tapped his earpiece. A moment later, Sejal's sleepy voice yawned in his ear.

"What's going on?" he said.

"Sejal, I need you to check the surveillance equipment," Kendi told him. "There's been an incident. Sufur's been murdered."

"Really? When's the party?"

"Just check the system," Kendi said tightly.

"Gimme a sec to call up the display, guy. Let's see, here . . . Hmmmm . . . Okay, this can't be good."

"What? What's going on?"

"The cameras are out. Hold on . . . hold on . . . Okay, I've got the image of you two leaving—you never did tell me what the hell was up with that—and then we've got . . . let's see . . . one hour . . . two hours . . . Shit! Now I've got nothing. The cameras went out two hours and twelve minutes after you left."

Kendi relayed this to Harenn and Ben. "So whoever killed Sufur knew the cameras were there," he said.

"Duh."

"Then maybe we should start with who knew the cameras were there," Lucia said.

Ben knew. The thought came unbidden into Kendi's mind. Disconcerted, he tapped his earpiece. "Thanks, Sejal. I'll be in touch." He disconnected.

Ben continued to rock Ara. He was still wearing the camouflage suit. "Now what?"

"Did you two leave any clues of your presence?" Kendi asked.

"No," Lucia said emphatically. "No DNA, no fingerprints, nothing. Ben left the computer running, but lots of people do that."

"At least tell me you know when Sufur was supposed to transmit the next code to the ship?"

"Ten thirty tomorrow night," Ben said. "But I don't know the ship's coordinates."

"We should go to bed," Kendi said. "Try to get a couple hours' sleep so we can tackle this with fresh minds."

"Gretchen's on that ship, and they'll space her if we don't find it in time," Lucia said. "I don't know how much sleep I'll get."

"Try," Kendi said. "You'll think better if you're not tired."

"I'll stay up with Ara a little longer," Ben said.

Kendi kissed the top of his head. "Then I'll see you at breakfast. In four hours."

Ched-Theree arrived during breakfast. Evan and Ara swung gently in identical baby swings in Salman's enor-

mous, sunny kitchen while Kendi served up scrambled
eggs with white cheese and red onions to Ben, Harenn,
and Lucia. Bedj-ka was already in class at the monastery.
The adults looked tired and drawn despite the lateness
of the morning hour. Kendi himself felt like his eyes
were full of sand. Ben filled in Harenn about the events
of the previous evening while Kendi set a plate of fluffy
yellow eggs in front of Lucia, who tasted them and nodded her approval. Kendi managed a wan smile. They
were eating scrambled eggs and toast on a sunny spring
morning while Gretchen was who-knew-where going
through who-knew-what.

Sufur was dead. This was the granddaddy of all mixed
blessings. On the one hand, Kendi couldn't wait for the
man's burial so he could perform a traditional Real People dance of some kind on his grave. On the other hand,
Ben and Lucia hadn't managed to get Sufur's codes,
which meant somewhere out there, a spaceship crew was
going to—

"—murder thirty-odd people if we don't figure out
what to do," Ben concluded.

Harenn gave a tight-lipped nod. "Then we must figure
out what to do."

"All right, troops," Kendi said, sitting down with his
own plate, "rescue plan time. Options?"

"Hey, guys," rasped Tan from the doorway. "Inspector Ched-Theree is here. She's insistent."

A chilly hand clutched Kendi's stomach. Ben shot
Lucia a quick look. She calmly forked up more eggs.
Harenn composed herself behind a sip of tea.

"She's here to see who?" Kendi asked casually.

"You and Ben," Tan said. "Should she come in?"

Kendi's eyes met Ben's. *Get it over with?*

Ben shrugged. *May as well.*

"Yeah," Kendi said. "Show her in."

Ched-Theree entered the kitchen, her heavy front claws
clicking on the wood floor. Her blue head cloth was freshly
pressed, and her silver Guardian medallion hung promi-
nently around her long neck. Tan stood to one side, both
hands behind her back, expression neutral.

"Can I offer you some breakfast?" Kendi said. "It's
human food, but—"

"Thank you, no," Ched-Theree interrupted with a dip of her head. "You know why I have come, of course."

"Actually, I don't," Kendi lied. By unspoken decree, he became spokesman for the group. "Unless it's to offer your sympathies on Senator Reza's loss last night."

Ched-Theree tapped her claws on the floor. "Father Kendi, I know of Padric Sufur."

Silence around the table. Every instinct Kendi possessed shrieked at him to grab Ben and flee. Instead he gave Ched-Theree a quizzical look. "Are you asking a question? I'm not sure what you want."

"Perhaps you should begin by telling me all you know about Padric Sufur's presence here on Bellerophon."

Kendi set down his fork. "Inspector, I'm getting the feeling that this has become an interrogation."

"Did you know he was here? I would advise you not to lie."

"Yes," Kendi said. "All of us knew. We were also watching his every move, though he rarely left his house. I imagine you've already spoken to the Vajhur family about the cameras."

"Why did you not tell me you knew of his presence?"

"We weren't sure it was him," Kendi said, working hard to keep his voice calm. "At first."

"Exactly when did you decide the inhabitant of that house was indeed Padric Sufur?"

Evan woke up and began to fuss. Ben plucked him from the swing and sat down with the baby in his lap.

"Inspector," Kendi said, "why don't you tell us what this is about? I—we—might be able to help if we knew what was going on."

"This morning the Treetown police received an automated alarm call. When they arrived on the scene, they found the body of an old man. He had been murdered."

"How?" Kendi asked.

"A neuro-pistol strike to the chest. Such a weapon would not set off a tactile proximity alarm. The man carried no identification, and at first we thought his name was Patrick Sulfur, the registered inhabitant of the house. A search of his home turned up his true identity. A scan of the surrounding neighborhood revealed numerous surveillance devices, which we tracked back to the Vajhur family."

"Have you arrested them?" Harenn asked.

"They have broken no law that we know of," Ched-Theree said.

"Why are *you* here?" Ben asked, still cradling Evan. "Sufur's house isn't on monastery property. It falls under police jurisdiction, not Guardian."

"We are performing a joint investigation," Ched-Theree said. "And I have interviewed all of you before. Can each of you please tell me where you were last night?"

"We were all here," Kendi said. "At the party. And then we went to bed."

Ched-Theree went around the table getting specifics. Everyone echoed Kendi, saying that they had attended the party and gone to bed late. Harenn and Ben added that they had gotten up to give night feedings to Evan and Ara, respectively, and no, they hadn't noticed anyone coming or going.

"And where is the senator?" Ched-Theree asked.

"At her office, I think," Kendi said. "The campaign is over, but she still has a senatorial seat and all the business that goes with it. She left before any of us got up."

"Why did you and Father Weaver visit Padric Sufur's home last night, Mr. Rymar?"

Kendi tensed. *Mr. Rymar,* not *Offspring.* Ben shifted Evan on his lap.

"What makes you say we were there last night, Inspector?" Ben asked.

"We confiscated the camera files and reviewed them," Ched-Theree said. "At eight thirty-seven last night, you and Father Kendi approached Sufur's home. He answered the door, and you went inside. You emerged thirteen minutes later. Your face, Mr. Rymar, was clearly angry. I would say it was even murderous. No one else was recorded entering before the cameras mysteriously went off-line at ten forty-nine. It is of interest to note that the medical examiner has put Sufur's death at sometime between eleven thirty p.m. and two thirty a.m., well after the cameras were deactivated. This seems to indicate that the killer knew the cameras were there."

Ched-Theree paused, and Kendi swallowed. Ben and Lucia had left for Sufur's house at a little after two in the morning. It only took twenty or so minutes to get to his house from Salman's, meaning it was possible Ben could have . . . have . . .

Killed Sufur, Kendi finished. He looked at Ben, who met Ched-Theree's gaze without blinking. Had Kendi suspected Ben from the start? The eggs churned in his stomach as he realized the answer was *yes*. Ben had hated—no *loathed*—Sufur, had made it clear that he wanted Sufur dead and that he wanted to see to it. Ben had set up the cameras, knew the location of each one, possessed the skill to disable them. Had he been at the party every moment last night? Kendi thought back and couldn't recall.

"You knew Padric Sufur was in that house, Mr. Rymar," Ched-Theree said. "You were keeping that knowledge a secret from the Guardians and the police. Understandable. Perhaps you went to confront Sufur about his creation of the Despair, and he made you angry. There is no shame in that. Perhaps you went back later, disabled the cameras that you yourself set up, went inside, and killed him. Also perfectly understandable. The man is a mass murderer. Thousands, perhaps millions, died because of him. Including your mother. You lost your temper and overreacted. Is that the way it happened?"

Kendi started to take a sip of tea, then stopped when he saw his hand was shaking. Ched-Theree's thoughts were echoing his own.

"Nothing happened," Ben said calmly. "I never went near Sufur's house after Kendi and I talked to him."

"What did you talk about?"

"The Despair. What a bastard he is. I . . . I hated him, right along with just about everyone else on Bellerophon, but I didn't kill him." Ben gave Evan to Harenn and held out both hands. "When you use a neuro-pistol set to kill, the backlash makes your hand shake for a day or two afterward. Mine are rock steady. See?"

Kendi looked at Ben's unmoving hands and felt relieved again. *But not everyone gets the shakes,* his treacherous mind pointed out.

"The symptom is common but not universal," Ched-Theree said. "You have a history of keeping secrets, Mr. Rymar, and I think you are keeping one now."

And a light flashed in Kendi's mind. He turned the idea over in his mind and saw nothing wrong with it. "You're right, Inspector," he said impulsively. "We *are* keeping secrets. And we need to come clean. Maybe we should do this in the living room?"

Ched-Theree dipped her head in surprise as Kendi rose. "Ken?" Ben said. "What—?"

"It's okay," Kendi said. "Come on."

They left the table, breakfast unfinished, and filed into the living room. Looking mystified, everyone took seats. Harenn and Ben held the babies. Ched-Theree sat on a floor cushion.

"I'll start at the beginning," Kendi said. "Yesterday I had a conversation with a Silent human in the Dream. His name was Frank Kowalksi. He told me that Padric Sufur has been arranging for various people—Silent and Silenced—to be kidnapped."

"Kendi!" Ben said. "You swore—"

"Sufur is dead," Kendi said. "And he was the one Frank was afraid of. With Sufur out of the picture, there's no reason to keep quiet."

Ched-Theree sat completely upright, head raised high on her serpentine neck. "Go on."

Kendi explained about the Silent Corridor and Sufur's plan to use the Silenced people as decoys back on SA Station so he could kill the remaining human Silent at leisure. He kept his reservations about the plan to himself, however. "The coordinates for the ship and the communication codes Sufur used are on his computer. All you have to do is turn the information over to the military, and they can rescue everyone."

"How do you know the codes are on his computer?" Ched-Theree asked.

"He told us when we visited him," Kendi said, falling back into the lie. "It was his way of taunting us because he didn't think we could stop him. You need to hurry—if the ship doesn't hear from him by this evening, they have orders to dump the hostages into space and run."

Ched-Theree seemed to deflate. Her head lowered. "Then I fear we have bad news. When our technicians attempted to access Sufur's computer this morning, they discovered an empty drive. At first we thought Sufur's killer had wiped the computer's drive, but then they discovered traces of a time-zone virus. The computer was programmed to wipe itself clean if Sufur did not access it by a certain time every morning."

Harenn put a hand to her mouth. "Oh."

"Gretchen," Lucia whispered, and grabbed automatically for the Irfan figurine she no longer wore around her neck. "What do we do?"

Ched-Theree rose. "I must report this to my superiors. If any of you remember anything, even the tiniest detail, contact me immediately. We have less than fourteen hours to find that ship."

Kendi stared at the blackened, creaking timbers that had been his and Ben's home. A wilting bouquet of blueflowers and a paper picture of a Ched-Balaar Kendi didn't know fluttered in the breeze, offerings left behind by die-hard Offspring idolizers. Slowly, carefully, testing every step, he picked his way across the surviving drawbridge and into the mess. It was like walking into a giant skeleton. Charcoal crunched underfoot, and the place smelled faintly of burned wood. Kendi figured he was standing in the living room, but it was hard to be sure. Work crews had removed all the salvageable possessions to the new house, and souvenir hunters had cleared out a lot of the loose pieces. How many chunks of charred wood hung on walls or sat on altars around Treetown now? "This piece belonged to the Offspring's house," says a proud owner. "It cured my daughter of her cold."

I came here to get something.

Kendi took a moment to orient himself. This was the entryway, which meant the living room was over that way and Ben's office was over there. Ara used to use that room for meditation and entering the Dream.

Moving as if he himself were in a dream, Kendi crunched over creaking, screeching floorboards. Part of the office wall had collapsed and burned, but Kendi easily found a particular spot on the floor and knelt there. Clumsily, he pulled aside a concealed section of flooring to reveal a safe hidden beneath.

Closure, maybe. I don't know.

Kendi stared at the locked safe. A little over a year ago—and how long ago that seemed—Empress Kan maja Kalii of the Independence Confederation had given Mother Adept Araceil Rymar an order: Determine if Sejal was a threat to the millions of lives that made up the Confederation. If, in Ara's judgement, Sejal posed a danger, Ara was to kill him.

Kendi had never learned what decision Ara had come to. Padric Sufur had spirited Sejal away, and then the Despair had struck, and Ara had leaped from a balcony. Sometimes, though, Kendi was sure that Ara had decided to kill Sejal, and the feelings of guilt that followed this decision—unfulfilled or not—had worsened the Despair for her, causing her to commit suicide. At other times, Kendi was positive Ara would never have tried to take an innocent life, that she had simply fallen victim to the Despair on her own, as so many other Silent had done. He would never know for sure.

A little gust of wind stirred the talltree leaves, and one or two drifted down to land beside Kendi. The safe had been Ara's, then Ben's, then Ben and Kendi's, and it appeared to have remained untouched by the explosion. In all the fuss and bother, he had completely forgotten about it and the weapons it contained—a needler and a neuro-pistol. He pressed his thumb to the plate, let it scan his retina, and recited a password for voice recognition. The door popped open, and Kendi looked inside.

The safe contained a needler and a box of ammunition. The neuro-pistol was gone.

Kendi's chest filled with ice. Slowly, carefully he closed the safe and stood on shaky legs. It wasn't true. It *couldn't* be true. Ben didn't—Ben couldn't—

A tiny sound caught his attention. He spun. Ben was standing a few paces away. The spring breeze tousled his red hair and brought the smell of charred wood. Kendi didn't move. Ben stared at Kendi with hard blue eyes, then turned and walked away, leaving Kendi standing in the wreck that had been their home.

CHAPTER EIGHTEEN

"It's hard to fight in silence."

—Irfan Qasad

"Where the *hell* have you been?" Tan demanded as Kendi entered Salman's living room. "I've got ten people out looking for you."

"Where's Ben?" Kendi interrupted. "Did he come back yet?"

"He went upstairs before we could finish bawling him out, love," Salman said from her place on the couch. "I've been talking to Ched-Theree, and we have the military—what's left of it—sweeping the system for that ship, but it's like finding a single leaf on an entire talltree."

"We've got barely two hours before that signal has to go out," Tan growled, "and you and Ben decide to disappear for—"

But Kendi was already heading up the stairs. The door to his and Ben's room was closed. Kendi stood outside for a long moment, then firmed his jaw and entered.

Ben sat in a chair by the window, caught in fading amber sunlight. The windows were all shut and the room felt stuffy. Kendi quietly shut the door.

"Let me tell you what you were thinking," Ben said without looking at him. "You were thinking about how much I hate Sufur and how you found me in the ruins of the house not long before he was murdered. You were thinking that since I set up the cameras around Sufur's house, I could easily take them off-line. You were thinking that I slipped out during Grandma's party, broke into Sufur's house, and killed him with Mom's neuro-pistol. Or maybe I just killed him when I went to his house with Lucia. That would be why I told her to wait outside. You were thinking I'm one of the few people whose hands don't shake after firing a neuro-pistol set to kill." He finally turned and faced Kendi. "You were thinking I broke my promise and that I killed a slimy, disgusting creature who deserved to die."

"Ben, I'm sorry," Kendi said. "I'm so sorry. But I had to know if the pistol was still there, and—"

It was the wrong thing to say. Ben's face set into a mask of stone, and he turned away again. Kendi stood there, filled with wretched uncertainty. All the clues pointed in Ben's direction, but Kendi didn't want to believe that Ben would break a promise and lie to him. He went over to the chair, knelt beside it, and took Ben's hand in his own.

"Tell me you didn't kill Sufur, and I'll believe you," he said.

"So you have to ask," Ben said.

"Ben—"

"I. Didn't. Kill. Him. Is that enough?"

Kendi nodded. "I believe you."

"Fine." But it clearly wasn't.

Long pause. "They still have Gretchen and all those other people," Kendi said. "We need to find that satellite and that ship."

"Yeah?" The hostility in Ben's voice remained. "How the hell are we going to do that?"

And Kendi lost it. All the weeks and months of being careful around Ben, of holding his tongue for fear of making Ben shut down, of being so careful and patient and understanding every moment—all of it smashed out into the open and rushed at Ben.

"You know what, Ben?" he snarled. "I'm really sick of this. I'm sick of the way you pick fights without picking fights, I'm sick of walking on eggshells around you, and I'm *goddammed* sick of solving all the problems around here." His voice rose, and he made no attempt to hold it down. "Who got our kids back? *Me.* Who figured out it who was trying to kill us? *Me.* Who caught on to Petrie's plot? *Me.* Who negotiated the game contract? *Me.* So who has to find Gretchen before Sufur's lackeys vacuum-dry her corpse? Apparently *me.* No one seems to have a fucking clue about what to do, but that's okay—good old Kendi will pull a trick out of his ass, don't you worry. Hell, no one even has to say *thank you*." Kendi was shouting now, his face contorted. "I'm sick of playing hero, and I'm sick of playing the detective, and I'm sick of the people who are supposed to be helping me always needing *me* to help *them*. For months I've been watching what I say and what I do around you, and you *still* get pissed at me. So maybe I should stop watching what I say. Or maybe I should just—just—"

And there he stopped. Some things shouldn't be said, even in the middle of white-hot anger. Ben's face had turned to stone. Every muscle in his neck and jaw stood outlined in stark, pale flesh. Kendi spun around, gulping in great breaths and trying to regain control. He heard Evan crying in the nursery up the hall, but for once he ignored the sound. Harenn or Lucia could handle it.

After several moments, Kendi's heart slowed, and he no longer felt like he was going to explode. Behind him, Ben hadn't said a word. Kendi turned around. He hadn't stirred from the chair. Of course he hadn't. Kendi fought the urge to grind his teeth.

"Gretchen," he said finally. "We have to find Gretchen. And I do have an idea."

Ben's only response was to relax his jaw. Kendi sat on the bed a fair distance away from him. "You said you called up both the logarithmic code and the coordinates for the ship and the satellite on Sufur's computer, right?"

"Right," Ben said shortly.

"That means you at least *saw* them, and *that* means the information is still somewhere in your head. All we have to do is find it."

"And how will we do that?"

The tension between them was so thick, it was almost visible, like a dirty fog hanging in the air. Kendi plunged on.

"You're not a Child of Irfan, so you didn't get the full mnemonic training at the monastery, but you've had the basics," he said. "Enough to do independent contract work. Your short-term recall is good enough to let you run letters and basic documents to other planets, but you're not certified to handle complex stuff like bank transfers and computer codes."

"Where is this going, Kendi?" Ben said impatiently. "I know what my limitations in the Dream are."

"The point is that we have a basis for getting those codes back," Kendi said. "For most Silent, including me, the information we transmit through the Dream fades within a day. We read it in the solid world, hit the Dream, relay it to another Silent, and forget it. If you were a fully trained Child, you could simply recite what you saw on the screen because your short-term memory wouldn't have let go yet. But you aren't fully trained."

"Meaning the information is gone."

"Meaning we just have to dig for it. In the Dream."

"It won't work."

"We have to *try*, Ben. Unless you have a better idea."

Ben shot him a hard look, then shrugged. "All right. We can try. Meet me on my turf." He produced a dermospray from the dresser and all but flung himself down on the bed. Kendi retrieved his spear and his own dermospray. Ben injected himself and shut his eyes without giving Kendi another glance. Kendi's temper rose again, and he found it hard to relax, even with the drug's help. He lost track of time, and it was quite a while before he found himself gliding on falcon wings through hot desert air. Far below lay the Outback. Kendi caught an updraft and cast out his mind. It took only three seconds to find Ben, and one second to sense the anger in his mind. Kendi's own temper rose in response. A dust devil whirled into existence beneath him, and Kendi beat his wings quickly to avoid it. Stupid. Thought became reality in the Dream, and unfocused anger took . . . unhealthy forms.

Outback sand butted up against a hard tile floor. Kendi glided along the boundary and reached out to Ben's mind. ~May I approach?~

~You may.~ Ben's mental voice was flat.

Kendi crossed the border and swooped downward. A ceiling faded into existence over him, and he reflexively dropped lower still. Ben stood in the center of an enormous room filled with electronic equipment. Organic data processing units wound up toward the ceiling, twisting in green-blue spirals. Data scrolled across holographic displays arranged neatly on shiny steel counters. Magnetic fields pulsed, lights flashed, metal gleamed. Transmission lines and data portals gaped in all directions, transmitting and receiving data at impossible speeds. Kendi dropped to the floor next to him and took the shape of a kangaroo.

"Let's get this started," Ben said. "I checked the time and we have fifty-three minutes to transmit Sufur's code."

"Right." Kendi leaned back on his tail. "I decided to try this here in the Dream because you're already in a trance when you're here. We just need to push you a little deeper, and you should be able to come up with what we need."

"Fine. What's the first step?"

"I'm new to this, too," Kendi said, trying to keep his temper from rising again. Ben wasn't being helpful. It was almost as if he *wanted* to fail. "I think you should try sitting down."

Ben raised a hand over the floor. The tiles softened and moved like warm clay, and a lounge chair rose out of them. It solidified with a noise like someone clenching a fistful of mud. Ben sat in the chair, and it reclined back so he was looking up at the ceiling.

"Close your eyes and relax," Kendi instructed. "Breathe deep and even . . . deep and even . . . your legs are relaxed . . . very relaxed . . . your torso is—"

"I don't need a lesson in relaxation, Kendi," Ben interrupted.

"All right," Kendi said through clenched teeth. "Why don't you relax yourself and then raise a hand when you're ready."

Ben didn't answer. Kendi waited. The computer terminals around him flickered and flashed unintelligible code. The air was still and a little chilly, despite Kendi's fur coat. He waited. His legs started to ache from lack of motion, and he shifted position slightly. Ben's eyes popped open.

"How can I relax when you keep making all that noise?" he said.

"Ben, I was only—"

"Why don't you turn into a . . . a blackfly or something? Then maybe I can—"

The anger roared over Kendi again, and this time he gave in. He reached out with his mind and *shoved*. Ben's turf vanished with a thunderclap, replaced by the featureless plain. Ben's chair disappeared as well, and Ben landed flat on his back. Kendi shoved again, and the Outback exploded into being around them. Thunder rumbled in the distance and uncharacteristic clouds blackened the sky.

"What the hell are you doing?" Ben shouted.

"I've *had* it with you," Kendi yelled back. The wind rose. "If you want a fight, you've *got* one!"

A dust devil sprang out of the ground and rushed at Ben. Ben's hand snapped up in a defensive gesture, and a rocky wall shot upward in front of him. The dust devil dashed itself to pieces against the stones. Kendi stamped a powerful hind leg, and the earth rumbled beneath him. Cracks sprouted and spread over the wall until it crumbled to rubble. Ben snatched at empty air, and a giant rocky hand formed out of the ground under Kendi's feet. It grabbed for him. Kendi sprang into the air, but the hand caught his tail with a jerk that wrenched his spine. Kendi's form blurred, and he became a falcon. He left two tail feathers in the stony grasp behind him as he clawed for altitude. The hand grew an arm that grew upward right behind Kendi. He stole a glance behind him and saw the rocky fingers grasping for him. Kendi changed direction, fled sideways. The arm lengthened and the hand followed him, leaving him no time to breathe or think. When had Ben learned this kind of control?

Kendi dove back toward the ground. The hand followed, its arm making a U-shape behind him. Kendi pulled in his wings and increased the speed of his dive as he headed straight for Ben. Only then did Ben realize what was happening. Kendi pulled out of his dive and shot to the left in a maneuver that left his wing muscles sore. The hand crashed into the ground where Ben was standing. A cloud of dust rose, then cleared, revealing that the fingers had spread open, forming a five-barred cage that surrounded Ben instead of crushing him. Ben gestured and the hand crumbled to dust, but Kendi's mind was already moving. The skies opened up, releasing a torrential rainstorm. Water gushed across the rocky ground, creating a flash flood. Kendi landed on a house-sized boulder, his feathers soaked through. The raging water rushed toward Ben. Ben snapped a motion at the ground, his red hair plastered to his skull. The earth around him rumbled open and dropped away, leaving Ben standing on an island in the middle of a great sinkhole. The flood waters rushed into the pit and swirled around Ben's island, leaving him untouched. Then Ben raised a fist in a gesture Kendi recognized as one Ara used to make. He leaped away from the boulder just in time to avoid the lightning bolt that crashed into the rock behind him. Bits of hot stone stung him, and the thunderclap sent him tumbling forward, his wet falcon feathers unable to get a good hold on the air. Desperately he changed shape again, becoming a wood duck. Was Ben really trying to kill him? He didn't believe it.

Another lightning bolt blasted down from the sky, sizzling the air only a winglength away. Another crash of thunder boomed against Kendi's bones, knocking him nearly senseless. He was falling. In a haze of semiconsciousness, he angled himself toward Ben's island. With one final burst of strength, he crashlanded on the stony ground at Ben's feet.

Now use the lightning, he thought, staring up at a giant-sized Ben.

Ben hesitated, looking down at Kendi. Rain poured down around them, and the water swirled angrily in the sinkhole. In a flash of inspiration, Kendi changed shape one more time. Abruptly Ben was standing over an enormous leathery crocodile. Ben started to react, but then there was a flash of movement from the crocodile, and he froze. The scene remained a motionless tableau—man, rain, crocodile. The crocodile's head was tilted upward, its jaws not quite closed.

"You wouldn't," Ben said.

"Guh wuh," Kendi said.

There was a pause. "What?" Ben said.

"Guh. Wuh."

"Give up?" Ben made a choking sound Kendi

couldn't identify. "Didn't . . . didn't your mother ever tell you not to talk with your mouth full?"

A laugh rose in Kendi's belly, and he snorted hard in an attempt to keep it in. If he laughed now Ben would lose his—

The choking sound from Ben intensified. Kendi could feel him quivering at the end of his snout. Ben was laughing, too.

"All right, you win," he gasped. "Now let go of my . . . just let go."

Kendi released his hold. Still laughing, Ben stepped back and adjusted his trousers. There was a small tear just below the belt line.

Kendi smacked his lips together. "Mmmmm. Tastes just like ch—"

"Hey!" Ben interrupted, and then started laughing again. Kendi started to make another remark and ended up bursting into a laughter of his own. The noise mixed with the sounds of pouring rain and swirling brown water.

"I can't . . . can't . . ." Ben gasped, and sat down hard as yet more laughter overtook him. Kendi's form blurred and shifted until a koala bear lay giggling on the wet, slippery stone. The sight made Ben laugh all the harder. Kendi felt the tension that had been growing between them melt like ice in hot chocolate.

"Can you . . . at least . . . shut off . . . the rain?" Ben asked between laughs.

Kendi blew up at the sky. The rain stopped and the clouds whisked themselves away, revealing a perfect azure sky. A bright, golden sun shone over them, and the floodwater drained away. Ben finally quieted. He scooted next to Kendi and put a hand on the damp brown fur covering his head.

"I'm sorry, Ken," he said. "I guess I've been acting like a prima donna lately."

"I'm sorry, too," Kendi said. "I should have known you wouldn't break your promise."

"I wish . . ." Ben trailed off.

"You wish what?"

"I wish you could be human in the Dream. It'd be weird to kiss a koala bear."

Kendi laughed again. "We're good for hugging, though. Even with these claws."

And Ben hugged him. It was decidedly odd. From Kendi's perspective, Ben was as tall as a tree, his arms as thick as branches. He smelled like rainwater and sunshine. Kendi burrowed close to Ben's chest and let Ben's arms surround him. For a long moment he had no worries, and everything was as it should be. He never wanted to move again. At last Ben set him down.

"Let's try those codes again," he said.

They banished the Outback and called up the computer lab. Ben lay in the lounge chair, closed his eyes, and relaxed. It was almost ridiculously easy. Koala-Kendi spoke softly, putting Ben into a deep trance. He took Ben back to the night he and Lucia had broken into Sufur's house.

"And now you're standing in front of Sufur's desk," Kendi said. "The computer is on, the data display hovering over the pad. The logarithm program activates, and it generates a code. You can see the code. What is it?"

Ben rattled off a series of letters and numbers. Kendi's own trained memory caught and held them.

"And now the computer displays the coordinates of the satellite. What are they?"

More numbers.

"And now the computer displays the coordinates of the ship. What are they?"

Still more numbers.

"And now the computer displays the communication codes Sufur transmitted to the ship. What are they?"

Ben's brow furrowed. Kendi waited, then repeated the command. Ben didn't respond for several heartbeats. Then he abruptly opened his eyes and sat up.

"The computer never displayed that code," Ben said. "I never saw it."

"Are you sure?"

"Positive."

"Shit," Kendi said. "Meet you out there." He shut his eyes. *If it be in my best interest and in the best interest of all life everywhere, let me leave the Dream.*

Kendi felt the butt of his spear pressing into his knee. He opened his eyes. Ben was already sitting up.

"How much time do we have?" he asked.

Kendi checked his fingernail and swore again. "They're going to space Gretchen in less than half an hour."

"Wake up."

A stinging slap cracked across Gretchen's face. She shuddered and opened her eyes. The blond man was looking down at her. The lip she had split for him was almost completely healed. He slapped her twice more.

Gretchen was cold again. She managed to turn her head and discovered she was lying in the cryo-unit. Again. Her body ached from the hit with the gravity beam. How long ago had that been? She didn't know. Her sluggish mind wasn't working right.

The blond man grabbed her by the arm and hauled her out of the cryo-unit. Her legs were shaky and wouldn't support her. She slumped to the ground and sprawled there. It was warmer out here. She drank in the heat and let herself shiver to warm herself up further.

"We didn't get the signal," the blond man said. "That means we get to space you and all the other Silent freaks. Then we're going to slip it all the way back to SA."

"Boomer," said the dark-haired woman. She was standing a few paces away. "This is a bad idea. You've seen how dangerous she can be."

"Shut up, Peg," Boomer shot back. "The bitch clocked me fucking *twice*. So now she's gonna pay for it."

"You got nothing to complain about," Gretchen managed. "Improved your looks."

Boomer grabbed her by the hair and yanked her head back. The room spun crazily. It wasn't the same cargo bay as before. This place was at least three times bigger, and the walls were painted an ugly lime green. More than two dozen cryo-units made a line of coffins across the floor in front of a cargo door big enough to drive a loader through. Gretchen's captors must have shoved her back into cryo-sleep and transferred her over here. Wherever "here" was. Gretchen looked defiantly up into Boomer's eyes.

"I get it," she said. "Power trip. You're supposed to space the hostages, but you want me to be awake for it so I can suffer, that it?"

Boomer yanked Gretchen's hair hard enough to make her eyes tear up. "We crack open the door, and I get to watch your blood boil. Should be a fun fifteen seconds."

"What about them?" Gretchen asked. Her mind was waking up now, and although it felt as if knives were driving through her every muscle, she could move them. "The cryo-units are tight. They'll survive in space just fine. Or are you going to wake them up, too?"

Boomer released his hold on Gretchen's hair so fast, she dropped to the deck plates again. Her muscles screamed pain at her.

"Gonna crack 'em open," Boomer said. "They won't feel it when the vacuum hits. But you will."

Gretchen's eyes darted around the cargo bay. There had to be a weapon, a tool, something she could use. Her gaze fell on the gravity beam holstered on Peg's hip. Peg, however, was too far away for a surprise grab. Boomer seemed to be unarmed. Gretchen lay on the floor, feigning greater weakness than she felt.

"What's in it for you, anyway?" she gasped, trying to keep him talking. "Why space all these innocent people?"

"Mr. Sufur's orders," Boomer said. "We didn't get the signal, which means the jig is up. Sufur is either dead or arrested, and the Corridor is done for. He still wants as many of you Silent freaks dead as he can arrange, so we get to kill you."

"Boomer," Peg warned. "We have shit to do."

"I'm not Silent," Gretchen said, getting to her knees and gasping with exaggerated effort. "I'm Silenced."

"Silent or Silenced. Who cares?" Boomer said. "You're still a freak."

Gretchen got to her feet, swaying like a drunken sapling in a stiff breeze. Over Boomer's shoulder she saw Peg tense. "You're a shit," she said. "No balls, either. I should know—I kicked you in them hard enough to—"

She lunged. Boomer was caught completely off-guard, and she plowed straight into him. Her momentum carried them both straight toward Peg. Her gravity beam

was already in her hand, but she couldn't hit Gretchen
with Boomer in the way. She aimed for a fruitless moment, then tried to leap aside, but it was too late.
Boomer smashed into her with Gretchen right behind.
Peg flew backward and hit the floor with a grunt in the
open doorway. Her gravity beam skittered across the
tiles. Gretchen landed on top of Boomer. She kneed him
in the stomach and the air whooshed out of him. Peg
scrambled to her feet and ducked into the corridor outside the cargo bay. Gretchen rolled away from Boomer
and her grasping fingers found the gravity beam. Boomer
got his breath back and leaped at Gretchen with a snarl.
Gretchen fired. The orange beam caught him square in
the chest. With a scream Boomer flew backward, crashed
into the wall, and slid to the floor. He landed near one
of the cryo-units.

Gretchen whirled and ran for the exit, but the door
slammed shut. Peg looked through the thick, round window. Her jaw was set hard as she reached down toward
controls Gretchen couldn't see. An alarm blared, and
the loader door began to grind upward.

"Peg!" Boomer screamed. "No!"

A cold breeze rose around Gretchen. Peg shrugged
and spread her hands with mock sorrow. The loader
door opened far enough to reveal black space, and the
breeze became a wind. Gretchen's ears popped. She
raised the gravity beam and fired orange at the window.
It didn't seem to have any effect. On the other side of
the window, Peg laughed.

The wind howled with hurricane force, dragging
Gretchen backward. Grimly she increased the power
and continued to fire. The cargo door grumbled steadily
upward, and the four cryo-units closest to it were
sucked out into the vacuum beyond. Boomer was
screaming something incoherent. The window cracked
into a spiderweb, and Peg ducked away. Gretchen fired.
She couldn't draw air into her lungs. The wind howled
in her ears, but she kept firing. Her entire world shrank
to keeping her balance and aiming the gravity beam.
The energy indicator said the power cell was almost
drained. Boomer was on his feet, staggering against the
wind and moving toward her. Two more cryo-units

vanished through the widening opening into space.
Boomer leaped.

And then the entire door gave way with a shriek of
tortured metal. It burst into the cargo bay on a fresh
blast of air. Gretchen flung herself to the floor. The door
sailed over her head and caught Boomer in midair. The
wind whipped away the cloud of blood and the sound
of Boomer's final scream as the door flung his half-
crushed body across the bay and out the loader doors.

Gretchen tried to crawl forward against the rushing
air, but her strength was giving out. It was all she could
do to keep herself from being swept backward to join
Boomer and the lost cryo-units. Desperately she checked
the gravity beam. A tiny spark of energy was all that
was left. With a flick of her thumb, she set the beam on
reverse, raised a shaky hand, and fired into the hallway
beyond. A green light shot from the beamer and hit
the corridor wall. Nothing happened for a moment, then
Gretchen felt herself being dragged forward by the
beam. A cramp spasmed her hand, but she grimly kept
her grip. The beam pulled her out of the cargo bay and
into the corridor. Then it sputtered and died.

Gretchen rolled to her left, away from the open doorway. Peg was nowhere to be seen. The wind, focused by
the tight confines of the hallway, shoved at Gretchen
like a living hand. She managed to crawl to the control
panel next to the door and slap the emergency close.
The loader door, which was halfway open, ground back
down again, more quickly than it had gone up. In a few
moments, it boomed shut, and the horrible wind
stopped.

Gretchen lay panting in the corridor, her lungs filling
with sweet, still air. She felt as if every inch of skin were
bruised, and when she rubbed a hand over her face, her
palm came away smeared with blood from dozens of
tiny cuts and scrapes caused by flying debris. In that
moment, the only thing she wanted was the chance to
collapse like a rag doll.

Grimacing, Gretchen forced herself to her feet. There
was no time to rest. Peg had no doubt already alerted
the rest of the crew, and Gretchen wasn't going to fool
herself into thinking that Peg was the only other person

on the ship. Even a skeleton crew would consist of at least four people. Gretchen staggered down the lime-green corridor, clutching the empty gravity beam. As she saw it, Gretchen had two options—try to hide or try to take over the ship. Although hiding had the advantage of giving her a chance to rest, it had the disadvantage of requiring her to know the layout of the ship. Trying a takeover in her current condition—wounded and unarmed—had its own set of difficulties. Dammit, why was everything in her life so *hard*? She wanted to howl and beat something—preferably Peg. Or Sufur.

Okay, get a grip, she told herself. *You have to keep moving so the crew can't find you. They're probably already on their way down here. Maybe you can bluff them with the gravity beam. They won't know it's empty.*

Gretchen reached an intersection and cautiously peered around the corner. Another empty hallway stretched ahead of her. Where the hell was everyone? She couldn't believe Peg and the as-yet-unseen crew were willing to let her wander around the ship. So why weren't they down here looking for her?

Hard tension stole down Gretchen's spine. "No!" she whispered, and forced her screaming body into a run. Her heart pounded. There had to be a staircase or an elevator someplace. She had to find the bridge before—

"Attention! Attention!" said a computer voice. "The ship will enter slipspace in thirty seconds."

"Shit!" Once the ship entered slip, it would be untraceable, destroying any hope of rescue. Peg and her crew knew that full well, which was why they were readying the ship for the jump into slipspace instead of trying to catch Gretchen. She found an elevator and slapped the control. No response. Peg must have locked her out.

Overhead, an intercom speaker chimed to life. *"So there you are,"* said Peg's voice. *"Don't worry, Gretchen—we'll come down to get you soon. No use fighting. There are eight of us up here, and we're all armed."*

Gretchen remained silent, unwilling to give Peg the satisfaction of an answer.

"Get ready," Peg said. *"We're entering slip in five . . . four . . . three . . . two . . . "*

The floor lurched, flinging Gretchen to her already bruised knees. Thunder rumbled over the ship, vibrating the plates beneath Gretchen's body.

"What the hell?" Peg said, apparently forgetting the intercom was still open.

"Attention, alien vessel," interpolated a new voice. *"This is the Bellerophon military ship* Irfan's Pride. *We have you in our gravity beam, and you are hereby ordered to stand down."*

"Aw, shit," Peg said, and Gretchen began to laugh.

CHAPTER NINETEEN

"The end is where lovers meet."

—Daniel Vik

Father Kendi Weaver picked up the empty cup. "More tea?"

"No," Gretchen said. "But we would like one of Lucia's croissants, please."

Kendi selected a plump, flaky croissant from the platter and efficiently sliced it in half with a bread knife. The entire household was gathered here in Salman's living room. Gretchen, bandaged like a war hero, had commandeered a chaise longue. Lucia was overseeing the enormous amounts of food piled on the coffee table. Tan lounged in her usual spot in the doorway. Ben and Harenn shared a sofa with Evan and Ara in their laps, and Salman occupied an armchair. She looked older, and tired. A great deal of her usual energy was absent, and Kendi found the change distinctly odd. He put the croissant on a small plate and started to hand it Gretchen.

"We prefer our croissants with orange marmalade," she sniffed.

Kendi made a mock bow. Ben laughed and jiggled Ara on his knee.

"Do not become accustomed to this," Harenn admonished. "I have the feeling that Kendi's goodwill will not last."

"And we intend to milk every last drop until it runs out," Gretchen said airily. "Not so much, Kendi. We have to watch our weight."

Kendi gave her the plate with another mock bow and sat on the thick carpet. The little, yellow lizards chirped softly and skittered about their cage.

"I'm just glad everything's over," Kendi said. "The

election results may have sucked, but at least we don't have to worry about them anymore. Sufur is dead—party scheduled for tomorrow—we stopped his weird little scheme, and the doctor said Keith is already getting better. Now all we have to do is finish moving into the new house. Me, I don't think I'm ever going out in public again."

"So what are you planning, Grandma?" Ben asked. "You've been really quiet."

Salman cleared her throat. "The race took more out of me than I thought," she said. "I think I'm just going to finish out my term in the Senate and retire. Maybe I can be a professional great-grandma."

Ben reached over and squeezed her shoulder. "You were *always* a great grandma."

"Thank you, my duck." But her tone was wan. "At least this entire incident has brought Ched-Pirasku around to my way of thinking. Sufur's scheme made it abundantly clear to everyone that Bellerophon can't afford to cut back on the military."

"How are the kidnap victims doing?" Lucia said. "I forgot to ask."

"They're fine," Gretchen said. "The *Irfan's Pride* found the cryo-units Peg blew out into space, no problem, and the rest were just sitting in the cargo hold. Most of the people didn't remember much after Boomer-boy and Peg knocked them out. The whole thing was actually harder on their families. And me."

"We'll be forever grateful to you," Kendi said. Gretchen snorted and took a big bite of croissant.

"Once you're on your feet again, Gretchen," Tan rasped from the doorway, "I've got a continuing assignment for you, if you want it. Election's over, but the Father and the Offspring will still need guarding."

Gretchen swallowed her croissant. "I'll think about it. Right now I just want to sleep for a month. In fact, I think it's time for our royal nap. Would someone be so kind as to help us upstairs?"

Lucia rolled her eyes. "Come along then, your majesty. I'll be glad to help."

"The babies need to be changed and put down for their naps," Harenn said, also rising. "Ben?"

"Let me take Ara up," Tan said suddenly. "I want to hold her for a while." When she realized everyone was staring at her, she added, "What? I can't be a grandma, too?"

Gretchen hobbled out of the room with exaggerated care on Lucia's arm, followed by Tan and Harenn, bearing babies. Kendi plucked Gretchen's plate from the coffee table and stuffed half the croissant into his mouth.

"I can't believe you want to retire, Grandma," Ben said. "It'll be . . . I don't know. Weird."

"I'm an old lady, love," she said. "Things aren't the same anymore."

"Change is the only constant," Kendi said, swallowing. "Even in the Dream."

"Is that a Real People saying?" Ben asked.

"Probably." Kendi reached toward the coffee table, intending to set the plate down. "The Real People said just about every—shit!" His hand slipped and the plate tumbled toward the floor. Salman automatically reached for it, then snatched her hand back. The plate struck the side of the table and broke in half. The rest of the croissant landed marmalade side down on the carpet. Kendi ignored it. His eyes met Salman's for a long moment. She stared defiantly back.

"Grandma?" Ben said softly. "Did I just see . . . ?"

Salman didn't move. Kendi glanced pointedly down at the old woman's lap, then met her gaze again. "Grandma?"

Slowly, with aching deliberation, Salman Reza held out her hands. For a moment they both remained steady. Then the right one began to shake. Ben let out a long breath. Kendi sat back on the sofa.

"How?" Ben asked. "Why?"

Salman abruptly straightened, and the room crackled with her old energy. "How can you of all people ask that, Ben?" she cried. "Padric Sufur was a *monster*. He engineered the deaths of thousands upon thousands of people. He destroyed my campaign. He killed . . . he killed . . ." Her voice fell into a cracked whisper. "He killed my daughter."

"I should have seen it," Kendi said. "You knew about

Sufur, you knew where the cameras were. You also knew about Ara's neuro-pistol. How did you get it?"

"I've always been cleared for Ara's safe," Salman said. "Just in case something happened to her. I never dreamed . . ." She looked down at her shaky hand. "It was surprisingly easy to tell everyone I was going to bed early. I'm an old lady who had just lost a major election."

"You gave most of your guards the evening off," Kendi recalled. "Not because you no longer needed the security but because you needed the chance to sneak out of the house."

"Yes."

"Then what happened?" Ben asked.

"I went over to Sufur's house with the pistol. He answered his own door, and I remember that surprised me. He didn't look startled to see me or anything. He just invited me in and sat in that chair. I asked him why he did it, why he created the Despair. He told me that humans are filthy and disgusting and that he wanted to stop us from killing each other. He looked so smug and righteous, sitting in that stupid easy chair, calmly explaining why he murdered my little girl. So I shot him. *That* surprised him, I could tell. He choked and clawed at the air, and I smelled his bladder let go. Then he died and I left. That was it."

Ben leaned forward. "Did it make you feel better?" he asked earnestly.

"I don't know," Salman whispered. "I'm still adjusting to the idea that I killed him." She paused. "Actually, that wasn't all that happened. Just before Sufur died, he looked at me and I . . . I swear he whispered something."

"What?" Kendi asked.

"I think . . . I think he said . . . *thank you*. It was the last thing I expected to hear, and I'm still not sure I heard him right."

"Thank you," Ben repeated softly.

"Are you going to turn me in?" Salman asked. "I suppose I'll understand if you do."

"I think I speak for both us when I say no," Kendi told her. "It's pretty clear to me that the only way to stop Sufur from hatching more . . . plans was to kill him. Someone had to do it. Why not you?"

"What about the police?" Ben said. "They did a DNA check to catch Petrie. Won't they catch you?"

"Ched-Pirasku isn't eager to let the world know that Sufur funded his campaign," Salman said. "I let him know that investigations often uncover certain sordid secrets, and he said that budgets will probably be too tight for the police to afford a DNA scan. Sufur Silenced Ched-Pirasku, too, so I'm not worried about the police."

Footsteps tromped down the stairs and toward the living room. Salman tucked her hands under her thighs as Lucia came into the room.

"The babies are fussy," she reported. "I think they want their daddies to say good night."

"Duty calls," Ben said with a paternal smile. Kendi grinned and followed him upstairs to rock their children to sleep, leaving Salman and the broken plate behind.

"I figured it out."

Ben rolled over and propped himself up on one elbow so he could look down at Kendi's furry face. "You figured out what?"

"What was bothering me about Sufur," Koala Kendi said. His eyes were wide and brown, and they reflected the stars. "That plan of his never had a chance, you know."

"Go on."

"There were thousands and thousands of human Silent before the Despair," Kendi explained. "Even now there are hundreds and hundreds. We have a lot here on Bellerophon, and Silent Acquisitions has a lot on their station, but even both groups together don't have anywhere near most of them. Not only that, Sufur was using only two operatives. He couldn't possibly have rounded up all the human Silent on Bellerophon with just Peg and Boomer. It would have taken decades to get everyone, and he *still* wouldn't have eliminated all human Silent from the Dream. Not with more Silent humans being born every moment."

"Huh." Ben lay back down. The sand beneath him was pleasantly warm, and gentle seawater lapped at his bare toes. Overhead, the moonless sky showed thousands of stars—milky diamonds pinned to black velvet. Even as Ben watched, another star flickered into existence, faded, then glimmered strong and bright alongside the others. "Maybe he was just crazy."

"It also didn't make sense for Sufur to come to Bellerophon in the first place," Kendi continued. It looked rather odd, a koala bear on a tropical beach, but Ben liked the effect. "Sufur could have overseen the whole thing from the ship or even from SA Station. It made no sense for him to come to a planet where just about everyone would want him dead."

Another star burst into being, shining more brightly than its fellows for a moment before fading into normal radiance. "So why did he come?" Ben asked. "I have the feeling you've got a theory."

"Sort of." Kendi scratched an ear with quick, fluttering movements. "It goes back to what Grandma told us Sufur said before he died."

"He said *thank you*," Ben said. "What does—oh. Oh!"

"Yeah."

A little wave, more ambitious than the rest, rushed up the beach and wet Ben's calves, licking them like a warm tongue. Ben remained silent for a while, then said, "So you think Sufur wanted to die."

"It fits," Kendi said. "He may not have even realized he was doing it, but Sufur set himself up to be killed. Putting together an impossible plan, living in a house in a neighborhood where someone was bound to see him, inviting people like us and Grandma into his home. And remember the way he talked to us? What he said? Pretty clear that he hated himself because he was a filthy human. I think he wanted to die but didn't have the courage—or maybe the cowardice—to kill himself. So he put himself in a position where someone else would do it for him. And if he took a bunch of Silent with him in the process, so much the better."

Two more stars slipped into the sky like shy children joining a party of adults. Ben shook his head. "It makes a twisted sort of sense. I guess we'll never know for sure."

Another long pause. Then Kendi said, "How do you feel about Grandma killing Sufur?"

Ben thought. "I'm glad Sufur is dead. Killing him didn't bring Mom back—I never thought it would—but now we know that he won't hurt anyone else. I guess I feel . . . relieved. Grandma got rid of him, so I don't have to worry about . . . about wanting to break my promise to you."

"Would you have broken it?"

"No. I would have worked hard to make you release me from it." Ben sighed. "Actually I'm kind of disappointed. Harenn was right—now that Sufur's dead, he's not suffering. If we'd kept him alive, we could have made him miserable."

"I think he was already pretty miserable," Kendi said. "A happy person wouldn't do the things he did."

"Let's talk about something else," Ben said. "We were supposed to come in here to relax."

A flicker of light heralded yet another star that joined the others. Ben lay there in silence next to Kendi, just enjoying the quiet beach, the night sky, and being with Kendi. He wondered how long it would be before Evan, Ara, and their other eventual children would join them in the Dream and what that would be like. Would Ara continue to be boisterous and loud like her Da? Would Evan be quiet and reserved like his Dad? Or would they change as they grew older?

"What are you thinking about?" Kendi asked.

"The babies," Ben admitted.

Kendi laughed. "So was I. So much for getting away from them for a while." He sat up and gave Ben a koala kiss on the cheek. "I love you, Ben Rymar."

Three stars popped into the sky like popcorn kernels. Ben grinned at Kendi. "I never thought I'd say it to a koala bear, but I love you, too."

They lay back again, staring up at the sky to watch as, one by one, new Silent entered the Dream.

DREAMER

A Novel of the Silent Empire

Steven Harper

0-451-45843-5

THE DREAM...
...is a plateau of mental existence where people are able to communicate by the power of their thoughts alone.

THE SILENT...
These people—known as the Silent—find that the Dream is threatened by a powerful Silent capable of seizing control of other people's bodies against their will...and may be causing tremors within the Dream itself.

THE RISK...
And if the "normals" learn of this, they will do anything to capture the Silent for use as a weapon— and the Dream itself may be shattered forever...

Available wherever books are sold or at
www.penguin.com

S572

The *Silent Empire* Series

NIGHTMARE
by
Steven R. Harper

0-451-45898-2

Kendi Weaver doesn't know he's a Silent. Hijacked into
slavery, he has resigned himself to a life of servitude.
Then the discovery of his innate gift for dream
communication changes everything. Suddenly Kendi is a
very valuable commodity. He is rescued by the Children
of Irfan, a society dedicated to freeing enslaved Silents,
and taken to their planet, Bellerophon.

But Bellerophon is hardly a safe refuge. A brutal
serial killer is murdering Silents in their
telepathic dreams, and Kendi is soon embroiled in a
world of madness and murder. To catch the killer,
he must enter the victims' dreams.

Also in this series:
TRICKSTER
0-451-45941-5

Available wherever books are sold or at
www.penguin.com

S825